Praise for #1 *New York Times* bestselling author Sherryl Woods

"During the course of this gripping, emotionally wrenching but satisfying tale, Woods deftly and realistically handles such issues as survival guilt, drug abuse as adolescent rebellion, and family dynamics when a vital member is suddenly gone."
—*Booklist* on *Flamingo Diner*

"Woods is a master heartstring puller."
—*Publishers Weekly* on *Seaview Inn*

"Once again, Woods, with such authenticity, weaves a tale of true love and the challenges that can knock up against that love."
—*RT Book Reviews* on *Beach Lane*

"Woods…is noted for appealing character-driven stories that are often infused with the flavor and fragrance of the South."
—*Library Journal*

"A reunion story punctuated by family drama, Woods's first novel in her new Ocean Breeze series is touching, tense and tantalizing."
—*RT Book Reviews* on *Sand Castle Bay*

"A whimsical, sweet scenario…the digressions have their own charm, and Woods never fails to come back to the romantic point."
—*Publishers Weekly* on *Sweet Tea at Sunrise*

Also by Sherryl Woods

For a complete list of all titles by Sherryl Woods,
visit www.sherrylwoods.com.

SHERRYL WOODS

Winter's Proposal

mira

mira

ISBN-13: 978-0-7783-0928-4

Recycling programs for this product may not exist in your area.

Winter's Proposal

Copyright © 2019 by Harlequin Books S.A.

The Cowboy and His Baby
Copyright © 1996 by Sherryl Woods

The Rancher and His Unexpected Daughter
Copyright © 1996 by Sherryl Woods

For questions and comments about the quality of this book, please contact us at CustomerService@Harlequin.com.

www.Harlequin.com

Printed in U.S.A.

CONTENTS

This one is for all the readers
who've embraced my characters and stories
through the years. You've been such a blessing in
my life and I treasure the friendship you've offered.

THE COWBOY
AND HIS BABY

1

Damn, but it was cold, Cody Adams thought as he chased down the last of the herd of cattle he was rounding up. Texas had never been this frigid, not even in the middle of January. He was surprised half the livestock hadn't flat-out frozen in the harsh Wyoming winter. They'd lost a few head of cattle, but nothing like what he'd anticipated the first time the temperatures had dropped below zero and the snow and ice had swirled around him.

The bitter cold and the frequent blinding snowstorms did serve one useful purpose, though. They kept him so busy—kept his brain cells so frozen, for that matter—that he hardly ever thought about home. He'd freeze his butt off and suffer frostbite on most any part of his anatomy for the blessing of a blank memory. He didn't want to think about Texas or his family. Most of all, he didn't want to think about sneaky, conniving Melissa Horton and the way she'd cheated on him.

It had taken him a long time to block out the image of his longtime girlfriend wrapped in his best friend's arms. Even now, more than a year later, that terrible, gut-wrenching moment sneaked up on him when he least expected it and reminded him that that kind of pain might hide out, but it seldom went away.

With the last of the herd rounded up and dusk falling, Cody gestured to one of the other hands that he was leaving and headed back toward the small but cozy line shack he'd insisted he preferred to the bunkhouse. He'd claimed it kept him closer to the cattle for which he was responsible, but the truth was, he craved the isolation.

For a man who had been a very social creature back in Texas—okay, a notorious flirt—it was quite a change and, for the time being, a welcome one. It was the only surefire way he could think of for staying out of trouble and avoiding the sort of heartache that falling for some woman just about guaranteed.

His boss, impressed by the fact that for years 28-year-old Cody had been running White Pines, his family's ranch back in Texas, hadn't argued with his idiosyncratic decision. Lance Treethorn had insisted only that a phone be installed so he could reach Cody on business. He was the only one with the number. He rarely used it. Cody dropped by the ranch house often enough to stay in touch.

On the tiny porch Cody stomped the snow off his boots, gathered up an armload of firewood and went inside. Within minutes he had a fire roaring and had shucked off his skeepskin jacket. He stood in front of the blaze, letting the heat warm his chilled body. Unfortunately, it couldn't touch the cold place deep inside him.

He'd been standing there for some time, lost in thought, when he noticed the stack of mail sitting on the table in the kitchen area of the one-room cabin. It was sitting atop a foil-covered pan that he suspected from the sinful, chocolaty aroma, contained a batch of freshly baked brownies. He grinned and ripped off the foil. Sure enough, brownies. Apparently, Janey Treethorn had been by again.

The fifteen-year-old daughter of his boss had a giant-size crush on him. Thankfully, though, she was painfully shy. She limited her overtures to dropping off his mail, always with a batch of brownies or his favorite apple pie. In the summer it had been fresh fruit cobblers. She was usually careful to stop by while he wasn't home. On the one occasion when he'd caught her, she'd blushed furiously, stammered an apology for intruding, and fled on horseback before he could even say thanks.

Unable to resist, he grabbed one of the brownies and ate it as he sorted through the few pieces of mail she'd left, putting the bills aside to be paid later. A small blue envelope caught his attention. Turning it over, he recognized his sister-in-law's handwriting.

As always, when anything came from a member of his family, his heart skipped a beat. Letters were rare enough to stir a pang of homesickness each time one arrived. Jordan's wife had been dutifully writing to him once every two weeks or so from the moment she and Jordan had gotten married. For a man who swore he wanted nothing to do with anyone or anything back home, it was downright pitiful how he looked forward to Kelly's chatty letters and the family gossip she shared with such humor and telling insight. This one was more than a week overdue. Since the others had come like clockwork, he'd been trying not to admit just how worried he really was.

He could tell right off there was something different about this one, too. It was stiffer, more like a card than a letter. He grabbed a second brownie, then carried Kelly's latest correspondence with him back to his chair in front of the fire.

When he ripped open the envelope, a tiny square dropped out of the card inside. He grabbed for it instinctively and found himself staring at an infant swaddled as tight as a papoose in a blue blanket. He caught himself grinning at the sight of that tiny, red, scrunched-up face.

So, Jordan was a daddy, he thought, amazed by the shaft of pure envy that shot through him. He'd known the baby was due any day now. Kelly had kept him apprised of every detail of her pregnancy, including his older brother's bemusement at the natural childbirth classes she'd insisted he take with her. He wondered if Jordan had made it through the delivery or if he'd fainted at Kelly's first big-time contraction.

He closed his eyes against the tide of longing that rolled over him. He was missing so damned much, he thought, once again cursing Melissa for the betrayal that had made staying in Texas where he belonged impossible.

He was missing seeing his other brother Luke and his wife Jessie's little girl grow. Angela had turned two back in December. Kelly had sent a picture of her with her face streaked with icing and her fist in the middle of the chocolate birthday cake with its two, fat pink candles. He'd tucked it in his wallet, along with the snapshot of Kelly's daughter from her first marriage, Dani, a little con-artist-in-training who could persuade penguins to buy ice, if she was of a mind to. Now he opened his wallet and inserted the tiny picture of this latest addition to the family.

He stared at the brand new baby one last time and

wondered if he'd ever see him. He'd been named Justin James, according to the information on the birth announcement.

"We're going to call him J.J.," Kelly wrote in the note accompanying the card. "We can't wait for you to see him. Jordan swears he hasn't slept a wink in the past week. I don't know how that can be, since I'm the one up every time the little monster screams in the middle of the night. I haven't noticed Jordan pacing the floor alongside me. I think he's been sleeping with a pillow over his head deliberately, so he can claim he never hears J.J. crying. He swears he only wakes up after I've already left the bed. The silver-tongued devil says it's missing me that wakes him. He thinks a line like that will make me more sympathetic to him. Fat chance.

"No, seriously," he read on, "your big brother has been a huge help. I think he's a little awed by fatherhood...or maybe it's just that mountain of diapers he's expected to wash every night."

Cody chuckled at the image of his button-down brother, the big-time oil company executive, changing diapers and warming bottles. Maybe he was taking to it better than any of them had anticipated, including Jordan himself.

"We're scheduling the baptism for the end of the month and we expect you to be here," the letter continued. "No excuses, Cody. It's time to come home."

It's time to come home. Kelly's words echoed in his head, taunting him, reminding him that nothing would ever make this beautiful, sprawling Wyoming ranch into home. Lance Treethorn was a kind, decent man. He'd become a good friend. His daughters were real little angels and they treated Cody like one of the family. Even so, it wasn't the same. Not that a little thing like being homesick mattered. Even though his heart ached for the life he'd left behind, he knew he could never go back. He'd rather eat dirt than get within a hundred miles of the traitorous Melissa ever again.

It had been over a year since he'd left Texas, eighteen months to be exact, but not even time had cured him of the rage that had sent him away from everyone and everything dear to him.

Mention Texas and he didn't think of his beloved White Pines, didn't think of his parents or his brothers, much as he loved them all. The only image that inevitably came to mind was of Melissa Horton. Sometimes not even an entire bottle of the best liquor in the store could blot out the memories of the woman who'd betrayed him with his best friend.

Even now the vision in his head of Melissa was so vivid he could practically feel the silky texture of her skin and the soft flow of dark auburn hair through his fingers. He could practically smell the sweet summer scent of her.

But along with the sensual memories came the blinding rage, as powerful now as it had been on the day he'd left Texas for good. Accompanying that rage was the anger and frustration of realizing that he was, in part, responsible for what had happened. Maybe if he'd told her he loved her, she wouldn't have turned to Brian Kincaid in the first place. Maybe if he'd had a clue just how much she mattered to him, instead of taking her for granted, he wouldn't be lying awake nights aching for her. He'd been a fool. She'd been a cheat. Quite a pair, the two of them. Maybe he deserved to be this miserable. She certainly did, though he had no idea if she was. She could be happily married to Brian now, for all he knew.

Before he'd realized what he was doing, he'd ripped the note inviting him to the baptism of Jordan and Kelly's baby to shreds. He couldn't allow himself to be tempted back, not even by something as important as this. He would not go back to Texas. Not now. Not ever.

The decision was firm, but it left him feeling heartsick and more lonely than he'd ever felt in his life. He was almost glad when the ring of the phone shattered the silence. He grabbed the receiver gratefully.

"Hey, boss, what's up?" he said, knowing it would be Lance Treethorn on the other end of the line.

The widowed father of three young girls, Treethorn had his hands full with trying to run the ranch and raise his daughters to be proper young ladies. He'd succeeded with the oldest. Janey was as prim and proper and dutiful as a father could ever want, but the two younger ones, ten and twelve, were terrors. Cody didn't envy the thirty-five-year-old man trying to get them raised and married without calamity striking.

"We got the herd rounded up today," he told Lance. "We only lost one more to the cold."

"Thanks, Cody, but I didn't call for an update."

Something in Lance's voice triggered alarm bells. "What's wrong?" he asked at once. "Are there problems with the girls?"

"No, it's nothing like that. We're all fine, but you had a call here at the house."

"I did?" He'd given the Treethorn number only to Jordan, with a direct order that it never be used except for a dire emergency. He knew his brother would never break that rule. His heart thudded dully as he waited for whatever bad news Jordan had imparted.

"Call home," his boss told him. "It sounded pretty urgent. Your brother asked how quickly I could get a message to you. Obviously Jordan still doesn't know you have a phone in your cabin."

"No," Cody admitted, grateful that his boss had never asked why he insisted on having such a buffer between him and his family. Lance was the best kind of boss, the best kind of friend. He was scrupulously fair. He lent support, but never asked questions or made judgments. There had been no hint of criticism in his voice when he'd commented just now on Cody's decision to keep his private phone number from his family.

"I'm sorry he bothered you," Cody apologized anyway.

"You know damned well it's no bother. I just hope everything's okay at home. Give me a call if there's anything I can do to help."

"Thanks, Lance."

Cody hung up slowly, thinking of the tiny picture that he'd placed in his wallet only moments earlier. Had something happened to Justin James? Or to Kelly? Why else would Jordan call? Damn, but he hated being so far away. What if… He allowed the thought to trail off.

"Stop imagining the worst and call," he muttered out loud, finally forcing himself to dial his brother's number, knowing that this call, whatever it was about, would shatter whatever distance he'd managed to achieve from his past.

Jordan picked up on the first ring. His voice sounded tired and hoarse.

"Hey, big brother," Cody said.

"Cody, thank God. I was worried sick you wouldn't get the message for days."

Jordan, the most composed man Cody had ever known, sounded shaken. The alarm bells triggered by Lance's call were clanging even louder now. "What's wrong?"

"It's bad news, Cody. Real bad."

Cody sank onto a chair by the kitchen table and braced himself. The last time Jordan had sounded that somber was when their brother Erik had been killed in an accident on Luke's ranch.

"Is it Dad?" he asked, hating even to form the words. Harlan Adams was bigger than life. He was immortal— or so Cody had always tried to tell himself. He couldn't imagine a world in which Harlan wasn't controlling and manipulating things.

"No, he's fine," Jordan reassured him at once, then amended, "Or at least as well as can be expected under the circumstances."

"Dammit, Jordan, spit it out. What the hell has happened?"

"It's Mother," he began, then stopped. He swallowed audibly before adding, "She and Daddy were out riding this morning."

He paused again and this time Cody could hear his ragged breathing. It almost sounded as if Jordan were crying, but that couldn't be. Jordan never cried. None of them did. Harlan had very old-fashioned ideas on the subject of men and tears. He had set a tough example for them, too. He hadn't shed a single tear when Erik died. He'd just retreated into stony, guilt-ridden silence for months after the loss of his son. The rest of them had coped with their grief dry-eyed, as well. If

Erik's death hadn't caused Jordan's cool, macho facade to crack, what on earth had?

"Jordan, are you okay?" he asked.

"No. Mother took a bad fall, Cody."

Cody felt as if the blood had drained out of him. Hands trembling, he grabbed the edge of the table and held on. "How is she? Is she…"

"She's gone, Cody," Jordan said with a catch in his voice. "She never woke up. She was dead by the time the paramedics got to the ranch."

"My God," he murmured, stunned. Forbidden tears stung his eyes. Ashamed, he wiped at them uselessly. They kept coming, accompanied by a terrible sense of loss. "Are you sure Daddy's okay? Why aren't you with him?"

"Luke and Jessie are over at White Pines now. Luke's got the funeral arrangements under control. Kelly and I will be going over right after I get off the phone. I wanted to stay here until you called back. How soon can you get here?"

Cody noticed his brother asked the question as if there were no doubt at all that he would be coming home. "I don't know," he said, struggling between duty and the agony that going home promised.

Disapproving silence greeted the reply. "But you will be here," Jordan said emphatically. "I'm telling Daddy you're on your way."

Cody rubbed his suddenly pounding head. "I don't know," he repeated.

"Look, this is no time to be indulging in self-pity, little brother," Jordan snapped impatiently. "Daddy needs you here, probably more than he needs any of the rest of us. He'll need you to take up some of the slack at White

Pines while he pulls himself together. He's always depended on you. Don't let him down now."

Cody said nothing.

Jordan finally broke the silence with a sigh. "We're scheduling the funeral for Saturday," he said. "Be here, Cody."

He hung up before Cody could reply.

Cody sat in the gathering darkness, silent, unchecked tears streaking down his cheeks. He had no choice and he knew it. Mary Adams might not have been the kind of warm, doting mother a child dreamed of, but Harlan Adams had worshiped her. He could not let his father go through this kind of grief without all of his sons at his side. It was the kind of loyalty that had been ingrained in him since birth. As badly as he wanted to pretend it didn't matter, he knew better. Nothing mattered more at a time like this.

He took some small comfort in the odds that said he would probably never even see Melissa. He doubted she would have the nerve to show up at the funeral. She certainly wouldn't have the audacity to show up at White Pines afterward. It would be okay. He could slip in and out of town before temptation overtook him and he sought out so much as a glimpse of her.

At least, that's what he told himself on the long, sad drive back to Texas after he'd cleared his departure with Lance. He'd chosen to drive to delay his arrival as long as possible. Maybe to come to grips with what had happened in private. He'd spend a few days with his family to grieve. A few days to do whatever he could for his father. A few days to spoil his nieces and hold his brand new nephew. A few days to soak up enough memories to last a lifetime.

With all that going on, Melissa would be the last thing on his mind.

The very last thing, he vowed with grim determination as he finally turned into the lane to White Pines.

He slowed his pickup and looked around at the land that he loved, the land he'd hoped one day would be his since Luke's mile-wide independent streak had sent him chasing after his own dream and his own ranch and Jordan was only interested in oil.

Even in the dead of winter, it was starkly beautiful, at least to him. He was home and suddenly, despite the sorrow that had drawn him back, he felt at peace for the first time since he'd driven away more than eighteen months before.

Melissa Horton took a break from her job behind the lunch counter at Dolan's Drugstore and perched on a stool with the weekly newspaper and a cup of coffee. Her attention was riveted to the story of Mary Adams's tragic riding accident.

The 55-year-old woman had always been incredibly kind to her. Melissa had figured Mary pitied her because she'd been mooning around Cody for most of her life. Once Mary had even tried to give her some advice. It had turned out to be lousy advice, but Melissa was certain Mary had thought she was doing her a favor.

Mary had sat her down one afternoon over tea and told her that Cody was taking her for granted. Not that that was news. At any rate, Mary had claimed that the only way Melissa would ever win him would be to make him jealous. Tired of being ignored except when it suited Cody, and taking the well-meant advice to heart, Melissa had tried to do just that by going out just once with Cody's best friend.

What a disaster that had been! Had she chosen anyone else, maybe the plan would have worked, but she'd foolishly selected the one man she'd figured wouldn't get hurt. Brian had known her heart belonged to Cody. He'd known their date meant nothing, that it was only a ploy to shake up Cody. He'd even tried to argue her out of it, warning her it could backfire, but her mind had been made up. She had risked everything, certain that Mary Adams was right. She'd seen it as the only way to get Cody to finally make a commitment to her.

She should have guessed that Brian understood Cody even better than she did. Every time she thought of the anger and hurt in Cody's eyes that night, it made her sick to her stomach. He had stared at them for the space of one dull, thudding heartbeat. He'd looked not at her, but through her. His gaze riveted on Brian, he'd said, "A hell of a friend you turned out to be."

He had spoken with a kind of lethal calm that had been more chilling than shouted accusations. Then he'd turned on his heel and walked away. He had taken off the next morning and never once looked back.

For the past eighteen months she'd had no idea at all where he was. Brian hadn't heard from him, hadn't expected to, for that matter. She hadn't had the courage to ask Cody's family for information. Her shame ran too deep.

There had been times when she'd considered being in the dark a blessing. It had kept her from chasing after him, from destroying what few shreds of pride and dignity she had left.

Now, though, she had no doubts at all that Cody

would be coming home. She might have driven him away with her betrayal, but his mother's death would surely bring him back.

Had he changed much? she wondered. Had he lost the flirtatious, fun-loving nature that had charmed her and half the women who'd crossed his path? Would she have to live with regrets for the rest of her life for turning him into a bitter, cynical man?

"No good'll come of what you're thinking," Mabel Hastings advised, coming up behind her to peer over her shoulder at the front page of the newspaper.

"How do you know what I'm thinking?" Melissa asked defensively.

Mabel shook her head, her tight gray curls bouncing at the movement. When Mabel had a permanent, she meant it to last. She'd been wearing the exact same hairstyle as far back as Melissa could remember. It did not suit her pinched features.

"I been reading you like a book ever since you set eyes on Cody Adams way back in junior high school," Mabel informed her huffily. "You seem to forget how many times you sat right here at this very counter making goo-goo eyes at him."

Melissa chuckled despite her irritation at the unsolicited interference. "'Goo-goo eyes'? Mabel, exactly how old are you? A hundred, maybe? Not even my mother would use an expression like that."

The older woman, who was probably no more than sixty, scowled at her. "Don't matter what you call it, the point is you've been crazy about that boy way too long and just look where it got you."

Melissa sensed the start of a familiar lecture. Listening to it was the price she paid for having a job that paid enough in salary and tips to keep her financially afloat and independent. She didn't have to take a dime from her parents.

"Okay, I get your point," she said, trying to avoid the full-scale assault on her sense and her virtue. "Drop it, please. I probably won't even see Cody."

She was bright enough to know it would be far better if she didn't. Her life had taken some unexpected twists and turns since he'd left, but it was settling down now. She was at peace with herself. There were no more complications, no more tears in the middle of the night over a man who didn't love her—at least, not enough— and no more roller coaster ups and downs.

No way did she want to stir up old memories and old hurts. One look into Cody's laughing brown eyes and she couldn't trust herself not to tumble straight back into love with him. She'd clearly never had a lick of sense where he was concerned.

Now, though, the stakes were way too high. Now she had more than her own heart to consider. She had someone else to protect, someone more important to her than life itself—Cody's daughter, the child he didn't even know he had.

2

The entire family was walking around in a daze. Cody had never seen them like this, not even when Erik died. He supposed they were all following Harlan's lead. His father hadn't spoken more than a word or two to anyone. He hadn't eaten. He wasn't sleeping. He had refused a sedative prescribed by the doctor. Not even his unusually subdued grandchildren, tugging on his sleeves and competing for his attention, drew so much as a smile. He looked haggard and lost.

On Saturday morning Cody found Harlan in his office, staring at nothing, his complexion a worrisome shade of gray. Cody walked over and perched on a corner of his desk.

"Hey, Daddy, are you doing okay?"

Harlan blinked, his gaze finally focusing. "Cody, have you been here long?"

The vague question startled Cody. Normally nothing went on at White Pines that Harlan didn't notice. "Actually, I got here yesterday."

His father's lips quirked for a fraction of a second.

"Hell, I know that. I haven't lost my marbles. I meant now. Have you been standing there long?"

Relief sighed through Cody. "Nope. Just walked in. Everyone's been looking for you."

"Must not have been looking too hard," Harlan grumbled in a manner that was more in character. "I've been right here all night long."

Cody was dismayed. "You didn't sleep?"

"Off and on, I suppose."

"Daddy, you should have been resting. Today's going to be rough enough without facing it exhausted."

His father shrugged. "I couldn't go upstairs."

"Damn," Cody muttered. Why hadn't any of them thought of that? Of course it was going to be hard for their father to spend time in the suite of rooms he had shared for so many years with his wife. It was hard for the rest of them just being in the house where their mother had reigned over every last detail. "I'm sorry. I'll go upstairs and bring some clothes down for you. It'll be time to go to the church soon."

He had barely reached the door when his father's voice stopped him.

"How could a thing like this happen?" Harlan murmured.

His choked voice sounded too damned close to tears. Cody was shaken by that as he hadn't been by anything else in his life.

"We were supposed to have so many years left," Harlan went on. "I had promised your mother we'd travel, that we'd see all the sights she'd been reading about over the years." He glanced at Cody. "Did you know she gave up a trip around the world for her college graduation to marry me? I promised to make it up to her one day, but I never got around to it."

Guilt sliced through Cody. His departure had kept them from going on those trips. His father had had to take over the running of White Pines again, just when he'd been ready to indulge all of his wife's fantasies.

"You can't think about that," Cody told him, partly because he couldn't bear to think about it, either. "You'll make yourself crazy. Think about the years you did have. You made Mother very happy. She loved being your wife. She loved being mistress of White Pines. She was wild about all those fancy ancestors of yours."

"She loved you boys, too," Harlan added quietly. "Oh, I know she didn't pay you the kind of attention she did me. I regret that. I regret that you all thought that meant she didn't love you."

At Cody's expression of shock, he added, "Don't deny it, son. I know you boys couldn't help feeling that way. Catering to me was just your mama's way. When you were little, I don't think she knew quite what to make of you. She was an only child. She wasn't prepared for the chaos of four rambunctious boys. But she cared about you and she was so very proud of the way you all turned out."

"Even me?" Cody asked, unable to prevent the question from popping out. He hated what it said about his insecurities. He had feared that turning his back on White Pines would cost him whatever affection either of his parents felt for him.

Harlan chuckled. "Are you kidding? You were her baby. There wasn't a day since you've been gone that she didn't worry about you and how you were getting along, when she didn't tell me how she missed hearing you thundering down the stairs or raising a ruckus in the kitchen."

"She hated it when I did those things," Cody protested.

"Only until they stopped," Harlan said softly. Sorrow had etched new lines in his face. The sadness behind the comment emphasized them.

Cody watched with amazement and new respect as his father visibly pulled himself up, gathering strength from some inner reserve that had been severely tested in the past few days. He stood, crossed the room and put a comforting arm around Cody's shoulders, sharing that strength with his son.

"Come on, boy. Help me figure out what to wear, so I won't put your mama to shame."

Together they climbed the stairs and went to prepare for the funeral of the woman Cody had adored and on occasion admired, but until just this morning had never understood.

Melissa watched the clock above the soda fountain ticking slowly toward noon. She would not go to Mary's funeral. She would not! If she did, she would be going for all the wrong reasons.

Drugstore owner and pharmacist Eli Dolan came out from behind the prescription counter, then peered at her over the rim of his reading glasses. "You going?"

"Going where?" Melissa asked.

He muttered something about women and foolishness under his breath. "To that funeral, of course. You ought to be paying your respects."

She didn't bother asking how Eli knew that she had been close to Mary at one time. Everyone in town knew everyone else's business. That's what had made staying here after her daughter was born so difficult. She doubted there was a single soul that didn't have their suspicions about the identity of Sharon Lynn's daddy, but as far as she knew only her own parents and Cody's brother Jordan and his wife knew the truth for certain.

She wouldn't have admitted it to Jordan and Kelly, but he had taken one look at the baby and guessed. She hadn't been able to deny it. Jordan had vowed to keep her secret and, as far as she knew, he'd been true to his word. She was ninety-eight percent certain that he'd never told Cody. Harlan had instilled a deep sense of honor in all of his sons. That included keeping promises, even when extracted under the most trying conditions.

She also had a hunch that if Jordan had told, Cody would have stormed back to Texas and raised a commotion that would have set the whole town on its ear. Or maybe that was just wishful thinking on her part.

"You'd better get a move on, if you're going to find a place in church," Eli prompted, clearly not intending to let the matter drop. "It's bound to be crowded. Folks around here think mighty highly of Harlan and his sons. They'll be there for them, even if most of them found Mary a little high-falutin' for their taste."

"I can't leave here now," Melissa hedged, taking another wipe at the already polished counter. "It's lunchtime."

"And who's going to be here?" he shot right back. "Everybody will be at the funeral. I don't expect we'll be doing much business. And you seem to forget that I was making milk shakes and sandwiches when you were still in diapers. I can handle things for the next couple of hours. If I make a mess of things, you can say you told me so when you get back."

He glanced over at Mabel and nodded in her direction. "Or she'll do it for you," he said with a sour note in his voice. "Now, go on. Do what you know is right."

Melissa didn't question the sense of relief she felt at being nudged determinedly out the door. If Eli didn't find it odd that she'd be going to the funeral, maybe no one else would, either. Maybe it would have been more noticeable if she'd stayed away.

Bracing herself against the brisk January wind, she rushed down Main Street, glad that she'd chosen to wear a dress to work rather than her usual jeans and T-shirt. Obviously some part of her had known even when she'd dressed that morning that she would change her mind about going to the service.

It was a dreary day for a funeral. Leaden clouds, practically bursting with rain—or, given the rapidly dropping temperature, more likely sleet—hung low in the sky. She tugged her coat more tightly around her, but gave up on keeping her long hair from tangling as the wind whipped it around her face.

All the way to the church she tried to keep her mind off Cody and on the service that was to come. Her best efforts, however, were a dismal failure. She kept envisioning Cody, wondering how he was holding up, worrying how he and all of his brothers were doing and regretting more than she could say that she couldn't take her place with them and offer the support she desperately wanted to give.

She was so late that she planned to slip into the back of the church and stand in the shadows. Cody would never know she was there. The last thing she wanted to do today was add to his misery.

She ran up the steps of the old church just as the bells were chiming in the tall white steeple. The sun peeked through the clouds for just an instant, creating a terrible glare. Going from that sudden bright sun outside into the church's dimly lit interior, she was momentarily blinded.

Apparently, whoever was hard on her heels was having the same problem because he slammed smack into her, his body rock solid as he hit her at full tilt. The contact almost sent her sprawling on the polished wood floor.

"Sorry," he said, gripping her elbows to keep her upright. "You okay, darlin'?"

Melissa's heart climbed straight into her throat. She would have recognized that voice, that automatic flirtatiousness, even if she hadn't heard it for a hundred years. The firm, steadying touch was equally familiar and just as devastating. If she'd brushed against a live wire, she couldn't have felt any more electrified.

"Cody?"

She spoke his name in no more than a whisper, but at the sound of her voice, he jerked his hands away as if he'd just touched a white-hot flame.

"Excuse me," he said, his voice instantly like ice.

As if she were a stranger, he shoved past her to make his way to the front of the church. No, she corrected, if she'd been a stranger, he would have been less rude, more solicitous.

Trembling from the unexpected face-to-face meeting, Melissa watched him stride up the aisle to join his father and his brothers in the first pew. In that single quick glimpse, she had seen new lines in his face. His sun-streaked, normally untamed hair had been trimmed neatly in the way his mother had always wanted it to be.

It was his eyes, though, that had stunned her. Once they'd been filled with so much laughter. Naturally she had expected to find sorrow today in the dark-as-coffee depths. What she hadn't anticipated was the cold antipathy when he recognized her, followed by an emptiness that was worse than hatred.

Well, she thought despondently, now she knew. Cody hadn't forgiven her. He'd looked straight through her as if he'd never known her, as if he'd never teased her or made love to her or shared his deepest, darkest secrets with her.

"Oh, God," she murmured in what could have been the beginning of a prayer, but instead simply died before completion. Their relationship was clearly beyond even divine intervention. She'd known it all along, of course, but she hadn't wanted to believe it. The last flicker of hope in her heart died like a candle flame in a chilly wind.

Though a part of her wanted to flee, she moved into the deepest shadows and stayed through the service, grieving not just for the woman lying in the flower-draped casket, but for the death of her own dreams.

"You went to the funeral, didn't you?" Velma Horton asked the minute Melissa walked through her mother's doorway to pick up her daughter after work.

"How did you know?" she asked, though it was easy enough to guess. The grapevine had probably been buzzing all afternoon and her mother was definitely tapped into that.

Her mother sniffed. "You think I didn't know why

you wore that dress today. I know what you said, some nonsense about all your jeans being in the laundry, but I'm not a fool, girl. I knew you wouldn't miss a chance to catch sight of Cody. So, did you see him?"

"Briefly," Melissa admitted.

"And?"

"And what? We didn't talk."

"Then you didn't tell him about Sharon Lynn."

Melissa shook her head. "He wouldn't care," she said with absolute certainty that was based on the way he'd looked straight through her for the second time in their lives.

To her surprise, her mother breathed a sigh of relief and some of the tension drained out of her expression. "Good."

There were times, like now, when Melissa didn't understand her mother at all. When Velma had learned her daughter was pregnant, she'd been all for chasing Cody to the ends of the earth and demanding he take responsibility for his actions.

"I thought you wanted him to know," Melissa said, regarding her mother with confusion. "There was a time you threatened to go to Harlan and demand that he drag Cody back here. You thought he owed me his name and his money. The only thing that stopped you was Daddy's threat to divorce you if you did."

Velma rolled her eyes. "Your father's got more pride than sense. Anyway, that was before Sharon Lynn was born, back when I didn't know how you'd manage by yourself. Seems to me you've done just fine. There's no sense in trying to fix what's not broke."

It was a reasonable explanation for the turnaround, but Melissa didn't entirely buy it. "There's something else, isn't there? Some other reason you don't want Cody to find out the truth?"

"There is," her mother admitted, an ominous note in her voice. "Harlan Adams is a powerful man."

"That's not news. What's your point? What does he have to do with this? It's between me and Cody."

"Not if Harlan gets it into his head to claim his granddaughter," her mother stated, a note of genuine fear in her voice. "There's no way we could fight a man like that."

Melissa was stunned by what her mother was suggesting. "Don't you think you're being a little paranoid? Jordan's known for almost a year now and he hasn't even spilled the beans. I suspect the rest of the family will react with just as much indifference."

Her mother didn't seem to be reassured. "Just watch your step. I'm warning you, Melissa, keep that baby as far away from Cody Adams as you can."

Though she didn't think the warning was necessary, Melissa nodded dutifully. "I don't think we have to worry about that. Cody will probably be gone before we know it."

Just then the sounds of her daughter's cheerful, nonsensical babbling echoed down the narrow hallway. Melissa smiled. Her heart suddenly felt lighter than it had all day. The baby had had that effect on her from the moment she'd been born.

"Did she just wake up?" she asked as she started toward her old bedroom.

"I doubt she's even been asleep. She didn't want to go down for her nap. I think she sensed the tension in both of us. You go on in. I'm going to fix your daddy's dinner."

Melissa went to pick up her daughter from the crib her mother had put up next to the twin bed Melissa had slept in for most of her life. Sharon Lynn was standing on shaky, pudgy little legs, hanging on to the crib rail. Her eyes lit up when she spotted her mother.

"Ma...ma...ma."

"That's right, darling girl," Melissa crooned, gathering her into her arms. "I'm your mama."

She inhaled the sweet talcum-powder scent of her baby and sighed as tiny little hands grabbed her hair and held on tight. "You've got quite a grip, little one. You must have gotten that from your daddy. I'm the original hundred-pound weakling."

"Da?" Sharon Lynn repeated, echoing a sound Melissa had taught her while showing her a snapshot of Cody. Her mother would have pitched a royal fit if she'd known.

"Oh, baby," she murmured, tightening her embrace. "Your daddy's right here in town. He has no idea what he's been missing all these months. He has no idea that he has a precious little girl."

Cody would have made a wonderful father, she thought with a sigh. He would have been too indulgent by far, too readily conned by sweet talk and a winning smile, but, oh, how he would have cherished and protected a child of his. Her foolish actions had cost him the chance to prove that. Worse, they had cost her daughter a chance to be loved by an incredible man. There were days when she almost made herself sick with regrets.

"We do okay by ourselves, though, don't we?" she asked, gazing into round, dark eyes that reminded her too much of Cody. The baby returned her gaze with the kind of serious, thoughtful look the question deserved.

Melissa wondered how many years it would be before that innocent contemplation turned to something far more accusatory because her mother had robbed her of any contact with her father.

"Don't," her mother pleaded, coming up behind her.

"Don't what?"

"Don't tell him."

"Who said I was going to?" Melissa asked.

"I know that look. You're making up pipe dreams about what it will be like when Cody finds out he has a baby girl. You're expecting him to declare he's never stopped loving you and sweep you off to get married."

Her expression turned dire. "It won't be that way, I'm telling you. If he cares about the baby at all, he'll take her from you. That's how much he hates you for what you did to him. You made a fool of him in front of the whole town by going out with his best friend. A man never forgets a betrayal like that. I don't care if it was just a bunch of foolishness on your part. The results were the same as if you and Brian had had something going."

"You don't know anything about Cody's feelings," Melissa argued, even though she had just seen with her own eyes that Cody did despise her. She didn't want to believe he could be cruel enough to try to take their daughter away from her.

"Are you willing to take that chance?" her mother demanded.

The baby whimpered, either because she was picking up on the sudden tension or because Melissa was holding her too tightly. "No," she whispered, fighting the sting of tears as she kissed her daughter's silky cheek. "No, I'm not willing to take that chance."

She had been weaving pipe dreams, just as her mother had guessed. The risk of trying to make them come true, though, was far too great. Rather than winning back Cody, she could very well lose her child. She would die before she let that happen. Sharon Lynn was the most important thing in her life.

All the way home she assured herself that she only needed a few days. If she kept the secret just a few more days, Cody would be gone and that would be the end of it.

Later that night she sank into the rocker beside Sharon Lynn's crib and set it into motion, hoping to lull the baby to sleep and to quiet all those clamoring shouts in her head that told her she just might be making the second worst mistake in her life by keeping silent. As much as she hated to admit it, her mother was right about one thing. If Cody did learn the truth from someone else, there was no telling what he might do to exact revenge.

3

For the past two days Cody hadn't been able to stop thinking about his brief meeting with Melissa at the funeral. She looked exactly as he'd remembered her, her long hair a tangle of fiery lights, her body slender as a reed except for the lush, unexpected curve of her breasts.

Even before he'd heard her voice, in that instant when he'd caught her to prevent her from falling, he'd known it was her just from the way his body had reacted to touching her. He had hated that reaction, hated knowing that his desire for her hadn't waned at all despite the months of self-imposed exile. That seemed like the cruelest sort of punishment.

Late that night after the funeral he'd been pacing downstairs when his father had come out of his office and caught him. Harlan had guessed right off that his agitation had to do with Melissa, though he'd been uncommonly cautious in broaching the subject.

"I thought I saw Melissa at the church today," Harlan had said casually after he'd pulled Cody into his office and they were both seated in comfortable leather chairs in front of a blazing fire, glasses of whiskey in hand. At the reference to Melissa, Cody had put his aside without tasting it. He'd feared if he got started, he'd never stop.

"She was there," he'd conceded, his voice tight.

"Did you get a chance to talk to her?"

"We have nothing to say to each other."

"I see," Harlan said. He'd let the silence build for a bit, taking a sip of his drink before adding nonchalantly, "I heard she's been working at Dolan's Drugstore, running the soda fountain for Eli. Doing a good job, too. Eli says business is up. The kids are hanging out there again instead of driving to the fast-food place out on the highway."

Cody hadn't even acknowledged the information. He'd just tucked it away for later consideration. Ever since, he'd been considering what to do about it.

He could drive into town, march into Dolan's and confront Melissa about what she'd done to him, something he probably should have done the very night he'd found her with Brian. He could raise the kind of ruckus that would be the talk of the town for the next year. It would go into the textbook of Cody Adams lore that had begun when he was barely into puberty. If half the tales had been true, he would have worn himself out by the time he was twenty.

Sighing, he conceded he couldn't see much point to adding another wild exploit to his reputation. A scene would only rake up old news, embarrass Melissa—not that he cared much about that—and tell anyone with half a brain that Cody wasn't over her. Otherwise, why would he bother to stir up the cold ashes of their very dead relationship?

No, for the sake of his own pride if nothing else, it

was better to stay the hell away from town. He repeated the advice to himself like a mantra, over and over, until he should have gotten it right.

Even as his old red pickup sped toward town late Tuesday morning, he was muttering it to himself, swearing that he'd have lunch with Luke and Jordan at Rosa's Mexican Café, then turn right around and go back to White Pines. A couple of beers and a plate of Rosa's spiciest food would wipe all thoughts of Melissa straight out of his head.

Unfortunately he hadn't counted on his brothers getting into the act. He'd been certain that they would leave the subject of his love life alone. He hadn't counted on the fact that both of them were now happily married and apparently intent on seeing that he took the plunge, too.

"Hey, Cody, why don't you drop by Dolan's as long as you're in town?" Jordan suggested after they'd eaten. He said it with all the innocence of Harlan at his matchmaking best.

"Any particular reason I should?" he inquired, refusing to fall into Jordan's trap.

He lifted the cold bottle of beer to his lips and took a long, slow drink just to show how unaffected he was by the prospect of seeing Melissa, whom Jordan clearly knew worked at Dolan's. This was probably the whole reason his brothers had suggested meeting in town in the first place rather than gathering at White Pines. They'd been plotting behind his back to try to force a reunion between Cody and his ex-lover.

"They still have the best milk shakes in the whole state of Texas," Luke chimed.

"We've just eaten enough food to stuff a horse," Cody stated flatly.

Luke and Jordan exchanged a look.

"Worried about your handsome figure?" Luke taunted.

Cody scowled at his oldest brother's nonsense. "No."

Luke went on as if he'd never spoken. "Because if that's it, I'm sure they have diet sodas in there, served up by the sweetest gal in all of Texas, or so I hear."

"I don't want a milk shake. I don't want a diet soda. There is nothing that drugstore has that I want," he said pointedly, scowling first at Luke and then at Jordan.

"Sounds to me like a man who's protesting too much," Jordan observed. "What does it sound like to you, Lucas?"

"Definitely a man who's scared out of his britches," Luke agreed.

Cody drew himself up indignantly. "Scared of what? A milk shake?"

"Maybe not that," Luke conceded. "How about Melissa Horton?"

Ah, a direct hit. Cody sighed. "I am not scared of Melissa," he said with extreme patience. "I feel absolutely nothing for Melissa."

"Cluck, cluck, cluck," Luke murmured, making a pitiful attempt to mimic a chicken.

The sound grated on Cody's nerves. He balled his hands into fists. He hadn't gotten into a rip-roaring fight with his big brothers in a very long time, but Luke was pushing every one of his buttons. And, from the teasing glint in his eyes, his big brother knew it, too. Even Jordan sensed that his patience was at an end. He eased his chair between them, a conciliatory expression on his face.

"Now, Luke, don't rile Cody," he said blandly. "If he

says he doesn't want to talk to Melissa, then who are we to interfere?"

Cody didn't exactly trust Jordan's sudden taking of his side. Jordan had a knack for sneak attacks that could cripple a business adversary before he even knew he was under seige. Cody eyed him warily.

"That's true," Luke conceded, his turnaround just as suspicious. "Daddy meddled in our lives enough that we should be more sensitive to Cody's feelings. Besides, Melissa probably doesn't want to see him any more than he wants to see her."

"Why? Is she involved with someone?" Cody asked, regretting the words the instant they slipped out of his mouth. The triumphant expressions on Luke's and Jordan's faces were enough to set his teeth on edge.

Jordan stood as if he'd just recalled a business crisis that couldn't be put off. "Come on, Luke. We've obviously accomplished our mission here," he said blithely. "The man is on the hook. Let's leave him to decide whether to wiggle off or take the bait."

"A fascinating metaphor," Luke commented, joining Jordan. He glanced back at Cody. The teasing glint in his eyes faded. "Don't be a damned fool, little brother. Go see the woman. You know you want to. It's time you settled things with her once and for all. We want you back here for good."

Cody finished the beer after they'd gone. He thought about ordering another one, but decided against it. It would only be delaying the inevitable. Some sick, perverse part of him wanted to see Melissa, just as Luke had guessed. He needed to know if that reaction he'd felt at the church had been a fluke or the undeniable

response of a man for the woman he'd belatedly realized that he'd always loved.

He paid the check—his damned brothers had stiffed
him on the bill, on top of everything else—and then
headed down Main Street. In the middle of the block
he hesitated, staring across at the front of the drugstore
that had been his favorite hangout as a teenager. His
and Melissa's.

Little had changed. Dolan's Drugstore was still
printed in neat black, gold-edged letters on the door.
A display of toys sat on the shelf beneath the big plate-
glass window, visible to any child passing by. A rack
of comic books stood off to the side. Cody suspected
they were the same faded editions that had been there
a decade before. The toys looked suspiciously familiar,
too. In fact, when he'd crossed the street for a closer
look, he was almost certain that there was a ten-year
layer of dust on the red, toy fire truck.

Telling himself he was fifty kinds of crazy for going
inside, he found himself turning the knob on the door
anyway. A bell tinkled overhead, alerting anyone working that a customer had entered.

The soda fountain was on his left, partially blocked
by a section of shelves with first-aid supplies and a
new display of condoms. Talk about times changing.
He couldn't think of a better example. He recalled the
first time he'd ever come into the store to buy condoms.
They'd been behind the pharmacy counter then. He'd
blushed brick red when he'd had to ask Mabel Hastings to give them to him. It was a wonder he'd ever
gone back. His only consolation had been that she'd
seemed even more embarrassed. After that he'd always

made sure Eli was on duty when he'd returned for a new supply.

A half-dozen teenage girls were sitting on one side of the U-shaped soda fountain, probably discussing schoolwork, or, more likely, boys. An equal number of boys was on the opposite side, tongue-tied and uncertain. The sight of them brought back a slew of memories best forgotten.

There was no sign of Melissa, though clearly someone had served the kids their shakes and hamburgers. Cody fought a bitter feeling of disappointment. He hadn't wanted to come here, but now that he had gathered the courage, he wanted to get this encounter out of the way. He wanted to shove the past behind him once and for all. He doubted a meeting would be enough to keep him in Texas, but maybe it would buy him some peace of mind.

"Hey, Missy, customer!" one of the boys shouted as Cody slid onto a stool close to the cash register.

"I'll be right there," a voice capable of raising goose bumps on any man past puberty sang out from the back.

The door to the storeroom swung open. Melissa emerged, her arms loaded with two trays of glasses piled atop each other. Her gaze zeroed in on Cody with impeccable precision. Every bit of color washed from her face. The trays wobbled, then tilted. Glasses crashed to the floor. Her gaze never wavered from his, despite the sound of breaking glass.

Several of the teenagers sprang to their feet and rushed to clean up the mess. Cody couldn't have moved if his life had depended on it. Apparently Melissa couldn't, either. Not even the swirl of activity at her feet caught her attention. He felt as if he'd been punched in the gut.

This definitely wasn't the reaction he'd been praying for. In fact, it was exactly the opposite. He'd wanted to look into those soft, sea green eyes of hers and feel eighteen months of hurt and anger boiling into a fine rage. Or, better yet, he'd wanted to feel nothing at all.

Instead it appeared his hormones were very glad to see her. Obviously they had a different sort of memory pattern than his brain.

"Missy, are you okay?" one of the boys asked worriedly. He scowled in Cody's direction.

"Fine," she murmured.

The youngster, who looked all of fourteen, clearly wasn't convinced. Just as clearly, he had a big-time crush on Melissa. "Is he a problem?" he inquired, nodding toward Cody.

Apparently the boy's itch to slay dragons for her got her attention as nothing else had. She jerked her gaze away from Cody and smiled at the teenager.

"It's okay, David. Cody and I have known each other a long time." She patted his shoulder. "Thanks for cleaning up the glass, you guys. Your sodas are on me."

"Nah, you don't have to do that," David said, pulling money out of his pocket and leaving it on the counter. "Right, guys?"

The other boys dutifully nodded and pulled out their own cash. Unless costs at Dolan's had risen dramatically, they were very generous tippers, Cody noted as all of the teens departed.

"See you tomorrow," David called back from the doorway. He lingered uncertainly for another minute, as if he couldn't make up his mind whether Cody was to be trusted. When Melissa shot him another reassuring smile, he finally took off to catch up with his friends.

"Quite an admirer," Cody said. "I think he was ready to mop up the floor with me."

"David is just testing his flirting skills. I'm safer than those girls in his own class. He knows I won't laugh at him."

"Maybe you should. Better to hurt him now than later," he said with unmistakable bitterness.

Melissa looked as if he'd struck her. "I'm not going to hurt him at all. He's just a boy, Cody." She straightened her spine and glowered at him. "Look, if you came in here just to hassle me, you can turn right around and go back wherever you came from. I don't need the aggravation."

Cody grinned at the bright patches of color in her cheeks. Melissa had always had a quick temper. He suddenly realized he'd missed sparring with her almost as much as he'd missing making love with her.

"Actually, I came in for a milk shake," he said, coming to a sudden decision to play this scene all the way through. He propped his elbows on the counter. He waited until he'd caught her gaze, then lowered his voice to a seductive whisper. "A chocolate shake so thick, I'll barely be able to suck it very, very slowly through the straw."

The patches of color in Melissa's cheeks deepened. She twirled around so fast it was a wonder she didn't knock a few more pieces of glassware onto the floor with the breeze she stirred.

With her rigid back to him, Cody was able to observe her at his leisure. Her snug, faded jeans fit her cute little butt like a glove. That much hadn't changed, he noted with satisfaction. With every stretch, the cropped T-shirt she wore kept riding up to bare an intriguing inch or so of a midriff so perfect that it could make a man weep. Her long dark hair with its shimmering red highlights had been scooped up in a saucy ponytail that made her look a dozen years younger than the twenty-seven he knew she was.

And, to his very sincere regret, she made him every bit as hard now as she had as a teenager. He squirmed in a wasted effort to get more comfortable on the vinyl-covered stool.

When she finally turned back, she plunked his milk shake onto the counter with such force half of it sloshed out of the tall glass. Apparently she wasn't entirely im-mune to him, either, and she wasn't one bit happier about the discovery.

She grabbed up a dishrag and began scrubbing the opposite side of the counter, her back to him. Given the energy she devoted to the task, the surface was either very dirty or she was avoiding him.

"So, how've you been?" Cody inquired, managing the nonchalant tone with supreme effort.

"Fine," she said tersely, not even glancing around.

He frowned. Why the hell was she acting like the injured party here? She was the one who'd cheated on him. Getting her to meet him halfway became an irre-sistible challenge.

"How are you, Cody? It's been a long time," he coached.

She turned and glared. "Why are you here?" she de-manded instead.

He could have shot back a glib retort, but he didn't. He actually gave the question some thought. He considered the teasing he'd gotten from Jordan and Luke. He considered his own undeniable curiosity. He even considered the size of his ego, which had found being cheated on damned hard to take. The bottom line was, he had no idea what had drawn him across the street and into the drugstore.

"I don't know," he finally admitted.

Apparently it was the right answer because her lush, kissable mouth curved into a smile for the first time since she'd spotted him at the counter.

"You mean to tell me that there's something that actually stymies the brilliant, confident Cody Adams?"

He nodded slowly. "It surprises the dickens out of me, too."

She leaned back against the counter, her elbows propped behind her. It was a stance that drew attention to her figure, though Cody doubted she was aware of it.

"You planning on sticking around?" she asked.

"A few more days, just till Daddy's got his feet back under him again." It was the same response he'd given everyone who'd asked. Now that he was right here with Melissa in front of him, though, he wondered if she might not be the one person who could change his mind.

At the mention of his father, her expression immediately filled with concern. "It must be horrible for him."

"It is."

"And the rest of you?"

"We're doing okay. Mostly we're worried about Daddy. He adored Mother. It's going to be lonely as hell for him with her gone."

"I'm surprised you're not staying, then."

He shook his head. "There's nothing for me here anymore," he said automatically, refusing to concede that he had evidence to the contrary in the tightening of his groin at the first sight of her.

She actually blanched at his harsh words. "I'm sorry," she whispered, looking shaken. "What about White Pines? You always loved it. You were building your whole future around running that ranch."

She was right about that. He'd fought tooth and nail to get Harlan to trust him with the running of the ranch. He'd spent his spare time building his own house on the property just to make the point that, unlike Luke or Jordan, he never intended to leave. Then in a matter of seconds after catching Melissa with Brian, he'd thrown it all away.

Now, rather than addressing his longing to be working that land again, he shoved those feelings aside and clung instead to the bitterness that had sent him away.

"There's no way I can stay here now," he said, unable to prevent the accusing note that had crept into his voice. "You ruined it for me."

Melissa swallowed hard, but she kept her gaze on him steady. Some part of him admired her for not backing down.

"Maybe we should talk about what happened, Cody. Maybe if we could put it behind us, you'd change your mind about staying. Your decision to stay or go shouldn't have anything to do with me."

Talk about finding her in the arms of his best friend? Analyze it and pick it apart, until his emotions were raw? Cody practically choked on the idea. Once he got started on that subject, he doubted the conversation would remain polite or quiet. Eli would be bolting out from behind the prescription counter and Mabel, whom he'd spotted lurking over toward the cosmetics, would get a blistering earful.

No, he absolutely did not want to talk about the past. Or the present. And most definitely not about the bleak, lonely future he'd carved out for himself.

He slid off the stool and backed up a step. "There's nothing to say," he said, hoping his tone and his demeanor were forbidding enough to keep Melissa silent. He slapped a five on the counter, then tipped his hat.

"It's been a pleasure," he said in a tone that declared just the opposite.

He had made it almost to the door when he heard a soft gasp of dismay behind him. He stepped aside just as Velma Horton opened the door and pushed a stroller inside. His gaze went from Velma's shocked expression to the chubby-cheeked little girl who promptly reached her arms up toward him, a thoroughly engaging smile on her face. He stared at the toddler in stunned silence, then pivoted slowly to stare at Melissa. Her face was ashen, removing any doubt at all that the baby was hers.

For the second time in a matter of minutes Cody felt as if he'd been hit below the belt. He could count backward as quickly as anyone in Texas. That darling little girl with the big eyes and innocent smile looked to be a year old, which meant she was Brian's.

His blood felt like ice water in his veins, but he forced himself to walk back toward the soda fountain. "I see congratulations are in order," he said so politely it made his teeth ache. "Your daughter is beautiful."

"Thank you," Melissa said so softly that he could barely hear her.

"I guess you and Brian were meant to be, after all,"

he said, then turned on his heel and bolted for the door before he made an absolute idiot of himself.

He brushed past Velma and the baby without giving them a second glance. Damn, Melissa! She'd turned him inside out again. For a fleeting moment he'd actually wondered if he could put the past behind him and move on, maybe get something going with her again since his body was as hot for her now as it had been eighteen months ago. He'd allowed old feelings to stir to life, indulged in a few quick and steamy fantasies.

One look at that baby had shattered any possibility of that. He should have known that Melissa and Brian were together. He should have guessed that the betrayal was more serious than the one-night stand he'd tried desperately to convince himself it was. He should have realized that neither of them would have cheated on him for anything less than powerful emotions they couldn't control. He should have given them credit for that much at least. He couldn't make up his mind, though, if that should make him feel better or worse.

It wasn't until he was back at White Pines, riding hell-bent for leather across the open land trying to work off his anger and his pain that he stopped to wonder why Jordan and Luke would have set him up for such a terrible sucker punch. Couldn't they just have told him and saved him the anguish of making a fool of himself over Melissa all over again?

Instead they had taunted him into going into Dolan's. They had poked and prodded at all of his old feelings for Melissa until he could no longer ignore them. Would they have done that if they'd known about Brian? If they'd known about the baby? Harlan had done his share of nudging, too. He'd been the first to plant the seed about finding Melissa at Dolan's.

It didn't make a lick of sense. How could they not have known? It was a small town. Harlan sure as hell knew everything that went on. And yet they had sent him like a lamb to slaughter, straight back to Melissa.

He reined in his horse and sat for a long time contemplating the possibilities. For once in his life he was oblivious to the raw beauty of the land surrounding him. Since he knew damned well his brothers weren't cruel, their actions had to mean something. At the very least, he'd bet that Melissa and Brian weren't married, after all. At the most...

He thought of that cute little girl who'd practically begged him to pick her up.

He didn't even want to consider the astonishing, incredible idea that had just popped into his head. What if she was his? What if he was actually a father?

He tried the idea on for size and realized that a silly grin had spread across his face. A father? Yes, indeed, the possibility fit as well as those tight little jeans had caressed Melissa's fanny.

Then his grin faded as he considered all the time he'd lost if it were true. If that little girl was his, he resolved there was going to be hell to pay.

4

Melissa stood over Sharon Lynn's crib and stared down at her sleeping child. The baby's cheeks were flushed, her dark blond hair curling damply against her chubby neck. Her blue nightshirt was sprinkled with tiny yellow ducks. A larger, stuffed duck was cuddled next to her. It had been her favorite toy ever since she'd been to a duck pond a few months before. She refused to go to bed without it.

A smile curved Melissa's lips as she watched her baby and fought the desperate need to pick her up, to cling to her. She hadn't been able to let her daughter out of her sight since that terrible moment in the drugstore when Cody had come face-to-face with his child. In that instant her heart had ricocheted wildly and her breath had caught in her throat as she'd waited for him to recognize Sharon Lynn as his, just as Jordan had the very first time he'd spotted her. She'd almost been grateful that the decision to tell Cody or not to tell him had been taken out of her hands.

But instead of promptly recognizing the baby as his, Cody had clearly leapt to the conclusion that someone else was the father. Given the cold glint in his eyes when he'd stepped back to the counter to congratulate her in a voice devoid of emotion and his comment about her relationship with Brian having been meant to be, he must have assumed the father was Brian Kincaid. It was a further complication in an already complicated situation.

She sighed as she considered the terrible mess she had made of things. She should have told Cody everything straight off, right then and there, but her mother's terrified expression and her earlier dire warnings had kept Melissa silent, too fearful of the consequences of blurting out the truth.

She couldn't imagine what her life would be like without her baby. As difficult as things had gotten after she'd learned she was pregnant, there had never been a single instant when she'd regretted having Cody's child. Every time she looked into that precious face, she saw a miracle that she and Cody had created together. Beyond that biological tie, however, Cody had no right at all to claim his child. She was the only parent Sharon Lynn had ever known. If only she could keep it that way.

Unfortunately, though, there was no way the truth could be kept hidden forever. Cody had already seen his daughter. His brother knew that Sharon Lynn was Cody's. Sooner or later the pieces of the puzzle would come together, and when they did, she didn't have a doubt in her mind what Cody's reaction would be. If he'd been furious when he'd thought she was cheating on him with his best friend, he would destroy her when he found out about the baby she'd kept from him. Maybe he wouldn't fight her for custody as her mother feared, but he would make her life into the hell she deserved for deceiving him in the first place.

She rubbed her knuckles against Sharon Lynn's soft skin and sighed again. There was so much of Cody in her daughter. She had the same stubborn tilt to her chin, the same dark blond hair that streaked with gold in the summer sun. And, for the most part, she had the same sunny disposition and laughing eyes Cody had had before he thought Melissa had betrayed him.

It had hurt today to glimpse the old teasing Cody, only to see him vanish in the space of a heartbeat at the first mention of the past. When he'd walked out of Dolan's, her heart had been heavy with the burden of guilt and fear.

"I have to be the one to tell him," she whispered finally, her fingers caressing that precious cheek. "I have to tell your daddy all about you."

Maybe by revealing the truth herself, before he learned it from someone else, she would have some small chance of earning his forgiveness. They could work out a solution together.

Tomorrow, she vowed. First thing tomorrow afternoon when she got off work, she would drive out to White Pines and tell Cody everything. And then she would pray that it didn't cost her the only person on earth she held dear.

Too restless to stay in one place for long as he contemplated how to go about discovering whether Melissa's baby was his, Cody drove over to visit Jordan and Kelly. Six-year-old Dani was always a distraction and he just might get a chance to hold that nephew of his. He had a hunch it would be a bittersweet sensation given what he suspected about Melissa's child being his own.

"Uncle Cody!" Dani screamed when she caught sight of him. She ran and leapt into his arms, planting kisses all over his face. "I really, really missed you."

The weight of her in his arms, the peppermint-sticky kisses, filled him with nostalgia and accomplished exactly what he'd hoped for. "I really missed you, too, pumpkin. I'm sorry I didn't get to take those kittens you had for me awhile back."

She patted his cheek consolingly. "That's okay. Francie had more. Want to see? One is all black with a white nose. I think you'll really, really like him."

He grinned. "I bet I will," he agreed. "We'll go see him later."

"We'd better go now," Dani protested. "Later it will be my bedtime."

"Give me a few minutes inside to say hello to your mom," he negotiated. "I'm sure it won't be your bedtime then."

Dani braced her hands against his chest, leaned back in his arms and studied him intently. "You promise you won't leave without going to see the kittens?"

"I promise," he said, solemnly crossing his heart as he put her down.

"Okay," she said cheerfully, and ran toward the house screaming, "Mommy, Uncle Cody's here and he says he's going to take one of Francie's kittens."

"Thank goodness," Kelly called back as she emerged from the house, a grin on her face. "Conned you again, huh?"

He chuckled. "If you're not careful, that child of

yours is going to be the biggest scam artist in the entire United States."

"I prefer to think she'll have a career in diplomacy or maybe negotiating strike settlements," Kelly said. "Come on in. Jordan's still at the office, but he should be home soon."

His sister-in-law surveyed him closely. "How are you? You look lousy."

"Obviously Dani isn't the only one in the family with a silver tongue."

Kelly didn't bat an eye. "Did you see Melissa today?"

"I'm sure you know perfectly well that your husband and Luke badgered me into it."

"They said they were going to try. I wasn't sure if it had worked."

"I saw her," he admitted. "And her baby." He watched closely for Kelly's reaction. She remained expressionless.

"I see," she said blandly, keeping her attention focused on the vegetables she was chopping. "How did it go?"

Cody thought she was working awfully darned hard to feign disinterest. "Fine for the first few minutes, ugly after that."

"Oh, Cody," she protested softly. "Isn't it time you settled things with her and came home for good?"

Suddenly he didn't want to pursue the topic. He needed a break from it. They could get into it again when Jordan got home. Hopefully his brother would have answers that Kelly couldn't or wouldn't give him.

"I don't want to talk about Melissa right now. First I want to catch a glimpse of that brand new baby boy of yours," he declared just as Jordan came in and dropped a kiss on his wife's cheek.

"Hey, little brother, what brings you by?" Jordan asked, sneaking a carrot from the pile Kelly had just cut up.

"He's going to take a kitten," Dani chimed in. "Can we go see them now, Cody? It's later."

Since going to see the kittens would keep him from having to deal with the subject of Melissa and her baby a little longer, Cody stood and headed for the kitchen door. Dani tucked her hand in his.

"You should probably take two kittens," she said on the way out. "One might get lonely."

"Listen, young lady, I said one kitten," he protested over the sound of Kelly and Jordan's laughter.

"But you were going to take two last time." Apparently she caught his stern expression because she gave a little shrug of resignation. "I bet you'll change your mind when you see them."

A half hour later he was back in the kitchen with two kittens in a box. Dani had been giving him very precise instructions on caring for them ever since they'd left the barn. Kelly's expression turned smug when she saw him.

"You are pitiful," Jordan said, shaking his head. "Is there a female on the face of the earth you can resist?"

"Who are you kidding?" Cody shot back, gesturing to the big tomcat that was curled in Jordan's lap purring contentedly. "You always hated cats and now you're surrounded by them. I don't hear you complaining."

"You may not hear it," Kelly said, "but it is almost the last thing I hear every single night. He says 'Good night, I love you, no more cats,' all in one breath."

"I do not," Jordan said, dislodging the cat and pulling Kelly onto his lap.

Cody listened to their banter and watched their undisguised affection with envy. Until he'd lost Melissa he'd never thought he wanted marriage and kids. He'd been as commitment-phobic as any one of those jerks who made the rounds of the talk shows. Ironically, ever since their breakup, all he'd been able to think about was settling down and having kids. He'd deliberately isolated himself in Wyoming so he'd be far from the temptation to try something at which he knew he'd inevitably fail.

After all, he hadn't appreciated Melissa when he'd had her and she was as sexy and generous, as kind and intelligent, as any woman he'd ever known. He'd had a roving eye, just the same. He'd taken her for granted, which everyone in the family had accused him of doing at one time or another. He suspected he'd do the same with a wife. What was the point of ruining some woman's life for his own selfish longing to have just a taste of the kind of love Jordan and Luke had found?

"How long are you sticking around? Have you told your boss when you'll be back in Wyoming?" Jordan asked after Kelly insisted Cody stay for dinner.

Kelly dished up a serving of stew for him and lingered at his shoulder. "You are not going back until after J.J. is baptized," she said emphatically.

Cody glanced up at her. "When is that again?"

"Next weekend, which you know perfectly well. I sent you an invitation. We're going ahead with it. Harlan insisted."

Something in his expression must have given him

away because she frowned. "You ripped it up, didn't you?"

Cody recalled the scattered pieces of the pretty blue invitation and felt a tide of red rising in his cheeks. Was the woman a damned witch?

"Of course not," he fibbed.

The response drew a disbelieving snort. "So you'll be here at least that long," she said.

Cody had a feeling once he learned the truth about Melissa's baby, he wouldn't be able to get away from Texas fast enough. He'd need to cool his temper for a good long while before confronting her with what he knew. He'd also need time to make up his mind exactly what he wanted to do about the baby she'd kept from him. He intended to learn that truth in the next twenty-four hours.

"Sorry," he said eventually. "I can't promise to stay that long."

Kelly glanced at Jordan, then back at him. "Your brothers said you were going to say no," she said.

"I had no idea I was so predictable."

"Lately you are," his sister-in-law said. "Lately, you've gotten downright boring."

He gave her a wry look. "More of that fatal charm, I see."

Kelly frowned at his teasing. "What if I told you that Jordan and I want you to be the baby's godfather?"

Something deep inside him shifted at the offer. He felt an unexpected warm glow. It was a feeling he told himself he didn't deserve, especially not if he had a real child of his own he'd never even acknowledged.

"I'd say you made a lousy choice," he responded.

"I told you he wouldn't even be gracious about

it," Jordan chimed in. "Leave him be, Kelly. He's as stubborn as the rest of us when he digs in his heels. He'll change his mind, if we let the idea simmer long enough."

"I won't change my mind," Cody said. "Sorry."

"You say that a lot these days," Jordan observed.

"Maybe I have a lot to be sorry for."

"Well, this is one thing you can check off the list," Jordan said.

He spoke in that matter-of-fact way that indicated he'd reached a decision and wanted no further argument. It was a tactic that might have served him well in business, but it grated on Cody's nerves.

"I want you here, little brother," Jordan stated emphatically. "And I want you to be the baby's godfather. It's settled."

Despite his annoyance at Jordan's attempt to snatch the decision out of his hands, Cody could feel himself weakening, feel that odd, empty sensation in the pit of his stomach that always meant the loneliness was taking hold again.

"Did you check it out at the church?" he inquired lightly. "They'll probably be worried about lightning hitting the steeple if I show my hide in there."

"There was some mention of that, but I believe there's a general consensus that your soul is still salvageable," Kelly said. "Please, Cody. We've missed you. It's only for a few days more. How bad can that be?"

A few days, one hour, any time at all would be hell, especially if he discovered in the meantime that he had a baby of his own. Still, Cody had never been able to resist his sister-in-law. Kelly had been coaxing him into trouble since they were toddlers. Jordan had been too

stuffy even at seven to fall in with some of her more outrageous mischief, though there had never been a doubt
in anyone's mind that Jordan was the one she loved.

"I'll stick around," he said eventually. "Long enough
to get that nephew of mine in good graces with the Lord.
Then I'm heading right back out. Understood?"

"Understood," Kelly said meekly.

Kelly meek? Every alarm bell in him went off. Before he could get too caught up in trying to figure out
her angle, she was gone. He was left alone with Jordan,
while Kelly went upstairs to tuck Dani into bed. Suddenly the questions that had been tormenting him earlier in the day could no longer be ignored.

"Kelly mentioned that you saw Melissa and her little
girl today, after you left Luke and me," Jordan said, his
gaze fixed on Cody's face.

The comment gave him the perfect opening. "Why
didn't you warn me?" Cody asked, trying to keep the
anger out of his voice. "You knew about the baby, didn't
you?"

Jordan sighed, then nodded. "I saw her once, about
eight months ago. She was just a baby." He scanned
Cody's face as if looking for answers. "What did you
think when you saw her?"

"I figured Melissa and Brian had more going for
them than I'd realized. I figured they were a happy little
family now." Cody threw out the possibility to gauge
his brother's reaction. If Jordan knew anything different, he'd find it out now.

The color washed out of Jordan's face. "Did you say
that to Melissa?"

"More or less," he admitted. "Along with offering
her my congratulations."

"What did she say?"

"Nothing."

"I see."

Cody lost patience for the game. He knew darned well that Jordan knew more than he was saying. He could see it in his eyes. His brother was looking everywhere in the kitchen except directly at him.

"You might as well spit it out," he told him finally.

"What?"

"Whatever has you looking like you'd rather be in Kansas."

A faint grin tugged at Jordan's mouth. "Maybe Houston, not Kansas," he said. He sighed. "How good a look did you get at the child?"

"Good enough," Cody said. He sensed that Jordan wanted him to reach a different conclusion than he'd just offered all on his own. He sucked in a deep breath. "She's mine, isn't she?"

Once Cody had actually spoken the words out loud, Jordan nodded, confirming everything.

Cody's heart pounded. An uncommon mix of hope and dismay swirled through him. "You know that for sure?"

"I saw it right off," Jordan admitted. "She was the spitting image of your baby pictures. I confronted Melissa about it straight out."

Cody felt an icy chill settle over him as Jordan's earlier comment came back to him. He stood and leaned down to look his brother in the eye. "And that was when? About eight months ago, you said?"

"Yes," Jordan replied softly.

"And Melissa confirmed your suspicions right then

and there?" he demanded, the hurt and anger of yet another betrayal slamming through him.

"Yes."

"Damn you, Jordan," he snapped, backing up to prevent slamming a fist in his brother's face. "How could you do that to me? How could you keep a secret like that? Didn't you think I had a right to know? Or was this another one of those big-brother-knows-best decisions?"

"She pleaded with me not to tell you," Jordan said simply.

Cody stared at him incredulously. "And your loyalty was with her and not me?"

"Why the hell do you think I've done everything in my power to get you back here? I didn't want to lay this on you when you were in Wyoming. I wanted you here, so you could see for yourself. I didn't want you to accuse me or her of making it up just to get you back here."

Cody wasn't buying it. "No, you were more concerned with keeping your promise to a woman who betrayed me than you were with doing what was right—giving me a chance to know my own child." He turned on his heel and headed for the door, the box of kittens in tow. "I can't believe you would do something like this. Maybe family loyalty doesn't mean anything once you're a big corporate executive. Is that it, big brother?"

"Cody, you have it all wrong," Kelly protested when she came back into the kitchen. Obviously she had overheard the tail end of the argument.

"I don't think so," he snapped, shooting her a look of regret. "Don't expect me at the baptism, after all. In fact, forget you even know me."

Kelly called out after him. He heard the screen door slam behind her, then Jordan murmuring something he couldn't quite make out. Whatever it was, though, it silenced her. When he looked back as he drove away, he saw them standing on the porch staring after him. He was sure it was only his imagination, but he thought he saw his brother wiping something that might have been tears from his cheeks.

He slowed the car momentarily and closed his eyes against the tide of anguish washing through him. Melissa had done it again. She had come between him and his family. He vowed then and there it would be the last time. This time he wouldn't run. He wouldn't let her control his destiny as he had before.

Forgetting all about his resolve to let his temper cool, an hour later he was in town, pounding on the Hortons' front door. Ken Horton, wearing a robe and slippers, opened it a crack. At the sight of Cody, he swung it wider, a welcoming smile spreading across his weathered face. Cody could see Velma's panicky expression as she stared over her husband's shoulder.

"Cody, what on earth?" Horton grumbled. "You trying to wake the whole neighborhood?"

"Where's Melissa?"

"She's not here," he said as his wife tugged frantically on his arm. When he leaned down, she whispered something in his ear, something that wiped any lingering expression of welcome from his face. "Go on home, Cody."

"Not until you tell me where she is."

"Don't make me call the sheriff."

"Don't make me pound the information out of you," Cody shot back belligerently.

Ken Horton regarded him sympathetically. "Boy, go on home and get some sleep. If you've got things to talk over with Melissa, do it in the morning, when you're calmer."

Despite his earlier promise to himself to think things through clearly, Cody realized he didn't want to be calm when he talked to Melissa. He wanted this rage to keep him focused, to keep him immune to the sight of her. He wanted to have this out with her while he was hot with anger, not lust.

"If I have to knock on every door in town, I'm going to talk to her tonight," he swore.

"There's nothing you have to say, nothing you need to know, that won't be settled just as readily in the morning," Horton repeated, still calm, still intractable.

Cody considered it as much as an admission that he and Melissa had serious issues to resolve, such as his relationship to that baby. He gathered from the warning look Horton shot at his now tearful wife that they didn't entirely agree on whether Cody had the right to know the truth.

"Where can I find her in the morning?" he asked finally, resigned to the delay. They all knew he wouldn't tear through town, creating yet another ruckus he'd never live down.

"She gets to work about nine," her father told him.

"I'm not talking to her at Dolan's," he said. "I don't want the whole town knowing our business."

Horton seemed about to offer an alternative when Velma piped up. "That'll just have to do," she said. "We're not telling you where she lives."

He couldn't decide if Velma was worried about him throttling Melissa or if she was simply being protective of her daughter's secret. Because he wasn't sure, he backed down.

"If you talk to her, let her know I'll be by the minute the doors open. Tell her to arrange with Eli for someone to cover for her unless she wants her personal life broadcast to everyone in town."

To his surprise, Ken Horton held out his hand. When Cody shook it, Melissa's father said, "For whatever it's worth, Cody, I think it's about time you two got everything out in the open. The two of you had something special once. Melissa's been punished enough for making one foolish mistake."

He gave his wife a defiant look. "And a man has a right to claim his child."

Velma Horton groaned and covered her face with her hands. Tears spilled down her cheeks. Cody wondered at the fear he'd seen in her eyes right before she placed her hands over them. She'd had the same terrified expression earlier in the day. He'd always thought Velma Horton liked him. Now she seemed to think he was some sort of a monster.

Was she blaming him for running out on her pregnant daughter? Or was it something more? He wondered what could possibly be behind the expression he'd read in her eyes.

Eventually, as he slowly walked back to his pickup, it came to him. She was actually afraid that he'd come home to take his baby away from Melissa.

Was that what he intended? He sat in his truck on the dark street in front of the Hortons' house, his head resting on the steering wheel. He honestly hadn't thought beyond discovering the truth and confronting Melissa with it.

Obviously, it was a good thing Ken Horton had prevented him from seeing Melissa tonight. He needed to get his thoughts in order. He needed to have a plan. For once in his life he couldn't act on impulse. Too many lives were at stake, his own, Melissa's, and that darling little girl's.

His heart ached every time he thought about his daughter. His arms felt empty, just as they did when Dani climbed out of them or he had to turn Angela back over to Jessie or Luke. He wondered about that vacant place he'd thought would always be inside him and realized that there was someone who could fill it, a child of his own.

Tomorrow he would claim her. He realized he didn't even know her name or how old she was or whether she could walk or talk. So many precious details. He sighed. Tomorrow he would fill in the gaps.

Tomorrow he would finally experience what it was like to feel like a father. Right now it was all too abstract, but in the morning he would hold his child in his arms. Whatever else happened between him and Melissa, he vowed that nothing would ever rip his baby away from him again.

5

Her mother had warned her. In fact, the first thing out of Velma's mouth when Melissa had dropped off her daughter for the day had been a detailed description of Cody's late-night visit. Based on Velma's panicked reaction, Melissa had been tempted to take Sharon Lynn and flee. She knew, though, that in his present mood Cody would only track her down.

Besides, hadn't she resolved just last night to tell him herself about Sharon Lynn? The decision on the timing had just been taken out of her hands. Of course, that also meant that his anger had had all night to simmer. She walked to work, dreading the confrontation that was clearly only minutes away.

She meant to ask Eli for an hour or so off to deal with a personal matter. She meant to be outside, on the sidewalk, when Cody arrived. She meant to do everything possible to ensure their conversation took place in private, away from prying eyes and potential gossip. She meant to be calm, reasonable, even conciliatory.

Cody took any chance of that out of her hands.

Before the door to the drugstore fully closed behind her, Melissa heard the bell ring loudly as the door slammed open again. Without even turning around, she sensed it was Cody. The air practically crackled with tension. She pivoted reluctantly and found him so close she could almost feel his breath on her face. She surveyed him slowly from head to toe, trying to gauge exactly how furious he was.

He looked exhausted. His mouth was set in a grim line. His shoulders were stiff. His hands were balled into fists. He also looked as if he'd slept in his clothes, perhaps in his truck, right in front of the drugstore. That would explain why he'd appeared right on her heels.

Despite all that, her heart flipped over. Her pulse scrambled. She had the most absurd desire to fling herself straight into his arms.

But she couldn't. More precisely, she didn't dare. It would only complicate an already impossible situation. She sucked in a deep breath and waited. The first move was going to have to be his.

As she waited, she was suddenly aware of every sound, every movement. She could hear the hum of the electric clock, the rattle of plastic bottles and *ping, ping, ping* of pills being counted out as Eli filled a prescription in the back, the swish of a mop as Mabel dusted the floor. Mabel rounded the aisle of shelves, caught sight of the silent tableau at the front of the store and stopped and stared.

Melissa felt like screaming. Mabel's presence was anticipated, but unfortunate. Of all the people in town, she was the most likely to spread word of every last detail of any encounter between Melissa and Cody. Her pale eyes sparkled as she watched the two of them.

Cody tipped his hat to Mabel, but didn't extend even

that much courtesy to Melissa before latching on to her arm and practically hauling her into the storage room, past the startled gaze of Eli Dolan. Cody kicked the door shut behind them, plunging them into darkness.

"Dammit, Cody, what do you think you're doing?" Melissa demanded, trying to wrench herself free and reach the light switch at the same time. She couldn't succeed at doing either one.

"We need to talk," he declared, seemingly oblivious to the lack of light.

"Fine. Then let's do it like two civilized adults. There's no need for your caveman routine."

He was close enough that she could see that his eyes sparked fire, but he released his grip on her. Melissa felt along the wall until she found the switch. She flipped it on, illuminating the room that was small under the best of conditions, but claustrophobic with Cody pacing in the cramped space.

Somehow he managed to neatly avoid the stacks of just-delivered boxes, metal shelves of inventory and a disorderly array of cleaning supplies. Melissa had the feeling that he was practically daring the inanimate objects to give him an excuse to knock them all to the floor. She couldn't recall ever seeing him quite so angry or quite so speechless. Cody's glib tongue was known far and wide, especially among women.

She kept silent and waited. Finally he stopped in front of her, his hands shoved in his pockets, legs spread, a belligerent expression on his handsome face.

"Whose baby is it?" he demanded in a tone that made her hackles rise.

Melissa made up her mind then and there that she wasn't giving in to his bullying or to any coaxing he might decide to try when that failed. Maybe that had been the problem in the past. She'd been too darned easy on him, too much in love to ever say no. She hoisted her chin a challenging notch. They were going to have a conversation on her terms for a change.

"Good morning to you, too, Cody."

Cody's gaze narrowed at the sarcasm. "Dammit, I asked you a straight question. The least you could do is give me a straight answer."

She wasn't sure where she found the courage to face him down, but she did. "Why should I, when you're acting like a bully?"

"I think I have a right to act any damn way I please."

"No," she said softly. "You don't. I told you before that we can discuss this like two civilized adults or I can go into the other room and go to work."

He raked his hand through his hair in a gesture that was vintage Cody. She'd always been able to tell exactly how frustrated or annoyed he was by the disheveled state of his hair.

"If that baby's mine, I have a right to know," he retorted, his voice starting to climb.

"I was under the impression that you already know the answer to that. You certainly carried on as if you did when you dropped in on my parents last night."

He didn't look even vaguely chagrined by the reminder of his outrageous behavior on her parents' doorstep. "I want to hear it from you," he snapped. "I want to hear why you kept it from me. If I am that child's father, I should have been told about her way back when you first discovered you were pregnant. I had a right to know. We should have been making decisions together."

Melissa met his gaze unflinchingly. "You gave up

any rights the day you left town without so much as a goodbye. You never got in touch. I didn't know where you were. How was I supposed to let you know?"

"Jordan knew where I was, but you made damned sure he wouldn't tell me, didn't you?"

"Because your leaving town the way you did told me everything I needed to know about how you felt about me. What was the point of dragging you back so you could tell me to kiss off?"

She could almost see his patience visibly snap.

"Dammit, Melissa, you know that I had more than enough cause to go," he practically shouted, slamming his fist into a box and sending it crashing to the floor. Judging from the shattering noise it made, it was the glasses Eli had bought to replace the supply she'd broken only the day before.

Eli opened the door a crack and peered inside, his expression anxious. "Everything okay back here?"

"Fine," Cody and Melissa said in unison. The response wasn't very heartfelt from either of them.

Eli glanced at the box on the floor and shook his head wearily. He backed away without comment and shut the door.

Throughout the interruption, Cody had kept his gaze fastened on her face, sending color flooding into her cheeks. "You know I'm right," he said more quietly the instant they were alone again. "You cheated on me."

She had known from the beginning that that was what he believed. She had even wanted him to believe it…up to a point. Even so, it hurt to hear him say it. "Still jumping to conclusions, I see. That was always one of your worst habits, Cody."

He shoved his fingers through his thick hair again.

"Jumping to conclusions," he repeated incredulously. "Did you or did you not sleep with my best friend?"

She was amazed at the speed with which the conversation had veered from the subject of their daughter to the real source of Cody's fury. He'd had well over a year to work up a good head of steam on the subject and clearly he intended to vent it now, unless she put a quick stop to it.

"I did not," she told him quietly.

"See—" he began triumphantly. His expression suddenly faltered as her reply finally penetrated his thick skull. "You didn't?"

"Never," she said emphatically, her gaze unflinching.

"But I saw…"

"You saw exactly what I wanted you to see." She shrugged. "Unfortunately, you leapt to the wrong conclusion."

He stared at her blankly. "I don't get it."

It was time—way past time—to spell it out for him. "Brian and I had one date. It wasn't even a date, really. It was a setup. Brian only went along with it because he knew I was crazy about you. You were supposed to get wildly jealous, realize you were madly in love with me, and propose. You were supposed to fight for me. You weren't supposed to haul your butt out of town without looking back."

"Jealous?" He stared at her in bemusement. "How the hell was I supposed to know that? You were in his arms. What was I supposed to think, that you were discussing the weather?" he asked in a tone loud enough to wake the dead.

"You're shouting again," she observed.

He scowled. "Well, so what if I am?"

Melissa chuckled despite herself. He was too darned stubborn to recognize even what was staring him straight in the face, much less the subtleties of the trap she had tried to spring on him. No wonder it had failed so miserably. She should have issued an ultimatum in plain English if she'd wanted him to marry her, not tried to trick him into recognizing his own feelings. As for right now, he obviously needed his present circumstances clarified for him.

"Mabel's probably taking notes," she stated patiently. "Eli may be calling the sheriff. Other than that, there's no reason to quiet down that I can think of."

Cody groaned and sank onto a stack of boxes. When he finally looked at her again, she thought she detected a hint of wonder in his eyes.

"Then the baby really is mine?" he asked quietly. "Jordan was right?"

"No doubt about it, at least in anyone's mind except yours."

His gaze honed in on hers and an expression of complete awe spread over his face. "I have a baby."

"Actually, you have a *toddler,*" she corrected. "She's thirteen months old."

"Whatever," he said, clearly unconcerned with the distinction. "Tell me everything. I want to know her name. How long you were in labor. What time she was born. I want to know what she likes to eat, whether she can talk, how many steps she's taken, if she has allergies, what her favorite toy is. I want to know every last detail."

The yearning behind his words struck her. He almost sounded as if he regretted missing out on so much. His eagerness was impossible to resist. Suddenly she couldn't wait to see him with his daughter. It was something she'd dreamed about since the first moment the doctor had confirmed her pregnancy.

"Wouldn't you rather just go and meet her?" Melissa inquired softly.

He nodded, apparently speechless again.

"I'll speak to Eli and be right with you," she promised.

"Don't try ducking out the back," he warned, but he was grinning when he said it.

"I'm not the one who runs," she reminded him.

His comment might have been half-teasing, but hers was not. She wanted him to know that she was stronger now than she had been when he'd abandoned her. She wanted him to know that she was tough enough and secure enough to fight him for her daughter, if she had to.

But she also wanted him to see that she was brave enough to allow him into his child's life, if he wanted a place there. This wasn't about her any longer. It wasn't about her feelings for Cody, though those clearly hadn't died. This was about her daughter and what was best for her. It was about giving her child a chance to know her father.

Even so, as they walked down Main Street toward the tree-lined street where her family had lived her whole life, Melissa couldn't help the vague stirring of hope deep inside her. The past year and a half of loneliness and regret had been wiped out of her heart in the blink of an eye. Left in its wake was anticipation, the eager-to-start-the-day anticipation of a woman in love. As dangerous an emotion as that was, she could no more have prevented it than she could have held back the wildness of a tornado's winds.

Cody was back and she might as well admit to herself one more truth. Time and distance hadn't dulled her feelings for him a bit. She wanted him every bit as fiercely as she ever had.

Cody was in a daze. He was only marginally aware of the woman walking beside him. Instead he kept seeing images of the child that he now knew without any doubt whatsoever was his. Melissa's confirmation kept echoing over and over in his head. He was a father.

The realization was both incredible and scary. What if he blew it? What if his daughter took one look at him and rejected him? Okay, the latter was unlikely. Just the day before she had reached for him as if she already knew who he was. He recalled the eager stretch of her arms in the air and the sensation of tenderness that had welled up inside him at her innocent smile.

On the walkway at the Hortons' he paused, his hand on Melissa's arm. "Wait."

She turned a quizzical look on him. "Second thoughts?"

"No." He swallowed hard. "What's her name?"

"Sharon Lynn."

He repeated it softly, just to hear how it sounded on his tongue. "I like it."

"I'm not sure she'll tolerate being called by both when she gets a little older, but for now that's what we call her. My father tends to call her Pookie. I'm trying to break him of the habit. I will not have my child go through life being nicknamed Pookie. Missy is bad enough."

He smiled at her and barely resisted the urge to reach over and brush a strand of auburn hair from her cheek. "I never called you Missy."

"For which I was exceedingly grateful. That's probably why I let you get away with so much."

"You never let me get away with a thing," he protested.

"That baby inside says otherwise."

"I'll have to remember that," he said, grinning. "If I just whisper your name in your ear, you'll do anything I ask, is that right?"

She frowned, probably at the sudden provocative note in his voice. He knew she didn't want him to guess how easily he got to her. She was going to fight him tooth and nail.

"That was then," she said staunchly, confirming his guess. "This is now and the tide has turned, cowboy."

He readily accepted the challenge in her tone. "Is that so, Me…liss…a?" He deliberately drew her name out. Before she could react to the teasing, he lowered his head and dropped a quick kiss on her parted lips. "See, it still works."

The startled, slightly dazed expression on her face almost tempted him to try again. That brief brush of his mouth over hers had been just enough to tantalize him. Memories of warm, moist kisses and stolen caresses slammed through him, turning teasing into something very, very serious.

How had he ever walked away from her? Why hadn't he stayed and fought, just as she'd demanded earlier? Had it been the gut-deep sense of betrayal that had driven him all the way to Wyoming? Or had it simply been the even more powerful fear of the commitment to which fighting for her would have led? He'd never thought of himself as a coward, but suddenly he was taking a long, hard look at his actions in a whole new light.

"Cody?"

He blinked and gazed down into her upturned face. Before he could question himself, he scooped his hand through her silky hair to circle the back of her neck. With his gaze fixed on her turbulent sea green eyes, he reclaimed her mouth, lingering this time, savoring, remembering.

He felt her hands on his chest, tentative at first, then more certain as she slid them up to his shoulders and clung. Her body fit itself neatly, automatically, into his, the movement as natural as breathing and far, far more exciting.

Cody couldn't believe he had ever walked away from this. He couldn't imagine how he had lived without the sweetness of her kisses or the heat of her body pressed against his. The swirl of sensations was overpowering, demanding…and totally inappropriate for a sidewalk in plain view, he realized as a passing car honked and the teenage driver shouted out encouragement.

Melissa backed away as if she'd been burned. Her face was flaming with embarrassment. A warning flashed in her eyes, turning them the shade of soft jade in sunlight.

"That can't happen again," she stated emphatically.

"It can and it will," Cody said with just as much certainty. "Count on it."

Alarm flared in her expression. "No, Cody, this isn't about you and me anymore."

"Sure it is, darlin'. It always was."

"No!" She practically shouted it, as if volume might make her edict clearer. "You and I are over. You saw to that."

Cody dropped his own voice to a seductive growl. "We'll see," he taunted.

"Dammit, Cody, do you or do you not want to see your daughter?"

"Of course I do," he said, amused that she seemed to think the two concepts were diametrically opposed. "Meeting Sharon Lynn has absolutely nothing to do with my intentions toward you."

"Yes, it does," she said stubbornly.

"You're not keeping me from my daughter," he responded emphatically. "And you're not going to put up much resistance, once I set my mind to winning you back."

A scowl darkened her face. "You are the most arrogant, most infuriating man on the face of the earth. It's too late, Cody. You couldn't win me back if you courted me from now till we're both tottering around in orthopedic shoes."

A grin tugged at his lips. "Is that a challenge?"

"That's a guarantee."

Chuckling at her sincere conviction that she could win a test of wills with him, he took her hand and headed for the house.

"You don't have a chance, sweet pea," he told her solemnly as he ushered her inside, where Velma was waiting, her gaze wary. He lowered his voice to taunt one last time, "You don't have a snowball's chance in hell."

Melissa never responded because her mother spoke up just then.

"You brought him," Velma said, her tone accusing.

"You knew I would," Melissa told her mother. "Where's Sharon Lynn?"

"Down for her nap," she said, a note of triumph in her voice. "There's no need to wake her."

Cody was aware of the undercurrents between mother and daughter. Clearly, Velma was angry about his presence. Once again he had the sense that she feared him having any contact at all with his child.

Melissa shot him a vaguely apologetic look. "I'll get her," she said.

He fell into step beside her. "Don't wake her. I'll come with you. Let me just look at her for now. Your mother's right. There's no need to wake her yet."

If he had expected the suggestion to gain Velma's approval, he failed. He should have saved his breath. An expression of doom on her face, she trailed along behind them. He had the feeling she would have thrown herself across the threshold to the bedroom if she'd thought it would keep him away from her granddaughter.

He couldn't waste time worrying about Velma, though. From the instant he stepped into the room his gaze was riveted to the child asleep in the crib. She was sleeping on her stomach, her legs drawn up under her, her butt sticking up in the air. He couldn't imagine the position being comfortable, but she was sleeping soundly.

Awestruck, he moved closer to the crib. Melissa stayed a few steps behind him. Her mother never budged from the doorway. He studied the tiny, balled-up fists. Her skin looked soft as down and her light curls feathered around her face like wispy strands of silk. Her mouth curved like a miniature bow of pink. She was perfect. Adorable.

An overwhelming surge of protectiveness spread through him. This was his daughter. *His!* He'd seen Luke with the newborn Angela. He had watched Jordan hold J.J., but he had never guessed the depth of emotions that his brothers must have been feeling. He'd never experienced anything like it before in his life.

"She's so beautiful," he whispered, his voice choked.

"She has your eyes, your hair," Melissa said quietly.

"And your mouth," he noted. "I had no idea."

"No idea about what?"

"That it was possible to create anything so perfect."

Melissa laughed softly. "You haven't seen her throw a tantrum yet."

He turned toward her and grinned. "Ah, so she has your temper, too?"

"Oh, no," Melissa protested. "You're not blaming me for that. Every ounce of stubbornness she possesses she got from you."

Gazing directly into her eyes, he slipped an arm around her waist and pulled her close. "Thank you."

"For?"

He wasn't certain how to explain all that he was grateful to her for. For having the baby, even without him in her life. For keeping her healthy and safe. For loving her. So many things.

"For our daughter," he said simply.

"Oh, Cody," she whispered, tears welling up in her eyes and spilling down her cheeks.

"Shh, darlin', don't cry," he said, pulling her close. "You're not alone anymore."

To his astonishment, he realized that after the loneliest year and a half of his life, he was no longer alone, either. He was just a visit to the preacher away from having a family of his own. And nothing or no one was going to stand in his way.

6

Still awestruck, Cody was knee-deep in mental wedding plans before he and Melissa walked out the front door of her parents' house. He was so caught up in thinking ahead to the day when Melissa and Sharon Lynn would move into his old house out at White Pines, that he almost forgot to ask Melissa to have dinner with him that night so he could officially propose and go over the details.

"Both of you," he told her as they stood in front of the drugstore a few minutes later. "You and Sharon Lynn. We'll go to DiPasquali's. I'll pick you up at your folks' place after you get off work."

Her lips set in a stubborn expression he knew only too well.

"Was there an invitation in there somewhere or did you mean it to sound like an order?" she asked.

He supposed they could quibble all morning over the difference, but he didn't see much point to it. They had far bigger issues to worry about, like setting a wedding date in the next week or so. Now that he'd seen his daughter, nothing was going to keep him from her.

The prospect of instant parenthood scared the daylights out of him, but he was eager to get started, anxious to make up for lost time. He considered Melissa part of the package, of course.

"An invitation, of course," he said, wise enough to pacify Melissa. He wanted her in a receptive frame of mind tonight. He didn't want her stubborn streak kicking in. "Would you like to have dinner with me tonight at DiPasquali's?"

"I think your daughter is a little young for pizza."

Based on the spark of amusement in her eyes, she might have been teasing, but Cody took her comment seriously. He hadn't thought of that. In fact, what he really knew about babies would fit on the head of a pin. That was easily corrected. He would buy a book on parenting at the first opportunity. He was going to be the best-prepared father on the face of the planet, even if he was getting a late start.

"There must be something on the menu there she can eat," he said. "Or is there someplace that would be better?"

"DiPasquali's is fine," Melissa soothed. "I'll feed her first. She can chew on a slice of bread while we eat. She'll be perfectly content. She loves to eat out. She gets a lot of attention."

"Fine, whatever," he murmured distractedly, already thinking ahead to what he needed to accomplish between now and dinnertime.

He wanted to buy an engagement ring. And that book on parenting, of course. If he couldn't find one in town, maybe Luke or Jordan would have one he could borrow. He needed to call Lance Treethorn and tell him he wouldn't be returning to Wyoming. And he should sit down with his father and work out an arrangement for taking over his old duties at White Pines. Harlan would probably be relieved to be sharing the workload again.

"Cody?"

"Hmm?" He glanced up and caught Melissa's serious expression. "What's wrong?"

"Nothing. I'm just glad you want to be part of your daughter's life."

He stared at her, uncertain what would have made her ever suspect he'd do otherwise. "Well, of course, I do."

Melissa shrugged. "I wasn't sure how you were going to feel. And Mother, well, she had this crazy idea you were going to fight me for custody."

Cody couldn't imagine why he would have to fight for custody. He was going to claim his daughter *and* Melissa. If he'd known about the baby eighteen months ago, he would never have left for Wyoming in the first place. The incident with Brian might never have happened. He and Melissa would have been married. Custody arrangements would never have become an issue. At least, he finally understood Velma's reaction to him.

"That explains why she's been looking at me as if I'm about to steal the silver," he said.

"Yes."

"Well, she can stop worrying. We'll settle everything tonight." He leaned down and dropped a kiss on Melissa's lips. "See you later."

"Settle everything?" she repeated, a note of anxiety in her voice. "Cody!"

He turned back.

"What does that mean, we're going to settle everything?"

He smiled. "Not to worry, darlin'. We'll talk about it tonight."

* * *

"Exactly what did he say?" Velma fretted as Melissa bathed her daughter and got her ready for their evening with Cody.

"He said we'd settle everything tonight." She grabbed Sharon Lynn's rubber duck in midair as her daughter hurled it from the tub.

"What does that mean?"

Melissa sighed. "I don't know what it means, Mother. I suppose I'll find out shortly."

"I don't like it. I think your father and I should be there to protect your interests."

"I doubt Cody intends to pluck Sharon Lynn out of her high chair at the restaurant and carry her off into the night," she said as she toweled her daughter dry. "Anything other than that, I can cope with just fine on my own."

"What if he does decide to take her?"

"He won't," Melissa repeated, not sure how she knew with such conviction that Cody wouldn't do something so outrageous. "Stop worrying. I can handle Cody."

"You couldn't handle him two years ago," her mother commented. "What makes you think things are so different now?"

Melissa thought carefully about that before she answered. She used the struggle to get Sharon Lynn into her red corduroy pants and a cute little flowered shirt to buy some time.

"I'm stronger than I was then," she said eventually. "I've had almost two years to see that I don't need Cody Adams in order to survive. Sharon Lynn and I are doing just fine on our own."

Her mother regarded her skeptically. "Are you saying you're immune to him now?"

The kiss they'd shared on the front walk burned its way into her awareness. "No," she admitted. "I can't say that."

Velma groaned. "I knew it. I knew it the minute I saw the two of you playing kissy-face on the front walk."

"We were not playing kissy-face," Melissa retorted, blushing just the same. "Maybe you and Mabel have the same vocabulary after all."

"Mabel saw you kissing, too?"

"No, she just accused me of making goo-goo eyes at him way back in junior high."

"If only you'd limited yourself to that," Velma said dryly.

Melissa frowned. "If I had, we wouldn't have Sharon Lynn," she reminded her mother quietly.

Velma retreated into silence after that. She was still looking anxious when Cody arrived to pick them up. Melissa had a feeling she had her father to thank for keeping her mother from racing down the driveway after them. He appeared to have a tight grip on her elbow and a glint of determination in his eyes as he waved them off.

The ride to DiPasquali's took only minutes. It was a wonder they didn't crash into a tree, though. Cody couldn't seem to take his eyes off his daughter. Sharon Lynn returned his overt inspection with shy, little peek-a-boo smiles. Apparently she'd inherited her father's flirtatious nature, too, Melissa thought with some amusement. Cody was clearly captivated. She should have been pleased, but the doubts her mother had planted kept her from fully relaxing and enjoying the way father and daughter were bonding.

At the small Italian restaurant where both she and Cody were well known, they were ushered to a back booth amid exclamations over Sharon Lynn's outfit and Cody's return. Melissa didn't miss the speculative looks sent their way by customers who knew their history only too well.

Though a high chair was set up at the end of the table for the baby, Cody insisted she was just fine beside him in the booth. Sharon Lynn stood on the vinyl seat next to him, bouncing on tiptoes and patting Cody on the top of his head.

He circled her waist with his hands and lifted her into the air, earning giggles and a resounding kiss for his trouble. Melissa watched the pair of them with her heart in her throat. When Sharon Lynn climbed into Cody's lap, studied him seriously for a full minute, then cooed, "Da," Melissa felt the salty sting of tears in her eyes.

Cody's mouth dropped open. "Did she just call me Da?"

Apparently sensing approval, Sharon Lynn repeated the sound. "Da, Da, Da."

"She knows who I am," he whispered incredulously.

Melissa hated to disappoint him, but she knew that her daughter tended to call every man that. Besides, she refused to admit that she had tried to teach Sharon Lynn that very word while showing her a snapshot of Cody. She seriously doubted her daughter had actually made the connection between that blurry picture and the man holding her now.

She almost told him not to get too excited over it. Sharon Lynn might not even remember to connect that word with him tomorrow. The look in Cody's eyes kept her silent. He clearly wanted to believe that he and his child had made some sort of cosmic connection.

As she watched the pair of them, something shifted inside Melissa. Her earlier doubts fled. Maybe there really was some sort of instinctive bond between father and child. She wasn't sure what to make of this softer, gentler Cody. He had always been filled with laughter, but there was something incredibly sweet and tender in the way he teased his daughter and kept her giggling. Pride shone in his eyes at everything she did.

"She's brilliant," he declared every few minutes over the simplest accomplishments.

Sharon Lynn was clearly basking in the praise and the attention. Melissa held her breath, wondering just when exhaustion would overtake her daughter and turn that cheerful demeanor into far more familiar crankiness and tears. She couldn't help worrying about how Cody would respond to his child then. Would he turn tail and run again the instant the newness of this experience wore off, just as he had abandoned a long string of women once he'd tired of them? She was torn between anticipation and panic as she waited to see how the rest of the evening would play out.

They made it through their pizza without calamity striking. Sharon Lynn yawned a few times, grabbed a handful of the mushrooms Melissa had removed from her slice and squished them. When Cody tried to wipe her hands, she began sobbing as if she were being tortured.

Cody stared at Melissa helplessly as Sharon Lynn batted his hands away. "What did I do?"

"You didn't do anything. She's tired."

"Are you sure? Maybe she's hurt. Maybe there was a piece of glass and she cut herself." He unfolded her tightly clenched fingers and examined each one.

"Any sign of blood?" Melissa inquired, barely hiding her amusement.

He scowled at her. "How can you be so calm?"

"Because this is a nightly ritual."

He blanched. "Nightly?"

She nodded. "Just about. She gets so tired she can hardly keep her eyes open, but she doesn't want to miss anything, so she fights going to sleep."

Cody was regarding the sobbing child as if she were an alien creature. "Want me to take her?" she offered.

"No," he said insistently. "I have to learn how to deal with this."

He lifted Sharon Lynn up and sat her on the edge of the table facing him. Huge tears rolled down her blotchy cheeks. "Okay, kiddo, let's try to figure out a solution for this little problem you have with bedtime."

"Cody?"

He glanced up at her. "Hmm?"

"I don't think reason and logic are going to work."

"Sure they will," he argued. "Just watch."

He began talking in a low, soothing tone, explaining very patiently that sleep was very important. He added a lot of nonsense about fairy princesses and treasures that didn't come from any storybook Melissa had ever read.

Whether it was his tone or the actual words, Sharon Lynn's eyelids began to droop. The next thing Melissa knew, she was cradled in Cody's arms, sound asleep.

"Amazing," she admitted. "I should hire you to do that."

"No need to hire me," he said, his gaze suddenly

fixed on her in a way that had her pulse scrambling. "I intend to be available for bedtime duty every night from now on."

Melissa swallowed hard against the tide of panic that swept through her. Surely she hadn't heard him right. "Excuse me?" she whispered.

"Once we're married, I'll get her to bed," he said, making his intentions perfectly clear.

"Married?" she repeated as if it were an unfamiliar concept.

"Well, of course," he said. "What did you think was going to happen?" He reached into his pocket, scooped something out and set it on the table between them.

Melissa stared at the small velvet box incredulously. She looked from it to Cody's face and back again.

"Go ahead," he encouraged. "Open it. If you'd rather have something else, we can go together tomorrow."

She shook her head, fighting the urge to grab that tempting little box and claim not only the ring inside, but the future Cody had obviously mapped out for them. This reaction of his to discovering he was a father wasn't even remotely what she had expected. Obviously he wasn't thinking clearly. He hadn't wanted to marry her two years ago. She was faintly insulted that it had taken a baby to drag a proposal out of him.

Actually, it wasn't even a proposal. It was another of those orders she hated so much. Issuing edicts was something he had learned at Harlan Adams's knee. Considering how he'd rebelled against his father, she would have thought he'd be more sensitive to the crummy habit.

"No," she said flatly, meeting his gaze evenly. She was very proud of herself for getting the word out, for keeping her voice and her resolve steady.

He blinked and stared. "No what?"

She drew in a deep breath and, before she could change her mind, blurted, "I will not touch that box and I will not marry you."

A red flush climbed up his neck. "Of course you will," he said just as emphatically. "Don't be stubborn, Melissa. It's the sensible thing to do."

"Sensible," she repeated in a low, lethal tone. "I do not intend to get married because it is *sensible!*"

She stood and jerked on her coat, then moved to pick up Sharon Lynn. Cody held his daughter out of her reach.

"Sit back down and let's talk about this," he ordered. "You're causing a scene."

"I don't care," she said emphatically, though she didn't dare look around to see just how many people were fascinated by their argument. "There is absolutely nothing to discuss."

"Please," he said, sounding slightly more meek.

Since when had Cody cared about scenes? Melissa regarded him suspiciously, but she did sit on the edge of the seat. She did not remove her coat.

"How about another soft drink?" he coaxed.

"Cody!"

"Okay, okay." He leaned toward her intently. "Maybe I didn't go about this quite right."

"I'll say."

He reached awkwardly around his sleeping daughter and picked up the velvet box. He flipped it open to display an impressive emerald surrounded by diamonds. Melissa fought to pretend that the ring didn't just about take her breath away. The size of the ring and the sparkle of those stones were not important. A marriage based on obligation was the real point here. She wouldn't have it.

"It reminded me of your eyes," Cody said. He grinned. "The way they are right now, when they're shooting off sparks."

Melissa's resolve wavered. A little voice in her head gathered steam, repeating *no, no, no* so loudly she couldn't ignore it. Hadn't she told herself just a few hours earlier that she'd always been too easy on Cody? Hadn't she made a fool of herself over and over again by giving in if he so much as smiled at her?

And hadn't she learned that she could take care of herself? She no longer liked the idea of relying on anyone, either financially or, even more importantly, for her happiness.

"You're wasting your time," she told him emphatically before her resolve could falter. "The ring is beautiful. You're a fine man. I'm thrilled that you want to be a part of Sharon Lynn's life. But I will not marry you."

He looked absolutely dumbfounded. If the conversation hadn't been quite so difficult for her, too, she might have smiled at his flabbergasted reaction.

"Why?" he demanded, staring at her, indignation radiating from every pore.

"Because I will not get married for all the wrong reasons."

"What wrong reasons? We have a child. I intend to be a father to her."

"That's fine. It doesn't mean you have to be a husband to me. I'm doing just fine on my own. You were apparently doing so fine on your own that you saw no need to come back for almost two years."

"That's it, isn't it?" His gaze narrowed. "You're just

doing this to get even because I left town and you had to face being pregnant all alone."

Melissa regarded him sadly. "No, Cody, I am not trying to get even. I'm just trying not to compound one mistake by making another."

He seemed thoroughly taken aback by the realization that anyone—and most especially the woman who'd always adored him—would consider marrying him to be a mistake. Obviously his ego hadn't suffered any during their separation. It was as solid as ever.

She reached across the table and patted his hand. "It's nothing personal."

He stared at her. "How can you say that? I think it's pretty damned personal."

"Once you've had time to think it over, you'll see that I'm right," she assured him. "Obligation is a terrible basis for a marriage."

This time when she stood and reached for Sharon Lynn, he didn't resist. He pocketed the ring and stepped out of the booth. "I'll take you home," he said, his voice flat.

Melissa directed him to the small house she'd been renting for the past year, since about a month after Sharon Lynn's birth. Cody showed no inclination to get out of the pickup, so she let herself out. She hesitated for a moment with the door still open.

"I'm sorry, Cody. I really am."

He didn't look at her. "I'll call tomorrow and we'll work out a schedule for me to spend time with my daughter."

The chill in his voice cut straight through her. For the first time she wondered if she had made a terrible mistake in alienating him. Even though she knew in her heart that her decision was the right one, the only one to be made under the circumstances, perhaps she should have found a way to be more diplomatic about rejecting him.

"Fine," she said. "Whatever works for you will be okay."

She closed the door and started up the walk. An instant later she heard the engine shut off, then the slam of the driver's door behind Cody. He caught up with her before she could even make it to the front stoop.

Before she realized what he intended, he hauled her into his arms and kissed her so hard and so thoroughly that her head spun. Then, as if he suddenly became aware of the child she was holding or possibly because he figured he'd made his point, he released her.

"Give her to me," he said. "I'll carry her inside."

"Cody, she's fine," Melissa protested. She didn't want him inside, not when her knees were shaking and her pulse was racing.

"I said I'd carry her," he repeated, plucking her neatly out of Melissa's arms. "Open the door."

Following her directions, he made his way to the baby's small room. Angrily shrugging aside Melissa's offer of assistance, he fumbled with his daughter's clothes. He scanned the room, picked out a nightshirt from a small dresser, changed her, then laid her down gently.

Only then did a sigh shudder through him. His hand rested for a moment on the baby's backside.

"Good night, sweet pea," he murmured, his gaze riveted to his sleeping daughter as he backed toward the door.

The sight of Cody with their child, feeling his pain and his longing as he'd tucked her in for the night, had shaken Melissa. She was leaning against the wall outside the room, trying to gather her composure, when he finally emerged.

His gaze caught hers, burning into her. "It's not over," he said quietly. "Not by a long shot."

Trembling, Melissa stood rooted to the spot, staring after him long after she'd heard the truck's engine start, long after Cody had driven away.

Cody was right. It wasn't over. More than anything, she feared the struggle between them for their daughter was just beginning.

7

Cody didn't get a wink of sleep the entire night. When he wasn't overwhelmed by the amazing experience of holding his daughter, he was thinking about Melissa's astonishing transformation.

He had never noticed before how stubborn she was, nor how self-confident and independent. In fact, as he recalled, there had hardly ever been an occasion when she hadn't been thoroughly accommodating to his every whim. She'd picked a hell of a time to change, he thought, thoroughly disgruntled over having been shot down.

Sometime shortly after dawn, he finally forced himself to admit that he actually found the new Melissa ever so slightly more intriguing than he had the compliant woman he'd left behind.

Kelly, Jessie and the others had always warned him about taking Melissa for granted. It appeared he should have paid more attention to their advice. Melissa had used his time away to develop a very strong sense of who she was and what her priorities were. He was beginning to wonder if there really wasn't room for him in her life anymore.

Tired of his own company, he walked into the dining room at White Pines the minute he heard the rattle of breakfast dishes. Unfortunately, the housekeeper was very efficient. Maritza had already retreated to the kitchen, but she had left an array of cereals, a large pot of fresh coffee, a basket of warm rolls, and a bowl of berries, banana slices and melon. He noticed there were no eggs or bacon, no hash browns or grits. Obviously Harlan hadn't won his war to get what he considered to be a decent breakfast served during the week.

Cody was just pouring himself a cup of coffee when his father came in. He surreptitiously studied his father's face. Harlan looked tired and sad, but his complexion no longer had that unhealthy-looking pallor it had had when Cody had first arrived.

"You're up mighty early," Harlan observed, his expression sour as he surveyed the food the housekeeper had set out. "Dammit, I can't seem to get a decent piece of meat in the morning anymore." He shot a hopeful look at Cody. "Want to drive into town and get a real breakfast? Maybe a steak and some eggs?"

"And bring the wrath of Maritza down on my head? I don't think so. The fruit looks good."

"I don't see you eating any of it."

"I'm not hungry."

"Late night?"

"Something like that."

"I thought you were past carousing."

"Who was carousing? I had dinner with Melissa." He paused and drew in a deep breath. It was time to test the words on his lips, time to test his father's reaction. It would be a good barometer of what others would have to say.

"And my daughter," he added.

Harlan merely nodded, clearly not startled by the profound announcement.

"About time," he said succinctly.

Cody stared at him, his blood suddenly pumping furiously. "You knew, too? Dammit, Daddy, you're every bit as bad as Jordan," he accused. "You kept it from me, just like he did. What is wrong with everyone in this family? I thought we were supposed to stick together." He was just warming up to a really good tirade when his father cut in.

"Settle down, son. Nobody told me, if that's what you're thinking. Didn't take much to add up two and two, once I'd seen that child. She's the spitting image of you at that age. I've got a picture of you boys on my desk that would have reminded me, if I hadn't seen it for myself." He shrugged. "Besides, Melissa never had eyes for anyone but you."

Cody couldn't think of a thing to say. Apparently his father had been willing to stand on the sidelines and wait for Cody to show up and discover he had a daughter. It didn't fit with his usual manipulative style. Either his father was mellowing or he had some other kind of devious scheme up his sleeve.

Harlan speared a chunk of cantaloupe, eyed it disparagingly, then ate it. "So," he began, his tone one of such studied indifference that Cody immediately went on alert. "Is that why you took off? Did Melissa tell you she was pregnant?"

Cody was horrified his father could think so little of him. Was that it? Had Harlan thought he'd already made his decision about marrying Melissa and being a father to his child?

"No, absolutely not," he declared indignantly. "Do you honestly think I have so little backbone that I'd run from a responsibility like that?"

His father shot a bland look in his direction. "I wouldn't like to think it, but the evidence was staring me in the face."

"What evidence?"

"You were gone. Your girl was pregnant. She quit college. She had to take that piddly job at Dolan's to make ends meet, which suggested that no one was paying a dime to support her or the baby. Didn't take a genius to add it all together and figure out that one."

"Well, your calculator malfunctioned this time," Cody snapped. "She never said a word, never even tried to track me down. The first I knew about that baby was when Velma Horton brought her into Dolan's when I was there the other day. Even then, I thought someone else had to be the father. It never crossed my mind that Melissa would hide something that important from me."

"I see." Harlan scooped up a strawberry, eyed it with disgust, then put it back. "Now that you know, what do you intend to do about it?"

"I proposed to her last night."

Harlan's eyes lit up. His expression was suddenly more animated than it had been in days. "Well, hell, son, why didn't you say so? Congratulations! When's the wedding?"

"No wedding," Cody admitted dully. "She said no."

Harlan's openmouthed expression of astonishment reflected Cody's feelings precisely.

"She flat-out turned you down?" his father said incredulously.

"Without so much as a hesitation," he said. "It was downright insulting."

Harlan chuckled. "Well, I'll be damned."

"You don't have to sound so amused," Cody grumbled.

"Sure, I do, boy. Seems tame little Melissa has grown up into a spirited young woman. The next few months or so ought to be downright interesting."

Cody glared at him. "Months? Forget it. I'm giving her a day, maybe two, to get over this contrariness. Then I'm hauling her to a justice of the peace."

His father started to laugh, then smothered the sound with a napkin. "Sorry," he mumbled, then gave up the fight and chuckled. "Son, you're going to be able to sell tickets to that one."

Cody's frayed temper snapped. He stood and tossed his own napkin back on the table. "Well, get out your checkbook, Daddy. The best seats in the house are going to cost you. Melissa and I might as well start off our married life with a nice little nest egg."

Melissa wiped down the counter at Dolan's after the last of the lunch crowd had left and eyed Cody warily. He'd been skulking up and down the aisles of the drugstore since noon, but he hadn't come near the soda fountain. He seemed unaware that Eli and Mabel were watching him with overt fascination. Thankfully, he was also unaware of what his presence was doing to her pulse rate. Who knew what he would do to capitalize on that little hint of a fissure in her resolve.

"Mabel, why don't you take the rest of the afternoon off," Eli suggested, playing straight into Cody's hands.

"What's wrong with you, old man?" Mabel grumbled. "You planning on shutting down business?"

Eli gave her a pointed nod in Melissa's direction. "Go on, Mabel. You've been wanting to check out the new seeds over at the hardware store so you can get your garden in at the first sign of spring. Go do it."

Melissa almost chuckled as she watched Mabel struggle with herself. She'd been talking about those seeds for a week, ever since the hardware store owner had told her they'd arrived. She also hated to miss out on something with the kind of gossip potential that Melissa's next confrontation with Cody was likely to have.

"Go," Eli repeated, shooing her toward the door and taking the choice out of her hands. "I might not feel so generous again anytime soon."

"Don't doubt that," Mabel retorted sourly.

Mabel got her coat and left, reluctance written all over her narrow, tight-lipped face. Cody inched a little closer to the soda fountain, as if an invisible barrier had been removed from his path.

"Melissa," Eli called. "I'll be in the storeroom, checking this morning's delivery. Call me if you need me."

"Traitor," Melissa mumbled under her breath.

Cody had moved close enough by now to overhear. "Nice talk," he commented. "He's just doing you a favor."

"Me?" She stared at him incredulously. "Oh, no. You probably paid him to get rid of Mabel and to disappear himself. I noticed the other night that you'd inherited Harlan's knack for manipulation."

Cody clearly wasn't crazy about the comparison,

but he let the charge roll off his back. "I'm not desperate enough to be paying anyone to give me time alone with you," Cody said, his grin widening. "I'm still relying on my charm."

"Take it somewhere else," she muttered.

"Tsk-tsk, Me…liss…a," he drawled, tipping his hat back on his head as he settled on a stool at the counter. "What does it take to get a little service around here?"

"More charm than you've got," she retorted. "Or cold, hard cash."

He plucked a twenty out of his wallet and set it on the counter. Then he winked. It appeared he was giving her a choice about which currency she wanted to accept. Melissa would have gladly taken the wink, if it meant she could shove that bill straight down his throat.

Since she couldn't, she snatched the twenty, tucked it into her pocket and withdrew her order pad and pen. "What'll it be?" she inquired in the same impersonal tone she used with other impossible customers.

Cody propped his elbows on the counter and leaned forward. "A kiss for starters."

"You wish." Her knees trembled despite the defiant retort. Why was it that temptation always entered a room right at Cody's side? Shouldn't she have been totally immune by now? Lord knows, she'd been lecturing herself on getting over him from the day he'd left town. Some of that advice should have taken by now. Apparently, though, it hadn't.

"Then I'll have a hamburger, fries and a shake," he said.

The mundane order was a disappointment. Melissa cursed her wayward hormones as she slapped the burger on the grill and lowered the fries into the hot grease.

She sloshed milk into a metal container and out of habit added two scoops of chocolate ice cream, even though Cody hadn't specified the kind he wanted. Half of the mixture splashed out when she jammed the container into place on the automatic shaker.

"Nervous?" Cody inquired.

He spoke in a smug, lazy drawl that sent heat scampering down her spine. She scowled at him. "What on earth do I have to be nervous about? You're the one who doesn't belong here. You're the one making a pest of himself."

Sparks flared in his dark eyes. "Want me to ask Eli how he feels about you making a paying customer feel unwelcome?"

He didn't have to. She already knew that Eli would have heart failure if he heard her trying to run Cody off with her rudeness. He'd already taken Cody's side once today by slinking off to hide out in the storeroom to give them time alone. She'd never before noticed that Eli held Cody in particularly high esteem. His behavior must be part of some instinctive male support system that kicked in whenever one of them sensed that a woman might be getting the upper hand.

She turned her back on Cody, finished fixing his food, then set it down on the counter with a jarring thud.

He grinned at her. "Service with a smile," he commented. "I love it. You earn a lot of tips this way?"

Melissa closed her eyes and prayed for patience. When she opened them again, Cody hadn't vanished as she'd hoped. "Why are you in here?" she inquired testily. "Shouldn't you be out roping cattle or something?"

"We have plans to make, remember?"

"I told you just to tell me when you wanted to see

Sharon Lynn. I'll make the arrangements so you can pick her up at my parents' anytime."

"Not those plans," he said complacently, picking a pickle off of his hamburger and tsk-tsking her, apparently for not remembering that he hated pickles.

"Sorry," she said without much sincerity. She should have dumped in the whole damned jar. "You could have eaten at Rosa's."

"I prefer the spice here," he retorted. "Now let's get back to those plans. I was thinking that a week from Saturday would be good."

Melissa was surprised he wanted to wait that long before seeing his daughter again. Maybe his fascination was already waning. At this rate he'd be moving back to Wyoming in a month. Surely she could wait him out that long. She'd probably be a tangled heap of frustrated hormones, but presumably her sanity would still be intact.

"Sure, if that's what you want," she said more agreeably now that she knew he was likely to be out of her hair in no time. "I'm off on Saturday, so you can pick Sharon Lynn up at my place."

"Not just Sharon Lynn," he corrected. "Can't have a wedding without the bride."

Melissa dropped the glass she'd been rinsing out. It shattered at her feet. Eli poked his head out of the storeroom, saw the glass and shook his head.

"I hope to hell you two settle this quick," the pharmacist said. "It's costing me a fortune in broken glasses."

"Don't worry, Eli," Cody consoled him. "I'll settle up with you." He fixed his unrelenting gaze on Melissa and added, "I always accept my responsibilities."

"Oh, stuff a rag in it," Melissa retorted, stripping off

her apron and opening the cash register to shove in the twenty she'd pocketed. "Eli, I'm leaving. Mr. Adams has already paid his check. Keep the change."

She made it as far as the sidewalk, still shrugging into her coat, when Cody caught up with her. If her refusal to kowtow to his wishes for a second time had ruffled his feathers, he wasn't letting it show. He fell into step beside her, his expression perfectly innocent.

"Going to pick up the baby?"

Actually Melissa had no idea where she was going. She'd been so anxious to get away from Cody that she'd walked out of the drugstore without the kind of plan she should have had. It was an unfortunate sign of weakness, one she couldn't allow him to detect.

"No, actually, I have things to do."

"Like what? I'll help."

"No, thanks. I can handle it."

"Come on, Me…liss…a," he coaxed, planting himself on the sidewalk in front of her, legs spread. He rocked back on the heels of his cowboy boots and peered at her from beneath the brim of his hat. It was a look that invited a woman to swoon. She ought to know. She'd done it often enough, flat-out making a fool of herself over him.

"Would spending a little time with me be so awful?" he inquired.

Awful? That wasn't the word she would have chosen. Dangerous, maybe. Stupid. Risky. There was a whole string of applicable words and none of them had anything to do with awful.

"I'd rather not," she said politely.

"Bet I can change your mind," he countered, grinning at her.

She scowled at him as he advanced on her step by step. "Don't try."

He shook his head. "I don't know. The temptation is pretty great. Your mouth is all pouty. Very kissable," he assessed, his gaze hot on her. He took yet another step closer, crowding her. "Your cheeks are pink. Just about the color of rose petals and twice as soft. It's all hard to resist."

As he spoke, her lips burned as if he'd kissed them. Her cheeks flamed, turning to what she was sure must be a deeper shade. Damn, it didn't seem to matter if he actually touched her or not. Her body reacted predictably just to the provocative suggestion.

"Go away," she ordered in a voice that was entirely too breathless.

His expression solemn, he shook his head. "I can't do that, Me...liss...a."

She sighed. "Why not?" she demanded far too plaintively.

He circled one arm around her waist and dragged her against him. She could feel the hard heat of his arousal.

"You know the answer to that," he whispered, his lips scant millimeters from hers. His breath fanned across her cheek.

"Cody." His name came out as a broken sigh, a protest that not even someone far less relentless than Cody would have heeded.

"It's okay," he consoled her. "Everything is going to turn out just fine."

He slanted his mouth over hers then, setting off fireworks in January. *Why, why, why?* her brain demanded. Why was her body so darned traitorous? Maybe it was like the tides. Maybe the way she responded to Cody was as immutable as the sun setting in the west.

She resisted the explanation. It meant she had no will at all to fight it. She put her hands on his chest and shoved with all her might. She might as well have been trying to topple a centuries' old oak. Cody didn't budge. He didn't stop that tender assault on her mouth.

For what seemed an eternity he coaxed and plundered, teased and tasted until she was shivering with urgent and almost-forgotten need. When she was weak with a desire she definitely didn't want to feel, Cody finally released her. She very nearly melted at his feet. In fact, she might have if he hadn't kept his hands resting possessively on her hips. Even through her coat, her skin burned at his touch.

"So, what are we going to do with the rest of the afternoon?" he inquired. The gleam in his eyes suggested he had an idea of his own. His lips quirked up in the beginnings of a smile.

"Not what you're thinking," she said curtly.

His grin spread. "Don't be so certain of that, sweet pea. It sounds an awful lot like a challenge and you know I never could resist a dare."

Desperate for space, she backed away from him. "Give it a rest," she said crankily.

He reached out and rubbed his thumb across her lower lip. The sensation sent fire dancing through her.

"I'm just getting started, darlin'," he murmured, his gaze locked with hers.

Melissa held back a sigh of resignation. "You're not going home, are you?"

"When I can be with you? No way."

"Come on, then."

His expression immediately brightened. Once more he fell dutifully into step beside her. "Where are we going?"

"To buy groceries," she said, plucking a boring chore out of thin air. "And after that, we're ironing." She slanted a look at him to judge his reaction. He didn't bat an eye.

"Sounds downright fascinating," he declared. He captured her gaze, then added slowly, "I've always been particularly fond of starch."

She ignored the provocative tone. "Oh, really?" she said skeptically.

"Yes, indeed," he swore. "In my shirts and in my women. And you, sweet pea, are full of it."

Melissa had a feeling it would take her weeks to puzzle out whether he meant that as a compliment. For the first time, though, she had this funny little feeling she was going to have the time of her life figuring it out.

8

Somewhere in the middle of the grocery store, Melissa lost track of Cody. She was aware of the precise instant when she no longer felt the heat of his stare or the sizzling tension of his nearness. She almost sagged with relief, even as she fought off a vague stirring of disappointment. Clearly his attention span was no better now than it had ever been.

Worse, he was getting to her. Despite her best intentions, she was responding to his teasing, to the allure of his body. She could not let that happen. Steering totally clear of him, however, seemed to be the only way she was likely to be able to avoid succumbing to that seductive appeal. Now seemed like a good time to make a break for it.

All she had to do was get through the checkout line and race home before he caught up with her. She could barricade the door. Or maybe just hide out in a bedroom until he was convinced she wasn't home.

She tossed a six-pack of soft drinks she didn't need into the cart, just in case Cody wasn't as far away as she hoped. She had to leave the store with more than a quart of milk or he'd know that this trip had been nothing more than a ploy to avoid being alone with him.

She had rounded the last aisle and was heading for the cashier when she spotted him. He was positioned in front of the baby food, studying labels with the intensity of a scientist in his lab. Apparently, though, he wasn't so absorbed that her presence escaped his notice.

"Which of these does Sharon Lynn like?" he asked, holding up competing brands of strained peas.

"Neither one."

His brow knit worriedly. "Doesn't she have to eat vegetables?"

"Yes, but she's past the baby food. She has her first baby teeth. She can chew soft food." She regarded him oddly. "Do you really care about this?"

"Yes," he said succinctly, and replaced the peas. "Fill me in on everything."

Melissa shrugged. "Okay. She can eat the junior brands. Like these," she said, plucking a couple of jars off the shelf. "There are some foods that don't have to be specially prepared. She can eat the regular stuff. Peas, for example."

To her surprise, he seemed to be taking in every word as if she were delivering a fascinating treatise on something far more significant than baby food. In the past he'd reserved that kind of attention for very little besides ranching.

"What are her favorite foods?" he asked, studying the larger jars intently.

"Ice cream and French fries."

Cody stared at her. "That's her diet?"

"No," she said patiently. "Those are her favorites." She gestured to the junior baby food. "This is what she gets most of the time. When I have time, I even blend some myself from fresh fruits and vegetables. She's particularly fond of squishing bananas."

Cody eyed the jars of carrots and meats and fruits, seemed to struggle with his conscience, and then turned his back on them. "Let's go."

"Where?"

"To the ice cream section," he said as grimly as if he were going into battle and the enemy had pulled a last-minute tactical switch. "I'm not bringing home jars of that disgusting-looking liver or those limp little bits of carrot if she'd rather have ice cream."

"Cody, I do feed her. You don't need to stock my refrigerator, especially not with ice cream."

He stopped in his tracks and turned to face her. "Don't you see, this isn't about you. It's about me and my daughter. You've had her to yourself for thirteen months. Now I want a chance to be important in her life."

"By stuffing her with chocolate-fudge ice cream?"

Instead of taking her well-intended point, he seized on the tiny sliver of information she'd imparted about their daughter. "Is that her favorite? I'll buy a gallon of it."

He sounded relieved to know that he wouldn't have to resort to another round of guesswork and label-reading. In fact, he was loping off to the frozen food section before Melissa could gather her thoughts sufficiently to argue with him.

Okay, she told herself, it was only a gallon of ice cream. So what? It wasn't as if he could buy their daughter's affection or ruin her health with one extravagant gesture of chocolate fudge.

She had a feeling, though, that this was only the beginning. Cody was not a man to do anything by half measures. His retreat to Wyoming, abandoning not only her but his beloved home and family, was a perfect example of that. He could have straightened everything out between them with a few questions or even by hurling accusations and listening to explanations. Instead he had leapt to a conclusion and reacted by impetuously fleeing to another state.

He was doing much the same thing now that he had discovered he had a daughter. He wanted to be in her life—completely—right this instant. He wanted to marry Melissa…right this minute. The concepts of moderation or patience had obviously escaped him.

She sighed as he appropriated the shopping cart. The two half gallons of chocolate-fudge ice cream had turned into four. And she didn't like the gleam in his eyes one bit as he turned the cart on two wheels and headed straight for the shelves of diapers.

She'd been right. He was going to take over and she had a sinking feeling in the pit of her stomach that there would be very little she could do about it.

Cody realized he had almost lost it there for a minute at the supermarket. He'd wanted to sweep entire shelves of baby food into the shopping cart.

As it was, in addition to the ice cream, they had left the store with five, giant economy-size packages of disposable diapers, a new toy duck for Sharon Lynn's bath, five storybooks he could read to her at bedtime and an astonishing selection of her favorite juices. Melissa had just rolled her eyes at the startled checkout clerk.

"New father?" the girl had guessed.

"New enough," Melissa had replied.

Let them make fun, Cody thought. He didn't care. This was the first step in his campaign to make himself indispensable to Melissa and his daughter.

"Where to now?" he asked when they'd piled all those diapers and the rest of the shopping bags into the back of his pickup.

"I'm going home to iron," Melissa said, sticking to that absurd story she'd told him earlier in a blatant attempt to get rid of him. "Unless, of course, you'd like to do it for me?"

He frowned at her. "What about Sharon Lynn?"

"She's with Mother."

"I'll drop you off and go get her," he suggested eagerly.

"She's probably still taking her nap," Melissa said.

She said it in such a rush he had the feeling she thought he intended to kidnap the baby and take off with her. As much as he resented the implication, he kept his tone perfectly even. "She won't sleep forever," he countered reasonably. "I'll bring her straight home. I promise."

"You don't have a car seat," she noted pointedly.

Damn, but there was a lot to remember. "We'll stop now and get one."

"All of that ice cream will melt."

He frowned at the obstacles she kept throwing in his path. "Not in this weather. It's freezing out. And if it does, I'll buy more."

"Couldn't you just drop me off at home?"

"No, you need to come with me. You can show me the best kind of car seat."

Melissa sighed heavily. "Cody, what's the point? They're expensive and you probably won't…"

He guessed where she was going. "Won't what? Won't be here long enough to use it? You can get that idea right out of your head."

He tucked a finger under her chin and forced her to face him. "I've quit my job in Wyoming. I am home to stay, Melissa. Get used to it."

She held up her hands. "Sorry. I didn't mean anything. I was just trying to keep you from wasting money."

"If it's for my daughter, it is not a waste of money," he said curtly. "Now, can I find the kind of car seat I need at the discount superstore out on the highway?"

She nodded.

He turned the truck around on a dime, spewing gravel. He drove ten miles before his temper had cooled enough to speak again. He'd set out today to woo Melissa into changing her mind about marrying him. His first overtures, however, appeared to have gone awry. He'd lost his sense of humor, right along with his temper. It was no way for the two of them to start over. He sucked in a deep breath and made up his mind to mend fences.

"Truce?" he suggested, glancing over at her. She was huddled against the door, looking miserable. She shrugged.

"I'm not an ogre," he stated. "I'm just trying to fit into Sharon Lynn's life." Her gaze lifted to meet his. "And yours."

She sighed. "We don't need you," she repeated stubbornly. "We were doing just fine before you came back."

He ignored the tide of hurt that washed through him at the dismissive comment. "Maybe I need you."

Melissa frowned. "Yeah, right," she said sarcastically. "As if Cody Adams ever needed anybody. Didn't you pride yourself on staying footloose and fancy free?"

He saw no point in denying something she knew better than anyone. "I did," he agreed. He thought about the agonizing loneliness of that cabin he'd sentenced himself to in Wyoming. "Maybe being alone for the past eighteen months has changed me. Maybe I'm not the selfish, carefree, independent cuss who stormed away from Texas."

"And maybe pigs can fly," she countered.

He grinned at her. "Maybe they can," he said quietly. "If you believe in magic."

"I don't," she said succinctly.

Cody heard the terrible pain in her voice, even if her expression remained absolutely stoic. Dear heaven, what had he done to her by running off and leaving her to face being pregnant all alone? He saw now what he hadn't observed before. Not only was Melissa stronger and more self-sufficient, she also had an edge of cynicism and bitterness that hadn't been there before. The blame for that was his, no one else's.

At the discount store, when Melissa would have grabbed the first car seat they came across, Cody stopped her, deliberately taking the time to read the package for every last detail on safety. If nothing else, he intended to impress on Melissa that he took his parenting responsibilities seriously. Nothing was too trivial, too expensive, or too complicated to tackle if it had to do with his daughter.

Nearly an hour later they finally loaded the new car seat into the truck.

"I think that salesclerk despaired of ever getting you to make a choice," Melissa said, the beginnings of a smile tugging at her lips.

"It wasn't for her kid," he retorted.

"Okay, forget the salesclerk. Should I point out that the one you ended up taking is exactly the same one I tried to get you to buy when we walked in?"

He scowled at her. "What's your point?"

"That I had already done the exact same research, reached the exact same conclusion. You insisted I come along because you claimed to want my advice. When it came right down to it, though, you didn't trust me."

Cody carefully considered the accusation before turning to meet her gaze. "You're right. I should have listened to you. It's just that this is new to me. I'm trying to get it right. I don't want to mess up with something this important."

Her expression softened. "Cody, I can understand that. Really, I can. I was just as obsessive when I first brought Sharon Lynn home from the hospital. Mother and Daddy thought I was a lunatic. I didn't trust a piece of advice they offered. I was convinced it was probably outdated. I had to do it all for myself. Talk about reinventing the wheel." She shook her head. "I wasted more time, only to find myself doing exactly what they'd suggested in the first place."

He grinned. "You're just trying to save me traveling over the same learning curve, is that it?"

"Exactly," she said. She reached over and patted his hand. "I'm not trying to keep you out of Sharon Lynn's life, or control your input, or anything like that. I promise."

The impulsive touch didn't last nearly long enough. Cody grabbed her hand and pulled it to his lips. He brushed a kiss across her knuckles and saw the instantaneous spark of desire in her eyes. "I'll try to watch the defensiveness, if you'll do something for me."

She regarded him with conditioned wariness. "What?"

"Bring Sharon Lynn out to White Pines this weekend," he coaxed persuasively. At the flare of panic in her eyes, he pulled out his strongest ammunition—her fondness for Harlan. "I think seeing her would do Daddy a world of good. With Mother gone, he needs something positive in his life, something to cheer him up. You should have seen the look in his eyes this morning when I told him she was mine."

The hint of wariness in her eyes fled and was promptly replaced by astonishment. "You told him?"

"I did. But it wasn't news. He'd figured it out the first time he saw her, the same as Jordan had."

Her mouth gaped. "And he didn't do anything about it? I'm amazed he didn't haul your butt straight back here or offer to set up a trust fund for the baby or something."

"Frankly, so am I. Maybe he's learned his lesson about manipulating."

Melissa's expression was every bit as skeptical as his own had to be. "Okay," he said. "He probably has a scheme we don't know about yet. Even so, are you willing to take a chance? Will you bring her out? It's time she learned something about her father's side of the family."

He was playing to her sense of fairness and it was

clearly working. He could practically read her struggle with her conscience on her face.

"I'll bring her," Melissa finally agreed with obvious reluctance. "On one condition—no tricks."

Cody regarded her innocently. Now that he'd gotten her basic agreement, he could go along with almost anything she demanded. "What kind of tricks?"

"No preachers lurking in the shadows. No wedding license all signed and ready to be filled in."

He feigned astonishment, even though he thought she might actually have a very good idea, one that hadn't even occurred to him until just that minute. "Would I do that?"

"In a heartbeat," she said. "And even if you had an attack of conscience, Harlan wouldn't. No conspiracies, okay?"

"Cross my heart," Cody said, already wondering if there was some way to pull off such a wedding.

Melissa's gaze narrowed. "Why doesn't that reassure me?"

"And you accused me of a lack of trust," he chided.

"I'm not the one whose brother threw a surprise wedding in place of a rehearsal," she said, reminding him of the sneaky trick Jordan and Kelly had pulled on his parents to avoid the out-of-control celebration his mother had planned for their wedding. The whole town had gossiped about that little stunt for weeks.

"I'm glad you mentioned that," Cody taunted. "It does give me some interesting ideas."

"Cody Adams, I am warning you…"

"No need, sweet pea. I'm not fool enough to take a chance on getting rejected in front of my family and the preacher. When you and I get married, it'll be because you're willing and eager."

"'When,' not 'if'?" she chided.

"That's right, darlin'. Only the timing is left to be decided," he declared with far more confidence than he felt. He unloaded the last of their packages under Melissa's irritated scrutiny. Apparently, though, his certainty about their future had left her speechless. He considered that a hopeful sign.

"See you on Saturday," he said, escaping before he had a chance to put his foot in his mouth. "Come on out about eight. You can have breakfast with us."

Besides, he thought, if Melissa was there by eight, that gave him most of the day to convince her to have a wedding at sunset.

Melissa debated bailing out on her day at White Pines. Handling Cody was tricky enough without having to worry about Harlan's sneaky tactics at the same time. Still, she couldn't very well deny Harlan the chance to get to know the granddaughter he'd just officially discovered he had.

That was what ultimately decided her, or so she told herself as she dressed Sharon Lynn in bright blue corduroy pants, a blue and yellow shirt, and tiny sneakers. She brushed her hair into a halo of soft curls around her face.

"Ma? Bye-bye?"

Proud of Sharon Lynn's expanding vocabulary, she nodded. "That's right, my darling. We're going to see your daddy and your granddaddy."

Sharon Lynn's face lit up. She reached for the new toy duck that was never far from sight. "Da?"

Melissa shook her head at the instant reaction. Obviously Cody had had an incredible impact on his daughter in just one visit. Did he have that effect on all women or just those in her family? She tickled Sharon Lynn until she dissolved into a fit of giggles.

"Yes, Da," she told her approvingly. "We're going to see Da." And she, for one, was nervous as the dickens about it. Sharon Lynn clearly had no such qualms.

When Melissa pulled her car to a stop in front of the house at White Pines, she drew in a deep, reassuring breath, trying to calm her jitters. It was going to be just fine, she told herself, even as she fought the overwhelming sense of déjà vu that assailed her.

How many times had she driven out here, filled with hope, anxious to spend time with the man she loved, only to leave bitterly disappointed by his refusal to commit to anything more than a carefree relationship? Everything had always seemed more intense out here, the air crisper and cleaner, the terrain more rugged, the colors brighter. Similarly, her emotions had always seemed sharper, too—the bitter sorrow as well as the blinding joy.

Once she had dreamed of this being her home, the place where she and Cody would raise a family. Now with the snap of her fingers and a couple of "I do's," her dream could come true. But Cody's proposal, forced only by the existence of a child for whom he felt responsible, had tarnished the dream. She doubted it could ever recapture its original, innocent glow.

"Da, Da, Da!" Sharon Lynn screamed excitedly, bouncing in her car seat as Cody strode across the front lawn. He was wearing snug, faded jeans, a T-shirt that hugged his broad chest and worn cowboy boots. He looked sexier and more masculine than any male model ever had in *GQ*.

Before Melissa could fight her instinctive reaction just to the sight of him, he had thrown open the door and lifted his daughter high in the air, earning squeals of delight for his effort.

"Hey, pumpkin, I could hear you all the way inside the house," he teased the baby. "Your grandpa Harlan said you were loud enough to wake half the county. He's thinking of getting you geared up for the hog-calling contest at the state fair. What do you think?"

Melissa noted he reported his father's reaction with unmistakable pride. He glanced her way just then and the humor in his eyes darkened to something else, something she recognized from times past as powerful, compelling desire. Whatever was behind his proposal of marriage, the one thing she couldn't doubt was Cody's passion. He wanted her and he was doing nothing to hide that fact from her.

"Thank you for coming," he said, his expression solemn.

"I told you I would."

He shrugged. "You never know, though. Sometimes things come up."

Suddenly, for the first time Melissa was able to pinpoint the most devastating problem between them. Neither of them had so much as a shred of trust left for the other.

She didn't trust Cody not to leave again. She didn't trust him not to rip her daughter away from her.

And worse, to her way of thinking because she knew he had a right to feel as he did, he didn't trust her to keep her promises. She had kept the secret of his daughter from him. He had to wonder if he could trust her to be honest with him about anything.

All at once she was unbearably sad. Regrets for the open, honest relationship they had once shared tumbled through her, leaving her shaken.

Before she realized he'd even moved, Cody was beside her, Sharon Lynn in his arms.

"Are you okay?" he asked, his expression filled with concern.

"Of course. Why would you think I wasn't?"

"Maybe it has something to do with the tears."

She hadn't even realized she was crying. She brushed impatiently at the telltale traces. "Sorry."

"You don't have to apologize, for heaven's sake. Just tell me what's wrong."

"An attack of nostalgia," she said, knowing it was only partially true. "Nothing to worry about." She plastered a smile on her face. "Come on. Let's go inside before Harlan falls out of that window he's peeking through."

Almost as if he'd heard the comment, the curtains fell back into place and a shadow moved away from the downstairs window. Cody grinned at her.

"He can't wait to meet Sharon Lynn. If you think I'm bad, wait until you see the room he's fixed up for her visits."

The implications of the lighthearted remark sent panic racing through Melissa. If Harlan had fixed up a room, then he clearly intended for Sharon Lynn to be at White Pines a lot. Was this visit just a prelude to the custody battle her mother had warned her about? Cody might not be willing to fight her in court, but Harlan was another matter. With Mary dead and his life stretching out emptily in front of him, who could tell what kind of crazy notion he might get into his head.

Apparently her fears must have been written on her face, because Cody halted again. "Melissa, you don't have to worry," he reassured her. "It's just a room. You know Harlan. Everything drives him to excess."

"You're sure that's all it is?"

"Very sure. You don't have anything to worry about from Harlan." That said, he winked at her. "I, however, am another matter entirely. I've given up on winning you with diapers and juice and toys."

"Oh?"

"I intend to win you with my sexy, wicked ways."

He was up the front steps and in the house before she had a chance to react. When she could finally move again, her legs wobbled and her pulse was scampering crazily.

Suddenly any threat Harlan might pose dimmed in importance. Cody was the one she needed to worry about. Always had been. Always would be.

9

At the precise instant that Cody and Melissa entered the front door at White Pines, Harlan stepped into the foyer. His prompt presence indicated that he had indeed been watching for Melissa's arrival and was eager for an introduction to his granddaughter.

Cody studied his father's face closely as Harlan's gaze honed in immediately on Sharon Lynn. For the first time since the funeral, there was a spark of animation in his dark eyes. And when he glanced at Melissa that animation included her, only to be quickly replaced by questions, unanswerable questions Cody hoped he wouldn't get into right off.

To stave them off, Cody crossed the wide sweep of wood floor and woven Mexican rug to stand in front of his father, Sharon Lynn still perched in his arms.

"Daddy, meet your granddaughter, Sharon Lynn."

The baby responded to the cue as if she'd been coached. A dimpled smile spread across her face as she held out her arms to be transferred to her new grandfather's embrace. Harlan accepted her with alacrity.

"You are a mighty fine young lady," he told her,

his expression sober, his eyes unmistakably welling up with rare tears. "I'm very glad to be welcoming you to the family." His gaze shifted then to encompass Melissa once more. "It's good to see you again, girl. We've missed you around here."

Cody saw the sheen of tears spring to Melissa's eyes and realized more than ever what he had cost them all by running off as he had. His parents had always accepted that Melissa would one day be his wife. They had approved of her spirit, her kindness and her unconditional love for him. Melissa had been present on most family occasions, welcomed as if their relationship had been sealed.

Though he'd never asked his parents if they had continued to see her, he had suspected Melissa wouldn't feel that same sense of belonging after he'd gone. He knew from his father's comment just now that she had indeed stayed away and that her absence had hurt them all, costing them a relationship they held dear. The severing of ties had been as complete as if he and Melissa had been married and then divorced in an incredibly acrimonious manner that had forced everyone to choose sides.

"Thank you, Harlan," she said, stepping closer to be enveloped in a fierce hug that included Sharon Lynn. "I've missed you, too. And I'm so terribly, terribly sorry about Mary."

"I know you are. Mary thought a lot of you, girl. She always hoped…" At a warning glance from Cody, he allowed his voice to trail off, the thought left unspoken.

It hardly mattered, though. The damage had already been done. Melissa's cheeks turned bright pink. Cody could feel the blood climbing up the back of his neck,

as well. His father surveyed them both, then gave a
brief nod of satisfaction as if he'd learned something
he'd hoped for.

"Come on, then," Harlan said, his voice laced with a
telltale trace of huskiness. "Let's go have some breakfast, before we all turn maudlin and start bawling."

To Cody's relief, his father left the subject of the
past untouched beyond that single, oblique reference.
Either he was far too fascinated by the child he held or
he recognized that it was not a conversation to be held
in the baby's presence.

There was no mistaking, though, that more questions
lingered in his eyes. Cody guessed they would be as
much about the future as the past. He also knew there
were no answers his father would like hearing, not yet
anyway. Harlan had the same impatience as his sons. He
liked things settled to his satisfaction. Between Cody
and Melissa nothing was settled at all.

Sharon Lynn patted her grandfather's face, then
glanced to her mother for approval. "Da?" she ques-
tioned.

Cody scowled as he realized that he wasn't unique in
his daughter's view. He caught Melissa's grin and realized how pitiful it was to be jealous of his own father.

Unaware, as Cody had been, that it was Sharon
Lynn's universal name for any adult male, Harlan
beamed at her. "Damn, but you're a smart one," he
praised. "You and I need to have ourselves a little talk.
What other words do you know?"

"Ma and bye-bye," Melissa offered. "It limits the
conversations tremendously."

Cody noticed that his father didn't seem to mind. He
seemed perfectly content to carry on a one-sided con-

versation with his granddaughter. It was probably the first time in years someone hadn't talked back to him.

The distraction also kept Harlan from touching the eggs and bacon he normally couldn't wait to eat on the weekends. Possibly that was the most telling indication of all of Sharon Lynn's power over this new male in her life.

"So, Sharon Lynn, have you ever seen a horse?" Harlan inquired.

Cody chuckled as his daughter tilted her head, a quizzical expression on her face as she appeared to give the question serious consideration.

"I'll take that for a no," Harlan said. "In that case, I think it's about time to fix that. Can't have a rancher's baby who doesn't know about horses. Maybe we'll even go for a little ride."

Cody glanced at Melissa to check her reaction to the instantaneous bonding between Sharon Lynn and his father. To his astonishment, the color had drained out of her face. Clearly the idea of Sharon Lynn going off with Harlan panicked her in some way. What he couldn't figure was why.

"Harlan, I really don't think—" she began.

"Don't worry about a thing," Harlan reassured her, cutting off her words. "I had every one of my boys up on horseback when they were no bigger than this. She'll fit right on the saddle in front of me. She'll be just fine. I guarantee I won't let her tumble off."

Harlan and the baby were out the door before Melissa could offer the firmer protest that was clearly on the tip of her tongue. Cody knew better than to argue with Harlan. He also knew that Sharon Lynn would be perfectly safe with his father. However, he could see that Melissa wouldn't believe it unless she witnessed their adventure on horseback with her own eyes. He put down his fork.

"Come on," he said. "You'll be worrying yourself sick, if you're not right alongside them."

"She's too little to be riding a horse," Melissa complained, her complexion still pale as she followed him outside. "She'll be terrified."

"I doubt that," Cody said. "You're projecting your feelings onto her. You never were much for horses. I guess you were more of a city girl than I realized."

She shot him a wry look. "Hardly that."

He grinned at her. "I don't know. About the only time I could get you into the barn was when I wanted to tumble you into the haystack."

"Cody Adams, that is not true," she contradicted, patches of bright color flaring in her cheeks. "Besides, that has absolutely nothing to do with Sharon Lynn and this crazy idea Harlan has of getting onto a horse with her."

"Stop fussing. She's just the right age to be introduced to riding. Kids her age have no fear. It's not like Daddy's going to put her on the horse, hit its rump and send her galloping around the paddock. He's going to be in the saddle, holding her."

"I suppose," Melissa said, but her gaze immediately sought out some sign of Sharon Lynn the minute the barn came into view.

The little cutie was hard to miss. She was squealing with delight from her perch atop the fence around the paddock. Misty, the oldest, smallest and gentlest of their mares, had come to investigate. Sharon Lynn's eyes were wide with excitement as she patted the white blaze on Misty's head.

"This is Misty," Harlan was explaining quietly, his grip firm on the horse's bridle. "Can you say that? Misty."

"Mi'ty," Sharon Lynn dutifully repeated, surprising all of them.

The horse neighed softly at hearing her name.

Cody glanced at Melissa and saw that she'd finally begun to relax. Her gaze was riveted on her daughter, though. He sensed that if Misty so much as shied back a step, Melissa was poised to snatch Sharon Lynn out of harm's way.

Just when he thought the worst of her reaction was past, she turned and looked up at him, anxiety and dismay clearly written all over her face. "How can your father even think about getting on a horse ever again?" she asked in a low voice, not meant to carry.

As if he'd been struck by a bolt of lightning, Cody finally realized why Melissa had been so upset by Harlan introducing Sharon Lynn to riding. The accident that had cost his mother her life hadn't even crossed his mind when Harlan had suggested bringing Sharon Lynn out to see the horses. But obviously the way Mary Adams had died had left an indelible image on Melissa's mind, as it might on anyone who didn't have the sensitivity of a slug, Cody chided himself. She had been fearful of horses to begin with. His mother's death could only have exaggerated that fear.

"Damn, no wonder you turned white as a sheet a minute ago when Daddy suggested bringing Sharon Lynn out here," he apologized. "You were thinking about what happened to Mother, weren't you?"

"Aren't you?" she asked, staring at him incredulously.

"No," he said honestly. "There's no point in blaming the horse for what happened to Mother. It was an accident and not an uncommon one at that. The horse was spooked by a snake. Even then, the fall might not have killed her. It was the way she landed."

Melissa shuddered. "Still, how can either one of you not think about it every single time you see a horse?"

"Because Daddy is a rancher, through and through. So am I," Cody said, trying to explain to Melissa what must seem inexplicable. "There are some things over which a rancher has no control. Rattlers spooking a horse is one of them."

He glanced at his father. "If he blames anyone or anything for what happened to Mother, it's more than likely himself for suggesting that ride in the first place. He also knows that the only way to conquer the fear after what happened is to get right back on a horse. He's been out riding over that same stretch of land every single day since she died."

Melissa clearly wasn't reassured. "I don't care about conquering fear. All I see is that your mother's death should be a damn good reason for him not to bring his granddaughter anywhere near a horse," she argued. "She's a baby, Cody."

Cody was beginning to see there was no reasoning with her on this. It was too soon after his mother's tragic accident. "If it's really upsetting you, I'll talk him out of it," he offered. "But sooner or later, Sharon Lynn will ride. She can't have a cowboy for a daddy and not learn."

Melissa rested her hand on his forearm. The expression on her face pleaded with him.

"Later, please," she said. "Just the thought of it after what happened to your mom makes me sick."

Cody could see that she wasn't exaggerating. Though he didn't agree with her, he could feel some compassion for the anxiety she was experiencing. He walked over and spoke to his father. Harlan shot a look over his shoulder at Melissa and gave an understanding nod.

"Of course," he apologized at once. "I didn't realize it would bother her so."

"Neither did I," Cody said. "But she's practically turning green."

"You take this little angel on inside, then. I'll be there in a bit."

Cody reached for his daughter, who let out a scream the instant she realized she was being taken away from the horse.

"Mi'ty!" she sobbed plaintively. "Mi'ty!"

"You'll see Misty another time," Cody promised. "Right now, I'm going to take you inside so you can see all of your new toys that Granddaddy bought you."

He wasn't sure if Sharon Lynn totally understood exactly what having Harlan Adams as a benefactor was all about until they reached the room he'd filled with everything from a set of white baby furniture with pink gingham sheets and comforter to every stuffed toy he'd been able to order straight from the biggest department store in Dallas. Even Cody had been bowled over by the assortment he'd assembled practically overnight. Melissa's mouth was agape as she surveyed the room.

"Did he buy out the store?" Melissa asked.

Before Cody could respond, Sharon Lynn was trying to scramble down, her gaze fixed on the rocking horse.

"Mi'ty, Mi'ty," she called joyously as she dropped from unsteady legs to her knees to crawl toward it. She pulled herself up beside it and tried to climb on. Cody lifted her up and settled her on the seat, keeping a firm grip on the waistband of her pants as she rocked enthusiastically.

He grinned at Melissa. "Told you she was going to be a natural on horseback."

"I think this one is a little more her size," Melissa retorted dryly. "The distance to the ground isn't quite so far."

Before he could comment on that, something else caught Sharon Lynn's eye and she twisted around and tried to clamber down. Cody lifted her off the rocking horse and set her back on her feet.

"How about you walk wherever you want to go this time?" he suggested.

Sharon Lynn clamped her fingers around his, wobbled precariously, then took an unsteady tiptoe step forward. With each step her confidence obviously mounted, though she kept that tight grip on his fingers.

"She's going to ruin your back," Melissa observed. "You're bent practically double."

Cody didn't give a hoot. This was the first time he'd witnessed his daughter's faltering, tentative footsteps. He'd bend over the rest of the afternoon and ache for a week, if she wanted to keep walking. With every minute he spent with her, every experience they shared, the powerful sense of connection he felt with her intensified.

Just then she stumbled and fell. Her eyes promptly

filled with tears. Certain that she must have broken something to be sobbing so pathetically, Cody knelt beside her and gently examined ankles, arms, knees and elbows. He even checked for a bump under her hair or on her forehead, though he knew perfectly well she hadn't hit her head. She'd landed squarely on her well-padded button.

Finally satisfied that she was more scared than hurt, he scooped her up, only to find Melissa grinning at him.

"And you thought I was overreacting. At this rate, you're going to be a wreck in a month," she chided, sounding smug. "Either that or you'll drive the emergency room staff at the hospital completely wild. They'll flee when they spot you coming."

He lifted his eyebrows. "Is this another chunk of that learning curve you're trying to help me skip?" he taunted.

To his amusement, she blushed furiously. "Stop teasing. I only took her in twice," she admitted defensively.

"Oh? When?"

"The first time I thought she'd swallowed the toy from a box of cereal."

Cody shuddered. He would have had her in for X-rays himself. "Had she?"

"No, I found it later in the crack between the refrigerator and the sink. I suppose she threw it across the room."

"And the other time?"

"She fell and bumped her head," Melissa said, shivering visibly at the recollection. "It terrified me. I'd never seen so much blood in my entire life. I was sure she was going to bleed to death before I got her to the hospital."

Cody's heart skidded to a halt. He anxiously studied

Sharon Lynn's face for some sign of such a traumatic injury. He smoothed back her hair to get a better look at her forehead.

"No stitches?" he asked when he could find no evidence of them.

Melissa shrugged. "Not a one," she confessed. "They put a butterfly bandage on it and sent us home. Apparently head injuries just bleed profusely. There was no permanent damage done."

Cody met her gaze and caught the faint signs of chagrin and laughter in her eyes. He also thought he detected something else, perhaps a hint of resentment that she'd been left to cope with such things on her own. Guilt sliced through him, even though part of the blame for his absence could be laid squarely at Melissa's feet.

"I'm sorry I wasn't here for you," he said, and meant it. He regretted every lost opportunity to share in the experiences—good or bad—of his daughter's first year.

The laughter in Melissa's eyes died at once. That hint of resentment burned brighter. "I handled it," she said abruptly, and turned away.

He watched as she walked over and knelt down by their daughter, listening intently to Sharon Lynn's nonsensical jabbering. The hard expression on her face when she'd turned away from him softened perceptibly. A smile tugged at her lips as she cupped her hand possessively behind her daughter's head, caressing the soft curls. Sharon Lynn looked up at her, an expression of adoration on her face.

In that instant Cody saw what it meant to be a family…and he wasn't a part of it. Melissa couldn't have shut him out any more effectively, any more deliberately, if she'd tried.

He stood there, so close and yet very much apart from them. Longing welled up inside him, longing to know all of these little details of Sharon Lynn's first months that Melissa shared so grudgingly.

There was so much more he yearned for, as well. He yearned to share their closeness, to have Melissa look into his eyes with something more than distrust.

He sighed then, because it all seemed so unlikely, so impossible, thanks to his own foolish decision to accept what he'd seen that fateful night at face value. If only he'd stayed. If only...

Wasted regrets, he chided himself. This was his reality—a child who barely knew him, a woman who wanted no part of him, who was willing to allow him glimpses of his child out of a sense of obligation, not love.

He thought then of the flicker of passion he'd caught once or twice in Melissa's sea green eyes, of the heat that had flared when he'd touched her, and wondered whether her disdain ran as deep as she wanted him to believe.

Reality and circumstances could change, he reassured himself. Sometimes for the worse, of course. Harlan knew all about the dramatic, unexpected, tragic turns life could take. He'd lost a son and his beloved wife when he'd least expected it. Those losses had taught a lesson to all of them.

Harlan had also taught his sons that they could control most aspects of their lives if they set their minds to it and fought for what they wanted. In fact, he'd turned out a dynasty of control freaks, it seemed. Luke had built his own ranch from the ground up, rather than take the share in White Pines that Harlan had wanted him to have. Jordan had fought his father bitterly for a career in the oil industry. Cody had battled for a share of White Pines, and now, it seemed, he had an even more difficult war to wage.

Cody's gaze settled on Melissa and his daughter once again. They were worth fighting for. Harlan had given him years of practice at battling for everything from permission to go to a dance to the right to build his own house on White Pines' land. Apparently it had all been preparation for a moment like this.

His mouth curved into a slow smile. He'd just have to think of Melissa's rejection not as a setback but as a challenge. It was an opportunity to utilize all those lessons Harlan had not-so-subtly instilled in them. He would have to seize the initiative and keep Melissa thoroughly off kilter until she finally woke up and realized that this time he wasn't running.

This time he intended to be the steadying influence in her life and he meant to be there always.

10

The morning had been far too intense, Melissa thought as she finally escaped the house and settled gratefully into a chair on the patio with a tall glass of iced tea. The day had turned unseasonably warm and though she still needed her jacket, it was pleasant to sit outside in the fresh, clean air with the sun on her face while Sharon Lynn napped.

Her emotions were raw. Coming back to White Pines had been far more difficult than she'd anticipated. Part of that was because she felt Mary Adams's death here in a way it hadn't struck her even at the funeral. Some of it had to do with Harlan's warmhearted welcome and the obvious delight he was taking in getting to know his new granddaughter. Most of it, though, undeniably had to do with Cody.

At White Pines she was on his turf. Like Harlan, he reigned over the operation of this ranch as comfortably as she served burgers at Dolan's. His self-confidence radiated from him in this environment. It always had.

Cody might have been wickedly flirtatious and carefree in his social life, but when it had come to work he'd been mature and driven to prove himself to his father. His early success as a ranch manager had smoothed away any insecurities he might have had living in Harlan Adams's shadow.

Cody's command of this privileged world, combined with seeing how easily Sharon Lynn had been accepted into it as Cody's child, had caused her to rebel. Earlier, as Sharon Lynn had taken a few faltering steps with Cody's help, Melissa had had this awful, selfish feeling that Cody was benefiting from having a daughter without having done anything to deserve it beyond making her pregnant in the first place.

He hadn't coached her through labor. He hadn't walked the floor with Sharon Lynn in the middle of the night. He hadn't fretted and cried trying to figure out a way to calm her, all the while convinced he was a failure at parenting. He hadn't been there to panic over the sight of the blood from that cut she had described to him earlier.

No, he had simply waltzed back into their lives and expected to claim his parental rights by flashing his charming grin and dispensing toys like some cowboy Santa. Well, she wouldn't have it. She wouldn't let it be that easy. He was going to have to earn a right to be a part of his daughter's life...and of hers.

That decided, she was troubled only by the realization that her demands were vague, that even she might not recognize when Cody had paid the dues she expected. Should she have a checklist? A timetable? Or would she finally know somewhere deep inside when she was through punishing him for being absent when she'd needed him the most?

"You okay?" Harlan asked, coming out of the house and studying her worriedly.

"Fine," she said, fighting not to take her annoyance at Cody out on his father.

Harlan was innocent in all of this. She had seen for herself the toll his wife's death had taken on him and she was glad that bringing Sharon Lynn here had given him some pleasure. She was sorry that she had so stubbornly resisted the temptation to announce to all the world long ago that her child was Cody's, just so that Harlan and Mary might have had the chance to know their grandchild from day one. The irony, of course, was that everyone in town had known it anyway.

"If you're so fine, how come you're sitting out here in the cold all by yourself, looking as if you just lost your last friend in the world?" Harlan asked.

"I didn't lose him," she said dryly. "I'm thinking of killing him."

Harlan's blue eyes twinkled at her feisty tone. "Ah, I see. Cody can be a bit infuriating, I suppose."

"There's no supposing about it. He is the most exasperating, egotistical…"

"Talking about me?" the man in question inquired.

He spoke in a lazy drawl that sent goose bumps dancing down Melissa's spine despite her resolution to become totally immune to him. Obviously she still needed to work harder on her wayward hormones.

"Which part clued you in?" she inquired. "Exasperating or egotistical?"

Harlan chuckled at the exchange, then promptly clamped his mouth shut in response to a dire scowl from his son. "Sorry," he said insincerely. "You two want to be left alone, or should I stick around to referee?"

"Stay," Melissa encouraged just as Cody said, "Go."

"Thank you, Melissa," Harlan said, winking at her. "I think I'll stay. The show promises to be downright fascinating. This time of day, good entertainment's hard to come by. Nothing but cartoons on TV."

"Daddy!" Cody warned.

"Yes, son?"

"We don't need you here," Cody insisted rudely.

"Speak for yourself," Melissa shot back.

Cody strolled closer until he was standing practically knee-to-knee with her. He bent down, placed his hands on the arms of the chair and said very, very quietly, "Do you really want him to hear our private, personal, *intimate* conversation?"

The gleam in his eyes was pure dare. Melissa swallowed hard. Surely Cody was just taunting her. She couldn't imagine him saying anything to her that Harlan shouldn't hear. And the truth of it was, she wanted Harlan here as a buffer just to make sure that the conversation stayed on a relatively impersonal track. She didn't trust those slippery hormones of hers. They were liable to kick in when she least expected it.

She shot a defiant look at the man who was scant inches from her face. "Yes," she said emphatically.

Cody appeared startled by the firm response. His lips twitched with apparent amusement.

"Suit yourself, Me…liss…a."

The breath fanning across her cheek was hot and mint-scented. The glint of passion in his eyes sent her pulse skyrocketing. She tried to avoid that penetrating look, but no matter how she averted her gaze she seemed to lock in on hard, lean muscle. Temptation stole her breath.

She saw the precise instant when Cody's expression registered smug satisfaction, and it infuriated her. It galled her that she responded to him, annoyed her even more that he clearly knew it.

She gathered every last ounce of hurt and resentment she'd ever felt toward him to slowly steady her pulse. With careful deliberation she lifted her glass of tea to her lips and took a long, deep swallow. She kept her gaze riveted to his as she drank, determined to show him that this latest tactic no longer had the power to rattle her. He would not win her over with his easy charm.

Yet even as she did, even as uncertainty and then a flash of irritation darkened Cody's eyes, she quaked inside and prayed he would back off before she lost the will for the battle. She was weakening already, her palms damp, her blood flowing like warm honey.

Just when she was sure she could no longer maintain the calm, impervious facade, Cody jerked upright, raked a hand through his hair and backed off.

"Score one for Melissa," Harlan said softly, his voice laced with laughter.

Cody whirled on him. "Daddy, I'm warning you..."

Harlan's dark brows rose. "Oh?"

Cody frowned. "Dammit, how come you two are in cahoots?"

"Not me," his father protested, his expression all innocence except for the sparkle in his eyes that was quintessential Harlan. "I'm just a bystander."

"An unwanted bystander," Cody reminded him.

"Speak for yourself," Melissa retorted once again.

Cody scowled down at the two of them for another minute, then muttered a harsh oath under his breath and stalked off. Only when he was out of sight did Melissa finally allow herself to relax.

"Whew! That was a close one," Harlan said, grinning at her. "Another couple of seconds and the heat out here would have melted steel. Scorched me clear over here. You sure have figured out how to tie that boy in knots."

To her amazement, he sounded approving. "Shouldn't you be on his side?" Melissa inquired.

"I suspect Cody can take care of himself," he observed. "I'm just relieved to see that you can, too."

Melissa met his amused gaze and finally breathed a sigh of relief. She grinned at him. "It's about time, don't you think?"

"Way past time, I'd say," he said, and reached over to pat her hand. "You want some advice from a man who knows Cody just about as well as anyone on earth?"

"I suspect I could use it," she agreed, wondering at the turn of events that had truly put her and Harlan Adams in cahoots, just as Cody had accused. Maybe Harlan's wisdom would be more effective than his wife's advice had been.

"Despite all these centuries that have passed, the caveman instinct hasn't entirely been bred out of us men," Harlan began. "Now I know that's not so politically correct, but it's the truth of it. A man needs to struggle to claim what he wants. It builds up his passion for it, makes him stronger. Call it perversity, but things that come too easily don't mean so much. Don't ever tell 'em I said so, but I made every one of my sons fight me to earn the right to become his own man. They resented me at the time, but in the end they were better for it."

Sorrow flitted across his face as he added, "Except maybe for Erik. He wanted to please too badly. I made a serious miscalculation by forcing him to work in ranching, one I'll regret to my dying day."

Listening to his philosophy about men, Melissa wondered if Mary Adams had put up much of a struggle. Her adoration of Harlan, her catering to his every whim, had been obvious to anyone who knew the two of them. Given Mary's advice to her about making Cody jealous, Melissa suspected she had given her husband fits at one time.

"Did Mary make you jump through hoops?" she asked.

"She did, indeed," Harlan told her, chuckling even as his expression turned nostalgic. "I knew the first minute I laid eyes on her that she was the woman I wanted to marry. She was smart as the dickens, beautiful and willful. She claimed later that she fell in love at first sight, too. She didn't let me know it for a good six months, though. In fact, for a while there I was convinced she couldn't stand to be in my presence. It was a hell of a blow to my ego."

He shook his head. "My goodness, the things I used to do just to earn a smile. That smile of hers was worth it, though. It was like sunshine, radiating warmth on everyone it touched. For thirty-six years, I was blessed with it."

"You're missing her terribly, aren't you?" Melissa said softly.

"It's as if I lost a part of myself," Harlan admitted, then seemed taken aback that he'd revealed so much. He drew himself up, clearly uncomfortable with the out-of-character confidences. "Enough of that now. You didn't come all the way out here to listen to me go on and on."

"May I ask you a question?" Melissa asked impulsively.

"Of course you can. Ask me anything."

"Did you know Cody had asked me to marry him?"

"He told me."

"Did he also tell you I'd turned him down?"

Harlan nodded.

She looked over at this man who had always been so kind to her, who'd treated her as a daughter long before she had any ties to his family beyond her hope of a future with his son. Did she dare ask him what she really wanted to know, whether Cody loved her for herself or only as the mother of the daughter he was so clearly anxious to claim? She hedged her bets and asked a less direct question.

"Was I wrong to say no?"

Harlan regarded her perceptively. "Are you afraid he won't ask again?"

She drew in a deep breath, then finally nodded, acknowledging a truth that was far from comforting.

"What would you say if he does?"

"Right now?"

"Right now," he concurred.

She thought it over carefully. Given the unresolved nature of their feelings, she would have to give him the same answer. "I'd tell him no," she admitted.

"Then there's your answer," he reassured her. "Look, I don't claim to know what happened between you and Cody that made him run off to Wyoming, but it's plain as day to me that it wasn't a simple misunderstanding. You keeping that baby a secret from him proves that. Feelings that complicated take time to sort out. Take as long as you want, just don't shut him out of your life in the meantime. Silence and distance aren't the way to patch things up."

Harlan's warning was still echoing in her head when she finally went in search of Cody. He was right, the lines of communication did need to remain open, for Sharon Lynn's sake, if not her own.

She suspected Cody was either in the barn or had taken off for his own place nearby. His father had promised to look in on Sharon Lynn and to entertain her if she awakened from her nap.

When she didn't find Cody in the barn, she set off across a field to the small house Cody had built for himself in defiance of his father's order that he should strike out on his own and work some other ranch, maybe even start his own as Luke had. Every board Cody had hammered into place, every shingle he had laid on the roof had been a declaration that he intended to stay and claim his share of White Pines.

Melissa had watched him night after night, at the end of long, backbreaking days running the ranch. She had helped when she could, bringing him picnic baskets filled with his favorite foods on the evenings when he'd skipped supper to keep on working until the last hint of daylight faded.

She had observed his progress with her heart in her throat, waiting for him to ask her opinion on the size, the style, the color of paint, anything at all to suggest he intended it to be their home and not just his own. Though he had seemed to welcome her presence and her support, those words had never come.

Even so, she had been there with him when the last detail was completed, when the last brushstroke of paint had covered the walls. Though she had only spent a few incredible, unforgettable nights under that roof, she had always felt as if this was home. It was the place Sharon Lynn had been conceived.

As she neared the low, rambling white structure with its neat, bright blue trim, she thought she heard the once-familiar sound of hammering. She circled the house until she spotted Cody in the back, erecting what appeared to be a huge extension off what she knew to be the single bedroom.

The sight of that addition didn't snag her attention, however, quite the way that Cody did. He had stripped off his shirt, despite the chill in the air. His shoulders were bare and turning golden brown in the sun. A sheen of perspiration made his muscles glisten as they were strained and tested by his exertion.

Sweet heaven, she thought, swallowing hard. He was gorgeous, even more spectacularly developed than he had been the last time she'd seen him half-naked.

"Cody," she whispered, her voice suddenly thready with longing.

She heard the loud *thwack* of the hammer against wood and something softer, followed by an oath that would have blistered a sailor's ears. The ladder he was on tilted precariously, but he managed to right it and climb down without further mishap.

His gaze riveted on her, he muttered, "Damn, Melissa, don't you know better than to sneak up on a man when he's halfway up a ladder?"

She knew his testiness had more to do with his injured thumb than her unexpected presence. She grinned at him. "I've been in plain view for the last half mile. You would have seen me if you were the least bit observant."

"I'm concentrating on what I'm doing, not scanning the horizon for visitors."

"Just what is it you're doing?"

"Adding on."

She gave him a wry look. "That much is plain. *What* are you adding on?"

"A room for my daughter."

Surprise rippled through her. "Isn't that room Harlan's prepared good enough?"

"I want her to have her own room in my home," he insisted, giving her a belligerent look that dared her to argue.

"Seems like a lot of work for an occasional visit."

He climbed down from the ladder and leaned back against it, his boot heel hooked over the bottom rung behind him. His chin jutted up belligerently. It should have warned her what was coming, but it didn't.

"We're not talking an occasional visit, Melissa," he declared bluntly. "I expect to have her here a lot. You've had her for more than a year. I'm expecting equal time."

A year, here with Cody? Away from her? A sudden weakness washed through her. "You can't be serious," she whispered, thinking of the warning her mother had given her at the outset. Had Velma been right, after all? Would Cody bring all of the Adams influence to bear to get custody of his child?

"Dead serious," he confirmed, his unblinking gaze leveled on her.

This was a new and dangerous twist to Cody's driven nature. Clearly he intended to go after his daughter with the same singleminded determination he'd devoted to securing his place at White Pines.

"Cody, she's not a possession," she said in a tone

that barely concealed her sudden desperation. "She's a little girl."

"A little girl who ought to get to know her daddy."

"I've told you—I've *promised* you—that we can work that out. I don't want to prevent you from spending time with her, from getting to know her, but to bring her to a strange house, to expect her to live with a virtual stranger... I won't allow it, Cody. I can't."

"You may not have a choice," he said coldly. "I don't want to get lawyers involved in this, but I will if I have to."

Melissa had no trouble imagining who would win in a court fight. As good a mother as she'd been, Cody and his family had the power to beat her. "There has to be another way," she said.

He nodded. "There is."

"What? I'll do anything."

His mouth curved into a mockery of a smile. "You make it sound so dire. The alternative isn't that awful. You just have to marry me."

The conversation she'd just had with Harlan echoed in her head. She couldn't marry Cody, not under these circumstances, especially not with him trying to blackmail her into it. What kind of a chance would their marriage have if she did? None. None at all.

She forced herself not to react with the anger or counterthreats that were on the tip of her tongue. Reason and humor would be more successful against the absurdity of what he was suggesting.

"Cody, half of the women in Texas would marry you in a heartbeat if you're anxious to have a wife," she said, refusing to consider the terrible consequences to her emotions if he took her up on what she was suggesting. "Why try to blackmail me into it?"

"Because you're the one who's the mother of my child," he said simply.

"But that's all I am to you," she replied, fighting tears. "It's not enough to make a marriage. At the first sign of trouble, what's to prevent you from bolting again, just like you did when you saw me with Brian? You don't trust me. You don't want me."

"Oh, I wouldn't say that," he said, straightening and walking slowly toward her with a look that flat-out contradicted her claim.

Melissa held her ground. If she backed down now, if she showed him any hint of weakness, he would win. The prize was more than her pride, more than her body. The prize they were warring over was her daughter.

Cody's advance was slow and deliberate. His eyes, dark as coal in the shadow of the house, seemed to sear her with their intensity. His lips formed a straight, tight line. Anger and frustration radiated from every masculine pore.

When he neared to within a few scant inches, the heat from his body enveloped her, tugging at her like a powerful magnet. And still she held her ground.

"I want you, Me...liss...a," he said quietly. "Make no doubt about that."

She shivered under his slow, leisurely, pointed inspection. Her skin sizzled under that hot gaze. The peaks of her breasts hardened. Moisture gathered between her thighs. Her entire body responded as if he'd stroked and caressed every inch of her. She ached to feel his fingers where his gaze had been. And still, unbelievably, she held her ground.

Her breath snagged, then raced. Her pulse skittered crazily. She longed for someplace to sit or lean, anything to keep her weak knees from giving away her shakiness.

"Tempted, Me...liss...a?"

"No," she squeaked, hating herself for not making the response firmer, more emphatic.

"Remember how it felt to have me inside you?" he taunted, hands jammed into his pockets, deliberately stretching faded denim over the unmistakable ridge of his arousal.

Her gaze locked on that evidence of his desire. A matching hunger rocketed through her. She swallowed hard, clenching her fists so tightly she was certain she must be drawing blood. But still she held her ground.

"In there, on that big, old, feather mattress," he reminded her silkily. "Our legs all tangled, our bodies slick with sweat. Remember, Me...liss...a?"

Oh, sweet heaven, she thought, desperately trying to replace his images with other, safer memories of her own. Memories of being alone and scared, when she realized she was pregnant. Memories of staring at a phone that never rang as day after day, then month after month ticked by. Thinking of that, she steadied herself and held her ground.

She leveled a look straight into eyes that blazed with passion and said, "It won't work, Cody. We can't resolve this in bed."

He reached out then, skimmed his knuckles lightly along her cheek and watched her shiver at the touch. "You sure about that, darlin'?"

She wasn't sure about anything anymore except the tide of desire she was battling with every last shred of her resistance. Her breathlessness kept her silent, afraid that anything she said or the whispered huskiness of her voice would give her away.

His fingers traced a delicate, erotic path along her neck, circling her nape, pulling her closer and closer still until their lips were a scant hairsbreadth apart, their breath mingling along with their scents; hers, wild-flower fresh, his, raw and purely masculine.

The touch of his mouth against hers, gentle as a breeze, commanding as the pull of the tides, sealed her fate. The ground she'd held so staunchly gave way as she swayed into the temptation of that kiss.

Cody gave a sigh that she interpreted as part relief, part satisfaction. He coaxed her lips apart, touched his tongue to hers in a provocative duet.

Melissa bowed to the inevitable then. She had no power or will to resist this lure. She gave herself up to the sweet, wild sensations that had always been her downfall with Cody. He knew every inch of her, knew how to persuade and cajole, how to tempt and tease until her body was his as it had always been.

Her heart, she prayed, she could protect a little longer.

11

The dare was backfiring. Cody knew it the instant he saw Melissa sprawled across his bed, her long auburn hair tangled on his pillow, her skin like smoothest satin, her coral-tipped breasts beckoning to him.

Until this moment it had only been distant memories that tormented him, fueling steamy dreams and restless nights. Now she was here and this throbbing hunger he felt for her was real. Powerful sensations he'd been telling himself that absence—and abstinence—had exaggerated were reawakened now with passionate urgency.

There might still have been a split second when he could have reclaimed sanity and reason, but if there was, he let it pass. His need for her was too great. His conviction that making love to her once again would bind her to him forever was too compelling.

The soft, winter sunlight spilled through a skylight above the bed and bathed Melissa in a golden glow. An artist might spend a lifetime searching for anything so beautiful, he thought as he stood looking down at her. An artist might spend an entire career trying to capture that same sensual vision on canvas and fail in the end. Cody certainly had never seen anything to equal the sight. He couldn't tear his gaze away.

Pregnancy had changed her body, gently rounding it, where before it had been all sharp angles and far more delicate curves. He swallowed hard as he absorbed the changes, regretting with every fiber of his being that he'd never seen her belly swollen with his child or her breasts when they were tender and engorged with milk.

He was aware of the instant when embarrassment tinted her skin a seashell pink from head to toe. She grabbed for a corner of the sheet, but before she could cover herself, he caught the edge and tugged it gently from her grasp. He stripped away his own clothes and sank down beside her, his gaze never leaving hers.

His breath eased out of him on a ragged sigh. "You are even more beautiful than I remembered," he said, touching his fingers to the pulse that hammered at the base of her neck, gauging her response. Her skin burned beneath his touch. Her pulse bucked like the most impatient bronco he'd ever ridden.

And her eyes, oh, how they pleaded with him. The delicate sea green shade had darkened with some inner turbulence. There wasn't a doubt in his mind that she wanted him with a desperation as fierce as his own.

He also knew with absolute certainty that she didn't want to desire him at all. Outside just now, she had fought her own passion valiantly, but nature and the inevitability of their mating were against her, just as they had been against him since his return to Texas.

He had always understood that internal war, perhaps even better than she did. Way back, when he'd waged his own battle to resist being hemmed in, when he'd struggled against commitment, his body had betrayed him, hungering for Melissa in a way he should have recognized as proof that they were meant to be. It had never been anywhere near as casual between them as he'd sworn to himself it was.

Now, with this second chance, his gaze intent, he skimmed his fingers over delicate skin, caressing new curves and exploring familiar planes. He scattered kisses in the wake of his touch, until her skin was on fire and her breath was coming in soft gasps and her eyes were the color of a stormy sea.

He wondered if he would ever understand the complex mix of raw, violent emotions she stirred in him. The primitive urge to claim and possess tangled with a more sensitive desire to awaken and give pleasure. He concentrated on the latter, judging the success of each stroke of his fingers, each dark and passionate kiss.

"Cody, please," she pleaded, her body arching upward, seeking his, seeking the very possession he held back.

"Not yet," he soothed, even as he intensified his touches, tormenting and teasing until he sensed that she was right on the edge of a shattering, consuming climax.

His own body was rigid with tension, his blood pounding hotly through his veins. He held his own satisfaction at bay with a will that was being tested beyond endurance. He had no idea if the torment was meant to incite Melissa or prove something to himself. Perhaps he was hoping for one last, tiny victory in his internal battle to demonstrate that she didn't have the power to captivate him so thoroughly, after all.

But of course, she did. And when her soft cries and his own demanding need could no longer be ignored, he slowly, *slowly* entered her, sinking into that moist, velvet sheath with a sigh of thrilled satisfaction. As the pace of his entry and retreat escalated, they rode each wave of pleasure together until willpower—his and hers—vanished in an explosion that made them one.

Afterward, still floating on the memories of that wild, incredible journey, Cody couldn't help thinking of the implication. Melissa was home at last, where she belonged...and so was he.

"I told you so," Cody murmured smugly sometime later, when the room was bathed in the last pink shimmer of a glorious sunset.

"Told me what?" Melissa asked, her eyes closed, her body tucked against his side.

"That being married to me wouldn't be so awful."

Her eyes blinked open and she rose up to lean on one elbow. "This isn't marriage, Cody," she reminded him with a scowl. "It's an interlude, one afternoon, nothing more."

He was stunned that she could be so cool, so dismissive, in the aftermath of such all-consuming heat and passion. "Are you saying that this meant nothing to you?"

"I'm saying it's not enough to make a marriage," she countered stubbornly. "Cody, if sex were all that mattered, you would never have left for Wyoming and we'd have been married long ago."

His temper snapped at that. "I would never have left for Wyoming if you hadn't deliberately tried to make me think you were becoming involved with my best friend," he shouted, flinging her responsibility for his leaving back in her face.

Even as he hurled the accusation, he climbed from the bed and yanked on his jeans. He stalked out of the bedroom, not sure where he was headed until he found himself outside on the deck, standing at the rail gazing over the land he loved. Not even such natural beauty had the power to soothe him now, though. Fury made his insides churn.

The quick escalation of the argument forced him to admit that Melissa was right about one thing: making love hadn't solved anything. If anything, it had complicated matters, because now they both knew that the explosive chemistry between them was as volatile as ever. It was going to be harder than ever to work things out with reason and logic, when the temptation was going to be to fall into bed.

He sensed Melissa's presence before he felt her slip up to the rail beside him. He glanced down and felt the sharp tug of desire flare to life all over again, proving the very point he'd just made to himself.

She had pulled on one of his shirts, which fell to midthigh, leaving her long, slender legs revealed. She'd cuffed the sleeves halfway up her arms. The sun turned her tousled hair to strands of fire. She looked part innocent waif, part sexy siren.

"It should never have happened," she said, meeting his gaze, her expression troubled.

"I don't—I *won't*—regret it." He studied her intently. "You do, though, don't you?"

"Only because it complicates everything," she said, echoing his own thoughts. "I want so badly to think clearly about all of this, to make the right choices this time. When you touch me, my brain goes on the blink. I'm all sensation and emotion and nostalgia."

"Stay here with me tonight," Cody blurted impulsively, suddenly wanting to seize the opportunity to force a resolution to their standoff. "Sharon Lynn will be fine with Daddy. Maritza will be there to help him look after her."

A wistful smile played around her mouth. "Haven't you heard a word I was saying?"

"All of them. I was just thinking, though, that we're both stubborn, strong people. Surely we could sit down and discuss all of this rationally and reach a sensible conclusion."

"Here?" she said doubtfully. "Within a few feet of that bed in there? Within a few feet of each other, for that matter?"

She was shaking her head before the last words were out of her mouth. "Forget it, Cody. It would never work. Besides, this isn't something we can resolve in a few hours or even a few days."

He sighed heavily. "So what do we do?"

"We give it time." Her expression turned rueful. "Preferably in very public places."

Cody wasn't wild about her solution. Now that he'd made up his mind to make the commitment he should have made two years earlier, Melissa's insistence on a delay was exasperating. He also feared that a decision reached on cold logic alone might not work in his favor. He wanted the heat of their passion on his side.

Of course, he reminded himself, their chemistry didn't necessarily confine itself to suitable locations. It could flare up just about anywhere, anytime, with the right look, the right caress. And there was something to be said for deliberately, provocatively stirring it up, when fulfillment was absolutely out of the question.

Yes, indeed, he decided with a renewed sense of anticipation, he could make things between himself and Melissa hotter than a day in the sweltering Texas sun. He could make it his business to drive her wild.

The plan had only one drawback that he could think of—it was very likely to drive him to distraction at the same time.

"Okay, you win," he said eventually, pleased when he noted the faint hint of disappointment in her eyes. A less diplomatic man might have reminded her to be careful what she wished for. Getting her way obviously wasn't quite as satisfying as she'd expected.

"Let's get dressed and see what's happening up at the main house," he said, deliberately making it sound as if they'd just shared something no more personal than a handshake. "Sharon Lynn's probably awake by now. You shower first. I'll clean up the tools I left outside."

Melissa nodded at the bland suggestion and turned toward the house with unmistakable reluctance. Cody grinned at the dejected slope of her shoulders.

"Hey, Melissa," he called softly.

She glanced back at him over her shoulder, her expression uncertain.

"I'll be thinking about you in that shower," he taunted. "All wet and slippery and naked."

Color flared in her cheeks. The sparkle returned to her eyes. A pleased smile tugged at her lips as she turned and sashayed into the house with a deliberate sway of her hips.

Oh, my, yes, he thought as he watched her go. This was going to get downright fascinating.

If there was a decidedly knowing gleam in Harlan's eyes when they eventually returned to the main house,

Melissa pretended to ignore it. What worried her more was that he might be getting ideas after their long absence that she and Cody had spent the time wisely and worked things out. Harlan believed strongly in family. He clearly wanted them to resolve things in a way that kept them all together. Despite what he'd said earlier about taking all the time she needed, hearing that they had not settled a thing would surely disappoint him.

"I think we'd best be getting back into town," Melissa announced within minutes.

"What's your hurry?" Harlan asked at once. "There's plenty of room here, if you want to stay the night. I'm rattling around in this big old place all by myself. It would be a pleasure to have company."

Melissa couldn't help thinking of another very recent invitation to stay at White Pines, one she had firmly declined. Her gaze caught Cody's and picked up on the gleam of anticipation in his eyes as he awaited her answer to his father's plea. She felt the web of Adams charm being woven snugly around her.

"No," she said, breaking free for now. "Another time."

She scooped up her daughter. "Time to get home, pumpkin."

Sharon Lynn promptly tried to squirm free, holding her arms out plaintively toward her grandfather. "Da?"

"You can come to see Granddaddy again very soon," Melissa promised, forcing herself not to see the equally wistful expression in Harlan's eyes as she refused to relinquish her daughter.

Harlan leaned down and kissed them both. "You're welcome here anytime," he told her. "Both of you. Don't stand on ceremony. Come whenever you have some time."

"I'll walk you out," Cody offered, falling into step beside her. "Don't wait up for me, Daddy. I might spend some time in town tonight."

Melissa didn't have to glance back to know that the comment had stirred a speculative glint in Harlan's eyes.

"Why did you say that?" she demanded of Cody the instant they were out of earshot of the house.

He regarded her with his most innocent look, the one only a fool would trust. "Say what?"

"That you'd be staying in town for a while?"

"Because it's true."

"No, it's not," she said firmly. "We did not discuss anything about you coming into town."

"Who said I'd be with you?" he inquired, leveling a gaze straight into her eyes.

"But you said... W-who?" Melissa sputtered. "Dammit, Cody, you did that deliberately."

"Did what?"

"Let your father assume that you intended to spend the evening, maybe the whole night, with me."

"Is that what I said?"

"It's what you implied."

"You sure you're not projecting your own desires onto me?"

"No, I am not," she practically shouted, causing Sharon Lynn to begin to whimper. Melissa kissed her cheek. "Shh, baby. It's okay. Your daddy and I are just having a discussion."

Cody chuckled. "Is that what it is? You sure do get riled up over a little discussion."

"I am not riled up," she insisted, keeping a tight rein on her frayed temper.

"Could have fooled me."

"Oh, forget it," she snapped as she put Melissa into her car seat and buckled her in. As she walked around the car, she heard the driver's door open and assumed Cody was simply being polite. Instead she found that he'd climbed in behind the wheel.

"Now what?" she asked, regarding him suspiciously.

"I thought I'd hitch a ride."

"Why would you want to do that? It'll leave you stranded in town."

"Oh, I'm sure I can find someone willing to bring me home," he said, then winked. "Eventually."

He said it in a smug way that had her grinding her teeth. "Is that a new technique you've learned for luring ladies out to your place?" she inquired testily. "You claim to need a ride home?"

"Let's just say I'm trying it out tonight."

"And what if no one responds to your plight?"

"Oh, I don't think there's much chance of that," he said confidently. He shrugged. "If it does, I'm sure you'd be willing to take me in for the night."

"When pigs learn to fly," she retorted, irritated beyond belief that mere hours after they'd made love he was going on the prowl again. "Get out, Cody."

"I don't think so."

"Cody Adams, do not make me march back into that house so I can borrow a shotgun from Harlan."

He chuckled. "I'm not real worried about that, darlin'. You'd never shoot a man in plain view of his daughter."

He was right, of course. But, lordy, how she was tempted. "Oh, for heaven's sake," she muttered, flinging open the back door. "If you want to behave like a horse's behind, go right ahead."

"Thank you," he said, and turned the key in the ignition.

Cody was the kind of driver who liked to tempt fate. Melissa clung to the door handle, while Sharon Lynn squealed with excitement as they sped around curves. She knew they were perfectly safe. Cody never tried anything unless he was confident of his control of the road, the car, or the situation. In fact, she suspected that was exactly the point he was trying to make.

Even so, she was pale by the time he finally pulled to a stop in front of Rosa's Mexican Café. She was faintly puzzled by his choice. It was hardly a singles hangout.

"This is where you intend to spend your night on the town?"

He shrugged. "I thought we could grab a bite to eat first."

"Uh-huh," she said, regarding him skeptically.

"Do you have a problem with that?"

"Not really, I suppose, but you could have asked."

"I just did."

"Funny, it didn't sound much like a question to me. Maybe I already have plans for the night."

His expression turned dark. "Do you?" he demanded, his voice tight.

She let him wonder for the space of a heartbeat, then shrugged. "No, but I could have."

"Melissa, I swear…"

"Tsk-tsk," she warned, enjoying turning the tables on him, albeit briefly. "Not in front of the baby."

He scowled at her, scooped Sharon Lynn out of her car seat and headed inside, leaving Melissa to make up her own mind about whether to join them or remain in the car and quibble over semantics. Sighing over this latest test of her patience, she reluctantly followed him inside.

On a Saturday night, Rosa's was crowded with families. Melissa spotted Jordan and Kelly with their kids right off. Cody apparently did not, because he was making a beeline for an empty table on the opposite side of the restaurant. He picked up a booster seat en route and was already putting Sharon Lynn into it by the time Melissa joined him.

"Didn't you see Jordan and Kelly?" she asked. "They were trying to wave us over. There's room at their table."

"I saw them," Cody said tersely.

Melissa studied the set of his jaw. "Okay, what's wrong?"

"I do not intend to spend the evening with my brother," he said. "If you can call him that."

"Cody," she protested. "Why would you even say something like that?"

He frowned at her. "Because he knew about Sharon Lynn and he didn't tell me."

Melissa flinched as if he'd struck her. "Because I swore him to secrecy," she reminded him. She didn't want this family split on her conscience.

"He should have told me," Cody repeated, his stubbornness kicking in with a vengeance.

Melissa regarded him with a mix of frustration and dismay. The last thing she had ever wanted was to cause a rift between the two brothers. Uncertain what she could do to mend it, she turned and walked away. Cody was on her heels in a flash.

"Where are you going?" he asked suspiciously, latching onto her elbow.

"To the ladies' room," she said.

"Oh." He released her at once. "Sorry."

Melissa rolled her eyes and continued on to the back, praying that Kelly would spot her and join her.

She was combing her hair when Jordan's wife came into the rest room. "What are we going to do about them?" Melissa asked at once.

"It's not Jordan," Kelly said. "He feels terrible about what happened. He doesn't blame Cody for being furious."

"Okay, then, how do I get through to Cody? It's my fault. I've told him that, but he says Jordan should have ignored my wishes."

"He probably should have," Kelly concurred. "I could have told Cody myself and I didn't. There's enough blame to go around. The point now is to make things right. I wanted it settled before the baptism tomorrow so that Cody could be J.J.'s godfather. But until this is resolved, Jordan and I have decided to postpone the ceremony. It was only going to be a small family gathering anyway."

"Maybe if Jordan made the first move," Melissa suggested.

Kelly shook her head. "It wouldn't work. This is Cody's call, I'm afraid. The trouble is, we're dealing with the stubborn Adams men here."

"Can you all stick around?" Melissa asked. "I'll think of something."

"Sure," Kelly agreed. "Our dinner's just now being served anyway. I can't imagine what you can do, but let me know if you think I can help." She paused on her way to the door. "By the way, it's good to see the two of you together again. How are things going?"

"Don't ask," Melissa said.

Kelly grinned. "That good, huh? Does that mean you haven't signed up at the Neiman-Marcus bridal registry yet?"

"No, and I wouldn't be holding my breath for that if I were you. I am not inclined to marry a man who is as thoroughly, unrepentantly, exasperating as Cody is."

"Interesting," Kelly murmured, a knowing twinkle in her eyes.

"Don't start with me. I've just been subjected to Harlan's knowing looks for the past few hours."

"Not another word," Kelly promised readily. "Nobody understands the perverse streak that runs in this family any better than I do."

After Kelly had gone, Melissa slowly put her comb into her purse and headed back to their table. She saw at once that Cody had been joined by Kelly's precocious six-year-old, Dani.

"I came to see the baby," Dani announced when Melissa had joined them. "She's cuter than my brother. I wanted a sister, but somebody got mixed up and gave me a brother instead."

Melissa grinned at her. "I bet you'll be glad of that when you're older. I always wished I had a brother who'd look out for me." She shot a pointed look at Cody when she said it.

Cody rolled his eyes. Clearly, he didn't think Jordan had done such a terrific job of looking out for him when it counted.

Dani stood closer to the table and leaned her elbows

on it, propping her chin in her hands as she regarded her uncle. "You know, Uncle Cody, I was thinking."

He visibly contained a grin. "What were you thinking, you little con artist?"

"Maybe Sharon Lynn should have a kitten of her own."

"Maybe she should." He glanced at Melissa. "What do you think?"

"I think you two were plotting this," Melissa charged, trying not to chuckle at the guilty expressions. "Sharon Lynn does not need a kitten. More importantly, a kitten does not need Sharon Lynn. She'd probably scare it to death."

Dani's brow knit as she considered the argument. "She's probably right, Uncle Cody. Babies don't understand about kittens. Francie thinks that my brother is a pest."

"A valid point," Cody agreed. "Maybe after Sharon Lynn gets to know how to behave around those kittens you talked me into taking, she can have one of her own."

"Good idea," Dani said. "Francie will probably have more by then."

"Over my dead body," Jordan said, arriving to stand behind his stepdaughter. "Hello, Melissa." He looked straight at Cody, who avoided his gaze. "Cody."

After a visible internal struggle, Cody nodded curtly.

Jordan stood there, looking uncharacteristically indecisive for another minute before sighing and saying, "Come on, Dani. Your dinner's getting cold."

When the pair of them were gone, Melissa said, "You were rude to him, Cody. He made an overture and you didn't even say hello."

Cody closed his eyes. When he opened them, his

stubborn resolve seemed to be firmly back in place. "I had nothing to say to him."

"Cody, I'm the one who betrayed you, not Jordan. I'm the one you thought had cheated on you. I'm the one who kept it a secret that I'd had your baby. You're speaking to me. You've forgiven me."

She studied him intently. "Or have you? Are you taking all the anger you don't dare express against me because of Sharon Lynn and projecting it on to Jordan?"

She saw by the way his jaw worked and his gaze evaded hers that she'd hit the nail on the head. She sighed. "Don't do this, Cody. Don't let what happened between us come between you and Jordan. Please," she pleaded.

When he didn't respond, she gave up. "Just promise you'll think about what I said, okay?"

"Yeah," he said tersely. "I'll think about it."

With great reluctance, Melissa finally conceded it was the best she could hope for. For now, anyway.

12

Sometime well after midnight, Melissa woke to the sound of Sharon Lynn whimpering. She tumbled out of bed, flipped on the hall light and raced into the baby's room.

Sharon Lynn was tossing restlessly. Her skin was dry and burning up.

"Oh, baby," Melissa soothed as she scooped her up. "Are you feeling bad? Come with Mommy. I'll get you some water and check your temperature."

She had barely made it into the kitchen and flipped that light on when the front door burst open, scaring her half to death. She grabbed the frying pan and peeked through the kitchen doorway, prepared to do battle with a lunatic. Instead it was Cody, his clothes rumpled, his hair tousled, who stood in the foyer.

"Cody, what on earth?" she demanded, trying to slow the pounding of her heart. She set the frying pan down, though she wasn't entirely convinced he couldn't do with a good whop upside the head for scaring her so badly.

"What's going on?" he asked, casting worried looks

from her to the baby and back. "I saw the lights come on. Are you okay?"

She ignored the question and tried to figure out what he was doing at her house in the middle of the night. The last time she'd seen him he'd been sitting at the bar in Rosa's. He'd declared his intention of starting his night on the town right there, clearly implying he intended it to end in someone's arms. She'd choked back her fury and tried to exit with some dignity, when all she'd really wanted to do was have a knock-down, drag-'em-out brawl with him. She was still itching for a fight, as a matter of fact, but right now Sharon Lynn's condition took precedence.

"Where have you been?" she asked, pleased that she was able to sound so cool when she was seething inside.

"On the porch," he admitted, taking his feverish daughter from her arms. As soon as he touched her, alarm flared in his eyes. "Good heavens, she's burning up. Have you taken her temperature?"

"I was just about to." She tried to remain calm in the face of his obvious panic and her own. She'd experienced rapidly spiking temperatures before and learned that it was a matter of course for children. Still, she'd never felt Sharon Lynn's skin quite so hot.

The thermometer registered one hundred and three degrees. Cody's face blanched when she told him.

"We're going to the hospital," he said at once, starting out of the kitchen.

Melissa blocked his way. "Not yet," she said far more calmly than she was feeling. There was no point in both of them panicking. "Let me give her a Tylenol and try bathing her with cool water to see if we can't bring that temperature down. If there's no change, then we'll call the doctor."

Sharon Lynn patted Cody's stubbled cheek weakly and murmured, "Da." She sounded pitiful.

Cody looked thoroughly shaken. "Melissa, I don't think we should wait. Something's really wrong with her."

"It's probably nothing more than the start of a cold or a touch of flu," she said. "Stuff like that reaches epidemic proportions this time of the year."

"Her temperature's over a hundred," he reminded her. "That can't be good for her."

"Babies get high temperatures. It's nothing to get crazy about," she insisted, amending to herself, *yet*.

She gave Sharon Lynn Tylenol, then ran cool water into the kitchen sink. "Bring her over here and let's get her out of that nightgown. It's soaking wet anyway. Why don't you go back to her room and bring me a clean one, along with a fresh diaper. We'll need those after I've sponged her off a bit with cool water."

Cody looked as if he might refuse to budge, but eventually he did as she'd asked. By the time he'd returned, Sharon Lynn was no longer whimpering. In fact she seemed to be relaxing and enjoying the cool water Melissa was gently splashing over her.

"Are you sure that's good for her?" Cody asked, worry etched on his face.

"It's exactly what the doctor and all the child-care books recommend. If you don't believe me, there's a book in the living room. Go read it." Anything to get him out of the kitchen again before he wore a hole in the linoleum with his pacing. Worse, she was feeling crowded with all of his hovering.

"No, no, I'll take your word for it," he said, standing over her shoulder and watching every move she made. "Maybe we should take her temperature again."

Melissa sighed and stepped aside to allow him to put the fancy new thermometer in Sharon Lynn's ear for a few seconds.

"It's a hundred and two," he proclaimed. "That's it. We're going to the hospital."

"It's down a whole degree," Melissa observed, blocking him when he would have snatched Sharon Lynn out of the bathwater. "The Tylenol's working."

"Not fast enough."

"Let's give it another half hour," she compromised.

Cody hesitated, then finally conceded grudgingly, "A half hour. Not a minute more."

He sat down at the kitchen table and fixed his gaze on the clock over the sink. Apparently he intended to watch each of those thirty minutes tick by.

"Da!" Sharon Lynn called out.

Cody was on his feet in an instant. "What's up, sweet pea? You feeling better?" he asked, caressing her cheek with fingers that shook visibly.

A smile spread across his daughter's face. "Da," she repeated enthusiastically.

A little color came back into Cody's ashen complexion. "She feels a little cooler."

Melissa agreed. "I'm betting when we check her temperature again, it'll be just about back to normal."

Twenty minutes later Sharon Lynn was no longer feverish. She was once again tucked into her crib. Cody, still looking shaken, stood over her.

"How do you stand this?" he murmured to Melissa. "I've never been so terrified in my life."

Melissa patted his hand. "It gets easier after you've been through it once or twice and know what to expect," she promised him, but he shook his head.

"I can't imagine it getting easier," he said. "What if her temperature hadn't gone down? What if you'd guessed wrong?"

"Then we would have called the doctor or gotten her to the hospital."

"It might have been too late."

"Cody, stop that," she ordered, not daring to admit that she'd been scared silly, too, that she always was, no matter what the books said. "It's over. She's going to be fine. It was just a little fever."

He closed his eyes and drew in a deep breath. "Okay, you're right. Just a little fever." He still sounded unconvinced. He definitely showed no inclination to budge from beside the crib.

Melissa grinned at him. "Cody, everything really is fine. You don't have to stand there and watch her all night."

"I am not leaving this house," he said, his jaw jutting out belligerently.

"Fine. You can sleep on the sofa." She yawned. "Good night, Cody."

"Where are you going?"

"Back to bed."

"How can you possibly sleep?"

"Because I'm exhausted. You must be, too." In fact, he looked as if he hadn't slept in days.

"I won't sleep a wink," he swore.

"Whatever," she murmured, and headed for her room. At the doorway she recalled that they'd never really talked about why he'd been on her front porch in the first place. "Cody, why were you here in the middle of the night?"

A sheepish expression spread across his face. "I figured if you found me on your doorstep in the morning, you'd give me a lift home."

She grinned. "Couldn't find another taker for that fabulous Adams charm, huh?"

"Never even tried," he admitted, then shrugged. "You've spoiled me for anyone else, Me...liss...a."

She studied his face intently, looking for signs that the comment was no more than a glib, charming lie. He appeared to be dead serious. A little flutter of excitement stirred deep inside her. Was it possible that Cody really did intend to stick around through thick and thin, through good times and bad?

For the first time since he'd come home from Wyoming, she dared to hope that he really had changed. If he had...

No, she cautioned herself at once. It was too soon to leap to any conclusions at all about the future.

"Good night, Cody," she whispered, her voice husky with a longing she would never have admitted.

"Good night, darlin'."

Cody felt as if he'd slept on an old washboard. Every muscle ached like the dickens. Every vertebra in his back had either been compressed, twisted or otherwise maimed by Melissa's sofa. He suspected she'd made him sleep there on purpose, knowing what it would do to him.

He also had the distinct impression that there was a tiny wanna-be drummer in his head flailing away without much sense of rhythm.

He groaned and opened his eyes, blinking at the sunlight streaming into the living room. That was when he realized that the loud clanging wasn't in his head. It was coming from Sharon Lynn's room. If that was the case, it just might be something he could stop before his head exploded.

Moving inch by careful inch, he eased to his feet and padded down the hall to the baby's room. When he opened the door a crack, he found her bouncing in her crib, banging a wooden block on the railing. The instant she spied him, a smile spread across her face.

"Da," she enthused, and held out her arms.

Cody wondered if he would ever get over the thrill that sweet, innocent gesture sent through him.

"Morning, pumpkin. I take it from all the commotion in here that you're feeling better."

"Ya…ya…ya."

"That must mean yes," he decided as he plucked her out of the crib and took the toy block from her as a precaution. His head was feeling marginally better, but another round of Sharon Lynn's musical skills would be a killer.

Her temperature seemed to be gone. He quickly changed her, then carried her into the kitchen. Once there, he was stymied. Was she old enough for regular cereal? Or was there some sort of baby food she was supposed to have? He didn't recall discussing breakfast when he and Melissa had shopped for groceries.

He settled Sharon Lynn into her high chair, found a soft toy bear to entertain her, and searched through the cabinets. Nothing conclusive there beyond an assortment of frosted cereals that seemed more likely to appeal to a one-year-old than her mother. Then again, he didn't know much about Melissa's breakfast habits, either. On the rare occasions when they'd slept in the same bed before he'd left for Wyoming, breakfast had been the last thing on their minds first thing in the morning.

A glance in the refrigerator suggested that juice might be a good place to start. He recalled buying an awful lot of apple juice at the store. He filled a bottle and handed it over. Sharon Lynn tossed her bear on the floor and accepted it eagerly.

Scrambled eggs struck him as a safe bet. Besides, he and Melissa could eat them, as well. Fixing one meal for all of them appealed to him. It struck him as cozy; a family tradition of sorts. Their very first.

He started the coffeemaker, popped four slices of bread into the toaster, put butter and jelly on the table, then broke half a dozen eggs into a bowl and whipped them with a fork until they were foamy. Suddenly he heard the faint sound of footsteps behind him. He pivoted around and discovered Melissa leaning against the doorjamb.

"My goodness, you've been busy," she murmured, yawning and bending over to pick up the bear Sharon Lynn had tossed aside in favor of her juice. "How long have you been awake?"

Goose bumps chased down his spine at the sleepy sound of her voice and the sight of that cute little fanny draped in a very short, very revealing, silk robe.

"Our daughter's better than any rooster I ever heard. She woke me at the crack of dawn."

"Obviously she's feeling better," Melissa said, going over to touch her hand to the baby's forehead. "No more temperature."

"Seemed that way to me, too."

"Did you take it?"

He shook his head, drawing a grin.

"Turning into an old hand already," she teased. "No more panicking."

"I wouldn't say that," he said, shuddering at the memory of that icy fear that had washed through him in the wee hours of the morning. "But I am going to borrow that book of yours and read it from cover to cover."

He reached for Melissa's hand and pulled her toward him. He was vaguely surprised that she didn't put up a struggle. Maybe he hadn't imagined the closeness between them the night before.

When she was standing toe-to-toe with him, he had to resist the temptation to tug the belt of her robe free. Instead he brushed a strand of hair back from her face and gazed into her tired eyes.

"You were wonderful last night," he said softly. "Not only were you good with Sharon Lynn, but you kept me from freaking out."

Her lips curved slightly. "Having you here helped me, too," she said, surprising him.

"Why?"

"Staying calm for your benefit kept me from freaking out myself," she admitted.

He stared at her in astonishment. "You were scared?"

"Terrified," she admitted. "But I knew I couldn't let you see it or you'd have insisted on borrowing your father's plane and flying us all to some critical care hospital in Dallas in the middle of the night."

"You've got that right." He grinned. "We're quite a pair, aren't we?"

"Just typical parents, Cody."

The simple words were no more than the truth, yet

Cody felt as if he'd just heard something terribly profound spoken for the first time. He was a parent, a certified grown-up, with responsibilities he couldn't slough off. Responsibilities, in fact, that he actually yearned to accept.

He wanted more Sunday mornings just like this one, waking up to the sound of his daughter making some sort of commotion to get attention, fixing breakfast for all three of them, sitting at the kitchen table across from Melissa. He renewed his vow to himself to do everything within his power to convince Melissa they ought to be a family.

After they'd eaten and after he'd cleaned up most of the scrambled egg Sharon Lynn had managed to rub into her hair or fling halfway across the kitchen, he sat back with a sigh of pure contentment.

"Don't get too settled," Melissa warned, a teasing note in her voice. "Your daughter needs a bath. I think I'll let you do the honors since that egg she's smeared everywhere was your doing."

"You sound as if that's punishment," he said. "What's the big deal?"

"You'll see," Melissa retorted a little too cheerfully to suit him.

She ran the inch or so of bathwater into the tub, then left him to it. It didn't take long for Cody to figure out why she'd had that smug expression on her face when she'd exited the bathroom.

Sharon Lynn really loved water. She loved to splash it. She loved to scoop it up by the handful and dribble it all over him. She loved to throw her toys into it, sending yet more splashes into the air.

She wasn't quite so crazy about soap. She wriggled

and squirmed, trying to get away from him. Slippery as an eel, she evaded capture until she'd managed to soak him from head to toe. In fact, he was fairly certain that he was wetter and soapier than she was.

Melissa chose that precise moment to reappear. He heard her chuckling as he tried to towel his daughter dry.

"You find this amusing?" he inquired softly.

"Mmm-hmm," she admitted. "I sure do."

He dipped his hand in the scant remaining water that was actually in the tub and splattered it straight in Melissa's smug face. A startled, incredulous expression spread across her face.

"You brat," she muttered, turning on the faucet in the sink and scooping up a handful of water to pour over his head.

Sharon Lynn squealed with glee as water splashed everywhere.

Cody nabbed a plastic cup from the counter behind him, dipped it into the bathwater and soaked Melissa's front. Only after the damp bathrobe clung to her body did he realize the mistake he'd made. His breath snagged in his throat at the sight of her nipples hardening beneath that suddenly transparent silk. He swallowed hard, aware of the tightening in his groin and the flood of color climbing into his cheeks—and equally aware of the impossibility of pursuing the desire rocketing through him.

Melissa's gaze locked with his for what seemed an eternity, then dropped to the unmistakable evidence of his arousal. A smile slowly tugged at the corners of her mouth.

"Serves you right," she taunted as she turned and padded off to her room.

Cody groaned and wished like crazy that he knew Melissa's neighbors so he could plead with them to baby-sit for the rest of the morning. He wanted to finish what she had started with that provocative taunt.

Instead he forced himself to concentrate on getting Sharon Lynn dried off and dressed. The task was somewhat complicated by the soaked condition of his own clothes. He was dripping everywhere.

As soon as he had his daughter settled in her playpen, he grabbed a towel, went into the laundry room, stripped, and tossed his clothes into the dryer. He wrapped the towel snugly around his waist and retreated to the kitchen to drink another cup of coffee while he waited for everything to dry.

When Melissa wandered in a few minutes later her mouth gaped. "Where are your clothes?" she demanded, her gaze riveted on his bare chest.

"In the dryer."

"Get them out."

"I can't wear damp clothes," he observed.

"Whose fault is it they're wet?"

"Yours, as a matter of fact," he said blithely. "You're the one who insisted I bathe Sharon Lynn. You obviously know what she's like in water."

She fought a grin and lost. "Yeah, I do," she admitted. "But, Cody, you cannot sit around in nothing but a towel."

"You have any better ideas?" He didn't wait for any suggestions from her before adding, "We could go back to bed."

"In your dreams."

He deliberately caught her gaze. "Absolutely," he said softly. "You have no idea how vivid my dreams have become lately."

From the fiery blush in her cheeks, he had the feeling, though, that he'd been wrong about that. He got the distinct impression that Melissa's dreams had been just as erotic as his own lately. He vowed that one day soon they'd compare notes…and make them come true.

13

The rapport between them lasted all the way back to White Pines. In fact, Cody had high hopes that he was finally beginning to make progress with Melissa. He was convinced that his presence during the previous night's medical crisis had started the difficult process of convincing her that he wasn't going to bolt out of their lives at the first sign of trouble.

It had been such a small thing, being by her side during those tense moments, but he'd heard the gratitude in her voice this morning, seen the first faint flicker of renewed faith in her eyes. He couldn't allow anything to shake that trust again, not until he'd had time to strengthen it.

As they drove up the long, winding lane at White Pines he was startled to see his father emerge from the house. It appeared Harlan had been watching for them and, from the too cheerful expression on his face and the contradictory worry in his eyes, Cody could only guess that there was bad news.

He stepped out of the car and faced his father warily. "Hey, Daddy, everything okay?"

"Fine, just fine," Harlan said too heartily. He darted a worried look at Melissa, then added, "You'll never guess who's here to see you, son."

Cody shot a desperate glance toward Melissa and saw that she was hanging on his father's every word. He couldn't imagine who might have turned up at White Pines uninvited, but experience with his father's demeanor suggested he was right to be concerned. He regretted more than he could say having Melissa here at this precise moment. He should have walked home, even if it was twenty miles. He would have if he'd had any idea that trouble was going to be waiting on the doorstep.

He drew in a deep breath and braced himself. "Who?" he asked just as the front door creaked open and a slight figure with cropped black hair and a pixie face emerged. Shock rendered him speechless.

"Janey? What the hell?" He looked to his father, but Harlan merely shrugged. Cody turned back to the teenager who'd apparently tracked him down and come after him all the way from Wyoming. "What are you doing here?"

Even as he sought answers for Janey's unexpected presence, he heard Melissa's sharp intake of breath behind him. Before he could turn around, the car door slammed with enough force to rock the sturdy vehicle on its tires. He knew what that meant. He forgot all about Janey as he tried to get to Melissa before she got the wrong impression and took off in a snit. Correction, she already had the wrong impression. He just had to stop her.

"Melissa," he protested just as the engine roared to

life. "Dammit, we need to talk. Don't you dare drive away from here!"

He might as well have been talking to the wind. The order was wasted. She'd already thrown the car into gear, then backed up, spewing gravel in every direction. He slammed his fist on the fender as she turned the car, shifted again and headed away from the house at a pace that would have done an Indy 500 driver proud.

"Terrific," he muttered. "That's terrific. Not five seconds ago, I actually believed she was starting to trust me and now this!"

"Cody," his father warned, nodding toward the girl who had stopped halfway down the sidewalk.

Sure enough, Janey looked as if he'd slapped her. Cody raked his hand through his hair and tried to get a grip on his temper. It wasn't the teenager's fault that his personal life was a mess. He crossed to Janey Treethorn in three strides and looked into a face streaked with tears and eyes that were as wide as a doe's caught in the cross hairs of a hunter's gun. His anger dissipated in a heartbeat.

"Janey, don't cry," he said softly, pulling her into a hug. "Shh, baby, it's okay."

"I'm s-sorry," she stammered. "I didn't mean to mess up everything."

"I know," he soothed, awkwardly patting her back as he cast a helpless look at his father. Harlan shrugged, clearly as bemused by this turn of events as Cody was.

"It's not your fault," he told her, even though he very much wanted to blame her for ruining his fragile truce with Melissa. "Come on, let's go inside and you can tell me why you came all this way. Does your dad know you're here?"

"Ye-es-s," she said, sniffling. "Your father called him last night."

Cody's heart sank. Obviously, Janey had run away from home, if last night was the first Lance had heard of her whereabouts. His former boss was probably fit to be tied. Janey was the least rebellious of his daughters. If she had pulled a stunt as crazy as this, the other two were likely to drive him completely over the edge. Lance needed a mother for those girls and he needed her in a hurry.

Inside, Cody suggested that Harlan go and see if Maritza could rustle them up some hot chocolate. He knew it was Janey's favorite. There had been many cold winter nights when she'd fixed it for him and her father, then lingered in the shadows listening to them talk.

Before he sat down, he went into the closest bathroom and gathered up a handful of tissues and brought them back to her. He was careful to sit in a chair opposite her, since he had the terrible feeling that her crush on him was what had brought her all the way to Texas. He'd never done a thing to encourage it, except to be kind to her, but apparently that had been enough to cause this impulsive trip to Texas.

"Feeling better?" he asked after a while, when she appeared to have cried herself out and had finished the mug of hot chocolate Maritza had served with barely concealed curiosity.

Janey nodded, but wouldn't meet his gaze. Her cheeks were flushed with embarrassment. She tucked her jeans-clad legs up under her and huddled on the sofa like a small child expecting to be scolded. She looked so woebegone that Cody was having a difficult time maintaining what was left of his dying anger.

"Janey, tell me what this is all about."

"I c-can't," she whispered.

"There must be a reason you left Wyoming and came all the way to Texas. How did you know where to find me?"

"I found the address in Dad's papers."

"Did something happen at home?"

She shook her head, looking more and more miserable. Finally she lifted her chin and met his gaze for barely a second, then ducked it again. "You left," she said accusingly. "One day you just weren't there anymore and you never said goodbye."

Even though his reason for leaving had been an emergency, he could see how it might look from her perspective. He knew that in her reserved way, she counted on him.

"Didn't your dad tell you why I had to come home?" he asked.

"He said your mother died."

"That's right."

"But I thought you'd be coming back," she whispered. "But then you never did. And then Dad said you'd called and that y-you'd q-quit."

Her tears started all over again. Cody went for more tissues and brought back the whole box to buy himself the time he needed to figure out how to explain things to this shy, young girl who'd so badly needed someone that she'd chosen a miserable, cynical cowboy from Texas who already had a lousy track record for reliability.

"Janey, when I got here there were things that I realized I had to do. I couldn't come back. I explained all of that to your father."

"But...not...to me," she choked between sobs. "I thought you were my friend."

Cody sighed. "I am. I always want to be your friend."

"Then you'll come back as soon as things are settled here?" she inquired, hope written all over her tear-streaked face.

"No, sweetie, I can't come back."

"Why not?" she asked.

Not sure how she was likely to react, he drew in a deep breath before admitting, "Because I found out that I have a little girl and I have to be here for her."

Dismay darkened her eyes. "A baby?"

"Not so much a baby anymore," he confided. "She's over a year old."

"And you didn't know about her?"

"No."

Despite herself, she was apparently fascinated. For the first time since he'd arrived home, there was a sparkle in her dark eyes.

"How come?" she asked, her expression alive with curiosity.

"It's a long story."

"Was that her mom in the car just now?"

Cody nodded.

"Uh-oh," she murmured. Guilt and misery replaced the sparkle in her eyes. "I'm sorry if I messed things up for you, Cody. I really am."

He grinned ruefully. "Oh, the list of my sins is pretty long as it is. One more thing won't matter all that much."

"Want me to tell her you didn't know I was coming here?"

He had a feeling that the less Melissa saw of Janey, the better for all of them. Janey might be only fifteen, but she was a beautiful young girl who looked older than her years. It was the very fact that her body had blossomed so prematurely that had contributed to her shyness.

Ironically, he suspected she had been drawn to him for the very reason that he hadn't acted like the over-sexed teens who attended school with her. She'd felt safe with him, free to talk about her dreams, and she had magnified that feeling into a giant-size crush.

"No, sweetie, I'll take care of Melissa. Now, let's think about getting you back home again. How'd you get here?"

"I used my savings for a bus ticket. Then when I got to town, I called the ranch. Your dad came and got me."

Cody shuddered when he thought of her traveling that distance alone by bus. He also suspected that Harlan had deliberately not tried to track him down when Janey turned up to give him more time with Melissa before throwing a monkey wrench into things.

"I'll talk to Daddy about having his pilot fly you back to Wyoming," he told her.

Her eyes lit up. "Really?"

Her instantaneous excitement told him that her heart was already well on its way to healing. Maybe all she'd really needed was closure, a chance to say goodbye and make sure that she hadn't lost a friend. If he'd been half so insistent on closure before he'd taken off from Texas, maybe he and Melissa would have been married by now, instead of trying to rebuild their shattered trust.

Janey would be okay. He was sure of it. In the meantime, though, he had another heart to worry about. He had a feeling patching up the holes in Melissa's trust wasn't going to be nearly so easy to accomplish.

* * *

Melissa broke three glasses during the breakfast rush at Dolan's on Monday. As each one shattered, she heard a heavy sigh of resignation from Eli. She knew exactly how he felt. She'd had her fragile hopes shattered—again—the day before when she'd arrived at White Pines to find an adorable, sexy woman waiting on the doorstep for Cody.

As she swept up the debris from her latest round of clumsiness, she wished it were even half as easy to tidy up the aftermath of a broken heart.

When she finished sweeping, she glanced up and discovered Mabel sitting at the counter, curiosity written all over her face. To try to forestall the questions that were clearly on the older woman's mind, Melissa grabbed the coffeepot and poured her a cup.

"How about a Danish, Mabel?" she asked. "We have cheese and cherry left."

"No, thanks. So, did you and Cody have another fight?" Mabel inquired point-blank.

"No," Melissa replied honestly. They hadn't fought. She had taken off before her disillusionment could come pouring out in a wave of accusations.

"Now, why is it I don't believe that?" Mabel murmured. "You never broke a glass until that boy came back into town. Since then, you've been smashing them up so fast poor Eli's liable to go bankrupt."

"I'm going to reimburse Eli for the glasses," Melissa told her stiffly.

"No need for that," Eli called, proving that he'd heard every word of the discussion of her love life. "Maybe Mabel and I ought to sit that boy down and give him a stern talking to, though."

Mabel shot their boss a sour look. "What would you know about straightening out a lovers' tiff, old man?"

"As much as you do about starting one," Eli shot back.

Melissa stared at them. For the first time she noticed that their bickering carried the unmistakable sting of two former lovers. *Eli and Mabel,* she thought incredulously. Surely not. Then again, why not? She knew of no one else in either of their lives. Maybe that was so because they'd spent years carrying the torch for each other, unable to heal some foolish rift.

"Maybe I'm not the one who needs an intermediary," Melissa suggested, observing their reactions intently.

"You don't know what you're talking about," Mabel snapped. She shot a venomous look at the pharmacist. "Neither does he, for that matter."

"I know what I know," Eli countered. "Besides, we're not talking about you and me now. We're talking about Melissa and Cody."

"I'd rather talk about the two of you," Melissa said hurriedly, dying to know the whole story of two people who'd worked together as far back as she could recall without giving away so much as a hint that there was anything personal between them.

"No," Mabel and Eli chorused.

Melissa winced. "Okay, okay. We'll make a pact. You stay out of my personal life and I'll stay out of yours."

Mabel gave an obviously reluctant nod. Melissa waited for Eli to concur, but instead he muttered, "Too late. Yours just walked in the door."

Melissa's gaze shot to the front of the drugstore. Sure enough, Cody was striding in her direction, a glint of pure determination in his eyes.

"Go away," she said before he could settle himself on one of the stools.

"Is that any way to greet a paying customer?" he inquired.

He slapped a twenty on the counter. At the rate he was throwing them around, he was going to go broke.

"I'm not leaving until I've spent every last dime of that or you and I have talked," he announced. "You pick."

Melissa poured him a cup of coffee, snatched the twenty and tucked it in her pocket. "The coffee's on me. I'll consider the twenty a tip for services rendered."

Flags of angry color rose in Cody's cheeks. His grip on his coffee cup tightened, turning his knuckles white. "There's a name for taking money for that, darlin'."

Mabel sputtered and backed off her stool so fast it was still spinning a full minute after she'd gone. Melissa had a hunch she wasn't all that far, though, more than likely not even out of earshot.

"How dare you!" Melissa snapped.

"You started this round, not me," he said tightly. "Care to back up and start over?"

"We can't back up that many years," she retorted.

Cody visibly restrained his temper. Melissa watched as he drew in several calming breaths, even as his heated gaze remained locked on her. Her blood practically sizzled under that look. No matter how furious he made her, she still seemed to want him. It was damned provoking.

"Believe it or not, I came in here to apologize," he said eventually, his voice low.

"What's to apologize for? Just because you didn't mention that you were involved with another woman—a woman who apparently traveled quite some distance to be with you—that doesn't mean you owe me an apology."

To her annoyance, amusement sparkled in Cody's eyes. "I don't have a thing to hide, sweet pea. Want me to tell you about Janey?"

Melissa did not want to hear about the gorgeous creature with the exotic features, elfin haircut and sad, sad eyes. Cody had probably broken her heart, too.

"I can see that you do," Cody said, taking the decision out of her hands. "First of all, yes, Janey is from Wyoming. Second, I had no idea she was coming. Third, our relationship—then and now—most definitely is not what you think it was."

"Yeah, right," Melissa said sarcastically.

"Fourth," he went on as if she hadn't interrupted. "Her father was my boss, Lance Treethorn."

He leveled his gaze straight at her, until she felt color flooding into her cheeks. "Fifth, and most important, she is a fifteen-year-old kid."

Melissa stared at him. "Fifteen," she repeated in a choked voice. "Cody, that's—"

He cut her off before she could finish the ugly thought. "What that is, is a shy, lonely teenager with a crush on the first guy who didn't slobber all over her due to adolescent hormones," he insisted adamantly.

Melissa wanted to believe him. In fact, she did believe him. Cody was far too honorable a man to do anything so despicable. Harlan might have raised stubborn, willful, overly confident sons, but he'd instilled a set of values in them that was beyond reproach. She was the one who ought to be horsewhipped for even allowing such a thought to cross her mind.

She moaned and hid her face in her hands. "God, I'm sorry."

Cody shrugged. "Well, she does look older than she is. That's been her problem. The guys ahead of her in school think she's a lot more mature than she is and try to take advantage of her. She's coped by hiding out at the ranch."

"And you were kind to her, so she developed a crush on you," Melissa concluded, feeling like an idiot. "Why didn't you do something to put a stop to it?"

"For one thing, I had no idea it would go this far. The most overt thing she ever did before was leave food for me. She bakes a brownie that makes your mouth water."

Melissa grinned. "You always were a sucker for brownies."

"It was the first thing you learned to bake, remember? You were twelve, I think."

She remembered all right. Even back then she'd been trying to woo Cody by catering to his every whim. She wondered if it was ever possible to get beyond past history and truly have a new beginning. She'd been facetious when she'd snapped earlier that they couldn't go back far enough to start over, but maybe it was true. Maybe there was no way to ever get past all the mistakes and the distrust.

Despondency stole through her as she considered the possibility that they would never be able to move on.

"Melissa?" Cody said softly.

"What?"

"What's wrong?"

"Nothing."

"I don't believe that. You looked as if you were about ready to cry."

She tried to shrug off the observation. "Don't mind me. It's probably just Monday blues."

"I know how to cure that," he said. "Come out to White Pines tonight. We'll have a barbecue. It's warm enough today."

Melissa didn't think spending more time with Cody was such a good idea, not when parting suddenly seemed inevitable. Maybe Janey Treethorn's presence had been innocent enough, but sooner or later some other woman would catch his eye. They always did.

"The temperature's supposed to drop later," she said by way of declining his invitation. "It might even snow overnight."

Cody's expression remained undaunted. "Then I'll wear a jacket to tend the grill and we can eat inside."

"You never give up, do you?"

"Never," he agreed softly, his gaze locked with hers. "Not when it's something this important."

"What is it that's important, Cody?" she asked, unable to keep a hint of desperation out of her voice. "What?"

"You, me, Sharon Lynn," he said. "I want us to be a family, Melissa. I won't settle for anything less this time."

She heard the determination in his voice. More important, she heard the commitment. He sounded so sincere, so convinced that a family was what he wanted.

"Will you come?" he asked again. "You and Sharon Lynn?"

Melissa sighed. She'd never been able to resist Cody when he got that winsome note in his voice, when that thoroughly engaging smile reached all the way to his dark and dangerous eyes.

"What time?"

"Five-thirty?"

"We'll be there."

"My house," he said. "Not the main house."

Thoughts of making love in that house flooded through her. Melissa shook her head. "No," she insisted. "Let's have dinner with Harlan, too."

"Scared, Me...liss...a?"

"You bet, cowboy. You should be, too." She lowered her voice. "The last time we were alone in that house, we made love and we didn't take precautions. I'm not risking that again."

Cody grinned. "Hey, darlin', that's something I can take care of right here and now," he offered. "I'm sure Eli can fix me right up."

Melissa's cheeks flamed at the prospect of having Eli and Mabel know any more of her business than they already did. "Cody, don't you dare. Besides, we decided that sleeping together only complicated things."

"Did we decide that?"

"You know we did. We have dinner at Harlan's or you can forget it."

"Okay, darlin', I'll let you win this round," he said, startling her with his lack of fussing. "See you at five-thirty."

It wasn't until she arrived at White Pines that she discovered the reason for Cody's calm acceptance of her edict.

"Where's Harlan?" she inquired suspiciously the minute she stepped into the too silent foyer of the main house.

Cody's expression was pure innocence as he gazed

back at her. "Oh, didn't I mention it? Daddy's gone to spend a few days with Luke and Jessie."

With Sharon Lynn already happily ensconced in her father's arms, with a huge stack of ribs just waiting to be barbecued, Melissa bit back the urge to turn right around and flee. This round, it appeared, had gone to Cody.

14

For the next two months, Cody won more rounds than he lost, much to Melissa's chagrin. Though she'd turned down his proposals every time he made them, he took the rejections in stride. He just redoubled his efforts to change her mind. Her resistance was in tatters. Her senses were spinning just at the sight of him. She was clinging to the last shreds of pride and determination she had left.

There were moments, she was forced to admit, when she couldn't even remember why she was so staunch in her conviction that marrying Cody was positively the wrong thing to do. He had done absolutely nothing since his return to indicate that he wasn't thoroughly absorbed in his relationship with her and their child. He was sweetly attentive to her. He doted on Sharon Lynn.

And still, for reasons she was finding harder and harder to fathom, she kept waiting for some other woman to come between them, for some blowup that would send Cody racing away from Texas, away from them. It didn't seem to matter that his roots at White Pines ran deeper than ever. He'd left his home and her once before. She never forgot that, wouldn't let herself forget it.

She put more obstacles in their path to happiness than championship hurdlers had ever had to jump. Cody, just as determinedly, overcame each and every one, without criticism, without comment. He just did whatever was asked of him.

The truth of it was that his thoughtfulness and consideration were beginning to wear on her. She figured it was an indication of the depths of her perversity that she longed for a good, old, rip-roaring fight.

She was already working herself into a confrontational state when she reached her mother's after a particularly exhausting day at work, only to find that Sharon Lynn wasn't there.

"What do you mean, she's not here?" she demanded, staring at her father. Her mother was nowhere in sight, which should have been her first clue that her life was about to turn topsy-turvy.

"Cody came by," her father admitted. "I let him take her."

"You what?" Her voice climbed several octaves. Was everyone in town on Cody's side these days? She'd thought for sure at least her parents would stick up for her. Instead her father had joined the enemy camp.

"Why would you do that?" she asked plaintively.

Her father regarded her with amusement. "He's the child's father, for starters. He wanted to spend some time with her. He said he'd drop her off at your house and save you the trip. I guess he didn't tell you that, though."

"No, he did not," she snapped. "Which is a pretty

Sherryl Woods

good indication of why Cody Adams is not to be trusted."

"If you ask me, he's been jumping through hoops to prove he can be trusted. Why don't you give the guy a break?" He patted her cheek. "Come on, ladybug. You know you want to."

"I can't," she said simply.

"Why not?"

"Because he'll leave again at the first sign of trouble."

"He left before, because you provoked him into it. I can't say I blame him for being furious about finding you out with Brian. Going out with him was a danged fool idea to begin with."

Melissa's anger wilted. "I agree, but Cody should have stayed and talked to me. He shouldn't have run."

"Don't you think he knows that now?" her father inquired reasonably. "Don't you think if he had it to do all over again, he would make a different choice?"

"I suppose," she conceded reluctantly. "He says he would anyway."

"And aren't you the one who made things worse by refusing to tell him about the baby?"

She scowled at her father, the man who had stood by her even though he disagreed with her decision to keep Cody in the dark. "What's your point?"

"He forgave you, didn't he? Isn't it about time you did the same for him?"

Melissa was startled by the depth of her father's support for Cody. "How come you've never said any of this before?" she asked.

Her father's expression turned rueful. "Because your mother seemed to be saying more than enough without me jumping in and confusing you even more. Watching you getting more miserable day by day, I finally decided when Cody showed up today that enough was enough. I told her to butt out."

Melissa couldn't help grinning. "So there'd be room for you to butt in?"

"Something like that. Go on, cupcake. Meet Cody halfway, at least. For whatever it's worth, I think he's a fine man."

Melissa sighed. "So do I."

She made up her mind on the walk to her own house that she would try to overcome the last of her doubts and take the kind of risk her father was urging. There was a time when she would have risked anything at all to be with Cody. The pain of losing him once had made her far too cautious. It was probably long past time to rediscover the old Melissa and take the dare he'd been issuing for months now.

She found him in a rocker on her front porch, a tuckered out Sharon Lynn asleep in his lap.

"Rough afternoon?" she queried, keeping her tone light and displaying none of the annoyance she'd felt when she'd discovered he'd absconded with her daughter. She sank into the rocker next to him and put it into a slow, soothing motion. She allowed her eyes to drift closed, then snapped them open before she fell completely, embarrassingly, asleep.

"Playing in the park is tough work," he said, grinning at her. "There are swings and seesaws to ride, to say nothing of squirrels to be chased." His gaze intensified. "You look frazzled. Bad day?"

"Bad day, bad week, bad everything," she admitted, giving in to the exhaustion and turmoil she'd been fighting.

"I know just how to fix that," Cody said, standing. He shifted Sharon Lynn into one arm and held out a hand. "Give me the key."

Melissa plucked it from her purse and handed it over without argument. As soon as he'd gone, she closed her eyes again. The soothing motion of the rocker lulled her so that she was only vaguely aware of the screen door squeaking open and the sound of Cody's boots as he crossed the porch.

"Wake up, sleepyhead," he urged. "Here, take this."

She forced her eyes open and saw the tall glass he was holding out. "Lemonade?" she asked with amazement. "Where'd you get it?"

"I made it."

Her eyes blinked wider. "From scratch?"

He grinned. "I didn't bake a chocolate soufflé, sweet pea. It's just lemonade."

They sat side by side, silently rocking, for what seemed an eternity after that. The spring breeze brought the fragrance of flowers wafting by. Hummingbirds hovered around the feeder at the end of the porch.

"This is nice, isn't it?" Cody said eventually.

"Not too tame for you?" Melissa asked.

"Don't start with me," he chided, but without much ferocity behind the words.

She thought of what her father had said and of her own resolution to start taking risks. "I'm sorry. I didn't mean to say that. I guess it's become automatic."

"Think you can break the cycle?" he inquired lightly.

Melissa met his gaze. "I'm going to try," she promised. "I do want what you want, Cody."

"But you're scared," he guessed. At her nod he added, "Can't say that I blame you. I spent a lot of years hiding from the responsibilities of a relationship. Once you make a commitment, there's a lot riding on getting it right. I never did much like the idea of failing."

"Can I ask you something?"

"Anything, you know that."

"What makes you so certain we can get it right now?"

He grinned at the question. "You know any two more stubborn people on the face of the earth?"

Her lips twitched at that. "No, can't say that I do."

"I pretty much figure if we finally make that commitment, neither one of us will bail out without giving it everything we've got." He slanted a look over at her that sent heat curling through her body. "Nobody can do more than that, sweet pea. Nobody."

He stood, then bent down to kiss her gently. "Think about it, darlin'."

"You're leaving?" she asked, unable to stop the disappointment that flooded through her.

"If I stay here another minute with you looking at me like that, I'm going to resort to seducing you into giving me the answer I want. I think it'll be better if I take my chances on letting you work this one out in your head."

He was striding off to his pickup before she could mount an argument. She actually stood to go after him, but a wave of dizziness washed over her that had her clutching at a post to keep from falling.

What on earth? she wondered as she steadied herself. Suddenly she recalled the occasional bouts of nausea she'd been feeling that she'd chalked off to waiting too long to grab breakfast in the mornings. She thought about the bone-deep weariness that had had her half-asleep in that rocker only a short time before. And now, dizziness.

Oh, dear heaven, she thought, sinking back into the rocker before she fainted. Unless she was very much mistaken, every one of those signs added up to being pregnant—again.

How could this have happened to them a second time? Melissa wondered as she left the doctor's office in a daze the following morning. How could she be pregnant from that one time they'd made love at Cody's? They'd been so darned careful not to repeat the same mistake. She'd held him at arm's length, refusing to make love again for that very reason, because neither one of them used a lick of common sense once they hopped into bed together. It was better not to let their hormones get out of hand in the first place.

She had no idea what was going to happen next, but she did know that this time she would tell Cody right away. There would be no more secrets to blow up in her face later.

Dammit, why couldn't everything have been more resolved between them? They were so close to working things out. She had sensed that last night in their companionable silence, in the way Cody had vowed to give her the time and space to reach her own conclusions about their relationship.

She knew exactly how Cody was going to react. Forget about time and space for thinking. He was going to demand they get married at once. She wanted that, wanted it more than anything, but not if he was only doing it because of the baby. Okay, both babies.

He was a fine father. He'd accepted his responsibility for Sharon Lynn wholeheartedly. That wasn't the issue. He'd been proving that over and over since the day he'd learned the truth about Sharon Lynn. She had seen the adoration in his eyes whenever he was with his daughter. She had watched his pride over every tiny accomplishment.

He had even behaved as though she were important to him, too. But never once, not in all these months, had he said he loved her. She would not marry a man who could not say those words. She would not marry at all just because she was pregnant.

It created an interesting dilemma, since there wasn't a darn thing she could do about being pregnant. There was nothing on earth that meant more to her than being a mother to Cody's children. And she knew from bitter experience that she could do it just fine on her own, if she had to.

Still, she had to tell him sometime....

She managed to hold off for a couple of weeks, but her symptoms were cropping up when she least expected it. She didn't want him guessing when he found her practically swooning in his arms.

After thinking it over, she chose the storeroom at Dolan's to tell him. Eli and Mabel were getting used to her dragging Cody into the back to talk. They'd probably heard enough muffled arguments and full-scale screaming matches to last them a lifetime.

At least, though, they would be there to intervene if Cody decided to try to drag her off by the hair to the preacher. At home she'd have no such protection. She doubted even her parents would stand up to him. Her father was already on Cody's side and her mother had maintained a stoic silence ever since her father's edict that she butt out of Melissa's and Cody's business.

She had one other reason for choosing the store-room. She had noticed that Eli and Mabel were off by themselves whispering who-knew-what at the oddest times. Melissa had the feeling that the two of them were patching whatever differences had separated them years before. Maybe the very visible ups and downs of her relationship with Cody had set an example for them. They might as well be in on the denouement.

When Cody walked through the door as he'd gotten into the habit of doing around closing every day, Melissa's hands trembled. This time nothing on earth could have persuaded her to so much as touch a glass in Cody's presence.

Not even giving Cody time to get settled, she drew in a deep breath. "We need to talk."

"Okay," he said, giving her that crooked smile that made her heart flip over. "What's up?"

"In the back," she said.

Cody groaned. "Not again."

She glanced at Eli and Mabel, who were both suddenly extremely busy, their backs to the counter. "Will you just come on?" she muttered, holding the door open.

Cody trailed along behind her and propped a booted foot onto an unopened shipment of new glasses. "What now?"

Melissa tried to gather her courage. Finally she blurted, "I'm pregnant."

Cody's eyes widened incredulously. "You're going to have a baby?"

She nodded, watching him carefully, not quite able to get a fix on his reaction.

"A baby?" Cody repeated.

"Yes."

"Oh, my God." He sank down on the box, which gave way just enough to shatter the two dozen glasses inside.

At the sound of all that cracking glassware, Melissa started to chuckle. Cody bounced to his feet, but there was no hope for the crushed shipment.

"You okay?" she inquired between giggles. "No glass in your backside?"

"Forget my backside. It's just fine. Tell me more about the baby. When is it due?"

"You should be able to figure that one out. We only slept together that once since you got back."

"I can't even add two and two right now. Just tell me."

"A little over six months."

He nodded. "Good. That's plenty of time."

Melissa regarded him suspiciously. "Plenty of time for what?" she asked, although she thought she had a pretty good idea of the answer.

"To get married," he said at once. "Finish fixing up my house at White Pines, decorate a new nursery."

Melissa held up her hands. "Whoa, cowboy. Who says we're getting married?"

A mutinous expression settled over his face. "I do. No baby of mine is going to be born without my name. It's bad enough that we haven't taken care of getting Sharon Lynn's name legally changed. I'm not doubling the problem."

"Okay, say I agree to get married—which I haven't," she added in a rush when she saw the instant gleam in his eyes. "Then what?"

He stared at her blankly. "What?"

"Are you planning for us to live happily ever after? Are you intending to get a divorce as soon as the ink's dry on the birth certificate? What?" *Please,* she thought to herself, *let him say he loves me. Please.*

"You know better than that," he said.

It was a wishy-washy answer if ever Melissa had heard one. "Do I?" she shot back. "How? Just because you've been here a few months now and haven't taken off?"

He raked his fingers through his hair. "Yes."

"Not good enough, cowboy," she said, exiting the storeroom and emphatically closing the door behind her.

Mabel and Eli were suspiciously close to the door, though their attention seemed to be thoroughly engaged in their work. Of course, Mabel was sweeping the exact same spot she'd swept not fifteen minutes earlier and Eli was dusting off a shelf, a task that usually fell to Mabel.

"I'm leaving," she announced, grabbing her purse and heading for the door.

Mabel trailed her outside. "Don't be a fool, girl. Marry that man and put him out of his misery."

"I can't," Melissa said, sounding pretty miserable herself.

"Why the devil not?"

"He's only thinking about the babies. He's not thinking about us at all."

"If that's all he cared about, he could file for joint custody, pick them up on Friday afternoons and send you a support check," Mabel countered. "I don't hear him talking about doing any of that. He's talking about marriage, has been ever since he got back into town."

"Because it's the right thing to do," Melissa insisted

stubbornly. "The Adams men are nothing if not honorable."

Mabel shot her a look of pure disgust. "Maybe you ought to be thinking about doing the right thing, too, if that's the case. Those babies deserve a chance at a real home. Cody's willing to give them that. Why can't you?"

Mabel's words lingered in her head as she walked over to pick up Sharon Lynn. They echoed there again and again as she fought every single attempt Cody made to persuade her to change her mind.

She told herself she wasn't the one making things difficult. All it would take to make her change her mind was three little words—I love you. They were about the only words in the whole English language that Cody never, ever tried.

15

From the instant he discovered that Melissa was pregnant again, Cody tried to persuade her to marry him. He coaxed. He wooed. He pitched a royal fit on occasion and threatened to hog-tie her and carry her off to the justice of the peace.

For six solid months he did everything but stand on his damned head, but Melissa seemed to have clothed her heart in an impenetrable sheet of armor. He surely didn't remember the woman being this stubborn. The whole town was watching the two of them as if they were better than any soap opera on TV. He found it mortifying to be chasing after a woman who acted as if he didn't even exist.

He also discovered that this new side of Melissa was every bit as intriguing as it was vexing. He realized that he'd always taken for granted that sooner or later she would admit she loved him and accept his oft-repeated proposal. That she was still turning him down with another baby on the way shook him as nothing else in his life ever had. Maybe this was one time when his charm wasn't going to be enough.

And the truth of it was, she seemed to be getting along just fine. He'd seen that for himself ever since he'd gotten back from Wyoming. She had made a nice life for herself and Sharon Lynn. She would fit a new baby into that life without batting an eye.

She was strong and self-sufficient, downright competent as a single parent. She had her job at the drugstore. She had friends who were there for her. She had parents who supported her in whatever decisions she made, though he sensed that her father was not quite as thrilled with this independent streak as her mother was.

In short, Melissa had a life, while Cody was lonelier than he'd ever imagined possible even in the dead of a rough Wyoming winter.

The thought of Melissa going into that delivery room with anyone other than him as her labor coach grated. The prospect of his baby—a second baby, in fact—being born without his name made him see red. He wanted to be a part of that baby's life so badly it stunned him.

What flat-out rocked him back on his heels, though, was the fact that he wanted to be with Melissa just as badly. Maybe he'd started out just saying the words, asking her to marry him because of Sharon Lynn and more recently this new, unborn baby. But sometime, when he hadn't been paying attention, he'd gone and fallen in love with the woman. Mature, adult love this time, not adolescent hormones and fantasy.

How the hell was he going to get her to believe that, though? Nothing he had done in the past eight and a half months since he'd come home to Texas had done a bit of good.

He'd been steady. He'd been reliable. He'd even managed to seduce her, which was what had gotten them into this latest fix. Melissa, however, had kept a stubborn grip on her emotions. She had refused to concede feeling so much as affection for him, much less love.

Cody was at his wit's end. He'd decided, though, that it was tonight or never. He was going to make one last, impressive, irresistible attempt to convince Melissa to be his wife. If it failed, he would just have to resign himself to this shadow role in the life of his children. Up until now he'd turned his back on his pride, but it was kicking up a storm for him to stop behaving like a besotted fool and give up.

He took hat quite literally in hand and went to visit Velma. He needed her help if his plan was to work. Responding to his knock on her door in midafternoon, she regarded him with her usual suspicion.

"What do you want?" she inquired ungraciously.

Cody lost patience. "I am not the bad guy here," he informed her as he stalked past her and stood in the middle of the foyer.

He could hear Sharon Lynn chattering away in the guest room. It sounded as if she were having a tea party. He longed to go down that corridor and spend some time with her. She was changing in one way or another every day and he hated to miss a single one. Today, though, he was on a mission here and he couldn't afford to be distracted.

"I came by to see if you could keep Sharon Lynn here tonight," he said.

"Why?" Velma asked bluntly.

"So that Melissa and I can have an evening together alone."

"Seems to me you two have found enough time to

be alone without my help in the past. She's about to have a baby again, isn't she? She didn't get that way in public, I suspect."

Her sarcasm grated. Cody held back the sharp retort that came to mind. If this was going to work out, it was way past time he made peace with Melissa's mother. "Exactly what has she told you about our relationship?"

Velma didn't give an inch. "She doesn't have to say a word. I can see plenty for myself."

"What do you think you see, then?"

"That you think your money and your power give you the right to be irresponsible. You've used my daughter, left her, then come back here and used her again without ever giving a thought to the consequences."

"Are you aware that I have been trying to persuade your mule-headed daughter to marry me since the very first instant I got back into town?"

Velma blinked, but she didn't back down. Talk about stubborn pride. Velma had it in spades, which probably explained Melissa's streak of it.

"Too little, too late, if you ask me," she retorted.

Cody started to tell her he hadn't asked her, but of course he had. "Look, I don't blame you for resenting me, but the fact of the matter is that I love your daughter, stubborn as she is, and I want to marry her and be a father to our children. I think she loves me, too, but she thinks she's a fool for doing it."

He saw from the set expression on her face that Velma had probably reinforced that belief. Maybe if he could win over the mother, she'd change her tune with Melissa and give him a fighting chance.

"You want her to be happy, don't you?"

"Of course I do," she said indignantly. "What makes you think I don't?"

"Because I think she's taking her cue from you. I think if she and I had just a little time alone, we could work this out, preferably before another one of our children is born without my name. Will you give us that chance?"

Velma spent the next minute or two in an obvious struggle with her conscience. "What is it you want, exactly?"

"Keep Sharon Lynn here tonight. Don't interfere with my plans. That's all."

"You think you can convince her in one night, when you haven't made any progress at all in the past nine months?" Velma inquired with a shake of her head. "You don't know Melissa half as well as you think you do."

She sighed heavily. "Okay, I'll keep Sharon Lynn for you," she relented to Cody's relief. "But it'll have to be for the whole weekend. If you ask me, it's going to take you that long, maybe even longer, to turn that girl around. She's scared spitless she'll admit she loves you and you'll turn around and leave again."

"I won't," he swore. He circled Velma's waist and spun her around. "Thank you. You're an angel."

She kept her lips in a tight line, resisting him to the bitter end, but Cody thought he detected a spark of amusement in her eyes. "See that you do right by her, young man, or I'll have your hide."

He kissed her cheek. "Not to worry, Velma. This is going to be a weekend to remember."

He was already making plans to sweep Melissa away

to a quiet, secluded cabin for a romantic weekend by the time he hit the driveway.

His first stop was her house, where he managed to sneak in without being caught by the sheriff or a neighbor. He rummaged through her drawers and closets to find lingerie and the prettiest, sexiest maternity clothes she owned. He packed them, along with perfume and cosmetics, praying that he got the right ones. He didn't want her dissolving into tears because she couldn't find her blush or her mascara. Her hormones had her reacting in the most bizarre ways these days. He figured he ought to get a whole lot of points for just managing to stick by her anyway.

He'd considered taking her off to someplace fancy, maybe the most expensive suite in Dallas, but then he'd decided that would put her too close to taxis or planes or other means of escape. He wanted her all to himself.

He fought all of his old past resentments—most of them, as it had turned out, unwarranted—and tracked Brian down in San Antonio, where he was practicing law. He pointed out that his former best friend owed him one for the scam he and Melissa had tried to pull on Cody years before.

"I'm just grateful that you didn't come after me with a shotgun," Brian said. "Anything you want is yours."

"Does your family still have that cabin by the lake?"

"You bet."

"Can Melissa and I borrow it for the weekend?"

"It's all yours," Brian said at once.

He told Cody where to find the key, offered some unsolicited advice on taming the reluctant Melissa, then added seriously, "I'm glad you called, buddy. I've missed you."

"Same here," Cody said. "Next time you're down this way, we'll have to get together. You do have your own woman now, don't you?"

Brian chuckled. "Do I ever. Good luck. You and Melissa should have worked this out long ago. I'd have told you the truth myself, but Melissa swore me to secrecy."

"Secrets are her specialty, it appears," Cody said. "Anyway, thanks again for the cabin."

Those arrangements made, Cody loaded groceries, flowers and nonalcoholic champagne into the back of the truck, then swung by Dolan's. He marched straight to the soda fountain, ignoring the startled gazes of the teens gathered there.

"Cody? Is everything okay?" Melissa asked as he rounded the corner of the counter and headed toward her.

"Just dandy," he confirmed, tucking one arm under her legs and the other behind her waist. He scooped her up, amid a flurry of outraged protests from her and that same pimply faced kid who'd defended her honor once before.

"It's okay, son," Cody assured him. "She wants to go with me."

"I do not!" Melissa protested.

"Eli, call the cops or something," the boy shouted, his face turning red as he bolted after Cody.

"Not on your life," Eli said, and kept right on filling prescriptions. Mabel held the door open, grinning widely.

Melissa huffed and puffed a little longer, but by the time Cody had driven to the outskirts of town, she'd retreated into a sullen silence.

"Was that caveman approach entirely necessary?" she inquired eventually.

"I thought so."

"I would have come with you, if you'd asked politely."

He shot a skeptical look in her direction.

"At least, I would have thought about it," she amended.

"That's why I didn't ask. You've been thinking entirely too much."

"Are we going to White Pines?"

"Nope."

"Luke and Jessie's?" she asked hopefully, the first little sign of alarm sparking in her eyes.

"Nope."

"Cody, where the hell are you taking me?"

"Someplace where we can be alone."

"Where?" she repeated.

"Brian's cabin."

Her eyes widened. "You talked to Brian?"

"I figured drastic measures were called for, and he promised the best and quickest solution." He glanced over at her. "I was willing to do anything it took to make this happen, sweet pea."

"Oh," she said softly, and settled back to mull that over.

It wasn't more than half an hour later when he noticed she seemed to be getting a little restless.

"You okay?" he asked.

She turned toward him, her lower lip caught between her teeth as she shook her head. Instantly, Cody's muscles tensed.

"Melissa, what's wrong?" he demanded. "Tell me."

"It's not a problem," she said. "Not yet, anyway. It's just that…" Her eyes widened and turned the color of a turbulent sea. She swallowed visibly. "Don't panic."

Cody panicked. "Melissa!"

"It's okay, really it is. It's just that it's entirely possible that I'm in labor." She sucked in a ragged breath, then announced, "Cody, I think we're about to have a baby."

16

Cody found his father already pacing the waiting room when he got Melissa to the hospital. He'd called him on his cellular phone, right after he'd spoken to the doctor. He'd asked Harlan to alert the rest of the family.

"Even Jordan?" his father had asked cautiously, aware of the friction between them.

Cody decided then and there it was time to get over the rift between him and his brother. This was a time for healing.

"Even Jordan," he'd confirmed.

He turned now to his father. "Did you reach everyone?"

"They'll be here in a bit. How is she?" Harlan demanded at once as the nurse wheeled Melissa away to prep her for delivery. "Is everything okay?"

Cody wiped a stream of sweat from his brow. "She says it is, but I don't know. You had four sons. Is labor supposed to be so painful?"

"How should I know? Your mama wouldn't let me anywhere near the delivery room. She said having babies was women's work." He glanced at Cody with an unmistakable look of envy. "Wish I'd had a chance to be there just once, though. Seems to me like it must be a flat-out miracle. You going in there with Melissa?"

"If she'll let me," Cody said. "She's still making up her mind whether to be furious at me for kidnapping her this afternoon." He moaned. "I must have been out of my mind. I didn't even think about the fact that she might go into labor."

"Cody, you weren't at the other end of the world," Harlan reassured him. "You'd barely made it out of town. You got her here in plenty of time. The only way you could have gotten here much faster would have been to park her in a room upstairs for the last month of her pregnancy. Now, settle down."

"It's easy for you. It's not your baby she's having."

Just then the nurse came out. "Mr. Adams, would you like to step in for a minute? We're getting ready to take Melissa to the delivery room."

Cody shot a helpless look at his father. "It sounds like she's not going to want me in there."

"Maybe it's time to stop bullying the girl and tell her how much you want to be there," Harlan advised.

Cody doubted it would be as simple as that. Indeed, Melissa shot him a look of pure hatred when he walked into her room. Of course, that might have had something to do with the whopper of a contraction she appeared to be in the middle of.

He accepted a damp cloth from the nurse and instinctively wiped Melissa's forehead with it.

"You're doing great," he said.

"How would you know?" she retorted.

He grinned at the fiery display of temper. "Okay, you

got me. I have no idea. No one's running around the halls panicking, though. That must mean something."

"They're used to this," she retorted. "I'm not. Besides, they're just observers. I'm doing all the work."

"If you'd let me take those natural childbirth classes with you, I'd be more help about now."

She latched onto his hand just then and squeezed. It was either one hell of a contraction or she was trying to punish him by breaking all of his knuckles. As soon as the pain eased, she glared at him again.

"Go away."

"I don't think so," he countered just as stubbornly. "I want to share this with you."

"You want to see me writhing around in agony," she snapped.

"No," he insisted. "Having a baby is a miracle. I missed out on Sharon Lynn's birth. I'm going to be with you for this one."

"Why?"

He regarded her blankly. "Don't you know?"

"Cody, I don't know anything except that you've been making a pest of yourself ever since you got back into town. What I don't know is why."

Before he could answer, the orderlies came to wheel her down the hall to the delivery room. He could tell by the set of her jaw that she was going into that room without him unless he could find the courage to tell her what was in his heart.

"Dammit, Melissa, I love you!" he shouted after her, just as they were about to roll her out of sight.

"Stop!" Melissa bellowed at the orderlies between contractions.

Cody reached her side in an instant. Even with her

face bathed in sweat, her lower lip bitten raw, she looked beautiful to him. She always had, always would.

"What did you say?" she demanded, then grabbed onto his hand with a grip so fierce he could have sworn that more bones broke.

He grinned through the pain—hers and his. "I said I love you."

A slow, satisfied smile spread across her face. "It's about time, cowboy."

"Haven't I been saying that for months now?" he asked, vaguely bemused that she hadn't heard it before.

"Not the words," she told him. "How was I supposed to believe it without the words?"

"Someone once told me that actions speak louder than words. I guess I was putting it to the test. I thought you needed to see that I wasn't going anywhere."

"I also needed to hear why that was so," she told him, wincing as another pain started and then rolled through her. "I didn't want you with me out of a sense of obligation."

Relief swept through him as he realized he'd risked everything and finally gotten through to her. "Does that mean you'll marry me?"

"Whenever you say."

Cody turned and motioned to the preacher he'd had Harlan call for him. He'd also had Harlan make a call to a judge to cut through the legal red tape. "Get to it, Reverend. I don't think this baby's going to wait much longer."

The minister had never talked so fast in his life, quite possibly because he was conducting the ceremony in the doorway of a delivery room. Cody figured as long as they didn't cross that threshold, the baby would have sense enough not to come until his or her parents were properly married.

The "I do's" were punctuated by moans and a couple of screams. And not five minutes later, Harlan Patrick Adams came into the world with an impeccable sense of timing, just as the minister pronounced his mama and daddy man and wife. Melissa was beginning to wonder if she was ever going to be able to hold her own baby. Between Cody and his father, she'd barely gotten a look at him. Cody had finally disappeared a half hour before, but Harlan was still holding the baby with a look of such pride and sadness in his eyes.

"I wish Mary could have seen him," he said softly as a tear spilled down his cheek.

"Wherever she is, I think she knows," Melissa told him. "And I'll bet Erik is right beside her, watching out for all of us."

Her father-in-law gave her a watery smile. "I can't tell you how proud it makes me to have you in this family finally."

"I'm glad to be a part of it finally," she told him. "Though given the way my brand new husband scooted out of here after the ceremony, I'm not so sure I made the right decision. Any idea where he went?"

There was no mistaking the spark of pure mischief in Harlan's eyes. "Can't say that I know for sure," he said.

Melissa didn't believe him for a second. The old scoundrel and Cody were clearly up to their ornery chins in some scheme or another. Before she could try to pry their secret out of him, the door to the room slid open a crack.

"Everyone awake?" Cody inquired lightly.

"Come on in, son," Harlan enthused. "We were just wondering where you'd gone off to."

Cody stepped into the room and winked at her. "Should I take that to mean that you suspected I'd run off on you already?"

"It did cross my mind," she admitted. "You turned awful pale there in the delivery room. I figured you might be having second thoughts about marriage and fatherhood."

"Not me," Cody retorted indignantly. "I just figured the occasion deserved a celebration. You know how this family likes to party. You up for it?"

She stared at him as he watched her uneasily. "What if I say no?"

"Then that's it. I send everyone away."

"Everyone? Who is out there?"

"Sharon Lynn, first of all. She wants to meet her new baby brother."

Melissa grinned. "Bring her in. Of course I want her to see the baby."

Cody opened the door and Sharon Lynn barreled in and ran toward the bed. Over the past few months she'd grown increasingly steady on her feet. In the final weeks of her pregnancy Melissa had had a heck of a time waddling after her.

"Mama! Mama!" Sharon Lynn shouted.

Cody lifted Sharon Lynn onto the bed beside her. "Harlan, bring the baby over so Sharon Lynn can get a look," Melissa said.

As Harlan approached with the baby, her daughter's eyes grew wide. "Baby?"

"That's right, pumpkin. That's Harlan Patrick, your baby brother."

As if she knew that newborns were fragile, Sharon Lynn reached over and gently touched a finger to her brother's cheek. "I hold," she announced.

"Not yet," Melissa told her just as there was a soft knock on the door.

Cody reached for the handle, but his gaze was on her. "You ready for more visitors?"

"Who else is out there?"

"Your parents," he said.

"Luke and Jessie," Sharon Lynn chimed in, clearly proud that she'd learned two new names. "And Jordie and Kelly."

Melissa chuckled as she imagined straight-laced Jordan if he ever heard himself referred to as "Jordie." She gave her husband a warm smile, silently congratulating him for ending the feud that never should have happened.

"Let them in," she instructed Cody. "If I'd known you were inviting half the town, I'd have insisted on that private VIP suite they have upstairs."

As the family crowded in, a nurse came along, wheeling in a three-tiered wedding cake. Melissa stared at it in amazement. "When did you have time to order that?"

"Right after you said 'I do' and delivered our son," he said. "I told the bakery it was an emergency."

Kelly leaned down to kiss her cheek. "You should have seen the look on their faces when I stopped to pick it up. Obviously, they'd never heard of an emergency wedding before."

Melissa swung her legs over the side of the bed and prepared to go over for a closer look.

"Stay right where you are," Cody ordered, looking panicked.

"I'm not an invalid," she informed him.

"It's not that," he admitted, casting a worried look at the cake. "Actually, it was a little late to come up with an emergency cake. Fortunately, they had a cancellation."

Melissa stared at him, torn between laughing and crying. "That is someone else's cake?"

"They got the other names off," Kelly reassured her. "Almost, anyway."

Sure enough, when Melissa managed to get near enough for a closer look, she could spot the traces of blue food dye across the white icing on the top layer. Love Always had been left in place, but below it were the shadowy letters unmistakably spelling out Tom And Cecily.

Melissa grinned. "Get on over here, Tom," she said pointedly. "Give old Cecily a kiss."

Cody didn't hesitate. He gathered her close and slanted his lips across hers in a kiss that spoke of love and commitment and all the joy that was to come.

"Okay, that's enough, baby brother," Luke said. "Give the rest of us a chance to kiss the bride."

Cody relinquished his hold on her with obvious reluctance. He stood patiently by as she was kissed and congratulated by all the others. Harlan grabbed a paper cup and filled it with lukewarm water from the tap.

"A toast, everyone," he announced.

When they all had their own cups of water, he lifted his cup. "To Cody and Melissa. This marriage was a long time coming. There were times I despaired of the two of you ever realizing that you belong together. Now that you have, we wish you every happiness for all the years to come."

"Hear, hear," Jordan and Luke echoed. "Much happiness, baby brother."

"Now it's my turn to kiss the bride," Harlan declared, giving her a resounding smack on the cheek.

Cody stole between them. "Get your own bride, old man. This one is mine."

"Maybe I will," Harlan said, startling them all.

Cody, Jordan and Luke stared at him in openmouthed astonishment while their wives all chuckled with delight.

"Do it," Melissa whispered in his ear, standing on tiptoe to give him a kiss. "Find a bride and live happily ever after. No one deserves it more. Mary would want that for you."

She had a feeling that when Harlan Adams set his mind to finding a woman to share his life, he was going to set all of Texas on its ear. And his sons were going to have the time of their lives getting even for all the grief he'd given them over their own love lives. Melissa was thrilled that she was going to be right in the thick of it all, where she'd always dreamed of being.

Her mother and father came over to her then. "You happy, ladybug?" her father asked.

She clung tightly to Cody's hand and never took her gaze from his as she whispered, "Happier than I thought possible."

"About time," her mother huffed.

Cody leaned down and kissed her soundly. "Stop fussing, Velma." He grinned unrepentantly at her mother's expression of shock. "One of these days you're going to admit it," he taunted.

"Admit what?"

"That you're crazy about me."

Her mother scowled. "You're too sure of yourself, Cody Adams. Somebody's got to keep you in line."

He turned his gaze on Melissa then. "And I know just the woman to do it," he said softly.

"What if I don't want to keep you in line?" Melissa asked. "I kind of like your roguish ways."

"Told you she didn't have a lick of sense where that boy was concerned," Velma announced loudly.

Melissa glanced at her mother just then and winked. After a startled instant, her mother chuckled despite herself and winked right back. She tucked her arm through her husband's and added, "Married one just like him myself."

"Then I guess Cody and I are going to be okay, aren't we, Mother?"

Her mother glanced pointedly at Sharon Lynn and the new baby. "Looks to me like you've got quite a head start on it."

Cody brushed a kiss across her cheek. "Indeed, we do."

Everyone began leaving after that. Finally Melissa was alone with her husband. "I love you," she told him.

"I love you," he echoed. His expression turned serious. "Do you really think Daddy's going to start courting?"

"Sounded to me as if he meant what he said. How would you feel about that?"

Cody hesitated for a minute, then grinned. "Seems like a damned fine opportunity to get even with him, if you ask me."

"That's what I love about you Adams men," Melissa taunted. "You are so supportive of each other."

"You don't think he deserves to be taken on a merry chase?"

"By some woman," she admonished. "Not by you, Luke and Jordan."

He sighed and folded his arms around her middle from behind. His breath fanned across her cheek. "I suppose standing on the sidelines and watching him fall will have its moments," he agreed. "He sure seemed to get a kick out of watching that happen to the rest of us."

"Then I suggest you prepare yourself for the ride," she told him. "Knowing Harlan, it's going to be a bumpy one."

"As for you and me," Cody proclaimed, "from here on out it's going to be smooth sailing."

* * * * *

THE RANCHER AND HIS
UNEXPECTED DAUGHTER

1

Harlan Adams walked out of Rosa's Mexican Café after eating his fill of her spicy brand of Tex-Mex food just in time to see his pickup barrel down the center of Main Street at fifty miles an hour. In the sleepy Texas town of Los Piños, both the theft and the speed were uncommon occurrences.

"Ain't that your truck?" Mule Masters asked, staring after the vehicle that was zigzagging all over the road, endangering parked cars and pedestrians alike.

"Sure as hell is," Harlan said, indignation making his insides churn worse than Rosa's hot sauce.

"That's what you get for leaving your keys in plain sight. I've been telling you for months now that times have changed. The world's full of thieves and murderers," Mule said ominously. "They were bound to get to Los Piños sooner or later."

Given the time it was wasting, Harlan found the familiar lecture extremely irritating. "Where's your car?" he snapped.

Mule blinked at the sharp tone. "Across the street, right where it always is."

Harlan was already striding across the two-lane road before the words were completely out of his friend's mouth. "Come on, old man."

Mule appeared vaguely startled by the command. "Come on where?"

"To catch the damned thing, that's where," he replied with a certain amount of eagerness. The thought of a good ruckus held an amazing appeal.

"Sheriff's close by," Mule objected without picking up speed.

Harlan lost patience with the procrastinating that had earned Mule his nickname. "Just give me your keys," he instructed. He didn't take any chances on Mule's compliance. He reached out and snatched them from his friend's hand.

Before the old man could even start grumbling, Harlan was across the street and starting the engine of a battered old sedan. That car had seen a hundred thousand hard miles or more back and forth across the state of Texas, thanks to Mule's knack for tinkering with an engine.

Harlan pulled out onto Main Street, gunned the engine a couple of times, then shifted gears with pure pleasure. The smooth glide from standing stock-still to sixty in the blink of an eye was enough to make a man weep.

In less than a minute his truck was in sight again on the outskirts of town and he was gaining on it. He was tempted to whoop with joy at the sheer exhilaration of the impromptu race, but he had to keep every bit of his energy focused on his pursuit of that runaway truck.

The chase lasted just long enough to stir his ire, but not nearly long enough to be downright interesting. Not a mile out of town, where the two-lane road curved like a well-rounded lady's hips, he caught up with the truck just in time to see it miss the turn and swerve straight toward a big, old, cottonwood tree. His heart climbed straight into his throat and stayed there as he watched the drama unfold.

He veered from the highway onto the shoulder and slammed on his own brakes just as the truck collided with the tree. It hit with a resounding *thwack* that crumpled the front fender on the passenger side, sent his blood pressure soaring, and elicited a string of profanity from inside the truck that blistered his ears.

"What the devil?" he muttered as he scrambled from the borrowed car and ran toward the truck. Obviously the thief couldn't be badly injured if he had that much energy left for cursing.

To his astonishment, when he flung open the driver's door, a slender young girl practically tumbled out into his arms. He righted her, keeping a firm clamp on her wrist in case the little thief decided to flee.

She couldn't be a day over thirteen, he decided, gazing into scared brown eyes. Admittedly, though, she had a vocabulary that a much older dock worker would envy. She also had a belligerent tilt to her cute little chin and a sullen expression that dared him to yell at her.

Taken aback by her apparent age, Harlan bit back the shouted lecture he'd planned and settled for a less confrontative approach. He could hardly wait to hear why this child had stolen his pickup.

"You okay?" he inquired quietly. Other than a bump on her forehead, he couldn't see any other signs of injury.

She wriggled in a game effort to free herself from

his grip. He grinned at the wasted attempt. He'd wrestled cows ten times her weight or more. This little slip of a thing didn't stand a chance of getting away until he was good and ready to let her go. He didn't plan on that happening anytime soon. Not until he had the answers he wanted, anyway.

"Must be just fine, if you can struggle like that," he concluded out loud. "Any particular reason you decided to steal my truck?"

"I was tired of walking," she shot back.

"Did you ever consider a bike?"

"Not fast enough," she muttered, her gaze defiantly clashing with his.

"You had someplace to get to in a hurry?"

She shrugged.

Harlan had to fight to hide a grin. He'd always been a big admirer of audacity, though he preferred it to be a little better directed. "What's your name?"

She frowned and for the first time began to look faintly uneasy. "Who wants to know?"

"I'm Harlan Adams. I own White Pines. That's a ranch just outside of town." If she was local, that would be plenty of explanation to intimidate her. If she wasn't, he could elaborate until he had her quivering with fear in her dusty sneakers for pulling a stunt like the one that had ended with his pickup wrapped around a tree.

"Big deal," she retorted, then let loose a string of expletives.

She either wasn't local or it was going to take a lot more to impress her with the stupidity of what she'd done. "You have a foul mouth, you know that?" he observed.

"So?"

"I'll just bet you don't talk that way around your mama."

The mention of her mother stirred an expression of pure alarm on her delicate features. Harlan sensed that he'd hit the nail on the head. This ragamuffin kid with the sleek black hair cut as short as a boy's, with the high cheekbones and tanned complexion, might not be afraid of him, but she was scared to death of her mother. He considered it a hopeful sign. He was very big on respect for parental authority, not that he'd noticed his grown-up sons paying the concept much mind lately.

"You're not going to tell her, are you?" she asked, clearly trying to keep the worry out of her voice and failing miserably. For the first time since she'd climbed out of his truck, she sounded her age.

"Now why would I want to keep quiet about the fact that you stole my truck and slammed it into a tree?"

A resurgence of belligerence glinted in her eyes. "Because she'll sue you for pain and suffering. I'm almost positive I've got a whiplash injury," she said, rubbing at her neck convincingly. "Probably back problems that'll last the rest of my life, too."

Harlan chuckled. "Imagine that. All those problems and you expect to blame them on the man whose truck you stole and smashed up. You and your mother have a little scam going? You wreck cars and she sues for damages?"

At the criticism of her mother's ethics, her defiance wavered just a little. "My mom's a lawyer," she admitted eventually. "She sues lots of people." Her eyes glittered with triumphant sparks as she added, "She wins, too."

An image suddenly came to him, an image of the new lawyer he'd read about just last week in the local

paper. The article had been accompanied by a picture of
an incredibly lovely woman, her long black hair flowing down her back, her features and her name strongly
suggesting her Comanche heritage. Janet Something-
or-other. Runningbear, maybe. Yep, that was it. Janet
Runningbear.

He surveyed the girl standing in front of him and
thought he detected a resemblance. There was no mistaking the Native American genes in her proud bearing, her features or her coloring, though he had a hunch
they'd been mellowed by a couple of generations of in-
terracial marriage.

"Your mom's the new lawyer in town, then," he said.
"Janet Runningbear."

She seemed startled that he'd guessed, but she hid it
quickly behind another of those belligerent looks she'd
obviously worked hard to perfect. "So?"

"So, I think you and I need to go have a little chat
with your mama," he said, putting a hand on the middle of her back and giving her a gentle but unrelenting little push in the direction of Mule's car. Her chin
rose another notch, but her shoulders slumped and she
didn't resist. In fact, there was an air of weary resignation about her that tugged at his heart.

As he drove back into town he couldn't help wondering just how much trouble Janet Runningbear's daughter managed to get herself into on a regular basis and
why she felt the need to do it. After raising four sons
of his own, he knew a whole lot about teenage rebellion and the testing of parental authority. He'd always
thought—mistakenly apparently—that girls might have
been easier. Not that he would have traded a single one

of his boys to find out firsthand. He'd planned on keeping an eye on his female grandbabies to test his theory.

He glanced over at the slight figure next to him and caught the downward turn of her mouth and the protective clasping of her arms across her chest. Stubbornness radiated from every pore. The prospect of meeting the woman who had raised such a little hellion intrigued him.

It was the first time since a riding accident had taken his beloved Mary away from him the year before that he'd found much of anything fascinating. He realized as the blood zinged through his veins for the first time in months just how boring and predictable he'd allowed his life to become.

He'd left the running of the ranch mostly in Cody's hands, just as his youngest son had been itching for him to do for some time. Harlan spent his days riding over his land or stopping off in town to have lunch and play a few hands of poker with Mule or some other friend. His evenings dragged out endlessly unless one or the other of his sons stopped by for a visit and brought his grandbabies along.

For a rancher who'd crammed each day to its limits all his life, he'd been telling himself that the tedium was a welcome relief. He'd been convinced of it, too, until the instant when he'd seen his truck barreling down Main Street.

Something about the quick, hot surge of blood in his veins told him those soothing, dull days were over. Glancing down at the ruffian by his side, he could already anticipate the upcoming encounter with any woman bold and brash enough to keep her in hand. He suddenly sensed that he was just about to start living again.

* * *

Janet Runningbear gazed out of the window of her small law office on Main Street and saw her daughter being ushered down the sidewalk by a man she recognized at once as Harlan Adams, owner of White Pines and one of the most successful ranchers for several hundred miles in any direction. Judging from the stern expression on his face and Jenny's dragging footsteps, her daughter had once more gotten herself into a mess of trouble.

She studied the man approaching with a mixture of trepidation, anger, and an odd, tingly hint of anticipation. Ever since her move to Los Piños, the closest town to where her ancestors had once lived, she'd been hearing about Harlan Adams, the man whose own ancestors had been at least in part responsible for pushing the Comanches out of Texas and onto an Oklahoma reservation.

The claiming of Comanche lands might have taken place a hundred years or more ago, but Janet clung to the resentment that had been passed down to her by her great-grandfather. Lone Wolf had lived to be ninety-seven and his father had been forced from the nomadic life of a hunter to the confined space of a reservation.

Even though she knew it was ridiculous to blame Harlan Adams for deeds that had been committed long before his birth or her own, she was prepared to dislike him just on principle. What she hadn't been prepared for was the prompt and very feminine response to a man who practically oozed sex appeal from every masculine pore.

He was cowboy through and through, from the Stetson hat that rode atop his thick, sun-streaked hair to the tips of his dusty boots. His weathered face hinted at his age, which she knew to be somewhere in his fifties, but nothing about his easy stride or his broad shoulders added to that impression. He had the bearing of a much younger man.

In fact, Harlan Adams strolled down the sidewalk, her daughter in tow, with the confidence of a man who was comfortable with himself and with the power his wealth had earned him. To dampen any spark of fascination he might arouse, Janet quickly assured herself it was more than confidence she saw. It was arrogance, a trait she despised. Since there was no mistaking his destination, she braced herself for his arrival.

A few minutes later, with the pair of them seated across from her, she listened with a sense of growing horror as Harlan Adams described the theft of his truck and the subsequent accident, which had clearly done more damage to the truck than it had to Jenny. Her daughter didn't even seem flustered.

"He shouldn't have left the damned keys inside," Jenny muttered.

"Watch your tongue, young lady," Janet warned.

A heartfelt apology rose to Janet's lips but before she could begin to form the words, she caught a surprising glint of amusement in Harlan's startlingly blue eyes. She'd been anticipating the same mischievous dark brown eyes each of his sons reportedly had, according to the fond reminiscences of the local ladies. They must have inherited those from their mother, she decided. Harlan's were the bright blue of a summer sky just rinsed by rain.

"Jenny, perhaps you should wait in the other room, while Mr. Adams and I discuss this," she said, sensing that the twinkle in those eyes might mean an inclination toward leniency that wasn't altogether deserved.

The last of her daughter's defiance slid away. "Am I going to jail?" she asked in a voice that shook even though she was clearly trying desperately to sound brave.

"That remains to be seen," Janet told her without so much as a hint that she thought jail was the last thing on this particular victim's mind.

"Are you going to be my lawyer?"

Janet hid her face so that Jenny wouldn't see her own smile. "If you need one," she promised solemnly, doubting that it was going to come to that.

Sure enough, the second Jenny was out of the room, Harlan Adams chuckled. "Damn, but she's a pistol. She's got the makings of one heck of a young woman."

"If she doesn't self-destruct first," Janet muttered wearily. "I'm not sure I understand why you find all of this so amusing."

He grinned at her and her heart did an unexpected little flip. There was something so unexpectedly boyish about that lazy, lopsided smile. At the same time, the experience and wisdom that shone in his eyes was comforting. Something told her at once that this was a man a woman could always count on for straight talk and moral support. A little of that misguided resentment she'd been stoking slipped away.

"Remind me to tell you about the time one of my boys rustled a bunch of my cattle to start his own herd," Harlan Adams said, still chuckling over the memory. "He was seven at the time. Try taking your daughter's mischief and multiply it four times over and you'll have some idea why I can't work up too much of a sweat over one stolen truck."

"She could have been killed," Janet said grimly, realizing as she spoke that she was shaking at the very thought of what could have happened to Jenny.

"But she wasn't," Harlan reminded her in a soothing tone that suggested he knew exactly the sort of belated reaction she was having.

"Then there's the matter of your truck. I'm just getting my practice off the ground here, but I can make arrangements to pay you back over time, if that's okay."

He waved off the offer. "Insurance will take care of it."

"But it's my responsibility," she insisted.

"The danged truck's not important," he countered emphatically. "The real question now is how to make sure that gal of yours doesn't go trying some fool thing like that again."

His unexpected kindness brought the salty sting of tears to her eyes. Janet rubbed at them impatiently. She never cried. Never. In fact, she considered it a point of honor that she was always strong and in control.

Suddenly, for some reason she couldn't fathom, she was not only crying, but actually considering spilling her guts to a total stranger. Harlan Adams was practically the first person in town to be civilized to her, much less kind. Truth be told, the move to Texas was not turning out anything at all the way she'd imagined it would.

"I'm sorry," she apologized. "I don't know what's wrong with me or with Jenny. I never cry. And she used to be such a good girl."

Harlan's expression remained solemn and thoughtful. "You know," he said, "I used to teach my sons that tears made a man seem weak. The past year or so, I've had a change of heart. I think it takes someone pretty strong to acknowledge when they're feeling vulnerable and then deal straight-out with the pain they're going through."

Janet guessed right off that it was his wife's death that had brought him to a change of heart. The word on Mary Adams was mixed, according to the gossip that folks had been eager to share. Some thought she'd been an elegant, refined lady. Others thought she was a cold, uppity witch. One thing no one disputed, however, was that Harlan Adams had adored her and that she had doted on him.

Janet had wondered more than once what it would be like to love anyone with such passion. Her own marriage had been lukewarm at best and certainly not up to the kind of tests it had been put through. She'd been relieved to call it quits, eager to move far from New York and its memories to the land Lone Wolf had described with such bittersweet poignancy. She had legally taken the name he'd dubbed her with as soon as she'd settled in town. A new name, a fresh start for her and Jenny.

She glanced up and realized that Harlan's warm gaze was fixed on her. He was regarding her with more of that compassion that made her want to weep.

"Why don't you tell me what's been going on with that girl of yours?" he offered. "Maybe we can figure this thing out together."

Surprised at the relief she felt at having someone with whom to share her concerns, Janet tried to describe what the past few weeks had been like. "I thought coming here was going to make such a difference for Jenny," she said. "Instead, she's behaving as if I've punished her by moving from New York to Texas."

"Quite a change for a young girl," Harlan observed. "She's at an age when leaving all her friends behind must seem like the end of the world. Hell, she's at an age when *everything* seems like the end of the world. Besides that, it's summertime. All the kids her age around here are caught up with their own vacation activities. Lots of 'em have to work their family's ranch. Must seem like she'll never have a friend of her own again."

Janet didn't like having a total stranger tell her something she should have figured out for herself. She'd been so anxious to get to Texas after the divorce, so determined to get on with her life and to get Jenny settled in a safer environment than the city streets of Manhattan that she hadn't given much thought to how lonely the summer might be for her daughter. She'd been thinking of the move as an adventure and had assumed Jenny was doing the same.

Now it appeared that the kind of energy that might have resulted in little more than mischief back in New York was taking a dangerous turn. She cringed as she pictured that truck slamming into a tree with her daughter behind the wheel. If her ex-husband heard about that, he'd wash his hands of Jenny once and for all. Barry Randall had little enough room in his life for his daughter now. If she became a liability to his image, he'd forget she existed.

"I have an idea," the man seated across from her said. "I don't intend to press charges for this, but we don't want her getting the idea that she can get away with stealing a car and taking it joyriding."

Janet was so worried by the prospects for Jenny getting herself into serious trouble before school started in the fall that she was willing to listen to anything, even if it was being offered by the exact kind of man she'd learned to distrust—a rich and powerful white man. A Texan, to boot. A sworn enemy of her ancestors.

"What?" she asked warily.

"I'll give her a job out at White Pines. She can earn enough to pay off the cost of the truck's repairs. That'll keep her busy, teach her to take responsibility for her actions, and wear her out at the same time."

"I said I'd pay," Janet reminded him.

"It's not the same. It was her mistake."

Just one of many lately, Janet thought with a sigh. Perhaps if Jenny hadn't shoplifted a whole handful of cosmetics from the drugstore the week before, perhaps if she hadn't upended a table in Rosa's Café breaking every dish on it, Janet might have resisted a suggestion that would have kept her in contact with this man who made her pulse skip. The kindness in his voice, the humor in his eyes, were every bit as dangerous to her in her beleaguered state of mind as Jenny's exploits were to her future. At the rate she'd been going since they got to Texas, she'd either end up in jail or dead.

"Do I have any choice?" she asked, all but resigned to accepting the deal he was offering.

He shrugged. "Not really. I could sue you, I suppose, but that gal of yours says you're the best lawyer around. You might win, and then where would I be?"

Janet laughed at the outrageous comment. A man who could keep his sense of humor in a circumstance like this was rare. She just might be forced to reevaluate Harlan Adams. And he might be just the kind of good influence her daughter needed. There was no question Jenny needed a stern hand and perhaps a stronger father figure than her own daddy had ever provided.

"Are you really sure you want to deal with a rebellious teenage girl for the rest of the summer?" she asked, but there was no denying the hopeful note in her voice as she envisioned an improvement in Jenny's reckless behavior.

"I'll take my chances," he said solemnly, his gaze fixed on her.

Janet trembled at the speculative gleam she saw in his eyes. She hadn't had this kind of immediate, purely sexual reaction to a man in a very long time. She'd actually convinced herself she was capable of controlling such things. Now not only was Jenny out of control, it appeared her hormones were, as well. It was a dismaying turn of events.

It also served as a warning that she'd better be on her guard around Harlan Adams. It wouldn't do to spend much time around him with her defenses down. He was the kind of man who'd claim what he wanted, just as his ancestors had. Whether it was land or a woman probably wouldn't matter much.

She adopted her most businesslike demeanor, the one she reserved for clients and the courtroom. "What time do you want her at White Pines?" she inquired briskly, prepared to temporarily sacrifice her emotional peace of mind for her daughter's sake.

"Dawn will do," he said as he rose and headed for the door.

He must have heard her faint gasp of dismay because he turned back and winked. "I'll have the coffee ready when you get there."

Janet sighed as he walked away. *Dawn!* If he expected her to be coherent at that hour, he'd better have gallons of it and it had best be strong and black.

2

"I've taken on another hand for the summer," Harlan mentioned to Cody when he stopped by just before dinner later that night.

His son sat up a little straighter in the leather chair in which he'd sprawled out of habit as soon as he'd walked through the door. Instantly Harlan could see Cody's jaw setting stubbornly as he prepared to argue against his father's unilateral decision. Harlan decided he'd best cut him off at the pass.

"Don't go getting your drawers in a knot," he advised him. "I'm not usurping your authority. This was just something that came up."

"Came up how?" Cody asked, suspicion written all over his face. "There's no budget for another hand. You told me that yourself when we talked about it just last week."

"It came up right after my truck was stolen and smashed up," Harlan explained. "Let's just say that no money will be changing hands. The thief will be working off the repair bill."

Cody's jaw dropped. "You hired the thief who stole

your car? Haven't you ever heard of jail time? If any of us had stolen a car and gone joyriding, you'd have helped the sheriff turn the lock on the cell."

"It didn't seem like the thing to do with a thirteen-year-old girl," Harlan said mildly. "Seemed to me this was a better way to teach her a lesson."

Cody fell silent, clearly chewing over the concept of a teenage girl as his newest ranch hand. "What the hell am I supposed to have her doing?" he asked finally.

"You're not her boss," Harlan said, amused by the relief that instantly spread across Cody's face. "I am. I just wanted you to know she'd be around. Her name's Jenny Runningbear."

"Runningbear? Is her mother…?"

"The new lawyer in town," Harlan supplied, watching as curiosity rose in Cody's eyes.

"Did you meet her?" Cody asked.

"I did." He decided then and there that he'd better be stingy with information about that meeting. His son had the look of a man about to make a romantic mountain out of a platonic molehill.

"And?"

"And, what?"

"What did you think of her?"

"She seemed nice," Harlan offered blandly, even as he conjured up some fairly steamy images of the raven-haired beauty who'd struck him as a fascinating blend of strength and vulnerability. *Nice* was far too tame a description for that delicate, exotic face, those long, long legs, and eyes so dark a man could lose himself in them.

"Really?" Cody said, skepticism written all over his face. "Nice?"

Harlan didn't like the way Cody was studying him. "That's what I said, isn't it?" he replied irritably.

"Just seemed sort of namby-pamby to me," Cody retorted. "I might have described her as hot. I believe Jordan said something similar after he spotted her."

Harlan bit back a sharp rebuke. His gaze narrowed. "Exactly how well do you and your brother know the woman?"

"Not well enough to say more than hello when we pass on the street. Never even been introduced. Of course, if we both weren't happily married, we'd probably be brawling over first dibs on meeting her."

"See that you remember that you are married," he advised his son.

"Interesting," Cody observed, his eyes suddenly sparkling with pure mischief.

"What's interesting?"

"The way you're getting all protective about the mother of a teenage car thief. What time are they getting here in the morning?"

"That's nothing you need to concern yourself about." He stood, glanced at his watch pointedly as he anticipated his housekeeper's imminent announcement that dinner was on the table. "I'd invite you to dinner, but I told Maritza I'd be eating alone. It's time you got home to your wife and those grandbabies of mine anyway."

Cody didn't budge. "They're eating in town with her folks tonight, so I'm all yours. I told Maritza I'd be staying. I thought maybe we could wrangle a little over buying that acreage out to the east, but I'd rather talk more about your impressions of Janet Runningbear."

"Forget it," Harlan warned. "Besides, since when does my housekeeper take orders from you?"

"FAST FIVE" READER SURVEY

Your participation entitles you to:
✳ Up to 4 FREE BOOKS and Thank-You Gifts Worth Over $20!

Complete the survey in minutes.

Suspense

Romance

Get Up to 4 FREE Books

Your Thank-You Gifts include up to **4 FREE BOOKS** and **2 Mystery Gifts**. There's no obligation to purchase anything!

See inside for details.

Please help make our
"Fast Five" Reader Survey
a success!

Dear Reader,

Since you are a lover of our books, your opinions are important to us... and so is your time.

That's why we made sure your **"FAST FIVE" READER SURVEY** can be completed in just a few minutes. Your answers to the five questions will help us remain at the forefront of women's fiction.

And, as a thank-you for participating, we'd like to send you up to **4 FREE BOOKS** and **FREE THANK-YOU GIFTS!**

Try **Essential Suspense** featuring spine-tingling suspense and psychological thrillers with many written by today's best-selling authors.

Try **Essential Romance** featuring compelling romance stories with many written by today's best-selling authors.

Or TRY BOTH!

Enjoy your gifts with our appreciation,

Pam Powers

To get up to
4 FREE BOOKS & THANK-YOU GIFTS:

* Quickly complete the "Fast Five" Reader Survey
and return the insert.

▼ DETACH AND MAIL CARD TODAY! ▼

"FAST FIVE" READER SURVEY

1	Do you sometimes read a book a second or third time?	○ Yes ○ No
2	Do you often choose reading over other forms of entertainment such as television?	○ Yes ○ No
3	When you were a child, did someone regularly read aloud to you?	○ Yes ○ No
4	Do you sometimes take a book with you when you travel outside the home?	○ Yes ○ No
5	In addition to books, do you regularly read newspapers and magazines?	○ Yes ○ No

YES! Please send me my Free Rewards, consisting of **2 Free Books from each series I select** and **Free Mystery Gifts**. I understand that I am under no obligation to buy anything, as explained on the back of this card.

❏ **Essential Suspense** (191/391 MDL GNTC)
❏ **Essential Romance** (194/394 MDL GNTC)
❏ **Try Both** ((191/391 & 194/394) MDL GNTN)

FIRST NAME	LAST NAME

ADDRESS

APT.#	CITY

STATE/PROV.	ZIP/POSTAL CODE

© 2019 HARLEQUIN ENTERPRISES LIMITED
® and ™ are trademarks owned and used by the trademark owner and/or its licensee. Printed in the U.S.A.

READER SERVICE—Here's how it works:

Cody grinned. "Ever since I was old enough to talk. I inherited your charm. It pays off in the most amazing ways. Maritza even fixed all my favorites. She said she'd missed me something fierce. I'm the one with the cast-iron stomach."

Harlan sighed as he thought of the hot peppers that comment implied. Between lunch at Rosa's and that darned accident, his own stomach could have used a bowl of nice bland oatmeal. It appeared he was out of luck.

"Well, come on, then. The sooner we eat, the sooner I can get you out of here and get some peace and quiet."

"You really interested in peace and quiet, Daddy? Or do you just want to make sure you get some beauty sleep before you see Janet Runningbear in the morning?" Cody taunted.

"Don't go getting too big for your britches, son," Harlan warned. "You're not so old that I can't send you packing without your supper. Push me hard enough, I might just send you packing, period."

"But you won't," Cody retorted confidently.

"Oh? Why is that?"

"Because so far only you and I know about this new fascination of yours. Send me home and I'll have the whole, long evening to fill up. I might decide to use that time by calling Luke and Jordan. They like to be up-to-date on everything that goes on around White Pines. They'll be flat-out delighted to discover that you're no longer bored."

Harlan could just imagine the hornet's nest that would stir up. He'd have all three sons hovering over him, making rude remarks, discussing his relationship with a woman he'd barely spent a half hour with up to now. They'd consider taunting him their duty, just as he'd considered it his to meddle in their lives.

"That's blackmail," he accused.

Cody's grin was unrepentant. "Sure is. It's going to make life around here downright interesting, isn't it?"

Harlan sighed. It was indeed.

"I don't see why I have to work for him," Jenny declared for the hundredth time since learning of the agreement her mother had made with Harlan Adams. "Aren't there child labor laws or something?"

"There are also laws against car theft," Janet stated flatly. "You didn't seem overly concerned about those."

A yawn took a little of the edge off of her words. No one in his right mind actually got up at daybreak. She was certain of it. Even though she'd forced herself to get to bed two hours earlier than usual the night before, she'd wanted to hurl the alarm clock out the window when it had gone off forty-five minutes ago.

She'd dressed in a sleepy fog. With any luck, everything at least matched. As for her driving, she would probably be considered a menace if anyone checked on how many of her brain cells were actually functioning. The lure of a huge pot of caffeinated coffee was all that had gotten her out the door.

At the moment she could cheerfully have murdered Jenny for getting them into this predicament. The very thought of doing this day after day all summer long had her gnashing her teeth. She was in no mood for any more of her daughter's backtalk.

"Why couldn't you just pay him?" Jenny muttered. "There's money in my account from Dad."

"It's for college," Janet reminded her. "Besides, I offered to pay Mr. Adams. He refused."

"Jeez, did he see you coming! I'm free labor, Mom. He'll probably have me scrubbing down the barn floor or something. I'll probably end up with arthritis from kneeling in all that cold, filthy water."

"Serves you right," Janet said.

At the lack of either sympathy or any hint of a reprieve, Jenny retreated into sullen silence. That gave Janet time to work on her own composure.

To her astonishment, Harlan Adams had slipped into her dreams last night. She'd awakened feeling restless and edgy and unfulfilled in a way that didn't bear too close a scrutiny. It was a state she figured she'd better get over before her arrival at White Pines. He had struck her as the kind of man who would seize on any hint of weakness and capitalize on it.

The sun was just peeking over the horizon in a blaze of brilliant orange when she arrived at the gate to the ranch. She turned onto the property with something akin to awe spreading through her as she studied the raw beauty of the land around her. This was the land Lone Wolf had described, lush and barren in turns, stretched out as far as the eye could see, uninterrupted by the kind of development she'd come to take for granted in New York.

"This is it?" Jenny asked, a heavy measure of disdain in her voice. "There's nothing here."

Janet hid a smile. No Bloomingdale's. No high rises. No restaurants or music stores. It was little wonder her daughter sounded so appalled.

She, to the contrary, was filled at last with that incredible sense of coming home that she'd wanted so badly to feel when she'd moved to Los Piños. She considered for a moment whether Lone Wolf's father might have hunted on this very land. It pleased her somehow to think that he might have.

"That's why they call it the wide open spaces," she told her daughter. "Remember all the stories I told you about Lone Wolf?"

"Yeah, but I don't get it," Jenny declared flatly. "Maybe I could just get a job in the drugstore or something and pay Mr. Adams back that way."

"No," Janet said softly, listening to the early morning sounds of birds singing, insects humming and somewhere in the distance a tractor rumbling. Did he grow his own grain? Or maybe have a nice vegetable garden? On some level, she thought she'd been waiting all her life for a moment just like this.

"I think this will be perfect for you," she added as hope flowered inside her for the first time in years.

Jenny rolled her eyes. "If he makes me go near a horse or a cow, I'm out of here," she warned.

Janet grinned. "This is a cattle ranch. I think you can pretty much count on horses and cows."

"Mo-om!" she wailed. Her gaze narrowed. "I'll run away. I'll steal a car and drive all the way home to New York."

"And then what?" Janet inquired mildly. Jenny knew as well as she did that there was no room for her in her father's life. Even though at the moment his selfishness suited her purposes, she hated Barry Randall for making his disinterest so abundantly clear to his daughter.

Jenny turned a tearful gaze on her that almost broke Janet's heart.

"I don't have a choice, do I?" she asked.

"Afraid not, love. Besides, I think you'll enjoy this once you've gotten used to it. Think of all the stories you'll have to write to your friends back in New York. How many of them have ever seen a genuine cowboy, much less worked on a ranch?"

"How many of them even wanted to?" Jenny shot back.

"You remember what I always told my clients when they landed in jail?" Janet asked.

Jenny shot her a tolerant look and sighed heavily. "I remember. It's up to me whether I make my time here hard or easy."

"Exactly."

A sudden gleam lit her eyes. "I suppose it's also up to me whether it's hard or easy for Mr. Adams, too, huh?"

Janet didn't much like the sound of that. "Jenny," she warned. "If you don't behave, you'll be in debt to this man until you're old enough for college."

"I'll be good, Mom. Cross my heart."

Janet nodded, accepting the promise, but the glint in her daughter's eyes when she made that solemn vow was worrisome. The words had come a little too quickly, a little too easily. Worse, she recognized that glint all too well. It made her wonder if Harlan Adams just might have bitten off more than he could handle.

One look at him a few minutes later and her doubts vanished. This was a man competent to deal with anything at all. When he rounded the corner of the house in his snug, worn jeans, his blue chambray shirt, his dusty boots and that Stetson hat, he almost stole her breath away.

If she was ever of a mind to let another man into her life, she wanted one who exuded exactly this combination of strength, sex appeal and humor. His eyes were practically dancing with laughter as he approached. And the appreciative head-to-toe look he gave her could have melted steel. Her knees didn't stand a chance. They turned weak as a new colt's.

"Too early for you?" he inquired, his gaze drifting over her once more in the kind of lazy inspection that left goose bumps in its wake.

"No, indeed," she denied brightly. "Why would you think that?"

"No special reason. It's just that you struck me as a woman who'd never leave the house with quite so many buttons undone."

A horrified glance at her blouse confirmed the teasing comment. She'd missed more buttons than she'd secured, which meant there was an inordinate amount of cleavage revealed. She vowed to strangle her daughter at the very first opportunity for not warning her. At least the damned blouse did match her slacks, she thought as she fumbled with the buttons with fingers that shook.

"Jeez, Mom," Jenny protested. "Let me."

Janet thought she heard Harlan mutter something that sounded suspiciously like, "Or me," but she couldn't be absolutely sure. When she looked in his direction, his gaze was fixed innocently enough on the sky.

"Come on inside," he invited a moment later. "I promised you coffee. I think Maritza has breakfast ready by now, too."

"Who's Maritza?" Jenny asked.

Her tone suggested a level of distrust that had Janet shooting a warning look in her direction. Harlan, however, appeared oblivious to Jenny's suspicions.

"My housekeeper," he explained. "She's been with

the family for years. If you're interested in learning a little Tex-Mex cooking while you're here, she'll be glad to teach you. She's related to Rosa, who owns the Mexican Café in town."

"I hate Tex-Mex," Jenny declared.

"You do not," Janet said, giving Harlan an apologetic smile. "She's a little contrary at this hour."

"Seemed to be that way at midday, too," he stated pointedly. "Not to worry. It would be an understatement to say that I've had a lot of experience with contrariness."

He led the way through the magnificent foyer and into a formal dining room that was practically the size of Janet's entire house. Her eyes widened. "Good heavens, do you actually eat in here by yourself?"

He seemed startled by the question. "Of course. Why?"

"It's just that it's so..." She fumbled for the right word.

"Big," Jenny contributed.

"Lonely," Janet said, then regretted it at once. The man didn't need to be reminded that he was a widower and that his sons were no longer living under his roof. He was probably aware of those sad facts every single day of his life.

He didn't seem to take offense, however. He just shrugged. "I'm used to it."

He gestured toward a buffet laden with more cereals, jams, muffins, toast and fruits than Janet had ever seen outside a grocery store.

"Help yourself," he said. "If you'd rather have eggs and bacon, Maritza will fix them for you. She doesn't allow me near the stuff."

"How come?" Jenny asked.

"Cholesterol, fat." He grimaced. "They've taken all the fun out of eating. Next thing you know they'll be feeding us a bunch of pills three times a day and we won't be needing food at all."

"There are egg substitutes," Janet commented.

"Yellow mush," he contradicted.

"And turkey bacon."

He shuddered. "Not a chance."

Janet chuckled at his reaction. "I'm not going to convince you, am I?"

"Depends on how good you are at sweet talk, darlin'."

Her startled gaze flew to his. Those blue eyes were innocent as a baby's. Even so, she knew in her gut, where butterflies were ricocheting wildly, that he had just tossed down a gauntlet of sorts. He was daring her to turn this so-called arrangement they had made for Jenny's punishment into something personal. The temperature in the room rose significantly.

Nothing would happen between them. Janet was adamant about that. She was in Texas to tap into her Native American roots, not to get involved with another white man. She'd tried that once and it had failed, just as her mother's marriage to a white man had ended in disaster exactly as Lone Wolf had apparently predicted when her mother had fled the reservation.

She drew herself up and leveled a look at him that she normally reserved for difficult witnesses in court. "That, *darlin'*, is something you're not likely to find out," she retorted.

Jenny's eyes widened as she listened to the exchange. Janet was very aware of the precise instant when a speculative gleam lit her daughter's intelligent brown eyes.

Dear heaven, that was the last thing she needed. Jenny was like a puppy with a sock when she got a notion into her head. If she sensed there were sparks between her mother and Harlan Adams, she'd do everything in her power to see that they flared into a blaze. She'd do it not because she particularly wanted someone to replace her father, but just to see if she could pull it off.

To put a prompt end to any such speculation, Janet forced a perfectly blank expression onto her face as she turned her attention to the man seated opposite her.

"Exactly what will Jenny be doing today?"

"I thought maybe I'd teach her to ride," Harlan replied just as blandly, apparently willing to let that sudden flare of heat between them die down for the moment. "Unless she already knows how."

"Oh, no," Jenny protested.

Janet jumped in to prevent the tantrum she suspected was only seconds away. "She doesn't, but riding doesn't sound much like punishment or work to me."

"She has to be able to get around, if she's going to be much use on a ranch this size," he countered. "I can't go putting her behind the wheel of a truck again, now can I?"

He glanced at his watch, then at Jenny. "You ready?"

Jenny's chin rose stubbornly. "Not if you were paying me a hundred bucks an hour," she declared.

Janet thought she detected a spark of amusement in his eyes, but his expression remained perfectly neutral.

"You scared of horses?" he inquired.

Janet watched her daughter, sensing her dilemma. Jenny would rather eat dirt than admit to fear of any sort. At the same time, she had a genuine distrust of horses, based totally on unfamiliarity, not on any dire experience she'd ever had.

"I'm not afraid of anything," Jenny informed Harlan stiffly. "Horses are dirty and smelly and big. I don't choose to be around them."

Harlan chuckled at the haughty dismissal. "I can't do much about their size, but I can flat-out guarantee they won't be dirty or smelly by the time you're finished grooming them."

Jenny turned a beseeching look in Janet's direction. "Mom!"

"He's the boss," Janet reminded her.

"I don't see you getting anywhere near a smelly old horse," Jenny complained.

"You'd be welcome, if you'd care to join us," Harlan said a little too cheerfully.

"Perhaps another time. I have to get to work."

"Why?" Jenny asked. "You don't have any clients."

Janet winced. The remark was true enough, but she didn't want Harlan Adams knowing too much about her law practice, if that's what handling one speeding violation could be called.

"Business slow?" he asked, leveling a penetrating look straight at her.

She shrugged. "You know how it is. I'm new to town."

He looked as if he might be inclined to comment on that, but instead he let it pass. She was grateful to him for not trying to make excuses for neighbors who were slow to trust under the best of conditions. Their biases made them particularly distrustful of a woman lawyer, who was part Comanche, to boot, and openly proud of it.

"What time should I pick Jenny up?" she asked.

"Suppertime's good enough. You finish up at work any earlier, come on out," he said. "We'll go on that ride. I never get tired of looking at the beauty of this land."

Janet found herself smiling at the simplicity of the admission. She could understand his appreciation of his surroundings. Perhaps even more than he could ever guess.

"Maybe I'll take you up on that one of these days," she agreed. She stood and brushed a kiss across her daughter's forehead. "Have a good time, sweetie."

"Is that another one of those things you tell all your clients who end up in prison?" Jenny inquired, her expression sour.

"You're not in prison," Janet observed, avoiding Harlan's gaze. She had a feeling he was close to laughing and exchanging a look with her would guarantee it. Jenny would resent being laughed at more than anything.

"Seems that way to me," Jenny said.

"Remind me to show you what a real prison looks like one of these days," Janet countered. "You'll be grateful to Mr. Adams for not sending you to one."

Janet decided that was as good an exit line as she was likely to make. She was halfway to the front door when she realized that Harlan had followed her. He put his hand on her shoulder and squeezed lightly.

"She'll be okay," he promised.

Janet grinned at his solemn expression. "I know," she agreed. "But will you?"

3

When Janet's car had disappeared from sight, Harlan turned and walked slowly back inside. For the first time he was forced to admit that his decision to haul Jenny Runningbear's butt out to White Pines to work off her debt wasn't entirely altruistic. He'd wanted to guarantee himself the chance to spend more time with her mother.

But now, with Janet on her way back to town and her taunt about his ability to manage Jenny ringing in his ears, he wondered precisely what he'd gotten himself into.

Raising four stubborn sons, when he'd had authority and respect on his side, had been tricky enough. He had neither of those things going for him now. If anything, Jenny resented him and she had no qualms at all about letting him know it.

He sighed as he stood in the doorway to the dining room and studied Jenny's sullen expression. If ever a teen had needed a stern hand, this one did. Whether she knew it or not, she was just aching for someone besides her mama to set some rules and make her stick to them.

It was a job her father should have been handling,

but he'd clearly abandoned it. It was little wonder the girl was misbehaving, he thought with a deep sense of pity. Typically in the aftermath of divorce, she was crying out for attention. Maybe she'd even hoped if she were difficult enough, she'd be sent back to her father for disciplining.

It took some determination, but Harlan finally shoved aside his inclination to feel sorry for her. It wouldn't help. He figured whatever happened in the next few minutes would set the tone for the rest of the days Jenny spent at White Pines.

"Thought you'd be outside by now, ready to get to work," he announced. "I won't tolerate slackers working for me."

Her gaze shot to his. "What does this crummy job pay anyway? Minimum wage, I'll bet."

"It pays for a smashed up pickup, period. Think of it as a lump sum payment."

"I'll want to see the repair bill," she informed him. "If the figures for my pay, based on the minimum hourly wage, are higher, I'll expect the rest in cash."

Harlan wanted very badly to chuckle, but he choked back his laughter. This pint-size Donald Trump wannabe had audacity to spare. "Fair enough," he conceded.

"And I'm not getting on a horse," she reminded him belligerently.

"That's something we can discuss," he agreed. "Meantime, let's get out to the barn and groom them. They've been fed this morning, but tomorrow I'll expect you to do that, too."

She stood slowly, reluctance written all over her face. Harlan deliberately turned his back on her and headed out through the kitchen, winking at Maritza as he passed. He didn't pause to introduce them. He had a feeling Jenny would seize on any delay and drag it out as long as she possibly could. She might even inquire about those Tex-Mex recipes she claimed not to like, if it would keep her out of the barn a little longer.

With her soft heart, Maritza would insist on keeping Jenny in the kitchen so she could teach her a few of her favorite dishes and coddle her while she was at it. That would be the end of any disciplining he planned. Until he'd laid some ground rules and Jenny was following them, he figured he couldn't afford to ease up on her a bit. Her very first day on the job was hardly the time to be cutting her any slack.

"Was that your housekeeper?" Jenny asked, scuffing her sneakers in the dust as she poked along behind him.

"Yes."

"How come you didn't introduce us?"

"No time for that now," he said briskly. "You have a job to do. You'll meet Maritza at lunch. She'll be bringing it out to us."

"We're going to eat in the barn?"

Harlan hid a grin at her horrified tone. "No, I expect we'll be out checking fences by then."

She scowled at him. "I thought you were rich. Don't you have anybody else working this place? I can't do everything, you know. I'm just a kid."

"Trust me, you won't even be scratching the surface. And yes, there are other people working the ranch. Quite a few people, in fact. They report to my son. They're off with the cattle or working the fields where we have grain growing." He shot her a sly look. "You had any experience driving a tractor?"

"The sum total of my entire driving experience was

in your truck yesterday," she admitted, then shrugged. "You want to trust me with a tractor after that, it's your problem."

He grinned. "You have a point. We'll stick to horses for the time being."

He led her into the barn, which stabled half a dozen horses he kept purely for pleasure riding. Jenny eyed them all warily from the doorway.

"Come on, gal, get in here," he ordered. "Let me introduce you."

"Isn't it kind of sick to be introducing me to a bunch of horses, when you didn't even let me say hello to the housekeeper?"

"You'll get to know Maritza soon enough. As for these horses, from now on they're going to be your responsibility. I want you getting off on the right foot with them." He pulled cubes of sugar from his pocket. "You can start off by offering them these. That'll get you in their good graces quick enough. Let's start over here with Misty. She's a sweetie."

Jenny accepted the sugar cubes but she stopped well shy of Misty's stall. "Why is she bobbing her head up and down like that?"

"She wants some of that sugar."

Jenny held out all of it. "Here. She can have it."

"Not like that," he corrected, "unless you want her to nip off a few fingers at the same time."

He showed her how to hold out her hand, palm flat, the sugar cube in the middle. Misty took the sugar eagerly. He grinned as Jenny's wary expression eased. "Was that so bad?"

"I guess not," she said, though she still didn't sound entirely convinced.

For the next two hours he taught her to groom the horses, watching with satisfaction as she began first to mutter at them when they didn't stand still for her, then started coaxing and finally praising them as she worked. He'd never known a kid yet who could spend much time around horses and not learn to love them. Jenny's resistance was weakening even faster than he'd hoped.

When he was satisfied that her fear had waned, he walked over to her with bit and saddle. "How about that ride now? Seems to me like Misty's getting mighty restless and you two seem to have struck up a rapport."

Jenny regarded the black horse with the white blaze warily. The gentle mare wasn't huge, but Harlan supposed she was big enough to intimidate anyone saddling up for the first time.

"I don't know," Jenny said.

"Let's saddle her up in the paddock and you can climb aboard for a test run. How about that?"

"You're not going to be happy until I fall off one of these creatures and break my neck, are you?" she accused.

"I'm not going to be happy until you try riding one," he countered. "I'd just as soon you didn't fall off and break anything, though I can pretty much guarantee that you'll get thrown sooner or later."

"Oh, jeez," she moaned. "My mom really will sue you if that happens. We'll ask millions and millions for pain and suffering. We'll take this whole big ranch away from you and you'll end up homeless and destitute." The prospect seemed to cheer her.

"I'll take my chances," Harlan said with a grin. "Come on, kid. Watch what I'm doing here. If you don't cinch this saddle just right, you'll be on your butt on the ground faster than either of us would like."

Jenny grudgingly joined him in the paddock. With trepidation clear in every halting move she made, she finally allowed him to boost her into the saddle on Misty's back.

"I don't know about this," she muttered, shooting him an accusing look. "What happens now?"

"I'll lead you around the paddock until you get used to it. Don't worry about Misty. She's placid as can be. She's not going to throw you, unless you rile her."

"Is there anything in particular that riles her?" Jenny inquired, looking down at him anxiously. "I'd hate to do something like that by mistake."

"You won't," he promised.

It only took two turns around the paddock before Jenny's complexion began to lose its pallor. Satisfied by the color in her cheeks that she was growing more confident by the second, Harlan handed her the reins.

Panic flared in her eyes for an instant. "But how do I drive her?"

"You don't *drive* a horse," he corrected. He offered a few simple instructions, then stood by while Jenny tested them. Misty responded to the most subtle movement of the reins or the gentlest touch of Jenny's heels against her sides.

"Everything okay?" he called out as she rode slowly around the paddock.

Jenny turned a beaming smile on him. "I'm riding, aren't I? I'm really riding!"

"I wouldn't let you enter the Kentucky Derby just yet, but yes, indeed, you are really riding."

"Oh, wow!" she said.

Harlan chuckled as she seemed to catch herself and fall silent the instant the words were out of her mouth. Clearly she feared that too much enthusiasm would indicate a softening in her attitude toward this so-called prison sentence she felt had been imposed on her.

"I'm ready to get down now," she said, her tone bland again.

Harlan patiently showed her how to dismount. "I think you're going to be a natural," he said.

She shrugged with studied indifference. "It's no big deal. I'd like to go inside now. Too much sun will give me skin cancer."

He hid another grin. "Run on over to the kitchen. Maritza will give you some suntan lotion. She might even have some of those cookies she was getting ready to bake out of the oven by now."

"Jeez, milk and cookies, how quaint," she grumbled, but she took off toward the house just the same.

"Be back here in fifteen minutes," he shouted after her.

"Slave driver," she muttered.

Harlan shook his head. If she thought that now, he wondered what she'd have to say when she saw the fence he intended for her to learn how to mend.

Janet wasn't sure what to expect when she drove back out to White Pines late that afternoon. She supposed it wouldn't have surprised her all that much to find the ranch in ashes and Jenny standing triumphantly in the circular driveway.

Instead she found her daughter sound asleep in a rocker on the front porch. Harlan was placidly rocking right beside her, sipping on a tall glass of iced tea.

He stood when Janet got out of the car and sauntered down to meet her. Her stomach did a little flip-flop as he neared.

To cover the tingly way he managed to make her feel without half trying, Janet nodded toward her daughter. "Looks like you wore her out, after all."

"It took some doing. She's a tough little cookie."

"At least she thinks she is," Janet agreed. She allowed herself a leisurely survey of the man standing in front of her. "You don't appear to be any the worse for wear. You must be a tough cookie, too."

"So they say."

He tucked a hand under her elbow and steered her toward the porch and poured her a glass of tea. Jenny never even blinked at her arrival.

"Business any better today?" Harlan asked only after he was apparently satisfied that her tea was fixed up the way she wanted it.

Rather than answering, Janet took a slow, refreshing sip of the cool drink. It felt heavenly after the hot, dusty drive. Her car's air-conditioning had quit that morning on her way back to town and she hadn't yet figured out where to go to have it fixed. The sole mechanic in Los Piños, a man with the unlikely name of Mule Masters, was apparently on vacation. Had been for months, according to Mabel Hastings over at the drugstore.

"My, but this tastes good," she said, sighing with pure pleasure. "It's hotter than blazes today. I thought I'd swelter before I got back out here."

"What's wrong with your car? No air-conditioning?"

"It quit on me this morning."

"I'll have Cody take a look at it when he comes in," he offered. "He's a whiz with stuff like that."

"That's too much trouble," she protested automatically. For a change, though, she did it without much energy. It seemed foolish to put up too much of a fuss just to declare her independence. That was a habit she'd gotten into around her ex-husband. Weighing her independence against air-conditioning in this heat, there was no real contest. Air-conditioning would win every time.

"Nonsense," Harlan said, dismissing her objections anyway. "It'll give Cody a chance to snoop. He's dying to get a closer look at you, so he can tell his brothers that I've gone and lost my marbles."

Startled, she simply stared at him. "Why would he think a thing like that?"

His gaze drifted over her slowly and with unmistakable intent. "Because I'm just crazy enough to think about courting a woman like you."

Janet swallowed hard at the blunt response. She could feel his eyes burning into her as he waited patiently for a reaction.

"Harlan, I don't want you to get the wrong idea here," she said eventually.

It was a namby-pamby response if ever she'd heard one, but she'd never been very good at fending off the few men bold enough to ignore all the warning signals she tried to send out. She'd ended up married to Barry Randall because he'd been persistent and attentive… until the challenge wore off.

With that lesson behind her, she should be shooting down a man like Harlan Adams with both barrels. Suggesting he might be getting the wrong idea hardly constituted a whimper of protest.

He reached over and patted her hand consolingly,

then winked. "Darlin', there is absolutely nothing wrong with the ideas I have. You'll have to trust me on that."

That, of course, was the problem. She didn't trust him or, for that matter, herself. She had a feeling a man with Harlan's confidence and determination could derail her plans for her life in the blink of an eye. She couldn't allow that to happen for a second time.

"You running scared?" he inquired, his lips twitching with amusement.

"Scared? Not me."

His grin broadened. "You sound like Jenny now. I didn't much believe her, either."

"Harlan—"

"Maybe we'd better get this conversation back on safer ground for the moment," he suggested. "Wouldn't want you getting too jittery to drive home tonight. Now, tell me about your day. You never said how business was."

Janet's head was reeling from the quick change of topic and the innuendos Harlan tossed around like confetti. With some effort, she forced her mind off of his provocative teasing and onto that safer ground he'd offered.

"I had a call from somebody interested in having me draw up a will," she told him. "They decided I was too expensive."

"Are you?"

"If I lowered my rates much more, I'd be doing the work for free, which is apparently what they hoped for. The man seemed to assume that since I'm Native American, I handle pro bono work only and he might as well get in on the 'gravy train,' as he put it."

Harlan's gaze sharpened. "You get much of that?" he asked.

He said it with a fierce undertone that suggested he didn't much like what he was hearing. Janet shivered at the thought of what Harlan Adams might do to protect and defend those he cared about.

"Some," she admitted. "I haven't been around long enough to get much."

"Maybe it's time I steered a little business your way."

She suspected that was an understated way of saying he'd butt a few heads together if he had to. She understood enough about small towns to know that a sign of approval from a man like Harlan would guarantee more clients coming her way. As much as the idea appealed to her, she felt she had to turn it down. Barry had always held it over her head that her career had taken off in New York because of his contacts, not the reputation she had struggled to build all on her own.

"No," she insisted with what she considered to be sufficient force to make her point even to a man as stubborn as Harlan appeared to be. "I need to make it on my own. That's the only way people will have any respect for me. It's the only way I'll have any respect for myself."

"Noble sentiments, but it won't put food on the table."

"Jenny and I won't starve. I did quite well in New York. My savings will carry us for a long time."

"If your practice was thriving there, why'd you come here?" Harlan asked.

"Good question," Jenny chimed in in a sleepy, disgruntled tone.

"You know the answer to that," she told her daughter quietly.

"But I don't," Harlan said. "If it's none of my business, just tell me so."

"Would that stop you from poking and prodding until you get an answer?"

"Probably not," he conceded. "But I can be a patient man, when I have to be."

Janet doubted that. It was easier just to come clean with the truth, or part of it at least. "My divorce wasn't pleasant. New York's getting more and more difficult to live in every day. I wanted a simpler way of life."

She shot a look at Jenny, daring her to contradict the reply she'd given. Her daughter just rolled her eyes. Harlan appeared willing to accept the response at face value.

"Makes sense," he said, studying her with that penetrating look that made it appear he could see straight through her. "As far as it goes." He grinned. "But, like I said, I can wait for the rest."

Before she could think of a thing to say to that, a tall, lanky cowboy strolled up. He looked exactly like Harlan must have twenty or so years before, including that flash of humor that sparkled in his eyes as he surveyed the gathering on the porch.

"Looks right cozy," he commented, his amused gaze fixed on his father. "Anything going on here I should know about?"

"Watch your mouth," Harlan ordered. "Janet and Jenny, this tactless scoundrel is my youngest, Cody. Son, this is Janet Runningbear and her daughter Jenny."

Cody winked at Jenny, who was regarding him with blatant fascination. "Don't tell Daddy, but just so you know, I'm the brains behind White Pines."

"If that were true, you'd have better control over your manners," Harlan retorted.

Janet chuckled listening to the two of them. Talk about a chip off the old block. There wasn't a doubt in her mind that any trait Cody possessed, he had learned it at his father's knee. That included everything from charm to arrogance. Still, she couldn't help responding to that infectious grin and the teasing glint in his eyes as he squared off against Harlan. The squabbles around here must have been doozies.

"Why don't you make yourself useful?" Harlan suggested. "Janet says the air conditioner in her car has gone on the blink. Do you have time to take a look at it?"

"Sure thing," Cody said readily. "Let me get a beer and I'll get right on it."

"I could get the beer," Jenny piped up eagerly.

Cody tipped his hat. "Thanks."

Janet speared her daughter with a warning look, then said to Cody, "If one single ounce of that beer is missing when it gets to you, I'd like to know about it."

"Yes, ma'am," Cody said, winking at Jenny, who blushed furiously.

When they were gone, Janet turned to Harlan. "If he were giving the orders, I suspect Jenny would be docile as a lamb the rest of the summer."

"But he's not," Harlan said tersely. "I am."

"Jealous of the impact your son has on the Runningbear women?" she inquired lightly, just to see if the remark would inspire the kind of reaction she suspected it would.

Harlan's expression did, indeed, turn very grim. "He's married."

She grinned. "I know. Heck, everyone in town heard about his courting of Melissa Horton. It was still fresh on their minds when I moved here. But last I heard, looking's never been against the law. I ought to know. I read those big, thick volumes of statutes cover-to-cover in school."

He scowled. "You deliberately trying to rile me?"

"I didn't know I could," she declared innocently.

"Well, now you know," he asserted.

Janet couldn't help feeling a certain sense of feminine satisfaction over the revelation. But hard on the heels of that reaction came the alarm bells. It was entirely possibly that she was enjoying taunting Harlan Adams just a little too much. She had a hunch it was a very dangerous game to play. He struck her as the kind of man who played his games for keeps.

4

Harlan hadn't liked the gut-deep jealousy that had slammed through him when he'd seen the amused, conspiratorial look Janet and Cody had exchanged. Her comment that checking a man out wasn't any sort of legal sin had grated on his nerves just as badly.

Even though he'd guessed that the woman was deliberately baiting him, his blood had simmered and his temper had bordered on exploding. It was an interesting turn of events. He hadn't expected to react so strongly to a woman ever again.

Oh, he'd been attracted to Janet Runningbear the moment he'd set eyes on her. He'd been convinced, though, that he'd deliberately set out to settle her into a corner of his life just to relieve the boredom with an occasional feisty exchange. She was doing that, all right, and more. In spades.

She was stirring up emotions he'd thought had died the day he'd buried his wife just over a year ago. He wasn't so sure he wanted that kind of turmoil.

Unfortunately, he was equally uncertain whether he had any choice in the matter. It had been his observation that when a man was hit by a bolt of lightning—literally or in the lovestruck sense of the phrase—there was no point in trying to get out of the way after the fact.

Given all that, he was almost relieved when Cody announced that the car's air conditioner was working. Janet declined a halfhearted invitation to stay for supper, insisting that she and Jenny had to get home. Harlan waved them off with no more than a distracted reminder to be there at dawn again.

"Well, well, well," Cody muttered beside him.

Harlan frowned at his son's knowing expression. "What's that supposed to mean?"

"Just that it's downright interesting to watch a woman twist you this way and that without even trying."

"I don't know what you're talking about."

Cody grinned. "Then you're in an even more pitiful state of denial than I imagined. Want me to call in Jordan and Luke? Among us we probably have enough experience with women to give you any advice you need. Goodness knows we denied our feelings long enough to drive just about everyone around us to distraction. No sense in you doing the same thing, when we can save you all that time."

"Go away."

"Not till I'm through watching the entertainment," Cody shot back as he sauntered over to his pickup. "'Night, Daddy. Sweet dreams."

Sweet? Harlan could think of a dozen or more words to describe the kind of dreams Janet Runningbear inspired and "sweet" would be very low on the list. Provocative. Seductive. Steamy. Erotic. He had to go inside the air-conditioned house just to cool off from the images.

He consoled himself with the possibility that their first two meetings might have been aberrations. Boredom could play funny tricks on a man. The first thing that came along to relieve it might get exaggerated in importance.

Yes, indeed, that had to be it, he decided as he settled into a chair in his office with a book he'd been wanting to read for some time. A good, page-turning thriller was exactly what he needed tonight. That ought to get his juices flowing better than a leggy, sassy woman.

But the words swam in front of his eyes. His thoughts kept drifting to the enigmatic woman who presented such a placid, reserved facade. He'd enjoyed sparking confusion in those dark, mysterious eyes. He'd relished making a little color climb into her cheeks. Janet Runningbear wasn't nearly as serene around him as she wanted desperately for him to believe.

He also had the feeling, virtually confirmed by her earlier, that there were secrets to be discovered, hidden reasons behind her decision to relocate to Texas.

As a kid he'd been fascinated by stories of buried treasure. He'd spent endless hours searching for arrowheads left behind by Native Americans who'd roamed over the very land on which White Pines had been built. Somewhere in the house, probably in Cody's old room, there was a cigar box filled with such treasures.

If Janet Runningbear had secrets, he would discover them eventually. He'd make a point of it.

And then what? He wasn't the kind of man who courted a woman just for sport. He never had been. He'd tried to instill the same set of values in his sons, tried to teach them never to play games with women who didn't fully understand the rules.

Everything about Janet that he'd seen so far shouted that she was a woman deserving of respect, a single parent struggling to put a new life together for herself and her daughter. If he was only looking for diversion, would it be fair to accomplish it at the expense of a woman like that? It was the one question for which he had an unequivocal answer: no!

So, he resolved, he would tame his natural impatience and take his time with her, measuring his feelings as well as hers. It was the only just way to go.

But even as he reached that carefully thought-out decision, the part of him that leapt to impetuous, self-confident conclusions told him he was just delaying the inevitable. He'd made up his mind the minute he'd walked into her office that he wanted her and nothing—not his common sense, not her resistance—was going to stand in his way for long. "Where the devil have you been?" Mule asked in his raspy, cranky voice when Harlan finally got back into town on Saturday after four whole days of trying to keep Jenny Runningbear in line. "Ain't seen you since that gal stole your truck."

Mule's expression turned sly. "Word around town is that you've got her working out at White Pines."

Harlan tilted his chair back on two legs and sipped on the icy mug of beer Rosa had set in front of him the minute he sat down. "Is that what you're doing with your time these days, sitting around gossiping like an old woman?" he asked Mule.

"It's about all there is to do since you dropped out of our regular poker game to play nursemaid to that brat."

Harlan accepted the criticism without comment. Mule grumbled about everything from the weather to politics. His tart remarks about Harlan's perceived defection were pretty much in character and harmless.

Mule's watery hazel eyes narrowed. "I don't hear you arguing none."

"What would be the point? You think you know everything there is to know about the situation."

"Meaning, you think I don't, I suppose. Okay, so fill me in. Why'd you hire her?"

"Because she owes me a lot of money for repairs to my pickup," he said simply. "You ought to know. I had it towed to your garage."

"Ain't had time to take a look at it," Mule said.

"When are you planning to end this so-called vacation of yours?"

"Who says I am? I'm getting so I enjoy having nothing to do. Maybe I'll just retire for good."

Harlan nodded. "You're old enough, that's for sure. What are you now, eighty?"

Mule regarded him with obvious indignation. "Sixty-seven, which you know danged well."

"Of course," he said. "Must be that boredom ages a person, lets his mind go weak."

"There ain't a thing wrong with my mind."

"Then I'd think you'd be itching to tackle a job like that truck of mine."

"I'll get to it one of these days," Mule said. "When I'm of a mind to."

"If you don't plan on going back to work, maybe you ought to sell the garage. The town needs a good mechanic. Cody had to fix Janet Runningbear's air-conditioning the other night, because you're on this so-called extended vacation of yours."

"Bet he ruined it," Mule commented with derision. "Air-conditioning's tricky."

"It's been working ever since," Harlan said, deliberately setting out to goad the old coot into going back to the job he'd loved. "You know Cody has a way with mechanical things. He's probably better than you ever were and he's not even in the business. Maybe I'll have my truck towed out to White Pines and have him take a look at it."

Mule set his beer down with a thump. "I told you I'd get to it."

"When?"

Mule sighed. "First thing on Monday."

"Fair enough."

"Just don't start bugging me about when it'll be done. Decent work takes time and concentration."

Which meant it might take months before he saw that pickup again, Harlan decided. Still, he couldn't regret his decision to have the truck taken to Mule's garage, rather than someplace bigger or fancier in another town.

His friend had closed up shop almost three months ago for no reason Harlan had been able to discern. He'd been on this strike of sorts ever since. He wasn't likely to be happy again until he had his head poked under the hood of a car.

"Don't look now, but that brat is heading this way," Mule announced. "With her mama. Whoo-ee, she sure is a looker, isn't she?"

Harlan tried not to gape as Janet came into Rosa's wearing a vibrant red sundress that bared tanned shoulders and swung loosely around shapely calves. Her straight, shiny hair hung halfway down her back like a shimmering waterfall of black silk. He stood automatically at the sight of her.

"You again?" Jenny greeted him irritably. "This is my day off. I thought I'd get a break. Shouldn't you be mucking out stalls or something? I hope you're not planning to leave 'em untouched all weekend and expect me to clean up the mess on Monday."

He grinned. "It's nice to see you, too," he commented, and winked at her mother. "Even nicer to see you. Care to join us?"

Janet glanced at her daughter's sour expression, then back at him. "I'm not sure that's such a good idea. The company might ruin your appetite."

"I'll take my chances," Harlan said. "By the way, this is Mule Masters."

"The vacationing mechanic," Janet said, smiling at him.

"Not anymore," Mule grumbled, ignoring the hand she held out. Apparently he had more resistance than Harlan did to Janet's dazzling smile.

"He'll be back on the job on Monday," Harlan explained. "Hopefully his manners will improve by then, as well."

"When a car's as old as mine, it pays to know a good mechanic and I hear you're the best around," she said.

Harlan was impressed that she apparently had not taken offense at Mule's deliberate slight. Maybe she'd been able to judge for herself that it wasn't personal. Mule was just a cantankerous old man. Could be, too, that she'd just weighed his manners against her need for a decent mechanic and decided to ignore his grumpiness.

At her praise for his skill, Mule shot Harlan a triumphant look. "Cody couldn't be that danged good, after all, if she's still on the lookout for somebody who knows his business."

"Cody was just doing me a favor," she acknowledged.

"You get what you pay for," Mule noted in a dire tone as Janet and Jenny sat down in the chairs Harlan pulled out for them.

"As you can see, Jenny's not the only one at the table with an attitude," Harlan commented. "I've been putting up with Mule for years, partly because he keeps my cars running, but mostly because he loses regularly at poker."

"I can play poker," Jenny chimed in. "You guys play for money?"

"Is there any other way to play?" Mule retorted. "Don't play with girls, though."

"Why not?" Jenny demanded. "That sounds like a sexist policy to me. Either open your game to girls or I'll have Mama see that it's closed down."

Mule stared at her in open-mouthed astonishment. Harlan chuckled at the reaction. Jenny had been throwing him off stride the same way all week long.

"Don't play with girls," Mule repeated irritably.

Jenny pulled ten dollars out of her pocket and slapped it on the table. "My money's good."

Janet sighed. "Jenny, that's your allowance for the entire week. If you lose it playing poker, you're out of luck."

Jenny's chin rose a notch. "I don't intend to lose," she declared, leveling a challenging look straight at Mule. "You scared to play me?"

"Dang, but you've got a mouth on you," Mule commented. He glanced at Harlan. "Think we should bring her down a peg or two?"

"No," Harlan said succinctly, his gaze fixed on Janet as he tried to gauge her reaction. "She's already in debt up to her eyeballs."

"That's okay," Janet said. "If she wants to risk her allowance, it's up to her. Of course, I'm going to hate like crazy having to defend all three of you, if you get caught gambling illegally."

"Won't happen," Mule informed her. "Sheriff eats over at DiPasquali's every day. He's sweet on the daughter. Can't budge him out of there for anything less than murder."

Jenny grinned. "All right. Where are the cards?"

Harlan sighed and resigned himself to teaching Janet's rebellious daughter yet another lesson. He glanced into Janet's surprisingly amused eyes. "You in?" he asked her as Mule shuffled the worn deck he'd pulled from his pocket.

"No, I think I'll just sit here and enjoy the competition. I try real hard not to deliberately break the law, even when there's not much chance of getting caught."

"And here I had you pegged for a risk-taker," Harlan taunted.

Color flooded her cheeks. "Depends on the risk and the odds," she snapped right back. "Some are worth taking. Some aren't."

He winked at her. "I'll bet it's going to be downright fascinating figuring out which are which."

She swallowed hard and turned away. "Rosa," she called. "A beer, please."

That choked voice had Harlan smiling. "Throat dry?" he inquired.

"Parched," she admitted, meeting his gaze evenly. She ran her tongue over her lips. "Absolutely parched."

Maybe the gesture was innocent. Maybe not. Harlan doubted he'd ever know for sure. One thing was certain, she could best him at his own game anytime. The sight of that pink tongue delicately sliding over those lush red lips turned his blood hotter than asphalt on a Texas summer afternoon.

It also rattled his concentration so bad that he lost the first hand of poker to Jenny. So did Mule, which suggested that the thirteen-year-old just might know a little more about the game and gambling than he'd suspected.

He glanced up from his second hand to find Janet's gaze fixed on him. She leaned forward, which caused her sundress to dip a provocative inch or so, revealing just enough cleavage to make his own throat go dry.

"Mind if I take a look?" she inquired, placing her hand over his and turning his cards in her direction.

Harlan sucked in a breath as every muscle in his body tightened at that innocent, cool touch. He glanced into her eyes and changed his mind. There was nothing innocent about that touch. She knew exactly what she was doing. He pulled his cards out of her grasp.

"Trying to rattle me, darlin'?" he asked, amused by the blatant tactic.

Her eyes widened. "Why would I do that?"

"Maybe to protect Jenny's allowance," he suggested.

She grinned and shrugged, clearly not the least bit guilty at having been caught. "Hey, us gals have to stick together."

Mule stood, his whole demeanor radiating indignation. "A man would get shot for cheatin' at cards."

Harlan shook his head at his friend's idea of saloon-style justice. "Sit down, old man. I believe Ms. Running-bear will behave from now on out." He met her gaze. "Isn't that right?"

"I'll be innocent as a lamb," she promised. "Hands on the table. Eyes straight ahead. Lips locked."

"I can hardly wait to see how long that lasts," Harlan commented.

To her credit, she did exactly as she'd sworn she would. Unfortunately for him, she hadn't mentioned a thing about any part of anatomy below her fingertips. Just as he was about to bet, he felt a knee nudge his…and stay there. The heat that rose through him this time could have roasted marshmallows. Turned them to ashes, in fact.

He found that he enjoyed the sensation a little too much to tattle on her. He folded and left Jenny and Mule to battle for the pot. Mule took it with a full house to Jenny's two pairs. To his everlasting regret, Janet's knee retreated to a safe distance. It was by far the most intriguing poker game he'd ever played in. So far, it had cost him five bucks.

He considered the money an investment in his future with Janet. He was learning more about her with every hand of cards they played. He doubted she knew how much she was revealing about herself. Maybe she was a risk-taker. Maybe she wasn't. But she was definitely someone who liked to win.

She was also protective as a mother bear with a cub, where Jenny was concerned. And she had an absolutely fascinating, wild flirtatious streak. Just wondering how far she'd take it made his pulse scramble in a way that was downright disconcerting.

"I really think you ought to ante up," he told her as

Jenny shuffled the cards for the third hand. He glanced at her daughter. "Deal your mother in this round."

Janet's expression turned faintly uneasy. "Really, I don't think…"

"Humor me," he taunted. "I'll spot you the fifty cents for the pot." He tossed two quarters into the middle of the table.

Jenny paused, waiting for her mother's decision before dealing out the hand.

"Okay," Janet said eventually. "But I haven't had as much practice as Jenny."

Jenny's mouth gaped. "Mom!"

"Quiet, dear. Deal the cards."

Harlan chuckled at the exchange. He had the distinct impression now that everything Jenny knew about poker, she had learned from her mother. It was just one more facet to Janet Runningbear to intrigue him. Apparently she was a bit of a gambler, after all.

She scanned her cards with a practiced eye, tossed two back onto the table and waited for Jenny to replace them. Harlan drew three and wound up with two pairs, but most of his attention was on the woman seated next to him. Her face was an absolutely expressionless mask, a genuine poker face.

Mule bet fifty cents. Harlan met his bet. He wouldn't have dropped out of this hand if they'd been playing for a hundred times that amount.

"That's fifty cents to you, darlin'."

She nodded, not even glancing his way. "Your fifty and fifty more."

Jenny looked from her mother to Harlan and back again. "I'll fold," she said.

"I'm out," Mule concurred, tossing his cards onto the table in apparent disgust.

Janet turned an expectant look on Harlan that had his breath catching in his throat.

"Are you in?" she inquired in a lazy, seductive tone that had him conjuring up images that could have melted concrete.

"You'd better believe it, darlin'. Your fifty and I'll raise you a buck."

"My, my, you are confident," she said, turning to wink at Jenny. "Shall I stay, do you think?"

Jenny grinned. "You can't quit now, Mom. He'll think you're chicken."

"True. We can't have that, can we?" She reached over and plucked five dollars from Jenny's pile of winnings. "I'll repay you in a minute."

Harlan studied her expression before matching the bet. He couldn't tell a thing about whether or not she was bluffing. He dropped his money on the table. "Call."

She placed her first card on the table, an ace of clubs. Her second card was a seven of clubs. Her third, a five of clubs. The fourth was a two of clubs. "Now what do you suppose I have here?" she inquired, lifting her gaze to clash with his.

"Either another club or more audacity than anyone else in Texas," Harlan quipped.

She winked. "Want to go double or nothing on this last card?"

"That ain't the rules," Mule complained.

"Some rules are made to be broken," Harlan said, his gaze never leaving Janet's. "Not double or nothing. How about loser cooks dinner for the winner?"

The flash of uncertainty in her eyes told him she'd

just realized that she'd overplayed her hand. Still, she didn't back down.

"You sure that's what you want? You could just quit now," she said, clearly determined to brazen it out.

"Not on your life. Get that card on the table."

She sighed, an expression of resignation on her face as she dropped an ace of hearts on top of the other cards.

Harlan chuckled. "Darlin', you would have made an outstanding stripper," he teased. "You know a heck of a lot about drawing out the suspense."

"But you can beat a pair of aces, can't you?"

He showed her his two pairs, fours and eights. "Sure can. So, when's dinner?" he inquired as he gathered up the pot.

Jenny chuckled. "You still think you won, don't you? Wait till you try Mom's cooking!"

"Jenny," Janet protested. "How's tomorrow? I'm sure I can grill a hamburger or something that will be edible."

"That'll be a first," her daughter retorted. She glanced at Harlan. "You might want to bring along a roll of antacids. Mom's still trying to figure out how to cope with life without takeout."

"I'm sure anything your mother cooks will be just fine," Harlan said staunchly. "I'll be there about six."

Mule cackled. "Think I'll let the rescue squad know to be standing by just in case."

They could all joke all they wanted, Harlan thought as he tilted his chair onto its back legs and studied the trio. Even if Janet's food tasted like cinders, he had definitely come out of this a winner.

5

The kitchen was in shambles. Janet stood amid the collection of messy bowls, streaks of chocolate cake batter and spatters of frosting and despaired of ever getting a meal on the table by six o'clock.

"Why did you let me do that?" she asked Jenny, who was standing in the doorway gloating. "Why on earth did you let me make a bet like that?"

"You sounded like you were on a roll, Mom. How was I supposed to know you just had a piddly pair of aces?"

"Because you know what a competitor I am. I always get caught up in the moment, start bluffing and get carried away. You were doubling your allowance playing poker with me when you were eight for that very reason."

"I know," Jenny said, grinning. "If you'd gotten any more carried away yesterday, the man would be moving in with us."

"Hardly," Janet denied.

"Mom, it's true. He leveled those baby blues of his

on you and you perked up as if he'd showered you with diamonds."

Janet winced at the accuracy of the accusation. She had enjoyed the challenge and the blatant masculine approval she'd been able to stir with a little teasing. Harlan Adams was the kind of man who could make any woman lose sight of her independent streak.

"All women are a little susceptible to flattery and the attention of an attractive man," she said to defend herself. "It's not something to be taken seriously."

"You've got my jailer coming to dinner in twenty minutes and you think that's not serious," Jenny retorted.

"Would you stop calling him that?" she implored. "Mr. Adams did you a favor, young lady. And the truth is, you're having fun at White Pines, aren't you?"

"Oh, sure, I just love spending my summer vacation breaking my back mucking out that stinky old barn."

"You should have thought of that before you stole his truck," she admonished for what must have been the hundredth time.

"How was I supposed to know that pickup belonged to a man who'd never heard of child labor laws? You probably ought to investigate him or something. He probably has little kids all over that ranch of his, working their butts off." She shot a sly look at Janet. "Little Native American kids, Mom."

Janet chuckled at the blatant attempt to try to push her buttons. "Forget it, Jenny. You can't rile me up that way. There is absolutely no evidence that anything like that is going on at White Pines."

"Isn't that why we're here, though? Aren't you supposed to be righting old wrongs, looking out for the descendents of the Comanches who rightfully belong on that land that Mr. Adams's ancestors stole? Jeez, Mom, we're in town for less than a month and you're practically in bed with the enemy."

"I am not in bed with anybody," Janet said. "Stop with that kind of talk and set the table."

"Okay, but I say you're selling out."

"And I say you have a smart mouth. I'd better not hear any of that kind of talk while Mr. Adams is here."

Jenny nodded, her expression knowing. "I get it. You don't want to tip him off too soon that his days on that land are numbered, right? You'll finish your research, then *bam,* file the papers and boot him off. That's good. I like it. Boy, will he be surprised when he finds out I belong at White Pines more than he does. Maybe I'll even make *him* clean the barn."

Janet was beginning to regret ever having told Jenny how the land that Lone Wolf's father had cherished had been taken over by white ranchers, while the Comanches were forced into smaller and smaller areas and eventually out of Texas altogether.

"Sweetie, there is no evidence that White Pines itself belonged to Lone Wolf's father," she explained. "True, he roamed all over west Texas and the Comanches believed that the land of the Comancheria was theirs, but it's not as if it was ever deeded to them and recorded as theirs."

"But that's just a technicality, right?" Jenny argued. "You're going to prove that possession was nine-tenths of the law stuff and that the government never had any right to force them out, right?"

Janet had to admit it was a dream she had had, a fantasy inspired by listening to Lone Wolf spin his sad tales. She had vowed at his grave, when she was younger than Jenny was now, that she would try to rectify what had happened to their ancestors.

When her marriage had failed, she'd been drawn to Texas at least in part to see if there was any way at all to fulfill that old promise. Now, while it seemed likely there was much she could do to assist the scattered Native Americans still living in Texas, reality suggested there was little chance she could return their old lands to them. While principle dictated the claims of the tribe were valid, individually their legal rights were murky at best.

"Jenny, you know that's what I want to do, but it's complicated. I can't just waltz into the courthouse and file a few briefs and expect a hundred years of wrongs to be righted. The system doesn't work that way."

"The system stinks," Jenny retorted, thumping the plates onto the table. "And just remember, Mom, Mr. Adams is part of that system."

Janet sighed. It wasn't something she was likely to forget. If the twinkle in his eyes or the fire stirred by a casual touch distracted her, she had only to gaze around at his land to remember what had brought her to Texas.

Every acre of raw beauty reminded her of Lone Wolf's broken father, forced to live as a farmer in an unfamiliar state when tradition and instinct made him a hunter.

In the abstract, it had been easy to hate the Texans who had made that happen. Now, faced with a man like Harlan Adams, who had shown her nothing but kindness, compassion and a hint of desire, it was awfully hard to think of him—or even his faceless ancestors—as the enemy.

So, what did she consider him to be? she wondered as she checked the cake she had baking. Her mother, a full-blooded Comanche, had barely survived a disastrous marriage to a white man. Janet was only half Comanche and her own marriage to a white man had been only minimally better. She'd convinced herself that returning to Texas to learn more about her Comanche heritage was the secret to happiness.

Was Jenny right? Was she selling out already by allowing Harlan Adams to assume such a significant role in their lives? It was not as if she'd had much choice, she consoled herself. Jenny had gotten their lives entwined from the moment she'd impulsively stolen that truck of his.

As for the way she responded to Harlan's warm glances, that was just hormones talking. Her good sense could overrule that anytime she chose—or so she prayed.

She reached into the oven to remove the cake. The pot holder slipped. Her thumb landed squarely on the pan.

"Damn," she muttered as the round pan clattered to the floor. A crack the size of the Grand Canyon appeared down the middle of the cake. Jenny appeared just in time to stare in dismay at the mess.

"Jeez, Mom, that cake was about the only thing this meal had going for it."

"Don't remind me," she muttered, sucking on her injured thumb. "I'll fill it in with frosting, so it'll look okay. We'll cut pieces from the outside edges. Harlan will never know."

"I don't know. I think after he gets a taste of that limp spaghetti and the wilted salad, he'll be expecting it."

Janet scowled at her daughter. "You're no help. A little encouragement would be welcomed about now."

"You need more than encouragement to bail you out," Jenny declared derisively. "How about a quick trip to DiPasquali's? I could be back before he gets here. He'll never know you didn't prepare every bite yourself."

Janet was sorely tempted to do just that. For some reason that probably didn't bear too close a scrutiny, she really had wanted this meal to go well. She surveyed the mess in the kitchen, then glanced at the clock. He was due in five minutes.

"There's no time," she said, resigned to serving a meal barely fit for human consumption.

"You call. I'll run," Jenny repeated. "If he's here when I get back, I'll slip in through the kitchen. Just keep him out of here."

Janet reached for her purse and pulled out a twenty. "Go," she said. A survey of the disaster she'd made of the kitchen had her adding, "And don't worry about coming in through the kitchen. I wouldn't let Harlan in here if it were burning down and he were the volunteer fireman."

When Jenny was gone and she'd placed the desperation call to Gina DiPasquali, she left the kitchen and closed the door behind her. If there'd been a lock, she would have turned the key.

At least the dining room looked presentable. Jenny had even picked flowers for the center of the table and had put out the good china and silver. For all of her grumbling about Harlan Adams, it appeared she wanted to impress him, as well. Janet was more pleased about that than she cared to admit.

She was just checking her makeup in the hall mirror when the doorbell rang. Precisely at six o'clock, she noted, checking her watch. She wondered if that was an indication of polite promptness or, perhaps, just a little eagerness. Her heart thumped unsteadily at the possibility that it might be the latter.

When she opened the door, she could barely glimpse Harlan through the huge bouquet of flowers in his arms.

"Did you buy out the florist's entire stock?" she asked, taking them from him.

He shrugged, looking faintly embarrassed. "It was late Saturday. She said it would all spoil by Monday anyway, so she gave me a deal," he said, confirming what she'd meant as a facetious comment.

"I see."

"I brought wine and candy, too. I wasn't sure which you'd prefer."

"The flowers would have been plenty," she assured him, wondering how the devil she was going to keep him out of the kitchen if she took them in there to put them in vases.

He grinned. "A little over the top, huh?"

"But sweet," she assured him.

"It's been a long time since I've gone calling on a lady."

She could tell. He looked about as at ease as a man making his first trip to a lingerie department. Not even his starched white shirt, expensive black trousers and snakeskin boots could combat the impression made by his anxious expression.

"You seem to forget that this isn't exactly a date," she said to reassure him. "You won dinner fair and square on a bet."

She waved him toward a chair. "Have a seat and I'll get these in water. What can I bring you to drink when I come back? Wine? A beer? Iced tea?"

"Iced tea sounds good. Why don't we sit on the porch? It's a nice night. Or is dinner just about ready?"

"No, dinner will be a while," she said in what had to be the understatement of the decade. However, sitting on the porch was out of the question. He was bound to spot Jenny returning from DiPasquali's. She grasped desperately for an alternative.

"Actually, I hate to do this to you, but my bathroom faucet has been leaking." Even though the tactic grated, she used her most helpless expression on him. "I don't know the first thing about changing a washer. Could you take a look at it?"

He latched onto the request as if she'd thrown him a lifeline. "Just show me the way."

She led him down the narrow hallway to the old-fashioned bathroom, which, thankfully, Jenny had straightened up after her shower. "I bought washers and there are some tools there," she said, pointing.

"I'll have this fixed in no time," he promised, already loosening his collar and rolling up his sleeves. "By the way, it's nice to walk into a house and smell dinner cooking. There's nothing like the scent of chocolate to make a man's mouth water." He glanced at her and winked. "Unless it's that sexy perfume you're wearing."

"I'm not sure it's perfume you're smelling," she said. "It's probably all these flowers."

He shook his head. "They were in the car with me all the way into town. That's not it. I'd say you're wearing something light with just a hint of spice. It's the kind of thing that could drive a man wild."

Janet could feel herself blushing. "Thanks. If you'll excuse me, I'll get these into water."

In the kitchen she put the flowers down on the only clear surface, the top of the stove, and drew in a deep breath. She hadn't realized what a sucker she was for charm. Maybe it was just the sweetly tentative way in which it was delivered.

She didn't doubt for an instant that Harlan Adams had always been a flirt, but she was also very aware that he was out of practice delivering compliments with all sorts of subtle innuendo behind them. Teasing a woman just to make her feel good was one thing. It was another to be experimenting with dating after so many years of marriage. It made what they were doing here tonight seem riskier and more significant for both of them.

She sighed and forced her attention to the flowers. It took three large vases to handle all of them. She scattered the arrangements around the living room, poured Harlan's iced tea, then traipsed back to the bathroom where she'd left him.

"I brought your tea," she said, keeping one ear attuned to any sounds from the kitchen that might indicate that Jenny had returned. "How's it going?"

"The washer's replaced," he said, his voice muffled. He had his head poked into the vanity under the sink. "Thought I'd check to make sure all the joints were sealed under here while I was at it."

He slid out and grinned at her. "No leaks under there."

She took one look at the streaks of grime on his face and shirt and winced. "Harlan, you're a mess. I'm sorry. I should never have asked you to do this for me, especially when you were all dressed up."

"Stop fussing. A little dirt never hurt anybody. I'll wash up."

"But your shirt…" she protested.

"It's not a problem," he insisted. He shot her a wicked grin. "Unless, of course, you object to a man coming to the dinner table looking like this. I could strip down and let you wash the shirt here and now."

He seemed a little too eager for her to grab at that solution. "Never mind," she assured him. "I'm the one responsible. I can hardly complain, can I?"

Just then she heard the kitchen door slam. She plastered what she hoped was an innocent expression on her face. "Oh, good, that must be Jenny. She's been out for a bit. Now that she's back, I'll get dinner on the table. Go on out to the porch after you've washed up, why don't you? Relax for a minute. I'll call you when everything's on the table."

"I could help," he offered.

"No, indeed. You've done more than enough. Besides, you won the bet. I can't have you helping."

She took off, trying to ignore the fact that there was something a little too knowing about his expression. He couldn't possibly have guessed what she'd done, could he? No, of course not. As long he remained far away from that kitchen, there was no way he could figure out that she hadn't prepared every dish herself.

Jenny was pulling aluminum pans of food out of paper bags when Janet got back to the kitchen.

"Gina said to warm the lasagna again for a few minutes before you serve it. I've already turned the oven on low. The salad's in that package. She put the dressing on the side, so you could toss it in your bowl." She reached into another bag and pulled out a loaf of Italian bread wrapped in foil. "Garlic bread. It goes in the oven, too."

Janet rolled her eyes at Jenny's instructions. "I could have figured that much out for myself."

"Who would guess?" Jenny quipped. "So how'd you keep Mr. Adams out of here?"

"I had him fixing the leak in the bathroom."

Jenny grinned. "Good for you. It's about time he sees what it's like to work for free."

"I don't think he thought of it quite that way. He was doing me a favor." She pointed to the bowl of frosting. "The cake should be cool enough by now. You ice it while I toss the salad."

Twenty minutes later they were seated in the dining room. Janet's heart was in her throat as Harlan took his first bite of salad. Would he be able to tell she hadn't prepared it? It was only lettuce, tomatoes and a few radishes. Surely he wouldn't suspect that even that much had been beyond her skill.

"Delicious," he said. "Jenny, I think you sold your mother short when you said she couldn't cook."

Janet shot a warning look at her daughter. Jenny shrugged.

"It's pretty hard to ruin a bunch of lettuce and some tomatoes," she retorted, avoiding Janet's gaze.

The lasagna was an equally big hit. "Can't think when I've had any better," Harlan enthused. "It's every bit as good as Gina DiPasquali's."

Janet groaned and covered her face. There wasn't a doubt in her mind that the jig was up. "You know, don't you?"

"Know what?" Harlan replied, trying to sound innocent and failing miserably.

"That Jenny picked up the salad, bread and lasagna from DiPasquali's."

He winked at Jenny. "Did she now?"

"How did you know?" Janet demanded.

"Saw her running in the front door of the restaurant as I drove through town," he finally admitted as Jenny chuckled.

Janet glared at the pair of them. "And you let me wriggle on the hook like a big old fish. Did you enjoy watching me squirm trying to keep you away from the front of the house till she got back?"

He nodded. "Sure did." He reached across the table and patted her hand consolingly. "That's okay, darlin'. I appreciate you going to all that trouble to impress me."

Janet moaned. "I did not do it to impress you," she declared adamantly.

"She did it to keep you from getting food poisoning," Jenny chimed in. "You should see—"

"That's enough, Jenny," Janet said sharply. She was determined to get through the rest of the evening with some dignity intact. If she wasn't careful, Jenny would be offering Harlan a tour of the kitchen.

"That chocolate cake sure does smell good," he said. "I know Gina didn't stop by and bake that."

"It's got a great big crack right down the middle," Jenny revealed. "I had to patch it together with icing."

Janet scowled at her. "Thank you for sharing that," she grumbled.

Harlan winked at her this time. "Don't fret, darlin'. With chocolate cake, it's taste, not looks, that count."

"I wouldn't hold your breath on that score, either," Jenny warned. "She probably left out something important."

If she could have, Janet would have sent Jenny to her room on the spot before she made any more embarrassing revelations. Unfortunately, she could see the injustice of such an act. She was just going to have to survive this debacle and hope that Harlan wasn't one to gossip. Fortunately, she was in town to practice law, not to do catering.

As it turned out, the cake was not only edible, but actually pretty good. At least Harlan ate two slices of it, his amused gaze fixed on her the whole time. He seemed especially fond of the inch-thick icing in the middle.

The minute dinner was over he shooed Jenny off by declaring that he would help clean up. Jenny didn't have to be asked twice. She was gone before Janet could protest.

"You cannot walk into that kitchen," she said adamantly, though short of stretching out her arms and trying to bar the doorway, she didn't know what she could do to stop him.

He ignored her, picked up an armload of dishes and headed across the dining room. "The sooner we get things squared away in there, the sooner you and I can sit on that front porch and enjoy the breeze."

To his credit, he didn't even blink as he walked into the midst of the mess she'd created trying to make dinner. Maybe he'd served time on KP in the military at some point, she decided as she watched the ease with which he set things right.

"Come here," he commanded when he'd washed the last dish and wiped down the countertops.

"I don't think so," she said, holding up the last plate she was drying as if to ward him off.

He grinned, shrugged and came to her. Before she realized his intentions, he slid his arms around her waist and held her in a loose embrace. "Thank you," he said softly, his breath fanning intimately across her cheek.

"For what?" she asked shakily. Her breath snagged in her throat as she met his gaze.

"For going to so much trouble."

"I told you—"

He reached up and brushed a strand of hair away from her eyes. "I know what you told me, but the fact is you could have served me whatever that was you cooked in the first place and tried to scare me off for good. Instead, you went to a lot of trouble that wasn't necessary. I don't scare that easily."

She sighed. "That's what I'm afraid of."

He studied her intently. The spark of mischief in his eyes raised goose bumps.

"You gonna fall apart if I kiss you?" he inquired.

An unwilling smile tugged at her lips. "I might."

He nodded. "I think I'll risk it anyway," he said softly.

He lowered his head until his lips were a tantalizing hairbreadth above hers. She trembled as she waited for him to close that infinitesimal distance. When, at last, their mouths met, she could have sworn fireworks exploded. She'd been expecting a kiss that was gentle and tentative. Instead, he plundered, claiming her mouth as surely as his ancestors had claimed Comanche land.

After the first startled instant, when she couldn't have moved if her life depended on it, Janet slid her hands from his shoulders into his thick hair, holding him, encouraging him to continue the assault that had her senses vibrantly, thrillingly alive for perhaps the first time ever. Nothing she had shared with her ex-husband compared to the consuming, white-hot fire raging through her just from Harlan Adams's incomparable kiss.

She willed it to go on forever, imagining all of the wicked places it could take her. But just as she was indulging in sensations so sweet her heart ached for them to continue, she heard a startled gasp behind her.

"Mom, how could you?" Jenny protested with all of the hurt and confusion a thirteen-year-old could experience.

The kitchen door rattled on its hinges as Jenny left far more noisily than she had entered.

"I'll go after her," Harlan offered, but Janet stilled him.

"No, it's up to me. You'd better leave, though. She won't want to see you again tonight and this could take a while."

He nodded, reluctance clearly written all over his face. "If you're sure."

"I am. I'll handle it."

"You'll be at White Pines in the morning, then?"

"That might be difficult," Janet said. "She might not want to be there after this."

"A deal's a deal," he reminded her, his expression intractable.

She saw then, what she should have recognized before. Harlan Adams had a will of iron when it came to the things he wanted. What worried her was that she'd just had unmistakable evidence that what he wanted was her.

6

Harlan was up before dawn the morning following his dinner with Janet and Jenny. By six he was pacing the front porch from end to end, wondering if they would show up and if they did, what kind of reception he might get.

He'd cursed himself a dozen different ways on the drive home the night before. As much as he'd been aching to kiss Janet, he never should have taken a chance on doing it where Jenny could walk in on them. Even a fool would have been smarter than that.

Now, not only had he put his relationship with the intriguing Janet Runningbear at risk, but it seemed likely he'd spoiled the fragile rapport he'd been building with her daughter.

When he finally heard the sound of an engine in the distance, his spirits soared, then crashed just as quickly when he saw that it was Cody's red pickup barreling down the lane.

Just what he needed. He doubted there was a chance in hell he could keep his perceptive son from guessing what was on his mind. And if Cody picked up on his mood, he'd be offering unsolicited advice to the love-lorn and enjoying every minute of it.

"Aren't you supposed to be up north today, checking those fence lines?" Harlan grumbled as Cody approached. "You're getting a mighty late start."

Cody eyed him warily. "You roll out on the wrong side of the bed, Daddy?"

"No, it's just that we could lose a lot of the herd if that fence doesn't get taken care of. I shouldn't have to be telling you a thing like that."

"I'm aware of what's at stake," Cody retorted as carefully as if he'd unwittingly walked into a mine field. "Which is why I sent Mac and Luis up there first thing yesterday morning. I didn't want to wait for today."

"Oh," Harlan said, and fell silent. It took everything in him, but he kept his gaze averted from the lane.

"How's Melissa?" he asked eventually since his son didn't seem inclined to venture any further conversation. He couldn't say he blamed him, given the reception he'd gotten so far.

"Fine."

"And Sharon Lynn and the baby?"

"Fine. Just about the same as when you saw them in church yesterday morning."

Harlan shrugged. "Never can tell with kids, though."

"True," Cody said, then suddenly chuckled.

Harlan scowled at him. "What's so blasted amusing?"

"You," Cody said. "What's the matter? Haven't they shown up yet?"

"Who?"

"The tax collectors," Cody retorted with heavy sarcasm. He shook his head. "You are so pitiful. I'm talking about Janet and Jenny, of course."

"No, they're not here yet."

Eyes sparkling with pure mischief, Cody added, "Heard you had quite a poker game with them on Saturday."

So the cat was out of the bag, Harlan thought, stifling a desire to groan. "I suppose Mule couldn't wait to report every detail," he said sourly, resigning himself to as much taunting as Cody cared to mete out.

"Actually, I heard about it from Maritza, who heard it from her cousin Rosa, who witnessed it all right there in her very own café." He grinned. "And just so you know, Luke's housekeeper also got the word from cousin Rosa, which means your oldest son knows every detail by now, too. He couldn't wait to check out the story with me."

"Damn, I knew it was a mistake helping that whole darn family to settle in Los Piños," he muttered, regretting the day he'd first hired Consuela, who was now working for Luke, and subsequently her cousin Maritza, his present housekeeper. He'd even cosigned the loan for Rosa's damned café. So much for loyalty. They apparently hadn't been able to wait to blab his business all over hell and gone. "Don't they have anything better to do than gossip?"

"Guess not," Cody said. "Especially not when the news is so fascinating. So, how was dinner with the loser?"

With the grapevine already abuzz anyway, Harlan didn't bother trying to contain a grin at the memory of the meal that Jenny had snuck in from DiPasquali's.

"Fascinating," he attested.

"So why the worried look when I drove up?"

He weighed telling his son the truth or at least part of it. Maybe if he swore him to secrecy with a promise of eternal damnation if he broke his vow, he could chance it. If he didn't talk about what had happened, he'd go plumb stir-crazy.

"This doesn't get repeated, okay? Luke already knows too much. I don't want him and Jordan hovering around here, trying to decide if I'm losing my mind."

"It may not be Luke and Jordan you need to worry about," Cody drawled. "If Jessie and Kelly get wind of it, they'll get matchmaking fever the likes of which west Texas has never seen."

"All the more reason for you to keep your trap shut," Harlan said, shuddering at the prospect of all that meddling. "Can you do it?"

Eyes dancing with renewed mischief, Cody solemnly crossed his heart. "Not a word. I swear it. What happened last night?"

"No guffawing, okay?"

"I wouldn't dream of it."

Harlan was doubtful about that, but he decided to chance it. "Okay, let's just say the evening ended on a more awkward note than I might have preferred."

Cody's mouth gaped. "You made a pass at her?"

He made it sound like Harlan was sixteen and had been trying to get into the drawers of the preacher's daughter. "It wasn't a pass, dammit. It was a kiss."

"Well, I'll be damned. I bet Luke you wouldn't have the guts to try that for at least another month."

Harlan groaned. "I knew this was a mistake. I knew it." He scowled fiercely. "You blab one word of this and I'll hang your hide from the oak tree out back just to set an example for your brothers."

Unfortunately, Cody didn't exactly seem to be intimidated. He chuckled even as he said, "Not a word. I already promised. Besides, do you think I want Luke to know I lost the bet? So what was so awkward?"

"Jenny walked in."

"Uh-oh."

"Uh-oh is right. She wasn't happy."

"She's a kid. She'll get over it. Surely her mom has been on dates before."

"Maybe. Maybe not. But it took me most of last week to get a civil tongue in that girl's head. Now I've gone and lost whatever ground I gained."

"What was Janet's reaction to all this?"

"Naturally she was upset."

"With you or Jenny?"

"I'm the supposedly responsible adult. I'm the one who caused the problem."

"Not if she kissed you back," Cody corrected. "Did she?"

Harlan couldn't help smiling at the memory. "She did, indeed."

"Then you'll find a way to work it out," Cody predicted, apparently satisfied that he'd completed his role as counselor. "I'm going inside for breakfast. All this advice has left me famished."

"You're always famished," Harlan observed. "Doesn't Melissa ever feed you?"

"Sure, but that was two hours ago," he said as he opened the front door. Just as he was about to step inside, he looked back. "Hey, Daddy?"

Harlan's gaze was already riveted on the lane again. "Hmm?"

"Remember what you used to tell us when we were dating?"

His head snapped around. "What?"

"It's not polite to kiss and tell," Cody taunted.

If he'd had something available, he would have thrown it at him. "Then see that you don't repeat my mistake," he warned emphatically. "There will be hell to pay for both of us, if you do."

By eight o'clock Harlan had just about accepted the fact that Janet and Jenny wouldn't be coming. He decided to let it pass for today, but if they didn't show up tomorrow, he vowed to have a little chat with Jenny about paying off debts and living up to obligations. If he was more concerned about his own selfish interests, well, that was something she wouldn't have to know.

He was in the barn saddling up his favorite stallion when he glanced up to see Jenny standing hesitantly in the doorway. Surprise kept him speechless, even as relief spread through him. When he could keep his tone matter-of-fact, he said, "A little late, aren't you?"

"Mother dropped me off on the highway. I had to walk the rest of the way up the lane."

"I see. Whose idea was that?"

Jenny's chin rose a belligerent notch. "Mine."

He would have guessed as much. It was probably her way of keeping him and her mother apart. The fire in her eyes dared him to make anything of it. He clamped a lid on his desire to challenge her. At least she was here. He considered that a good sign.

"The lane's pretty long," he offered blandly. "Must be close to two miles. You thirsty?"

"A little," she admitted, scuffing her sneaker in the dirt and avoiding his gaze.

"Then, run on in the house and have Maritza give you something cool to drink."

She didn't dash off as he'd anticipated she would.

"Are you going riding?" she asked.

He nodded. "I was about to."

"Can I come?"

"Of course."

"You'll wait?"

"I'll wait," he agreed, trying to remain as nonchalant as she was when he was filled with questions about what had happened after he'd left last night. Her odd mood wasn't telling him much, but at least she didn't appear to be holding that kiss against him. She simply appeared determined to stave off a repeat.

"I'll hurry," she promised, and took off.

He stared after her, confusion teeming inside. Would he ever figure out the workings of that girl's mind?

Jenny was polite, but quiet for the rest of the day. She did everything he asked of her, if not eagerly, at least without complaint. By the end of the day he was longing for a little of the more familiar sass.

"Is your mama picking you up at the house or are you meeting her out by the highway?" he inquired eventually.

"At the highway," she said, shooting a belligerent look at him that confirmed his earlier opinion that this was her way of keeping him and Janet separated.

"You'd better get going then. It'll take you a while to get out there. The humidity's up. Maybe you'd better borrow a baseball cap and get a thermos of water to take along," he said, deliberately emphasizing that the walk would seem even hotter and longer than it had in the cooler morning air.

He let that sink in for a minute, then added casually, "Or I could drive you out."

He could tell from her expression that she was struggling with the offer, weighing the advantages of the quick, cool ride with the disadvantages of having him possibly bump into her mother.

"I suppose that would be okay," she conceded grudgingly. "I don't want to get heatstroke."

"Good thinking," he said. He glanced at his watch. "Should we leave now? It's almost five."

She nodded and followed him to his car, a luxury model he kept in the garage. Her mouth dropped open when she saw it. "How come you drove that pickup, when you had this?"

"It was more practical. I'm always hauling stuff for the ranch."

"Oh." She touched the leather interior almost reverently. "I like this. It's really soft. I'm going to have a car just like this someday."

"I'll bet you will," he agreed. "Are you planning to earn it or steal it?"

"Hey, that's not fair," she protested, frowning. "I'm really not a thief."

"You couldn't prove that by me."

She grimaced. "It's not like I have a criminal record or something. What happened was just like an impulse or something. The truck was there. I could see the keys inside. I took it. I figured it served you right for leaving the keys inside."

He nodded, hiding a grin. It was a bad habit he and all of his sons had. Half of Los Piños was aware of their reckless pattern. This was the first time, though, that anyone had taken advantage of them.

"I suppose it did," he admitted.

She shot a look at him. "Does that mean I'm off the hook?"

"Not on your life. Even if I'd gone off and left it sitting wide open with the engine running, it wouldn't give you the right to take what's not yours."

"Oh." She looked more resigned that surprised.

At the end of the lane she started to climb out of the car. "It's awful hot out there," Harlan observed. "Not much shade, either. Why don't I wait? You can sit in the air-conditioning."

She promptly shook her head. "I'll be okay. Mom ought to be here any minute."

"What if she got held up?"

"By what? A traffic jam?" she asked sarcastically.

"Maybe a client," Harlan said.

"Yeah, right."

"You never know."

"Oh, for Pete's sake, if you want to wait, wait." She closed the door, settled back in the seat and folded her arms around her middle, her gaze directed out the passenger window toward town.

"You want to talk about it?" he asked eventually.

"About what?"

"What you saw last night?"

"No," she said succinctly.

Harlan weighed everything he knew about raising kids and decided once more to let it pass for now. Let Janet hash it out with her first. If they couldn't settle it, then he'd step in and try to clarify what that kiss had been about…assuming he had it figured out by then.

"There she is," Jenny announced, flinging open the car door. "See you."

Her quick flight precluded any opportunity for him to exchange so much as a word with Janet. He rolled down his window and managed a wave that was returned half-heartedly before the car backed onto the highway and disappeared from view as quickly as it had come.

He chafed at letting a thirteen-year-old interfere in his life. He figured Janet ought to be mad as hell about it, too, but she seemed to have accepted Jenny's right to stand squarely between her and him.

For the rest of the week he only managed to eke out bits and pieces of information about Janet from her sullen, tight-lipped daughter. He couldn't seem to break the pattern that had been established on Monday. Janet never came any closer than the end of the lane. Her aloof behavior left him rattled and irritable.

He couldn't recall the last time he'd been so fascinated by a woman. It must have been when he'd first met Mary, though. Not once in all the years since then had he ever strayed in thought or deed.

Mary had been a good wife, devoted to a fault. Sometimes he'd almost regretted the way she'd doted on him to the exclusion of their sons. He'd never doubted her love for Luke, Erik, Jordan and Cody, but she'd focused all of her attention on him. He'd felt cherished and, in return, he had made her the center of his life, as well.

Ever since her death, there had been this huge, empty space inside him. And, despite the attempts of his sons to fill the endless hours of the day, he'd been lonely. He hadn't really recognized that until he'd suddenly felt so alive the minute he'd walked into Janet Runningbear's office after that heart-in-his-throat spectacle of her daughter crashing his pickup into a tree. He wasn't going to give up the feeling she stirred in him without a fight.

By Friday he was at his wit's end. He figured the only way to get back on speaking terms with Janet was to get her clear up to the house. And the only way to do that was to see to it Jenny wasn't waiting at the end of that lane for her.

On Friday morning he enlisted Cody's help. "How about taking Jenny with you this afternoon? It's about time she got a real look at the workings of this place."

If Cody guessed his father's intentions, he didn't let on. "I won't be back until dark," he warned.

"That's okay."

"Won't Janet be expecting to pick her up at five as usual?"

"I'll keep Janet entertained."

Cody grinned. "If you say so. I'll come back for Jenny at lunchtime."

"Thanks, son."

"Don't mention it."

Jenny rode off with Cody just after noon, looking as besotted as if she'd just been granted a date with her favorite movie star. Harlan spent the next few hours catching up on paperwork in his office, then dressed for his meeting with Janet as eagerly as if they were going out on a date. His sons would have laughed their fool heads off if they'd seen him debating what to wear, only to end up in a pin-striped dress shirt with the sleeves rolled up, jeans and his best boots. A pile of discards worse than any Mary had ever left strewn around covered the king-size bed.

Promptly at five he took a pitcher of iced tea, two tall glasses, a bowl of Maritza's *pico de gallo* and some tortilla chips onto the porch. Leaning back in a rocker, his boots propped on the porch railing, he settled back to wait. He wondered how long it would be before Janet guessed that he wasn't bringing Jenny to the end of the lane and resigned herself to driving to the house to pick her up. He figured fifteen minutes.

He was off by five. At ten minutes past five she came flying up the lane, sending up a cloud of dust. She leapt out of the car, her expression half frantic.

"Where's Jenny? Has something happened to her?"

"She's fine," he soothed. "She's off helping Cody this afternoon. She won't be back for a while yet. Come on up and join me."

Janet regarded the tea and tortilla chips suspiciously. "What's all that?"

"Just a little something to tide us over while we wait. Figured you might be thirsty and hungry this time of day."

"Exactly when are you expecting them back?"

"Seven or so."

She stared at him incredulously. "Seven? Why didn't you tell me?"

"I just did," he said, holding out the glass of tea.

Janet ignored it. Hands on hips, she stared him down, practically quivering with indignation. "What kind of game are you playing, Harlan Adams?"

"I could ask you the same question. You've spent the past five days avoiding me. Whose idea was that? Yours or Jenny's?"

She sighed and sank down onto the top step. She finally accepted the glass of tea and took a long swallow. "A little of both, I suppose."

"Shouldn't you have told me?" he said, mimicking her tone.

"I just did," she said, and chuckled. "I'm sorry."

"No need to be sorry. For a pair of grown-ups we are pretty pathetic, aren't we? Seems to me we should be past resorting to games or letting a teenager rule the way we live our lives."

"We should be," Janet concurred. "It's my fault. I should have insisted on bringing Jenny all the way to the house on Monday, but she was still so upset I gave in and dropped her at the end of the lane. After that, it became a pattern, I suppose. I couldn't seem to break it."

"Don't go taking all the blame. I'm the one who put you in an awkward position in the first place." He looked her over, admiring the creamy silk blouse she wore with a pair of tan linen slacks and a few pieces of expensive gold jewelry. She was all class, there was no mistake about that. "You haven't dated much since the divorce, have you?"

"Not at all."

"So Jenny's still very protective. Is she hoping you'll get back together with her father?"

"No, she knows better than that. He doesn't have time for either one of us anymore. I think that's really the problem. She needs all of my attention right now."

Her expression turned speculative. "It may be that she needs all of yours, too. You're providing a father figure for her. Maybe she's not ready to share you."

"But what do you need?" he inquired softly. "Do you need a man in your life?"

She shook her head. "It's not in my plans right now."

He thought of his sons and how hard they'd fought falling in love. In the end, when the right woman came along they hadn't had a choice, any more than he had when he and Mary had met.

"I wasn't aware you could plan for a thing like that," he said.

"You can certainly avoid putting yourself at risk," she countered.

"Is that what you've been doing since you got to Texas, avoiding risks?"

She nodded.

"Must have been a lousy plan, since we met anyway," he observed, grinning. "Or do you suppose fate just had something else in mind?"

"I don't know what to think," she admitted, then gazed at him imploringly. "Harlan, this can't go any further than it already has."

The wistfulness in her voice contradicted the statement and gave him hope. "I think we both know that's not so," he said. "But I'm willing to slow down and take things nice and easy, if that'll give you some peace of mind."

"Why is it that peace of mind is the last thing I feel around you?" she asked plaintively.

He winked at her. "Darlin', I think that's exactly what we're going to find out. Now, why don't you and Jenny stick around for dinner? Let's see if we can't get things on an even keel again."

Janet protested, but she didn't put much *oomph* in it. After seeing her resort to takeout the Sunday before, he could see why. Any meal she didn't have to prepare herself must have seemed like a godsend. Just like any meal he didn't have to eat alone these days was a genuine pleasure for him.

If he had his way about it, there were going to be a whole lot more evenings starting off just like this one.

7

Janet couldn't quite decide whether or not to be irritated at Harlan's high-handedness in sending Jenny off to work with Cody. She knew he had done it just so he could end the stalemate she had started following that devastating kiss.

Jenny's shocked reaction had been partly responsible for her retreat, of course. But it was her own response that had truly shaken her. She wasn't sure she was ready to deal with a man as strong-willed and compelling as Harlan Adams, a man who made her heart pound and her blood sizzle with lust and temper in equal measure. She resented the fact that he had forced her into confronting the issue by facing him again.

Still, once dinner was on the table, her exasperation dwindled at an astonishing rate. Apparently she could be bought for a decent meal she didn't have to cook herself. Tender chicken-fried steak, mashed potatoes and gravy, a salad, vegetables—it was heaven.

Jenny wasn't nearly so easily won over. She sat at the dining room table in stubborn silence, glaring from Janet to Harlan and back again. Apparently she had belatedly guessed that the price of her afternoon with Cody was this unwanted reunion. By the end of the meal Janet's nerves were raw from the tension in the room.

"I think we should go," she said the minute they'd finished dessert. The housekeeper had served a chocolate silk pie that had almost inspired Janet to ask for the recipe until she'd reminded herself what a disaster she'd make of it. "I know eating and running is impolite, but we have things we should be doing."

Harlan regarded her with undisguised amusement. "Such as?"

"Homework," she retorted automatically. "Jenny's doing some make-up assignments so she'll be ready to take advanced English in the fall. She fell behind at the end of the term at home."

"Mom, it's Friday night," Jenny protested, then clamped her mouth shut the instant it apparently dawned on her that speaking out might mean staying at White Pines longer.

Janet hid a smile. "I suppose we could stay a little longer," she said, her expression innocent.

Alarm flared in Jenny's eyes. "No, you're right," Jenny contradicted hurriedly. "I should get my homework done. I have a big project due next week. It'll probably take me hours and hours, maybe the whole weekend. I won't get any sleep at all."

"Sounds like a tough assignment," Harlan agreed. "What is it?"

Jenny looked trapped. "A paper," she finally blurted in a way that said she was ad-libbing as she went along. "On Edgar Allan Poe."

Harlan leaned back. "Ah, yes, Poe. Now there was

a writer. Pretty scary stuff, it seemed to me when I read him."

"You read Poe?" Jenny asked in an insulting tone of disbelief that suggested she was surprised to discover that Harlan read at all.

"Poetry, short stories, just about all of it, I suppose," he said, clearly unoffended. "Of course, by today's standards, I suppose he seems pretty tame. Not nearly as graphic as some writers. It always seemed to me there was something to be said for leaving things to the reader's imagination, the way Poe did."

Jenny's expression brightened. "That's what I thought," she said eagerly, then caught herself. "Never mind. You probably don't care about what I think."

Janet's breath caught in her throat as she waited for Harlan's reply. Her ex-husband had never been interested in hearing his daughter's thoughts on much of anything. For the most part, Barry had believed children should be seen and not heard, unless showing Jenny off had had some professional benefit. He'd enjoyed being perceived as an up-and-coming lawyer and proud family man. When Jenny's grades had slipped in direct proportion to the amount of arguing going on at home, he'd lost what little interest he'd ever had in her school days.

For a time, Janet had been fooled by her ex's superficial evidence of concern and pride. Now that she'd observed Harlan Adams for a couple of weeks, especially when Cody was around to banter with him, she had seen what a genuine family was all about. What she and Barry and Jenny had shared had been a mockery of the real thing, more feigned than substantive.

She watched now as Harlan fixed an attentive look on Jenny. That was the gaze Barry had never quite mastered, an expression of real interest. Seeing it warmed Janet through and through and further endangered her already shaky determination to keep Harlan at a distance.

"Of course I'm interested in your opinion," he assured Jenny. "And if you're going to be in an advanced class, you must be pretty smart."

"My teacher in New York said my short stories and essays are really good," Jenny admitted, pride shining in her eyes. "She said I could probably be a writer someday, if I want to be."

"And do you want to be?" Harlan asked.

Jenny nodded, her expression suddenly shy as she revealed a dream that Janet knew she'd shared with almost no one. It was a tribute to the fragile trust flowering between Jenny and Harlan that she was telling him.

Once again, Janet couldn't help thinking that the theft and subsequent accident that had brought Harlan Adams into their lives was turning out far better than she'd had any right to expect, especially for Jenny. It made her more determined than ever not to do anything to shake the trust the two of them were establishing, even if it cost her a chance with Harlan for herself.

"I'm going to write about Native Americans," Jenny said. "I want to tell all the stories that Lone Wolf told Mom."

"And who was Lone Wolf?"

"He was my great-great-grandfather. He died way before I was born."

Harlan glanced at Janet. "But you spent time with him?"

"Just one summer," she admitted sorrowfully. "My father didn't want me spending time with my Comanche relatives. He said I'd grow up wild and out of control. One year, though, my mother insisted. She sent me to stay with Lone Wolf on the reservation in Oklahoma. It was the best summer of my life."

"Which almost explains why you ended up in Texas when your marriage ended," Harlan said. "Why here and not Oklahoma?"

Janet flushed guiltily and avoided Jenny's knowing gaze. "Because he talked about Texas a lot and the days when our ancestors lived here," she said, leaving it at that.

Harlan didn't appear convinced. "Something tells me there's a lot more to it," he said.

"Not really," she denied. "I'm just following a little girl's dream."

He shrugged, finally accepting her at her word. "Then we'll leave it at that for now," he said.

There was no mistaking the implication that he wouldn't leave the topic alone for long. Janet wondered how well her resolve would stand up to any real grilling by this man with the coaxing eyes and persuasive charm.

And more and more she was wondering whether she'd be able to go on battling the warm feelings he was stirring in her, the kind of feelings she'd vowed never to allow to deceive her again.

Harlan Adams struck her as a complicated man of many passions. She could only guess how well she would fare if she became one of them. For her own sake, as well as Jenny's, she hoped the moment of truth would be a long time coming.

"Maybe you should think about spending the weekend here," Harlan suggested just then, startling her. Her panic must have shown because he quickly added, "I've got a whole library filled with works by Poe. Jenny could do all the research she wants right here."

As generous and innocent-sounding as the offer was, Janet was shaking her head before the words were out of his mouth. "No, really, it's impossible. We're not prepared for an overnight stay."

His gaze settled on her in a provocative way that made her pulse race. "The closet's always filled with extra toothbrushes, if that's what has you worried," he said.

Janet felt her cheeks flame. He knew precisely what had her worried, and it definitely wasn't toothbrushes or the lack of them. "Thanks for the offer, but no," she said firmly.

"Come on back in the morning then," he said.

In giving in more gracefully than she'd expected, he almost left her feeling disappointed. Obviously she needed to work a little on her backbone. It was apparently as limp as an overcooked strand of spaghetti.

"Jenny can do her research and you and I could go riding," he prodded when she remained silent. "You still haven't seen all of White Pines."

Janet felt Jenny's wary gaze on her, but she avoided meeting her daughter's eyes. There were a lot of reasons to accept Harlan's offer, beginning with the chance it would give her to explore the very land that her ancestors had once hunted on. Jenny couldn't fault her for that.

There was also one very big reason to turn him down: he made her stomach do the most amazing flip-flops every single time he looked at her. If he could manage that after a few relatively brief encounters, what kind of havoc could he wreak during a whole day's outing? In private? Without Jenny's watchful gaze on them every minute?

Would there be more of those bone-melting kisses like the one that had thrown her so off stride on Sunday night? Without a doubt. The heated promise was in Harlan's gaze every time he looked at her. Temptation heated her blood. Longing made her heart thump unsteadily. And the combination had her saying yes before she could stop herself.

Once the single affirmative word was out of her mouth, Janet wasn't sure which of the three of them was most stunned. A pleased smile hovered on Harlan's lips. Jenny retreated into sullen silence. And Janet considered whether a steel rod implant was necessary to stiffen her spine to the degree it needed.

"Shall we get an early start?" Harlan inquired. "Or are you one of those people who likes to laze in bed on the weekends?"

There was just enough seductive innuendo in the question to make her voice unsteady when she vowed that she could be there at any hour he liked.

He grinned. "Brave words," he taunted. "I'll give you a break just this once, though. You get here by ten. I'll have Maritza pack us a picnic to take along."

"For three," Jenny said, scowling at her mother. "I want to come, too."

"Thought you had a big paper to do," Harlan said, but his eyes were glinting with amusement at Jenny's obvious ploy to play chaperone once again.

"I'll need a break," she said. "Otherwise, my brain will probably bust."

"Then by all means, you'll come, too," he replied. "Can't have a tragedy like that on my head."

If he was disappointed, he didn't let it show. Clearly, he understood how important it was for Jenny to feel she wouldn't be intruding.

For that, Janet decided, he would always have her gratitude. And, if he kept up the sweet gestures and the blatant provocation, he might very well wind up with her heart after all. Only time would tell just how terrible or incredible that fate might be.

Janet Runningbear was skittish as a brand-new colt, Harlan decided midway through their ride on Saturday. He'd never met a woman so determined to avoid being alone with a man.

Of course, Jenny was playing right into her mother's hands by acting like the overprotective adult, rather than the other way around. He might have found it amusing and rather gratifying, if it hadn't been so blasted frustrating.

He wanted to get to know this woman, but whenever he steered the conversation in a personal direction, she scooted it onto some other topic faster than a tornado could rip apart a house. He supposed for the first time in his life he was going to have to learn to be patient. His usual habit of making quick decisions and acting on them wasn't going to work with Janet. If he pushed too hard, he knew right now he'd scare her out of his life entirely.

He kept a close eye on her as they rode. She handled herself well in the saddle. Clearly, this wasn't her first ride on horseback. She didn't bat an eye when he picked up the pace. In fact, she shot him a daring look, dug in her heels and sent the mare he'd chosen for her into a flat-out gallop.

Laughing, Harlan didn't even try to keep up. He was enjoying the view from behind too much. She was leaning low over the horse's back. Her long black hair was caught up in a single, severe braid, but tendrils had escaped to curl defiantly along the back of her elegant, exposed neck. A longing to press a hot, lingering kiss to that bare skin washed through him with the ferocity of a summer storm, stunning him with its intensity.

She slowed after a bit, letting him and Jenny catch up.

"Where'd you learn to ride like that?" he asked. "Not in Central Park, I'll bet."

"Jeez, Mom, you never said you'd been on a horse before," Jenny said, looking a little awestruck.

"I learned in Oklahoma that summer. It all came back to me. I remembered how it felt to have the wind in my face. It's exhilarating."

"It shows," Harlan said quietly, his gaze locked with hers. "You've got some color in your cheeks for a change and your eyes are sparkling."

Jenny shot him a suspicious frown, as if not quite certain whether he was making another pass at her mother right under her eyes.

"It's the God's truth," Harlan insisted with a touch of defiance. "Jenny, take a good look at your mom. Have you ever seen her look so happy?"

Apparently by drawing Jenny into the appraisal of Janet's appearance, he managed to allay her fears. She studied her mother, then nodded. "You do look spectacular, Mom. You should do this more."

"Anytime," Harlan said quickly, capitalizing on the

small, inadvertent opening. "No need even to call first. If I'm not around, just leave me a note in the barn or let Maritza know you're taking one of the horses out."

"Thank you," she said, rubbing the mare's neck. "I may take you up on the offer. This has been incredible."

Harlan locked gazes with her once more, refusing to break eye contact as he said, "And it's just the beginning."

Janet swallowed hard under his intense scrutiny. He enjoyed the knowledge that she was responding to him despite whatever reservations she might have. He was finally reassured that this attraction he'd been feeling from the beginning was returned, albeit with great reluctance.

"Come on, you two. I know the perfect spot for our picnic. It's about a mile ahead."

They ambled along at a comfortable pace for the next few minutes, picking their way through a denser stand of trees until they emerged on the shaded bank of a creek. It was too late in the season for the bluebonnets that usually dotted the area, but it was a tranquil, lovely setting just the same. Harlan had always enjoyed coming here when he needed to ponder some puzzle in his life. The serenity seemed to clear his head.

It was also a romantic spot for a picnic. He and Mary had stolen away here a time or two before she'd decided picnics were for youngsters and they needed more sedate and elegant entertainment. He'd always regretted that they no longer shared this spot and the simplicity of the hours they had once spent here.

He kept a close eye on Janet to gauge her reaction. A soft smile lit her face as she took in her surroundings. She sighed then with what looked to be sheer pleasure.

"Lone Wolf used to tell me about incredibly beautiful places just like this," she murmured, lifting her eyes to meet his again. "I dreamed of finding one. Thank you for bringing us here."

As if she sensed that the undercurrents between her mother and Harlan were getting too provocative and too intense, Jenny cut in. "I don't see what's so special. It's just a dumb old creek. I saw the Atlantic Ocean a couple of times when Mom and Dad actually stopped working long enough to take me. Now that's impressive," she said, shooting a defiant look in his direction.

He grinned at her, refusing to take offense. "It is something, isn't it? But appreciating the magnificence of one doesn't mean you can't recognize the beauty of the other. That would be like saying if you like Monet, you can't like Grandma Moses. Or if you enjoy Bach, it's not possible to appreciate the Beatles."

He pointedly fixed his gaze on Janet when he added, "Seems to me the more experiences you open your heart to, the richer your life will be."

Color rose in her cheeks as his implication sank in. Satisfied that she'd gotten his message, he nodded and busied himself with taking the picnic from the packs Maritza had prepared. He handed Janet a red-checked tablecloth.

"You pick the spot for that," he suggested, then watched as she headed unerringly for his favorite place beneath an old cottonwood. It was the exact spot where he often sat, his back braced against the trunk of the tree as he waited for the sun to set and his tangled thoughts to unravel. He'd come a lot after Mary's death, hoping for understanding and acceptance of the tragedy that had taken her.

Today, for the first time, with Janet and Jenny by his side, he thought maybe he'd found the reason for God's choice. One door in his life had closed and another had opened. He couldn't help wondering with a sense of tremendous anticipation what awaited him on this new adventure.

"You suddenly seem very far away," Janet said quietly as she came to stand beside him.

Harlan noticed that Jenny had already stripped off her shoes and socks and was wading in the creek. For the moment he and Janet had a bit of privacy. He lifted his hand to her cheek in a light caress.

"No more," he murmured. "Now I'm right here, with you."

Worry darkened her eyes at once. "Harlan—"

He touched a finger to her lips. "Shh. For once, don't argue. Let's just see where this takes us. No promises. No commitments. No guarantees. Just be open to the possibilities. Can you do that?"

He felt her tremble beneath his touch, felt her skin heat and saw the glitter of excitement in her eyes. A sigh hovered on her lips before she finally nodded.

"I can try," she agreed, looking anything but certain even as she spoke.

"That's all anyone can ask." He glanced toward the bank of the creek and saw that Jenny was still in view, even though she had her back to them for the moment.

He dropped his voice even lower. "I want very much to kiss you." He allowed the thought to linger between them, allowed the color to climb in her cheeks and the anticipation to shine in her eyes before adding, "But I won't. Not with Jenny so close by again."

It might have been his imagination or wishful thinking, but he thought he detected disappointment shadowing the depths of her eyes even as she murmured her thanks.

He grinned. "That doesn't mean I can't tell you what I think kissing you would be like. Your mouth is soft as a rose petal, Janet Runningbear, and your breath is just as sweet. I love the way your eyes darken when my mouth is this close to yours," he said, leaning down to within a hairbreadth of her lips, then retreating almost at once. This time he heard the shock of her indrawn breath and knew, absolutely knew, that what he saw in her eyes was disappointment.

He ran his thumb along her lower lip. "There will be other times," he assured her. "Private times."

He released her then, amused that she stood as if his hands were still on her, quiet and shaken. He hoped his own emotions weren't half so apparent. One thing for sure, he wasn't half as frightened of what the future might hold as she appeared to be. For the first time since they'd met, she seemed truly vulnerable.

For the life of him, he couldn't decide if that was good or bad. Until he could figure it out, he settled for taming the electricity arcing through the air so they could get through the rest of the day without giving Jenny something more to fret about.

He winked at her. "Come on, woman. Why are you standing there? We've got fried chicken and potato salad and coleslaw to serve up. You must be starving after that ride."

She visibly shook off the uncertainties that had held her still. "You're right. I am famished." She scanned the creek bank until she found Jenny, then called her, just a hint of desperation in her voice. "Come on, sweetie. Lunch is ready."

Harlan settled himself in his favorite position against the tree and listened to Janet and Jenny chatter through lunch. If there was a nervous edge to the conversation, he chalked it up to the electricity that his best effort had failed to diffuse. For better or worse, the attraction humming between Janet and him was powerful stuff. It needed only a chance look, a casual touch, to set it off.

"Is the creek deep enough to swim in?" Jenny asked after they'd eaten. "I wore my suit under my jeans."

"How'd you know about the creek and guess we'd be coming here?" Harlan asked, more amused than ever by her earlier grudging comparison of the creek to the ocean.

"Cody showed me," she said, shrugging, her expression all innocence. "He said it was your favorite place. When you invited Mom to go riding, I knew you'd end up here."

That explained the swimsuit and her earlier derisive reaction. The creek had probably looked much more interesting when she'd been here with Cody, Harlan decided. It also explained her determination to come along today. She hadn't wanted her mother alone with him in such a romantic setting.

"Can I go in the water, Mom?"

"Not right after lunch," Janet said at once.

"She'll be fine," Harlan said. "The creek's only waist high at its deepest."

Janet still seemed uneasy—about the swim or being left alone with him, it was hard to tell—but she gave permission.

"You could go in, too," Harlan said when Jenny had run off.

"I didn't wear my suit," she said.

"That's not a problem. Strip down over behind those trees. I won't peek. Cross my heart."

"Yeah, right," she said, amusement making her eyes sparkle.

Harlan's pulse bucked like a bronco. She looked ten years younger all of a sudden. That was the way of flirting, he decided. It lifted spirits and drained away problems, at least for a moment in time. It brought back that starry-eyed anticipation that regrettably seemed to fade once youth had passed by.

"If it's all the same to you, I'll stay right here, where it's safe," she said.

"Darlin', if you think it's safe here with me, your judgment has more problems than that old car of yours."

To his surprise, she grinned. "But you're an honorable man and you've already promised that absolutely nothing will happen as long as Jenny is around."

"That promise didn't allow for the temptation factor. You keep taunting me and I can't be responsible for my actions."

"Then by all means, let's change the subject. Tell me about White Pines."

He leaned back against the tree and linked his hands behind his head just to keep himself from reaching for her.

"It's been in my family since the time of the Civil War," he said, thinking back to all the history that Mary had loved so deeply. She'd been far more fascinated by the Adams legacy than he had been. He'd just loved the land and ranching. It was as deeply ingrained in his blood as whatever DNA there was to identify him.

"That's how it got its name," he continued. "My ancestors moved here from the South and called it White Pines, just like the plantation that had been burned to the ground by Yankee soldiers. Texas seemed like a land of opportunity back then, I suppose. They came here with very little, but with grit and determination the next generations added to that beginning until it became what you see today. The Mexican settlers in the area named the town Los Piños after the ranch, which provided work for so many of the families."

At some point as he talked, a change came over Janet's face. Suddenly she was more aloof than ever and a kind of seething resentment burned in her eyes.

"Is something wrong?" he asked, thoroughly bemused by the change in her.

"Not really," she said, and stood, brushing off her jeans.

The innocent gesture drew attention to her shapely rear end and had Harlan's blood sizzling like an adolescent boy's. But he was too puzzled by the abrupt change in her demeanor to enjoy his reaction for very long.

"Janet?"

"We'd better be getting back."

"You'll stay for supper," he said, making it more a matter-of-fact statement than a question.

She hesitated for just an instant, clearly wrestling with indecision, her expression uncertain, then shook her head. "No. That wouldn't be a good idea."

"Why?"

"It just wouldn't, that's all. We've taken up too much of your time as it is."

Harlan frowned. "What the devil is that supposed to mean?"

"Forget it," she muttered. With that, she bolted in the direction of where Jenny was swimming in the creek. "Jenny, come on now, sweetie. It's time to go."

Janet's strange mood lasted all the way back to the house. For the life of him, Harlan couldn't figure out what had gone wrong. One thing was certain, though. Janet was far more of a mystery than the woman who'd been his mate for more than thirty-five years.

She was strong, as Mary had been. But she was also fiercely independent, burned by what he could only guess had been a lousy childhood and an even lousier marriage. There were apparently other dark secrets he hadn't even begun to discover.

Whatever those secrets might be, he had the feeling her heart had turned to ice in the process. Knowing that might have discouraged some men, but not him. He had a hunch that melting it was going to be downright interesting.

8

No amount of persuading had been able to convince Janet and Jenny to stay for supper on Saturday or to return on Sunday. Harlan decided he must be losing his touch. He thought he'd tried some very inventive arguments, along with a little subtle flirting and a few dares. There had been a brief spark in Janet's eyes at one point, but she'd still managed to decline the invitation, albeit with a satisfyingly obvious hint of regret in her voice.

Watching them leave, he resigned himself to waiting impatiently for Monday morning when Janet would return to drop off Jenny. Maybe then Jenny would be able to shed some light on her mother's abrupt shift in mood.

In the meantime, the hours stretched out ahead of him, promising nothing but tedium. Now that he was starting to feel alive again, he was even less tolerant of the prospect than he had once been.

Short of booting Cody out of his position as ranch manager, he wasn't sure what to do about it. Los Piños was too small a town to need an influential citizen meddling in its affairs. State or national politics had never intrigued him. In fact, the only things that had ever mattered to him were his family and the ranch.

After church on Sunday, he spent most of the remainder of the morning wandering through all the empty rooms at White Pines, trying to remember the days when his sons had made the kind of racket that drove Mary nuts, trying to imagine the big old house echoing with laughter once again.

Jenny's presence lately had given him a delightful hint of what it might be like, at least when she let down her guard long enough to act like a regular thirteen-year-old. Occasionally she and some of Maritza's younger relations would whoop it up in the kitchen, usually when she counted on him being out of earshot. The joyous sound, when he happened to catch it, brightened his day.

Now, though, he tried to picture the generations before him, who had built the ranch into a thriving enterprise. He knew almost nothing about those early days beyond the scant information he'd shared with Janet. Mary had always been exasperated with him for caring so little about the past. He'd been more concerned with the future, with making White Pines into a legacy for his sons and their children.

Ironically, only Cody had really cared about his heritage. Ranching was in his blood, just as it had been in Harlan's. Luke had loved ranching well enough, but he'd had a milewide independent streak that pushed him into starting up his own place, not just as proof that he could succeed at it, but to best his father. Cody had the same goal, it seemed to him. He was just more willing to fight Harlan one-on-one, on his home turf. He seemed to thrive on the war of wills.

Jordan and Erik hadn't been interested in White Pines or ranching at all. In fact, it had been attempts to force Erik into a life that was never right for him that had ultimately led to his death. Riding a tractor one day at Luke's, he'd gotten careless. The tractor had rolled over on him and killed him, leaving Jessie a widow and expecting his child.

Ultimately, Luke had claimed both mother and child, a beautiful Christmas baby named Angela. As happy as they were, Harlan wondered sometimes if they'd ever forget the cost at which that happiness had come.

With Jordan in the oil business and living at the ranch that had belonged to his wife Kelly's family, now only Cody and Melissa and their kids remained at White Pines. Even they, however, lived in their own home, rather than in one of the suites that had been created to house new generations at a time when Harlan had imagined spending his golden years surrounded by family. They were close by, but not nearly close enough to keep him from rattling around in these lonely old rooms.

Only a few hours after his uncommon bout of self-pity, Harlan cursed himself for regretting the lack of company. It just proved that a man should be careful what he wished for.

Cody and Melissa arrived on his doorstep first with their kids, Sharon Lynn and Harlan Patrick. He could tell right off this was no drop-by visit for a quick hello. They seemed ready to settle down for a bit. They'd brought along enough paraphernalia for the kids to entertain them until nightfall.

Luke and Jessie were hard on their heels with precious, sweet-faced Angela. Jordan and Kelly turned up within minutes after that with Dani and Justin James.

It was a conspiracy, no doubt about that. He didn't believe for a second they'd all shown up just to get a decent meal from Maritza.

Apparently his housekeeper had known they were coming, though. He noticed that she'd set places for every traitorous one of them at his table.

"So, Daddy, anything interesting going on around here?" Luke inquired after Maritza had served a prime rib big enough to feed an expected crowd, but far too big to pass off as something she'd prepared just for one. Not even his impudent housekeeper was brazen enough to suggest she was having to stretch the lavish spread of food to accommodate unexpected guests.

"Other than the lot of you showing up to beg a meal?" he retorted. "Not a thing."

"Have you met the new lawyer in town?" Jordan inquired with a perfectly straight face. "What's her name? Janet Runningbear? I've spotted her a couple of times myself. She's gorgeous. You thought so, too, didn't you, Cody?"

Harlan scowled at Cody and Melissa, who were looking about as innocent as a couple of tattletales could. If he'd had any doubts about his youngest son having the biggest mouth in the family, his proof was sitting around his dining room table right now.

It was obvious Luke and Jessie and Jordan and Kelly knew every last detail of his fledgling fascination with Janet Runningbear. They'd probably been told the second Cody had finished listening to all of his confessions about that night in Janet's kitchen. That poker game at Rosa's hadn't helped. What Cody hadn't blabbed himself, Rosa had.

"We've met," he admitted tersely, trying hard to

avoid making the kind of revelations that would invite more taunting.

Cody chuckled, then covered his face with a napkin to hide his smile.

"Damn your hide, boy," Harlan said to his youngest. "You got any control whatsoever over that mouth of yours?"

"I can't imagine what you mean," Cody declared, feigning a hurt expression that was about as believable as the ones he'd worn on his chocolate-streaked face when he'd sworn he'd never been near the cookie jar.

"If anyone's to blame, it's you," Cody added, trying to pass on the guilt. "You're the one who made a spectacle of yourself at Rosa's. It was the hottest story on the Los Piños grapevine for a solid week. Mule filled in any gap Rosa left in the story. Seemed to enjoy it, too. All I did was confirm a few facts, when asked directly."

"It was a poker game, not a spectacle," Harlan retorted defensively. "Playing cards wasn't a crime last time I checked."

"From what I heard, poker wasn't exactly the only game being played that afternoon," Jordan chimed in with a wicked grin.

Harlan resigned himself to sitting back and taking whatever they were of a mind to dish out. To his surprise, though, he found an unexpected ally in Jessie. She reached over and patted his hand.

"I think all of you should leave your father alone," she protested to the others, a twinkle in her blue eyes. "He obviously doesn't require your meddling in order to have a social life."

All three of his sons hooted. "Meddling?" Luke said to his wife. "You call this meddling? This is child's play compared to what he put all of us through. You and me included, in case you've forgotten."

"I still think you should leave him alone," Jessie repeated firmly.

"Thank you," Harlan said. "But I think you're wasting your breath with this band of hooligans."

"I still have a little influence with one of them," she said, shooting a pointed look at Luke, who was seated on her other side.

"Right," Jordan said. "And I suppose those bags you toted upstairs a little while ago don't indicate that you and Lucas intend to stay right here until morning, just so you can catch a glimpse of Janet Runningbear and her daughter. I'd be happy to describe her, if you'd like to turn right around and go back home. Tall, slender, mid-thirties, long black hair. Is that what you were wondering about?"

"It's a start," Luke confirmed.

This was definitely a turn of events Harlan hadn't counted on. Janet was skittish enough around him without having to face his whole darn family. He scowled at Luke. "You're staying?"

"Just till dawn," he said with a grin. "I'd hate to make that long drive back tonight. I might fall asleep at the wheel. Besides, you don't get to see nearly enough of Angela. She misses her granddaddy. Isn't that right, sweet pea?"

The toddler dutifully scrambled off her chair and ran around to be picked up so she could deliver sticky kisses to Harlan's face. "Miss you, grandda," she asserted enthusiastically.

"Did you coach her to do that, just so I wouldn't toss you out on your ear?" Harlan grumbled.

Jordan glanced across the table at his wife. "Maybe we should stick around, too. What do you think?"

"I think Luke is perfectly capable of tormenting your father without any help from you," Kelly retorted.

"Thank you," Harlan said to her.

"But I want to stay," Dani protested. The seven-year-old's expression turned wily. "I can help baby-sit Angela. Aunt Jessie says I'm really, really good."

"Oh, for goodness' sake, the whole darn lot of you might as well move back in," Harlan declared.

"Don't tempt us, Daddy," Luke advised. "We just might do it, at least until we see where things between you and Janet Runningbear are heading. By the way, have you been locking up all the cars now that her daughter's around here all the time?"

Harlan groaned. He'd always wanted a tight-knit family. He'd always done his darnedest to make his sons feel welcome at White Pines, even after they'd gone on to lives of their own. It appeared he was going to live to regret not booting them all into another state. For the second time in a little more than an hour, he reminded himself to be very, very careful what he wished for in the future.

Janet took one look at the assembled members of Harlan Adams's family as she drove up to the house on Monday and very nearly turned tail and ran. She didn't have a doubt in the world that she and Jenny were the main attraction that had drawn them onto the porch at daybreak. All of the family, she guessed from the size of the gathering, right down to the youngest grandchild. Even her intrepid daughter seemed a little awed by all the attention riveted on them.

"Who are all those people and why are they staring at us?" Jenny asked, regarding the bunch of them warily.

"Now you know how Custer must have felt when he made his last stand," Janet said dryly, then added, "My guess is they're all here to try to figure out if we have designs on their father."

"You mean like wanting to marry him or something?" Jenny asked, astonishment written all over her face.

"That would be my guess," Janet confirmed.

Jenny's mouth gaped. "You don't, do you?"

"I don't," Janet said emphatically.

She wished she could speak with as much certainty about Harlan's intentions. He was the first man in aeons who wasn't the least bit put off by her prickly, independent nature. Even after she'd turned moody on him on Saturday, he'd remained flirtatious and placid.

In fact, if anything, the glint in his eyes burned even brighter in the face of her contrariness. He wanted her and that, in his opinion, was that. He clearly thought it was just a matter of time until he got his way.

Apparently his sons thought as much, too, or they wouldn't be here this morning trying to check out the woman who'd caught their father's eye.

"Go on and hop out," she advised Jenny.

"You're going to leave me here alone with *them?*" her daughter protested, clearly aghast at the prospect. "I don't think so."

"Jenny, I'm sure they're all very nice people."

"Then why are you running away?"

"Because they obviously have an agenda I don't want to deal with," she said.

She cast a quick look to see if she could turn her car

around in this unoccupied corner of the driveway or if she was going to be forced to circle all the way around in front of the house, in front of all those fascinated, prying eyes.

Jenny folded her arms over her chest and lifted her chin. Defiance radiated from every pore. "I am not getting out of this car without you."

"Sweetie, please," she implored.

"No way."

"You'll embarrass Harlan."

"And your taking off won't?" Jenny flung back. "Get real, Mom. They're here to check you out even more than me. Maybe you should prepare a little speech denying any interest in Mr. Adams. Maybe then they'd go away."

Janet sighed and threw the car into park and shut off the engine. "Traitor," she muttered at her daughter.

"Don't blame me. Blame Mr. Adams."

Janet glanced in Harlan's direction. He looked every bit as miserable as she felt. "I seriously doubt that this was his idea of a good time," she observed.

"Then he should have kicked them out," Jenny retorted. "If he can't control his own kids, how come you think he's such a good influence on me?"

"It's hardly the same," Janet replied.

"I don't see why. If I'm going to turn out all nosy like them, I'd think you'd want to get me away from here as fast as you could."

Before Janet could come up with an adequate answer for that, Harlan was opening her door.

"I'm sorry," he said in a hushed tone. "I didn't know they were coming yesterday and I sure as hell didn't know they were staying. I couldn't shake 'em out of here to save my soul. I thought about starving them out, but my housekeeper would have fed them behind my back, I'm sure."

His genuine discomfort relieved some of her own tension. "Jenny thinks you have a serious inability to control your own kids."

He grinned. "I couldn't have said it better myself. I'm still not sure where I went wrong." He held out his hand to her. "Come on. We might as well get this over with. Give it five minutes and you can swear you have a major client coming and that you have to get to town."

She suddenly found his desire to be rid of her in such a hurry a little insulting. "Are you afraid to let them spend too much time with me?" she asked irritably.

His mouth gaped. "With you? Are you crazy? I'm scared silly you'll take one look at the lot of them and never show your face around here again."

She grinned at his adamant tone. "I'm made of tougher stuff than that," she declared. "So is Jenny." She leaned back in. "Out, young lady."

Jenny rolled her eyes. "Oh, all right. But I'm not playing cute for anybody, okay?"

"There was little doubt of that," Janet said dryly, exchanging a pointed look with Harlan, who looked as if he wanted very badly to burst out laughing.

As they approached the porch, three young women came down the steps to meet them.

"Hi, I'm Jessie," the first one said. "We're sorry about all of this, but there's no controlling these guys when they get together to harass their father. We couldn't have gotten them out of here last night if we'd set off a canister of pepper spray in the house. Believe me, I thought about it. So did Kelly and Melissa."

"I even had one in my purse," Kelly said. "I bought it when I lived in Houston. Never had a need for it there, thank goodness, but I thought it might come in handy here last night."

"Too many babies, though," Melissa added. "I'm talking about the ones in cribs, not the ones we're married to. You'd think they hadn't learned to share, the way they've been carrying on about meeting the woman who's stealing their daddy's affection."

Janet warmed to the trio of smiling women immediately. They clearly understood what it meant to hook up with an Adams man. "Believe me, I am not out to steal their daddy's affection or anything else, for that matter."

"It's not entirely up to you," Jessie declared with the kind of clear-thinking logic that cut straight to the heart of Janet's dilemma. "Our husbands may be the stubbornnest set of men in Texas. Not a one of them knows how to take no for an answer. Who do you guess they learned that from?"

"Hey," Harlan protested. "Watch your tongue."

"It's true, Harlan, and you know it," Kelly and Melissa chimed in, laughing at his disgruntled expression.

Janet considered the teasing comments to be very discouraging news. Apparently Harlan detected her discomfort, because he slipped her arm through his.

"Come on," he said. "We might as well get the rest of this over with. Ladies, go tell your husbands to be on their best behavior."

"Don't expect us to accomplish what you couldn't," Kelly teased.

Jenny rolled her eyes. "I told you, Mom."

Harlan glanced at her. "What did you tell your mother?"

"That you must not be half so tough as you try to pretend, if your sons walk all over you."

The sons in question hooted at that.

"Guess she has you pegged, doesn't she, Daddy?" Cody taunted.

"If her mama's half as smart, you're in for it," Jordan agreed, grinning at Janet as he shook her hand.

Luke crowded in next, a sympathetic glimmer in his eyes. "Don't let all the fuss scare you to death. We're not half as intimidating as we sound."

"A bunch of soft touches?" Janet asked doubtfully.

He nodded. "And Daddy's the easiest of all."

"You start giving away all my secrets and that prize bull of mine you want to breed next year won't get anywhere near those cows of yours," Harlan warned.

Luke held up his hands and backed off. "Not another word," he vowed.

The teasing went on for another ten minutes, though, as the three oldest grandchildren raced around the yard. Jenny seemed thoroughly bemused by all the commotion. It made Janet wonder whether she'd been so wrong to insist to Barry that she wanted no more children. Left unspoken had been the fact that she didn't want them with him. Within months of Jenny's birth, she had already sensed that their marriage wasn't going to last the distance. It had taken her more than twelve years to finally cut the ties.

When Melissa shoved a baby into her arms, so she could chase after her daughter who was vanishing around the side of the house, Janet felt a stirring of maternal instinct that was so overwhelming it brought tears to her eyes. She quickly handed the baby over to Jessie, who was standing nearby.

"I have to get to work," she announced to no one in particular.

Harlan was at her side in a heartbeat. "We'll talk later," he said as he walked with her to her car. "I'll come up with some way to apologize for all this."

"It's not like you threw me into a den of starving wolves," she reminded him. "It wasn't that bad. They're nice people, all of them. And they clearly love you and worry about you."

He grinned at that. "Do I look like a man who needs people fussing over him?"

She couldn't help smiling at that. "I doubt they see you the same way I do," she said.

"Oh, really," he said, sounding absolutely fascinated all of a sudden. "And how do you see me?"

"Never mind. Your ego's big enough as it is," she said, and closed the car door in his face.

"We'll finish this discussion tonight," he shouted as she drove away.

The challenge in his voice and the gleam in his eyes stayed with her the rest of the day. At least a dozen times, as she talked with the few potential clients who called, an image of Harlan's face popped into her head. His strength and compassion, along with that taunting, unmistakable desire, kept her from regretting the day she'd moved to Texas.

Too many of the calls were from people only interested in hiring her if she'd work free, or from people with ugly accusations to make about her being an uppity Indian. She found the atmosphere of bias and distrust both discouraging and infuriating.

By the time she returned to White Pines to pick up Jenny, she had a thundering headache and a chip on her shoulder the size of a longhorn. The sight of Harlan waiting on the porch for her, a pitcher of tea ready, along with more of Maritza's culinary treats, brought tears to her eyes. She lingered in the car for a moment for fear he'd see how despondent she was and try to jump in and fix things for her. After a day like the one she'd just had, it would be too easy simply to let him.

Even though she'd taken the time to gather her composure, Harlan wasn't fooled. He took one look at her and reached out to gather her into his arms. She hesitated only an instant before accepting the comfort he offered.

"Bad day?" he asked.

"Is it that obvious?"

"To me, it is. Want to talk about it?"

She wrapped her arms a little tighter around his waist and rested her head on his chest. "No, but this is nice."

Too nice, she reminded herself sternly. Too easy. It was a dangerous trap. With a sigh, she pulled away. "Thanks."

"You could stay right where you are," he said. "These are mighty broad shoulders. Might as well make use of 'em, if you've got troubles."

"Nothing I can't handle," she said, and forced herself to step away from what he was offering.

When she would have turned away, his voice stopped her.

"Janet?" he said in little more than a whisper.

She lifted her gaze to his and felt her heart skip a beat at the blazing heat in his eyes. She swallowed hard. "Yes?"

"Jenny's off with Cody again. They're going to be a while. Care to take a chance on another kiss?"

She almost wished he hadn't asked at all, that he'd just swept her back into his arms without giving her any say in the matter. But she couldn't deny that a part of her was glad he'd reassured her of Jenny's whereabouts first.

"I can't," she protested halfheartedly, even as she swayed toward him.

He stroked a finger along her cheek. "Talk about mixed messages, darlin'."

She shook her head ruefully. "I know. I'm pitiful."

"Never pitiful," he argued. "Strong, sassy, impossible, maybe, but never pitiful."

His touch on her face lingered. There were a hundred questions in his eyes, but only one that really mattered: had she meant yes or no? Both, depending on whether he asked her head or her heart, she decided.

And just this once she was going with her heart. She stood on tiptoe to lift her lips to his. Her touch was tentative, but it was all it took to set passion blazing. So much tenderness. So much heat, she thought as he held her head still and plundered her mouth.

The rightness of it stunned her. He was everything she'd once been taught to hate by Lone Wolf—a Texan and a rancher. And yet, in his arms, as she was right now, she felt at home. At peace.

At least that was how she felt deep in her heart. Her head was another matter entirely. She had a hunch that struggle was far from over.

9

"Hot," Janet murmured eventually, backing away from Harlan as if he were a stove and she'd been standing over it too long. If she'd owned a hankie and it wouldn't have been a dead giveaway of how affected she was by his touch, she would have patted her brow with it.

"I'll say," he agreed, his eyes twinkling with amusement

"I was referring to the temperature," she insisted as embarrassment made her face flush even hotter. At this rate she'd wind up as a little puddle of mortified genes right at his feet.

"Of course you were," he said perfectly innocently. "So was I."

"The weather, dammit!"

He nodded. "If you say so."

She turned her back on him and headed across the porch, trying not to mutter out loud about his impudence. On the way, she grabbed a glass of iced tea and held it against her feverish brow.

This attraction was getting out of hand. She was

slipping into a pattern that had all the earmarks of sur-
render. It would be just her luck that she'd fall head-
over-heels in love with Harlan Adams and then he'd
discover that she was out to find a way to reclaim some
of his land for the Comanches. He'd blow a gasket,
blow her off, and they'd both wind up being hurt and
feeling used.

She heard his booted footsteps as he crossed the
porch to join her. He was moving slowly, almost as if
he wanted to give her time to prepare. By the time he
paused beside her, her nerves were jittery all over again.
Damn, why did it have to be this particular man who
made her feel like a whole, vibrant, sexy woman again?

"You still wrestling with yourself?" he inquired in
that lazy tone that raised goose bumps up and down
her spine.

"Wrestling, hell," she admitted. "It's all-out war."

He chuckled at that. "Good."

"You don't have to sound so complacent about it."

"Sure I do. That's the nature of an Adams man."

Despite herself, she laughed and shifted until she
could look into his eyes. "Big egos, huh?"

"I prefer to think of it as self-confidence."

"You would. Arrogance by any other name is still
a flaw, Harlan."

"I'm entitled to one serious defect, don't you think?"

She held back another urge to laugh. "Just one?
That's all you're admitting to?"

"I'm not a fool, darlin'. I'm not admitting to a single
one you haven't already discovered. You're searching
so hard for more, I'd hate to spoil your fun."

"How altruistic," she retorted sourly, wondering
when she'd become so transparent. Or was it just that

Harlan had an innate knack for reading her, a knack that stemmed from fascination and concentration? Few men had ever studied her quite so intently, that's for sure. Barry had never even scratched the surface of her emotions. She couldn't decide whether to feel flattered or cornered that Harlan could.

He settled himself onto the porch railing, then pulled her between his thighs. She didn't even have the strength of will to resist.

The provocative position, the glitter of desire in his eyes, sent shivers of pure longing dancing through her. As dangerous as the reaction was, she couldn't have pulled back if her life depended on it.

He kept his hands loosely settled on her hips as if to convey she was free to go, if she chose…if she could.

"Your skin turns to fire when you're close to me like this," he observed.

"How polite of you to point it out," she said, but without nearly as much venom as she should have mustered. Besides, it was true. That was what had forced her away from him only moments before.

"Why does that bother you so much?" he asked. "Men and women have been attracted to each other from the beginning of time. It's natural."

"Sometimes the attraction's to the wrong person."

"You think I'm wrong for you?"

She nodded. "And I'm just as wrong for you."

"Why?"

She sighed, unwilling to spell it all out for him. "It's complicated. You'll just have to take my word for it."

Drawing in a deep breath, she leveled a serious look straight into his blue eyes. "If you can't, I'll have to stop coming around. I'll keep Jenny away, too. We'll find another way to pay for the repairs to your truck. I'll work it out with Mule."

"Your debt's not with Mule. It's with me," he insisted stubbornly.

"He's making the repairs, isn't he?"

"Forget the blasted bill," he said, his exasperation apparent in his tone. He lifted her aside and stood. "Your daughter stole my truck. I didn't call the sheriff because you agreed to let her work off the debt out here."

She stiffened at the reminder. "I wonder how the sheriff would feel about your taking the law into your own hands, devising your own brand of justice?"

He scowled at her. "You want to test him and find out?"

Janet had a feeling that—laws or no laws—he knew the justice system in Los Piños and could manipulate it far better than she ever could with her legal expertise and law school degree.

"Why are you making this so difficult?" she snapped. "Hasn't anyone ever turned you down before?"

A ghost of a smile played around his lips. "Haven't asked anyone until you came along, not for more than thirty-five years."

That sucked the wind right out of her sails. She reached up impulsively and placed her hand against his cheek. "Harlan Adams, you don't play fair."

"That's right, darlin'. I play to win."

Before she could reply to that, his mouth was moving over hers again, coaxing, persuading, claiming.

It was a hell of a kiss by anyone's standards. By Janet's, it was devastating. A bone-melting, breath-stealing crack of thunder deep inside her. It raised goose bumps from head to toe and had the hair on the back of her neck raised on end.

"I think I'd better be going," she murmured when it was over. As badly as she wanted to sound serene and unfazed, she couldn't seem to get her voice above a shaken whisper. She glanced around anxiously, trying to spot the purse she'd dropped somewhere.

"Without Jenny?" he inquired, laughter dancing in his eyes.

"Oh," she murmured. "No, of course not." She drew in a deep, supposedly calming breath. It didn't help a whit.

"How soon will she and Cody be back?" she asked a little desperately.

"Not for a while," he reported complacently. "You might as well settle back and relax."

Relax? It would take an entire bottle of tranquilizers to get her to relax as long as Harlan was in the vicinity. She didn't have so much as a single pill to her name. She sipped at the only available distraction, her iced tea, but it didn't go far in terms of settling her nerves or soothing the thirst that kiss had aroused.

"You look as if you could use a nice, cool shower," Harlan said after a bit.

Her head snapped up. "What?"

"A cool shower," he prompted, grinning. "Alone, if that's the way you prefer."

"Here?" she asked incredulously.

"Why not? It's a big house. There are lots of bathrooms. If I'd put in that pool the boys were always plaguing me to, I'd suggest that, but a shower is all I have to offer."

The offer might have been part generosity, part seduction, but Janet was intrigued just the same. Maybe an ice-cold shower would get her through the wait, she decided thoughtfully. It would wash away some of the hot day's dust and cleanse her wicked thoughts at the same time.

And maybe not. She weighed just how far she could trust Harlan to stay right here where he was, rather than following her inside.

Don't be an idiot, she lectured herself. Of course, he would stay here. The man was a gentleman…when it suited his purposes.

As if he'd read the temptation in her eyes, he said, "Use the bathroom in Luke's suite. It's the first one upstairs on the right. I think Jessie probably left some of that fancy, perfumed bubble bath she likes, if you'd prefer to relax in a tub for a while."

The suggestion conjured up images so steamy her brain should have been x-rated. "A shower will be fine," she said, bolting to presumed safety.

Inside Luke's suite, with the door locked, and inside the bathroom with *that* door locked, she leaned back against it and released a pent-up breath. Safe at last, she thought. What was yet to be determined, however, was whether she was hiding from Harlan's pursuit or her own increasingly dangerous longings.

Damn, but she was a stubborn one, Harlan thought to himself the following morning as he surveyed the disaster Jenny had made of his toolshed. Almost as stubborn as her mama.

Janet's abrupt retreat to hide out in Luke's suite until Jenny's return the night before had left him chuckling on the front porch. Frustrated as hell, but amused just the same. There'd been no mistaking how grateful Janet had been to be given a reason to escape his provocative company for a bit.

Jenny had shown up finally, looking for her mama. When Harlan had told her she was inside taking a bath, Jenny's shocked expression suggested she was making far more of that than she should have. Thank goodness Cody wasn't with her or he'd have had a few choice words to add to the conversation for sure.

Harlan had instantly regretted any inferences Jenny might have made, but he hadn't been able to think of any way to correct her mistaken impression without adding to the problem.

"Tell her I'm waiting in the car," she'd said stiffly, and stalked away, her back as straight and proud as any Comanche chief he'd ever seen pictured in the art museums around the Southwest.

"Sure you don't want a glass of tea or maybe some of the oatmeal-and-raisin cookies Maritza baked earlier?" he'd called after her. He'd seen his plans for an evening with the two of them vanishing in a puff of smoke. Janet was scared spitless of being around him and Jenny clearly resented whatever was happening between him and her mother.

The offer of cookies went unanswered, just one indication of how upset she'd been. When he'd relayed her whereabouts to her much cooler-looking, if no less rattled mother, Janet had grabbed her purse and taken off without so much as a goodbye.

"Well, that certainly went well," he'd muttered as he'd watched the trail of dust settle in their wake.

Apparently their evening hadn't gotten any better, if Jenny's sullen mood this morning was any indication.

She wouldn't even meet his gaze, which made him wonder just what Janet had told her about their little set-to the night before.

At midmorning, as soon as she'd picked disinterestedly at the snack Maritza had prepared for her, she'd stalked out of the kitchen and disappeared, sparing him little more than a glare.

He hadn't seen her for another hour or so. Hadn't even looked that hard, truthfully. He'd figured she needed time to settle down and get her bearings again without him hovering over her with a lot of questions.

Then, not more than five minutes ago, he'd spotted her sneaking away from the toolshed with suspicious streaks of yellow paint on her clothes. It was not a good sign, he'd decided as he went out to the shed.

The shambles he found triggered an explosion that could have been heard in the next county. Toolboxes had been upended, yellow paint had been splattered hither and yon, and nuts, bolts and nails were scattered like birdseed all over the floor.

"Damn that girl's hide!" he bellowed, even as he wondered precisely what had set her off this time. He'd long since discovered that Jenny only acted out when she was feeling threatened in some way.

Taking off in the direction he'd seen her heading, he followed her trail all the way to the creek. He found her sitting at the edge, her feet in the water, tears streaming down her face.

He lowered himself to the ground next to her and waited, biding his time until she felt like talking.

"I don't care if you do send me to jail," she said eventually in a voice choked with barely contained sobs.

"Actually, I hadn't considered that possibility," he

said. "I was thinking you could spend the rest of the day back there cleaning up the mess you made."

He looked her in the eye and saw thirteen years of hurt and loneliness there. "First, though, why don't you tell me what's on your mind?"

"Nothing."

"You just decided to tear up things inside the toolshed for fun?"

"So what if I did?" she said belligerently.

"I suppose everybody gets in a foul mood on occasion for no reason and needs to let off a little steam," he agreed, then slanted a look at her. "Just seems to me as if something must have set you off."

"Well, it didn't, all right!"

He shrugged. "If you say so."

For the next few minutes they sat there side-by-side in total silence except for the sound of birds singing in the trees overhead and the soft splash of the creek as it ran past.

"You just gonna drop it?" she asked, regarding him with a mix of surprise and wariness.

"I thought there was nothing you wanted to say. Of course, maybe if you tell me, you'll feel better. That's how it works sometimes. Sharing the load goes a long way toward making it seem a little lighter."

Her shoulders slumped dejectedly as she picked at the frayed edge of her cut-off jeans. "You'll get mad."

"So it has something to do with me?"

She nodded, looking miserable.

"Is it me and your mom?"

Her head gave an almost imperceptible little bob. "I think she likes you," she mumbled finally. "She says she doesn't, but I can tell."

Harlan considered the observation a promising sign. He didn't tell Jenny that. She obviously disagreed.

"Would that be so terrible, having your mom like me?" he asked instead, hoping to get to the root of her displeasure. Did she resent the possibility of a replacement for her father? Was it just him in particular she disliked? He had a feeling the answer might hold the key to his future.

"It's not that exactly," she admitted. "I mean, you're okay, I guess. A little bossy, but okay. It's just that my mom and me, we've been a team ever since the divorce. We don't need anybody else."

"Maybe I do," he said quietly.

The concept seemed to intrigue her. "What do you mean?"

"Just that it's been awful quiet around here the past year or so, ever since my wife died. My sons are all grown and living their own lives now."

"Maybe Cody and his kids could move in with you," she suggested, either in an attempt to be helpful or an attempt to get her and her mother off the hook.

He could have given some glib reply to that, but he decided she needed honesty from him. She needed to be treated like an adult, at least on this issue. "Oh, the truth of it is, Cody and I would butt heads constantly. And Melissa should be able to run her own house the way she wants without worrying about the way things were always done around here."

She nodded thoughtfully. "That could be a problem, I guess. So how come you like having me and my mom around so much?"

"For one thing, you're a pretty special kid, in case you didn't know. I knew it the second you climbed down out of that truck of mine, spitting mad and taking your own foolishness out on me."

He slanted a sideways look at her. She appeared to be listening intently, so he went on. "As for your mom, she's made me laugh again. That's mighty important. It's always seemed to me that folks weren't meant to go through life without a companion, someone who thinks they're terrific. I don't know a lot about what happened between your parents, but divorce is never easy. I think you and your mom deserve someone who'll put your needs first. And I could sure use someone to liven this place up."

Jenny looked torn between wanting him to feel better and her own distinctly opposite needs. "Maybe you could just play the radio real loud or 'Geraldo' and 'Oprah.' Wouldn't that work?"

He grinned. "It's not the same."

"You mean you just want people to talk to, stuff like that?"

"More or less."

"Oh." She seemed to be considering the idea, then she lifted her chin and stared him straight in the eye. "I thought you wanted sex with her."

The blunt and far too perceptive remark sent blood climbing up the back of his neck. He had to choke back a chuckle. "That's a whole other issue and one I do not intend to discuss with you, young lady," he said sternly.

"My mother and I talk about everything. She doesn't keep secrets," she said, regarding him with a sly look. "Not from me, anyway."

"I'll bet she'll keep this one," Harlan countered. It was beginning to seem to him, though, that there were too damned many people fascinated with his love life these days.

"So?" he asked. "What's the verdict? Do you object to your mom and me seeing each other?"

"Would you stop if I did?"

"Probably not," he admitted. "But I'd work like crazy to make you change your mind."

"Would you let me off this prison sentence you imposed?"

He grinned at the ploy. "Is being out here really so terrible?" He fixed a steady gaze on her. "Tell the truth."

"No," she said with an air of resignation. "It's just the principle of it. You get to boss me around and I have to take it."

"That's right," he said. "That's the way it works in the real world."

"Yeah, but in the real world you get paid. I'm doing slave labor."

He nodded. "Okay, maybe I didn't set up the rules quite right. How about we go back to the house and figure out how much you owe me for the truck—and the toolshed," he added pointedly. "Then we'll set a salary for your chores around here. You can pay me back out of your earnings each week."

"Will I have to pay you every dime?"

He chuckled at her negotiating skills. He'd raised one son who'd had the same knack for getting his way. He was head of an oil company now. He suspected Jenny could share a similar fate if she put that quick thinking of hers to good use.

"We can negotiate that," he suggested. "We'll work out an appropriate payment schedule. Of course, that might mean you won't be paid off at the end of summer. You might have to keep coming out here."

She weighed that for several minutes before nodding. "Okay."

He held out his hand. "Shall we shake on it?"

The instant they had solemnly shaken hands on their new deal, Jenny stood and whooped with undisguised glee. "I know exactly how I'm going to spend my money, too," she declared.

"How?" he said, anticipating a litany of CD titles and video games.

"I'm going to buy back Lone Wolf's land and give it to Mom."

He thought the plan might be a bit overly ambitious, given her debt and her likely wages, but who was he to discourage her. "And where is Lone Wolf's land?"

She grinned at him. "You're sitting on it."

10

This had been her great-great-grandfather's land? Harlan couldn't have been more stunned if Jenny had announced she and her mother had robbed a bank. He gazed around at the lush, verdant banks of the creek and beyond to the rolling landscape he'd always considered his home.

"You sure about that?" he asked, trying to piece together all of the implications. Was that why Jenny had stolen his truck in the first place, just to wrangle a meeting with him? Or maybe in some twisted way to get even with him for the perceived theft of her ancestor's land? It was certainly one explanation for the resentful expression he'd caught on Janet's face the day they'd gone riding over the ranch's acres.

It was several minutes before he realized Jenny hadn't answered. When he looked at her, he saw that she was scuffing the toe of her sneaker in the grass and looking guilty as sin. Since things like theft and destruction didn't stir that expression, he couldn't help wondering what had.

"Jenny?" he prodded. "How do you know that this was your great-great-grandfather's land?"

"Mom told me," she admitted, reluctance written all over her face. "I wasn't supposed to say anything, though. Please, don't say I told. Please."

There could only be one reason for keeping such a secret that he could think of. Janet had some cocka-mamie plan to right an old wrong and get this land back. He'd heard of court battles like that, efforts to reclaim Native American lands stolen by individuals or the government.

He didn't know of too many that had been successful, though. The government's treatment of Native American rights might have been shabby, but there were probably legal documents a foot thick to prove that the Native Americans had been compensated for every bit of land taken from them.

The thought that Janet might try, though, was enough to make his blood run cold. The knowledge that she had insinuated herself into his life without ever saying a word about her intentions infuriated him. He would have sworn Janet Runningbear didn't have a duplicitous bone in her body. It appeared his judgment had been impaired after all.

"Don't worry," he reassured Jenny with icy calm. "I won't say a thing to your mother."

No, he was going to sit back and wait for her to make her move. He would be ready for her, though. And he would make her regret the day she ever tried to tangle with Harlan Adams.

Later that night, alone in his den, he fought against the wave of disappointment rushing over him. He'd been so hopeful that Janet and her rebellious daughter were the answers to his prayers. Now it appeared that Janet, at least, was nothing more than a liar and a cheat.

He didn't like the prospect of sitting idle, waiting for her to strike. That wasn't his way.

And maybe he couldn't admit to all he knew and involve Jenny, but he could try to force Janet's hand. Maybe it was time he found out once and for all if it was him she was attracted to, or, as he was beginning to believe, the land she thought belonged to her.

With cold deliberation, he sat behind the desk where he'd kept White Pines books for so many years and plotted a strategy for making sure that not one single acre ever left Adams ownership. Janet Runningbear might be the smartest, slickest lawyer ever trained, but she was no match for him.

Except maybe, he thought, in bed. As icily furious as he was about Jenny's innocent revelations, he couldn't seem to tame the desire Janet aroused in him. Maybe sex was the way to force the issue. He could satisfy this growing hunger that had him aching to touch her morning, noon and night. A woman revealed a lot when she made love to a man. He was almost certain he would know once and for all what was really in Janet's heart, if he could just get past her emotional defenses.

He sipped on a glass of bourbon, pleased with his plan. His pulse kicked up just thinking about it. There was nothing like the prospect for steamy sex or a good battle of wills to make a man feel alive. He had Janet to thank on both counts, he thought with a trace of bitterness. He'd have to be sure to express his gratitude when all was said and done.

Janet glanced up with surprise when the door to her office opened at midmorning and Harlan stepped across the threshold onto the threadbare carpet she couldn't afford to replace until business picked up. Something in his expression alarmed her. She'd seen him looking determined. She'd seen him defiant. Both traits were evident now, but there was a cold, calculating gleam in his eyes that was something new and not entirely reassuring.

"What brings you into town?" she asked warily.

"I thought maybe you and I could get a word alone here."

She hadn't noticed that he had all that much difficulty getting her alone at White Pines when he was of a mind to, but she just nodded. "Something important come up?"

"In a manner of speaking," he said, perching on a corner of her desk, his jeans-clad knees scant inches from hers.

It seemed to Janet that he was deliberately crowding her. In fact, it was just more evidence of his odd mood. He had been acting weird all day. She'd noticed it first when she'd dropped off Jenny.

Now that she thought about it, Jenny had seemed awfully subdued since yesterday evening, as well. Had she gotten into more trouble? Was Harlan fed up with playing surrogate daddy? Had he come to tell her that he wanted to end their arrangement?

"Jenny's not giving you trouble, is she?" she asked, regarding him uneasily. Jenny, for all of her grumbling, would be heartbroken if her days at White Pines and with Harlan were over.

"None that I can't handle," he said.

The response relieved her mind on that score at least, but there was something. She was sure of it. "Then, what is it?" she prodded.

His gaze locked with hers. "I think we should go away together," he announced.

Oh, boy, she thought as the breath whooshed right out of her. This was the last thing she'd expected. Well, not the last thing, but certainly she hadn't anticipated such an invitation coming so soon. Janet felt her cheeks flame as she battled temptation and embarrassment.

"Go away together?" she repeated dazedly. "You and me? Why? I mean, we haven't even had a real date. Don't you think we're getting a little ahead of ourselves here?"

"We had dinner at your place. We've had dinner at my place. We've been on a picnic down by the creek. You don't call that dating?"

"No," she insisted. She didn't have a better name for it, but she'd been swearing to herself for days now that she was not dating Harlan Adams and that's the way she intended to keep it. "Even if those meals counted as dates, that's hardly a sufficient basis for assuming I would go off on some romantic tryst with you."

"I figured those kisses were a clue that you might at least consider the offer."

"Then you leapt to a wrong conclusion," she said adamantly.

An expression of pure frustration crossed his face. "Your daughter is asking me if I'm interested in having sex with you. My sons are practically salivating over every development in our relationship. I'd just like to get to know you someplace out from under their watchful eyes."

She stared at him with growing horror. "Jenny asked you about sex?" she asked with a sinking sensation in the pit of her stomach.

"Indeed she did," he said. "Not the workings of it, of course. Just whether that was the only reason I was interested in you."

"Oh, sweet heaven," she murmured. "I'm sorry."

He didn't seem to care about an apology. In fact, he seemed torn between exasperation and admiration for her child's audacity. She'd noticed that about him. Almost nothing threw Harlan Adams off stride. He was confident in a way that didn't require controlling other people. For all of the teasing she'd witnessed between him and his sons about his manipulation, she noticed that each of them had gone their own way, apparently with their father's blessing.

"I can't go away with you," she finally said with some regret. "I won't leave Jenny, for one thing. For another, I can't afford the damage to my reputation. I'm having enough difficulty getting the people in town to trust a woman lawyer, who's part Comanche, to boot, without giving them anything more to speculate about."

Harlan's expression promptly clouded over. "Are people still giving you a hard time? I thought that would be a thing of the past by now."

"It's no worse than I expected," she repeated emphatically, regretting taking that particular tack with him again. She knew better than to get his white knight tendencies stirred up.

"Who's bothering you?" he demanded, ignoring her low-key attempt to sidetrack him. "I'll have a word with them."

"No. You will not! We've been all through this. I will not have you fighting my battles for me. We're talking about my career. I can handle it."

He seemed ready and eager to rush off and slay a

few dragons for her, but he finally backed down at her adamant tone. It was another thing she liked about him. He didn't just listen to her. He actually *heard* what she was saying.

Somewhere in a corner of her heart she was beginning to recognize that Harlan Adams wasn't like any other man she'd ever known. And all of those sturdy defenses that had served her so well the past few years were slowly but surely beginning to topple.

"Let's talk a little more about you and me, then," he suggested, shifting gears so quickly it left her head reeling. "Where do you see us heading?"

Janet wished she had prepared herself better for this moment. She had known a conversation like this was inevitable. Harlan wasn't the kind of man to be satisfied for long by evasive answers and rushed, skittish departures. She had no idea what had triggered this particular confrontation at midmorning in her office, rather than some evening out at White Pines, but apparently he'd reached a decision about the future and intended to put his plan into motion.

"I don't know where we're heading," she said, which was too close to the truth to suit her and too wishy-washy an answer to suit Harlan.

"You ever think about marrying again?" he asked.

She swallowed hard. "You mean, getting married to you?"

His gaze was riveted on her. "Or anyone," he conceded grudgingly.

Her throat went dry. She couldn't have croaked out a reply if she'd had one handy.

"Something wrong?" he inquired. "Cat got your tongue?"

An odd note in his voice triggered an alarm some-where deep inside her. "Is there some reason you're forcing this issue now?"

"I just thought it was time to get our cards on the table." He studied her pointedly, then added, "All of our cards. Call the bet, so to speak."

Panic flooded through her. What exactly did he know? Had he somehow figured out her intentions about the Comanche lands? She'd been doing legal research in all her spare time, but no one knew about that, she reassured herself.

No one, except Jenny. Surely her daughter wouldn't have said a word. She knew how important silence was, especially when there was every chance in the world that nothing would come of her plans.

She studied Harlan's face and tried to guess what was going on behind that enigmatic expression. She had a feeling whatever decision she reached about that was critical. If she jumped to the wrong conclusion, said the wrong thing, it could ruin everything.

"My life's an open book," she said in what she hoped was an innocent-enough tone.

"Is it really?" he said, then shrugged. "I wasn't think-ing so much of the past. I'm more concerned with the future."

"Harlan, I'm just a single mom struggling from day to day to make ends meet."

The comment sounded a little ingenuous even to her own ears. Harlan responded with a lift of his eye-brows, indicating that he wasn't fooled by it, either. Janet sighed.

"Okay, what do you want me to say?"

"How about the truth?" he said with a surprising edge in his voice. "Start to finish."

The last suggested for the second time in a matter of minutes that he knew something, or thought he did. "Harlan, is there something specific on your mind?"

"I've told you what was on my mind. It's your head that remains a mystery." He stood. "Why don't we go grab lunch and see if we can clarify a few things over a cold beer and some of Rosa's enchiladas?"

"The last time you and I went to Rosa's, I got the impression people were hanging on our every word and reporting it afterward. Why would you want to go there now?"

He shrugged. "I was hoping the beer would loosen your tongue."

She stared at him in exasperation. "I'm being as honest here as I can be," she protested.

"Darlin', if this is your idea of being candid, I'd trust you to keep my deepest, darkest secrets." He stepped behind her and pulled back her chair. "Come on. Let's see if a beer will work any magic or not."

"I hate beer."

"Then you'll drink it down right quick, sort of like medicine," he said, a glint of amusement in his eyes for the first time since he'd entered her office.

Janet still couldn't help thinking there were undercurrents here, deep ones, that she might never figure out. Something told her, though, that her future might depend on her trying.

A half dozen heads snapped up when Harlan escorted Janet through the door at Rosa's. Mule rolled his eyes in disgust.

"You two hooked up together again? Don't expect me

to get involved in another poker game with the likes of you," the mechanic warned, scowling at Janet.

"Don't worry," Harlan informed him. "We're here for a little private conversation."

He passed right by his regular table and urged Janet into a booth all the way in the back. It wasn't quite out of the sight of prying eyes, but it was the best he could come up with under the circumstances.

"That was a little rude, don't you think?" Janet said when they were seated, a half dozen pairs of eyes staring at them. "Just the kind of thing that will stir up more gossip."

"Oh, will you stop fussing about gossip? Seems to me you have more important things to be fretting about."

"Such as?"

He reached across the table and touched a finger to her lower lip, all the while keeping his gaze locked with hers. "Such as the way your skin burns when I touch you like this."

He could feel her trembling even as she blinked hard and deliberately looked away. So, that much was real, he decided. She couldn't be faking a reaction like that, for devious purposes or otherwise. Which meant her reluctance to commit to anything more than the casual encounters they'd shared thus far was pure cussedness on her part.

Or perhaps a belated attack of ethical considerations, he amended. Maybe she'd decided she couldn't get any more involved with a man she intended to try to fleece out of his land. He supposed even would-be thieves had a code of honor they wouldn't breech.

He finally allowed his hand to drop away. "You trying to tell me that doesn't mean anything?" he chided.

"It doesn't," she insisted stubbornly.

"I don't believe you."

"Okay, I'm attracted to you," she snapped. "Is that what you wanted to hear? Does it make your heart go pitty-pat? Is your oversize ego satisfied?"

He chuckled at her irritation. "As a matter of fact, yes on all counts."

She lifted the menu and pointedly retreated behind it.

"You two planning on arguing all afternoon or were you thinking of ordering lunch?" Rosa inquired, not even trying to hide her amusement.

Harlan wondered with a sigh exactly how much she'd heard before she spoke up. He supposed whatever it was, his sons would know every word before nightfall. He wondered idly if Rosa's silence could be bought. He glanced up and studied her speculatively.

"Rosa, darlin', what would it take to keep you from telling Maritza or any of your other myriad relatives in Los Piños that I was even in here today?" he asked.

Janet peeked around her menu, curiosity written all over her face. "You're trying to bribe Rosa to keep silent?" she demanded.

"You bet," he muttered grimly. "Come on, Rosa, what will it take?"

The heavy-set Mexican woman shook her head as she regarded him with an expression of pity. "You cannot buy loyalty, old friend."

"I can't seem to get it, either," he grumbled. "Whatever you heard here today, just forget it, okay? That's not so much to ask, is it?"

Rosa's expression was perfectly bland. "But I heard nothing."

Harlan sighed. "I'll bet."

Not trusting her one whit, he still dropped the subject and asked Janet what she wanted. When he'd placed the order, he leaned back and focused once more on the woman seated opposite him.

The color in her cheeks was high. That was probably a sign of guilt, he decided. She'd wound her hair into some sort of prim knot on top of her head, but she'd done it in a way that made a man's fingers just itch to tug it free. He considered it another contradictory message in a whole sea of them he'd been getting lately.

As irritated and suspicious as he was, he wanted her with a hunger that stunned him. He'd been comfortable in his marriage with Mary. He'd enjoyed the physical side of their relationship. There'd still been plenty of passion to it. More than a lot of people shared after being together more than thirty-five years, from what he'd heard.

But these feelings he was experiencing now were a far cry from that. His pulse quickened just at the prospect of seeing Janet. His body responded like some randy adolescent's at the most innocent touch. A kiss was enough to trigger a desire so thorough and overwhelming, it was a wonder he hadn't busted the zipper of every pair of jeans he owned.

None of those reactions had eased just because he now suspected her of trying to cheat him out of his ranch. Was that because on some level he couldn't believe that's what she meant to do? Was he thinking with his testosterone and not his head? He wouldn't be the first man to fall prey to that sort of foolishness.

He met her gaze and tried to read her intentions in her dark brown eyes, but in the restaurant's shadows they were more inscrutable than ever.

"Harlan, what's really bothering you?" she asked, sounding more worried about him than frightened for herself. She didn't sound like a woman with secrets she feared might have been uncovered.

"I told you, I'm trying to get a grasp on what the future holds," he said, making the response enigmatic enough to cover anything from their relationship to the future of White Pines.

"Is that something you need to figure out today?" she asked, amusement lurking in her eyes. "Couldn't you just take it day by day as it comes, the way most of us mortals do?"

"I've never much liked surprises," he admitted.

"So it's true, then," she teased. "You do like to control everyone and everything around you. Your sons and daughters-in-law were right about that."

The truth chafed, especially when it was being used to suit the purposes of someone who didn't want to reveal her own intentions. "What's wrong with wanting to shape your life, with wanting to take charge and make it the best it can be?"

"You miss out on the serendipities," she observed.

"Like Jenny stealing my pickup, I suppose."

She grinned. "It's true. If you didn't make it a habit to leave your keys in plain view, that wouldn't have happened. Maybe you're more open to risks than you know."

"I don't mind a few risks, when I've had time to weigh the odds," he countered pointedly. "For forty years those keys had never been a temptation to anyone in Los Piños. Now those are odds worth taking a risk on."

He looked her straight in the eye. "You seem like a good risk to me, too."

She didn't seem pleased by the observation. "You make me sound like a filly you might bet on in the fifth race at Belmont."

He waved off the comparison. "That's just money. I'm talking about fate here, Janet. Yours and mine. You've been talking a lot about my willingness to take risks. What about you? How do you feel about serendipity?"

He watched her closely as she seemed to struggle with the question. Whatever internal war she was waging struck him as a pretty good indication that she did have things to hide.

"I'm all for it," she said eventually.

"Oh, really? Then why aren't you seizing my offer to take you away to some romantic spot for a few days?"

She scowled at him. "I explained that."

"Not to my satisfaction."

She stood then and threw down her napkin. "Not everything in this world has to meet your satisfaction, Harlan Adams. You'd do well to remember that."

With that she turned and sashayed straight out of Rosa's, ignoring the gaping expressions of Mule and all the others following her departure. To his everlasting regret, Harlan's body turned rock-hard just watching her go.

When she was finally out of sight, he sighed. That woman's defiant streak was going to be the death of him yet. Worse, he didn't know a damn bit more about what was going on in her head now than he had before he'd forced this confrontation. Yep, it was just as he'd suspected. He was definitely losing his touch.

11

"Mom, did Mr. Adams seem weird to you today?" Jenny asked as she watched the hamburgers she had frying on the stove for dinner.

"Weird, how?" Janet replied, even though she thought she knew exactly what Jenny was talking about. He'd struck her as weird, impossible, arrogant and a whole lot more. She was interested, though, in just which vibes Jenny had picked up on.

"Like he was mad or something. I don't know. He was just awful quiet, not bossy like he usually is. And he took off in the middle of the morning without giving me anything to do. He said I could just go into his library and read, if I wanted to."

"That must have been when he came into town to see me."

Jenny put the spatula down, turned and regarded her worriedly. "How come?"

Janet had been wondering the very same thing ever since he'd appeared on her office doorstep. Their lunch hadn't really enlightened her. Even though Harlan had plainly stated that he wanted to discuss their future, there had been those odd undercurrents, as if he were really looking for evidence of some treachery. She couldn't share that with her daughter, so she simply said he'd wanted to talk.

"About what?" Jenny persisted. "Me?"

The last was said with a plaintive note that Janet found worrisome. "Why would you think he wanted to talk about you? Have you been making trouble out there?" When Jenny remained silent, Janet's heart sank. "Okay, what happened?"

"Nothing."

"Jenny?"

"Okay, okay. Don't bust a gut. I did make sort of a mess of his toolshed yesterday," she finally admitted.

"I see."

"But I cleaned it up," her daughter said in a rush. "I even painted it. Bright yellow, in fact. It's awesome."

Janet couldn't work up much enthusiasm over the color scheme of the toolshed, especially since Jenny herself seemed to be the reason it had needed painting.

"Why did you wreck it in the first place?" she asked, even though she thought she already knew from what Harlan had mentioned about Jenny's questions to him. "Did it have something to do with your being worried that Mr. Adams and I might be sleeping together?"

Jenny groaned and turned beet red. "He told you, didn't he? Jeez, Mom, he swore he wasn't going to blab."

"He didn't blab, at least not the way you mean. It just sort of came out in a conversation we were having."

"About the two of you?"

Janet nodded.

"So, are you?"

"Are we what?"

"Sleeping together," Jenny said impatiently. "He wouldn't say exactly."

"And neither will I," Janet said. "That's not a subject that's any of your business."

"How can you say that? He's the enemy."

Janet grinned at Jenny's determination to cling to that label. Her daughter was even more stubborn than she was. She'd conceded days ago that Harlan was no more the enemy than some descendant of Custer's might be.

"You don't believe that any more than I do," she chided.

"You're giving up?" Jenny said, staring at her incredulously. "You're not going to fight him for Lone Wolf's land?"

"I'm still researching whether there's any legal way to get the land. Besides, I told you before that I don't have evidence that Lone Wolf's father was ever on Mr. Adams's land. We may never know for sure. And the way things worked back then, it wasn't like the Comanches had deeds on file."

"But I told him—" Jenny turned pale. "Whoops."

Janet felt as if she'd been whacked over the head by a two-by-four. Of course! That explained those odd undercurrents she'd felt with Harlan. With her thoughts in turmoil, the odor of meat burning barely even registered. At the moment the fate of the hamburgers was the last thing on her mind.

"You told him what?" she asked carefully.

"Nothing," Jenny muttered, backing away from the stove and clearly trying to put some distance between herself and her mother at the same time.

"Jennifer!"

"Okay, I might have let it slip that his ranch was sitting on Lone Wolf's land."

"You might have?"

"I did, all right?" she said belligerently. "I don't know what difference it makes. He was going to find out sooner or later anyway."

Janet clung to her temper by a thread. "But it might have been nice if he found out about it from me. Now he must think I've just been playing some sort of sick game by hanging around out there. He probably thinks we're out to betray him."

"Aren't we?" Jenny asked simply. "Isn't that why we're in this godawful state, instead of back home in New York, where we belong?"

With that she whirled and ran from the kitchen, leaving Janet to take the burned hamburgers from the stove. No longer the least bit interested in food, she dumped the frying pan, burgers and all, into the sink, then went out to the front porch to sit in a rocker and think.

Should she go out to White Pines first thing in the morning and tell Harlan everything? But, if he already knew most of it, why had he been trying to back her into a corner about their future earlier today? Why hadn't he been blasting her as the deceitful traitor she felt like? Would she ever understand the workings of this man's mind? Or any man's, for that matter?

And why, dear heaven, did it suddenly seem to matter so much to her that Harlan Adams not think ill of her? Was it possible that he had come to mean more to her than that elusive dream she'd formulated as a child and held on to so tightly ever since?

She could still recall Lone Wolf telling her about the Comanches known as Penateka or Honey-Eaters, who'd occupied a stretch of the Comancheria from Edwards Plateau to Cross Timbers. His telling had been further preservation of the oral history of his forefathers.

Even now she shook with indignation at his description of the 1840 meeting in San Antonio during which the Comanche leaders who'd come to discuss peace had been slaughtered in what had come to be known as the Council House Massacre. There had been nothing after that to indicate to the tribe that Texans could ever be trusted.

Slowly but surely settlers had been given more and more of the Comanche lands, until Lone Wolf's ancestors had been forced from Texas altogether. Could she ever achieve retribution for something that had occurred so long ago and even now seemed so complex? Everything she'd read indicated it would be difficult, if not impossible, to make any legal claim.

The questions kept her up most of the night. The answers didn't come at all.

In the morning, she didn't have a chance to act on any of the myriad possibilities that had occurred to her. When she and Jenny got to White Pines, Harlan was nowhere to be found. It was Cody who waited for them on the front porch.

"Come on, short stuff," he said to Jenny, who brightened immediately. "You and I are going out to look for stray calves this morning."

"Oh, wow!" Jenny said, clearly pleased to be asked to help her idol with such an important task. It was the first time Janet had seen a smile on her face since their argument the night before.

"Where's your father?" Janet asked Cody, hoping that her heart wasn't sitting in plain view on her sleeve.

He shrugged. "Beats me. He left me a note to take Jenny with me today. Didn't say where he was heading or when he'd be back. He took his plane, though. He might have had business over in Dallas or something."

"Oh." Janet fought against the tide of disappointment that washed through her as Cody headed over to the two horses he'd saddled and had tethered to a fence rail. She should have been relieved, but she wasn't. She brushed a kiss across Jenny's forehead, ignoring her daughter's embarrassed protest. "Have a good day, pumpkin. See you tonight."

"Yeah, Mom. Bye," Jenny said, already rushing off to keep up with Cody's long strides.

Feeling abandoned on all fronts, Janet stood where she was until Cody and Jenny had ridden off. Only after they'd gone did she admit to herself that she would rather have had Harlan screaming at her than ignoring her this way. There was little doubt in her mind that he'd deliberately made it a point not to be at home this morning.

Maybe he really had had unexpected business to take care of, just as Cody had suggested, she consoled herself as she drove into town. Right, she scoffed right back. Without telling Cody the details? No way. He was very careful not to step on his son's managerial toes. No, the truth of it was, he was avoiding her because his discovery of her treachery was eating at him.

She resigned herself to waiting until Harlan turned up again before settling matters between them. The delay wouldn't make much difference. She doubted she'd have any clearer an idea how to handle it hours or days from now than she did right this minute.

Harlan had spent half the night after his aborted meeting with Janet reading through every book in his library on the Comanches and their days in the southern Great Plains. Nothing he found there was conclusive proof that Janet's ancestral claim to his land was solid. In fact, it seemed to him that Lone Wolf's father had probably been a typical nomadic hunter, before being sent off to the reservation in Oklahoma.

It had been well into the wee hours of the morning when he'd decided to do a little more investigating by going to Oklahoma to see what he could discover there. His meetings with folks at the Bureau of Indian Affairs and with tribal elders who agreed to see him were inconclusive, as well. He sensed that Janet would never find the proof she sought unless she hoped to stake her claim for all Comanches and not just for her great-grandfather and his descendants.

Still, the meetings had given him much to think about, a historical perspective on his own family's actions when they'd moved to Texas to flee the war that had destroyed their home in the South. In seizing an opportunity for themselves, had they stolen it from others? He found he could understand Janet's actions far more clearly now and he could do so without feeling the rancor of betrayal.

Perhaps, if Janet ever opened up to him, they could reach some sort of compromise. In the meantime, though, he'd decided that she enriched his life too much for him to walk away without fighting for their future. It was a decision weighed and reached with years of maturity, rather than the angry, instantaneous, hot-blooded reaction he might have had a couple of decades earlier.

Also, the more he thought about the desperate plea he had made to Janet to run away with him, the more he realized that she had been exactly right to turn him down. The place to court her was right in Los Piños, in plain view. He didn't ever want a soul to think he was sneaking around with her because he wasn't proud to be seen with her. There were too many people ready with quick bias for him to be adding to that sort of rotten speculation about her morals or his own.

As soon as he'd set down his plane at the local airfield, he marched straight down Main Street, walked into her office and hauled her off to have dinner at Di-Pasquali's.

"Harlan," she protested, even as she hurried to keep pace with him. "What about Jenny? She's going to be waiting for me at White Pines. She'll be worried."

"I called Melissa from the airport. Jenny will have dinner with her and Cody. Sharon Lynn and baby Harlan love having her around. You can pick her up there."

She halted in her tracks and scowled at him. "Do you always have to manipulate everything to get your own way?"

He grinned unrepentantly. "Always," he assured her. "Get used to it."

He linked her arm through his and gently, but insistently, escorted her the rest of the way to the restaurant. It seemed to him her footsteps dragged a bit reluctantly, but at least she didn't bolt on him.

Inside DiPasquali's, he directed her to a table right smack in front of the window, in plain view of anybody coming or going inside the restaurant or passing by on the street outside. She regarded him with a curious look, but sat where he'd indicated.

Gina DiPasquali joined them at once with their menus, winking at Janet as she handed one to her. If he hadn't already known about their conspiracy over that dinner at Janet's, he would have wondered what the two of them were up to.

"Are you thinking of having the lasagna?" Harlan inquired innocently, his gaze fixed on Janet's face.

Gina chuckled as Janet's cheeks turned pink. "Caught you, didn't he?"

"Before he'd taken two bites," Janet admitted. "Then he rubbed it in for the rest of the evening."

"I did not," Harlan protested, feigning indignation. "But I couldn't very well let you go on thinking you'd put one over on me, though, could I? It would have set a dangerous precedent. I might never have gotten the upper hand again."

"Who says you ever had it," she shot right back. "Besides, no gentleman would have embarrassed a hostess by pointing out what he suspected. You should have been oohing and aahing over my supposed culinary skills."

Gina rolled her eyes. "If you were counting on that, I could have told you not to bother. Harlan's only a gentleman when it suits his purposes."

"Besides which, you'd have felt guilty as sin if I offered high praise for a dish you knew you hadn't prepared," he asserted. "I was just saving you that."

"How considerate," Janet retorted a trifle sourly.

Gina apparently decided to let them resolve the issue of etiquette they were debating, because she stuffed her order book back into her pocket.

"You two can sit here and battle wits from now till the cows come home," she said. "Let me choose dinner tonight, so you won't have something more to quibble about. I'll have Tony fix you something special."

"Perfect," Janet said.

Harlan decided she was apparently no more eager to choose from the menu than she was to cook in her own kitchen. It was a wonder she wasn't skin and bones.

When Gina had gone, he did an appreciative survey of Janet. Whatever her disinterest in food, she managed to have a perfectly rounded figure that could fill a man with lust. He dragged his attention away and stared at the ceiling in what was only a partially successful attempt to bring his hormones under control. The reaction only confirmed what he'd guessed earlier, that he couldn't walk away from her.

"Everything okay?" she inquired with a half smile that was all too knowing.

He caught the undisguised mirth in her eyes. "Fine," he lied. "How about you? You looked put-out when I turned up at your office a little while ago. Something on your mind?"

"Just your habit of appearing without notice and expecting me to drop everything to accompany you. Haven't you ever heard of the telephone?"

"Sure, but it's harder for you to turn me down face-to-face."

"What makes you think that?"

"Watching you stammer around for excuses a few times."

"I never stammer," she retorted irritably. "Still, I can't keep taking off at the drop of a hat, just because you get some whim to feed me."

"You have a lot of work piled up?" he inquired doubt-fully.

"That's not the point."

"Sure it is. No sense in you sitting around in your office pretending to be busy, when you could be having a nice meal with me."

"What about a nice meal with my daughter?"

"Who'd cook?"

She frowned at him. "You really do have a rotten streak, Harlan Adams."

"Just speaking the gospel truth. It's not even hearsay. Don't forget I saw the state of your kitchen that night and you never even dared to put that meal on the table. Makes me wonder how the two of you have survived this long. Must have been the takeout available from all those fancy New York restaurants."

She looked a little like a chicken who'd had her feathers ruffled by that comment, but she kept her mouth clamped firmly shut. Harlan watched the temper flare in her eyes, then slowly diminish before she finally seized on another topic.

"Where did you go so early this morning?" she asked in a perfectly neutral tone.

He grinned. "So, you did miss me. I'm gratified to hear it."

"I did not say I missed you. It was a simple question, Harlan. Just a little polite conversation, okay? If it's some big secret, just say so."

He got the impression he might be pushing her a little too hard with his teasing. He opted for giving her the truth, or at least a select portion of it. "I had some unexpected business to take care of."

"I thought Cody took care of all the ranch's business these days."

"Doesn't mean I can't stick my nose into it, when I'm of a mind to," he said. "By the way, did I mention you're looking particularly beautiful today. That red blouse suits you."

"Thank you," she said, but her gaze narrowed suspiciously. "You're up to something, aren't you?"

"I could ask you the same thing with more cause," he retorted, enjoying the unmistakable guilt that darkened her eyes.

He decided there was something to be said for tormenting her. Maybe he wouldn't tell her about that trip to Oklahoma, not until she came clean with him. Surely a man was entitled to some secrets from a woman who had the ability to tie him in knots without even trying.

Gina played straight into his hands by turning up just then with a platter of antipasto and two glasses of Chianti. It got them both off the hook, which was probably to the good, he decided as he watched Janet nervously shoving a couple of olives around on her plate. Let her stew for a bit.

"You get any clients today?" he asked after a while.

She looked up, her expression revealing unmistakable gratitude for the change to a more innocuous topic. "As a matter of fact, yes. Mule came by."

Harlan's mouth gaped. "What the devil did he want?"

"That's a matter of client confidentiality," she said, obviously pleased that she'd not only stunned him, but stirred his curiosity.

"Well, I'll be damned. You sure he didn't want to get in a few quick hands of poker? He might have been running short of cash, since he's had that garage of his closed for so blasted long."

"Sorry," she said blithely. "I can't talk about it."

"Mule tells me most of his business anyway," he said, trying to coax her into telling, when he knew perfectly well that she was too ethical to ever say a word. He was enjoying aggravating her too much to stop just yet.

"Then you'll have to ask him about this," she retorted. "Now, stop prying."

"Just making polite small talk," he shot right back, echoing her earlier jab.

She rolled her eyes. He couldn't help chuckling at her exasperated expression. "You are a treasure, you know that, don't you?"

The compliment seemed to throw her off-balance. "Where did that come from?" she asked in a tone that said she didn't think she deserved it.

"Just an observation. A man's entitled to make one every now and again, isn't he?"

"Of course."

"Shall I make a few more?" he inquired, leaning forward and lowering his voice to a seductive whisper.

She swallowed hard and shook her head. "I don't think so."

He grinned. "How come?"

"Because I don't think this is the time or the place to be discussing whatever it is you have on your mind."

"Now that's an interesting bit of speculation on your part," he observed, trying to keep the amusement out of his tone. "Just what is it you think I have on my mind that would be unsuitable for discussion in a public place?"

She blushed furiously. "Never mind. Perhaps I was wrong."

Harlan shook his head. "Now, you don't strike me as a woman who admits lightly to being wrong. Maybe you ought to say what's on *your* mind. Could just be you're right on track."

"Why are you doing this?" she demanded. "A gentleman—"

"We've already established that I'm no gentleman, not when it comes to affairs of the heart, so to speak."

He allowed his gaze to sweep over her, lingering long enough to keep her color high and her nerves jittery. The game turned on him, though. The next thing he knew his own heartbeat was racing and the blood was rushing straight to a portion of his anatomy where its unmistakable effect could prove downright embarrassing. He wanted her with an urgency that drove out all other thoughts. Visions of taking her here and now took up residence in his brain and clamored for action.

Apparently he'd been wrong about one thing, though. He was just enough of a gentleman not to act on such a desperate, wicked longing. But Janet Runningbear could thank her lucky stars that he'd chosen DiPasquali's for dinner tonight instead of White Pines. He doubted he'd have been anywhere near so restrained in the privacy of his own home.

He met her gaze and thought he read a mix of passion and uncertainty in those dark brown depths. Soon, he silently promised her and himself. He would claim her soon.

As if she could read his mind, an audible sigh eased through her. A sigh of satisfaction perhaps? Or maybe anticipation? Whichever it was, Harlan could only share in the sentiment.

To him the future was as clear-cut as a pane of glass or a ten-carat diamond. Whatever Janet Runningbear's original agenda had been in coming to Los Piños, he had a feeling it was only a matter of time and subtle persuasion before he'd have her seeing the years ahead as vividly as he did.

12

The bouquet of flowers that arrived in Janet's office the next morning was so huge that the only surface big enough to accommodate it was her desk. She was still staring in astonishment at the arrangement of splashy yellow mums, vivid orange tiger lilies, Texas bluebonnets and fragrant white roses when the man responsible for sending it walked in.

She didn't get it. Why was he lavishing all this attention on her, now that he knew the truth? Why had he kept so silent about what Jenny had told him? Was he planning to set her up to take a tremendous fall? If that was it, it was a pretty diabolical plan; one she couldn't imagine Harlan resorting to.

She was still trying to puzzle it out when he came up behind her, spanned her waist with his hands, brushed aside her hair and planted a kiss on her nape.

"I see it got here," he said, sounding extremely pleased with himself.

"Just a few minutes ago," she said, unable to take her eyes off the lavish display. She couldn't quite decide whether to be awed or appalled. She settled for adding, "The flowers are beautiful."

He released her, stepped in front of her, then examined her face intently. Apparently her expression gave her away. He frowned.

"Too much?" he inquired.

"It's not that…exactly," she said, not wanting to trample on the sentiment behind the overdone gesture. She'd discovered long ago that men required all the positive reinforcement possible, if a woman expected flowers and candy not just for special occasions, but as impulsive gifts for no reason at all. This wasn't a habit she wanted to break, just to modify. And this was an improvement over that first floral excess he'd brought to the house.

She gestured helplessly at the arrangement's take-over of her desk top. "Where am I supposed to work?"

He nodded. "Definitely a problem." He settled an innocent look on her. "So, take the day off."

She couldn't help laughing at his mischievous expression and at the outrageous suggestion. "Was that why you sent such a huge bouquet, so I wouldn't be able to work?"

"Actually, no, but I'm a man who can think on his feet. I could see your dilemma right off and came up with what I consider to be the perfect solution—play hooky."

She studied him suspiciously. "Seems a little convenient to me that you turned up here just in time to make a suggestion like that."

"You've obviously been hanging around with too many criminals. You lack trust."

Janet perched on the only available corner of her

desk and studied him intently. "Okay. If—and that's a very big if—I were to take you up on your suggestion, what exactly do you have in mind?"

"Lunch," he said at once.

"It's barely nine-fifteen in the morning."

"In Dallas."

She stared at him and tried to keep her mouth from gaping. "You want to go all the way to Dallas for lunch? Isn't that a little extravagant?"

He had a ready answer for that, too, apparently. "We could shop," he said without so much as a hesitation.

"For?"

He shrugged, his expression vaguely uncertain. "Beats me. I just figured all women loved to shop. And much as I love Los Piños, I can see that it's not exactly loaded with those fancy little designer boutiques, where a hankie costs an arm and a leg."

"I can't afford a boutique where hankies cost a hundred times what I'd pay for a pack of tissues."

"But I can."

She grinned at his persistence. "You want to fly to Dallas to buy me lunch and a hankie?"

"Or maybe a fancy outfit to wear to a party," he said, watching her with another of those exceptionally innocent expressions that wouldn't have deceived anyone with even half a brain.

Janet's gaze narrowed. "What party?"

"The one I'm throwing on Saturday night to introduce you to a few of my friends."

"Harlan, I told you I do not want you trying to drum up business for me."

He scowled, his exasperation apparent. "This isn't about business, darlin'. This is strictly personal."

For some reason she didn't find that nearly as reassuring as she should have. It struck her as being too... personal, she decided, using his own word to describe it. Too intimate. Especially given that unspoken subject hanging in the air between them. Why, why, why? she wondered again. What was he up to?

"I don't know—" she began, only to have him cut her off.

"It's no big deal," he reassured her. "There are a lot of people I owe for inviting me to dinner and stuff. I figured one big bash would take care of all those obligations. I can't have a big to-do without a proper hostess, can I?"

"And that's me?" she said skeptically. "The woman who can't cook a lick."

"I have Maritza and all of her relatives for that."

"You also have three very lovely daughters-in-law who would be happy to play hostess, I'm sure."

He waved off the suggestion. "I want a woman of my own."

She cringed at the possessive description, but let it pass. "Half the people in town barely say more than hello to me," she noted pointedly.

"That'll change when you're with me."

Knowing that he was right about that grated. "Harlan, I have to win people over myself."

"You will. I'm just opening the door, so they'll give you a chance to show 'em what a brilliant, witty, warm woman you are." He reached behind her desk and grabbed her purse. "Come on. You can think it over while we fly to Dallas."

"What about Jenny? What have you done with her since I dropped her off?"

"She's helping Melissa out with the kids today. I'm paying her ten bucks an hour to baby-sit. She says minimum wage is too cheap for the trouble those kids get into. Had to admit she was right about that."

Janet shook her head. "This is the oddest brand of punishment I've ever seen."

He shrugged. "So I'm lenient, sue me. Any more excuses?"

She was about to muster the last of her resolve and say no when she took a good, long look into his eyes. They were bright with excitement. He genuinely wanted to do this for her. How could she possibly disappoint him, when he'd already been so good to her and to Jenny? Besides, an unplanned trip to Dallas was exactly the sort of impulsive act she'd indulged in far too rarely.

"Okay, let's go for it," she said at last.

At the same time, she swore that she would do everything in her power not to take advantage of him. Lunch was one thing. A party outfit was something else entirely. She would buy that for herself, if she could convince herself that one of the dozens of cocktail dresses already in her closet from what seemed like another lifetime wouldn't do.

For a man who claimed not to know much about shopping, Harlan guided her around the best shops in Dallas with the ease and familiarity of an extravagant tour guide. He seemed to have his heart set on a particular kind of dress and, after trying on dozens, all she knew for certain was that it wasn't baubles, bangles or beads he was looking for.

"I think I know just the place," he said at last, and led her to a boutique carrying designer Western wear.

He gazed around at the fancy Western-cut shirts and rhinestone-studded jeans and nodded in satisfaction. "Yep, this is it."

Janet shook her head. "You knew all along this was what you wanted me to wear, didn't you?" she accused.

"I wasn't sure," he claimed.

"Harlan, there is no comparison between those cocktail dresses and this," she said, gesturing to the displays. "Why'd you waste three hours taking me to those stores, so I could try on silk and lace?"

"I thought all women liked to dress up in pretty clothes. Besides, I thought you might find something you couldn't resist." He shook his head. "You're a tough nut to crack, though. I never once saw a glimmer of longing in your eyes."

"Because I wore those kinds of dresses to more social functions than I care to recall back in New York. My closet is crammed with them. If I never wear another one, it will be okay with me."

He chuckled at that. "That's another thing I love about you. You've long since figured out who you are."

Janet denied his assessment with a quick shake of her head. "You're wrong. I know who I don't want to be anymore. I don't want to be a big city lawyer, living in a pressure cooker. I don't want to go to parties because I might meet someone important," she said pointedly, then added with a touch of wistfulness, "But I'm still discovering who I am."

Harlan listened to all that intently, then asked softly, "Any room in the picture for a rancher?"

The direct question took her by surprise. Her heart thumped unsteadily as she considered all the implications of what he was asking. "Maybe," she said eventually, her gaze locked with his.

"That's good enough," he said quietly. "For now."

She finally forced herself to break eye contact by feigning a sudden interest in a fancy denim outfit.

"Janet," Harlan said, drawing her attention back to him. "If there's one thing I've learned the past few years it's that life is unpredictable and often far too short. Don't get the idea I'm going to leave you much room to maneuver for long."

Her breath caught in her throat at the silky tone. "Is that a threat?"

He touched his fingers to her cheek in a light caress that set off fireworks in her midsection.

"It's a promise," he declared, then winked. "Now, try on that outfit you've been eyeing since we walked in the door. And while you're at it, take a look at that skirt and blouse with the sparkly doodads on it."

"Rhinestones?" she teased.

"That's the one. Looks perfect for square dancing."

"We're going to be dancing on Saturday?"

"Darlin', you can't have a big to-do in this part of the world and call it a party, unless there's dancing."

"I had no idea."

"That's why you have me," he reassured her. "I'm going to see to it that you fit right in in no time."

"I do so admire a man with a mission," she said as she grabbed the selected clothes off the racks and carried them into a nearby dressing room.

Inside the room, she shut the door and leaned against it, drawing in a deep breath. With every single minute she spent in Harlan Adams's company, she realized she was coming closer and closer to losing her heart. The day when she would have to choose between that and her own personal mission was clearly just around the corner.

On Saturday, Harlan fussed over every detail as the time for guests to start arriving neared. Maritza was beginning to mutter in Spanish, her tone suggesting it would be far better if he didn't try to translate. Her cousin Consuela, who'd been the original housekeeper at White Pines until Luke had lured her off to his ranch, finally backed him out the kitchen door by waving a dish towel in his face.

"Go, go. You stay out now," she ordered, barring the doorway. "You are only in the way in here."

"Damn, but you're bossy," he grumbled affectionately. "Who's running that house of Luke's? You or him?"

Her dark eyes flashed fire. "You remember that I can walk out before this affair of yours begins," she threatened, her own tone just as fond. "I will take Maritza and the others with me. How will you manage then, *señor?*"

"With my charm," he quipped.

She turned her gaze toward heaven as if praying for patience. "It will not feed this crowd you have invited," she reminded him. "Now, go and talk with your sons or play with your grandbabies."

"I'll go out and check to see if the tent's set up right," he said.

"No," she ordered at once. "The men have everything under control." She tilted her head at him. "I do not recall you making such a fuss over details in the past. This party is important to you?"

He nodded, feeling sheepish. "Silly, huh? We must

have thrown a hundred parties in this house, but this is the first time I've ever been a wreck."

Consuela's expression sobered at once. "It is because you no longer have Mary by your side," she said sorrowfully. "I should have thought, Señor Harlan. You must miss her very much at a time like this."

That was part of it, he supposed. But he'd come to terms with his loss in the past few months. Though he was likely to miss Mary until the end of his days, he had moved on. No, this sense that he was standing at the edge of a precipice and that the slightest misstep would send him over was due to another woman entirely.

"No," he corrected softly. "It is because I want everything to be perfect tonight."

Consuela's eyes widened. "For the *señorita,* yes?" At his startled look, she explained, "Rosa told me she has seen you together in town many times and then Luke and Jessie described meeting her. They say your eyes light up when you are in the same room. You care for this woman?"

He nodded, even though that was a pale description of his feelings. "Deeply," he admitted.

"Then Maritza and I will see that this party impresses her. Leave it to us, okay?"

He grinned. "Do I have any choice?"

"No," she conceded, and disappeared into the kitchen from which she had just banished him.

Left at loose ends, he paced. When that failed to calm him, he retreated to his office and fiddled with papers, none of which caught his full attention. He was trying for the third time to add up a simple column of figures when he realized he was no longer alone. He glanced up and found not one, but six pairs of prying eyes studying him with amusement.

"What's the matter with the bunch of you?" he grumbled, staring sourly at his sons and their wives. If he could have kept them away from this event, he would have, but he hadn't wanted to send the wrong message to Janet. He was very aware of how sensitive she was about not being accepted in Los Piños, despite the cavalier attitude she had expressed on the subject.

"We heard you were driving the entire staff nuts," Luke said. "Consuela thought you might need company."

"Consuela is a busybody." He noticed Jordan and Cody rolling their eyes. "And you two can be uninvited, you know."

"Us?" Jordan said innocently, exchanging a look with his younger brother. "What did we do?"

"We're giving him a taste of his own medicine," Cody retorted, clearly undaunted by the threat. "Looks like he can't take it."

Harlan heard the sound of footsteps clattering down the stairs. "Aren't those your little hellions I hear?" he demanded. "Damn, but they make a racket. Can't you control them?"

"Those are your precious grandchildren," Luke corrected. "And you're the one who said you wanted this to be a family event. How come, Daddy? You have big plans for tonight? Maybe an announcement of some kind?"

Harlan was startled by the suggestion, even though he could see how they might have leapt to that conclusion. "Don't go getting ideas. This shindig's just to let Janet get to know the family and some of my friends."

"How big's the guest list?" Jordan prodded, his expression entirely too smug.

"Two hundred, okay?" Harlan retorted, frowning at him. "Once I got started, I figured I might as well invite everybody at once."

"I hope Janet's not expecting an intimate little gathering," Jessie said worriedly. "I'll never forget that birthday party you threw for me when I was first married to Erik. I'd never seen that many people gathered together outside of a church revival in my entire life."

"Well, we'll know soon enough," Kelly stated. "She and Jenny are just pulling up." She grinned at her father-in-law. "Did you tell her to come early to play hostess?"

Harlan shook his head in disgust at their teasing. "Never mind what I told her," he said as he strode past them.

"He must not think we're up to the responsibility," Kelly said to Jessie and Melissa. "Think we should stage a protest?"

"I'm for it," Melissa teased.

Harlan turned back and glared at the lot of them. "If you all don't behave tonight, I'm disowning every one of you."

"I win!" Cody said with a whoop.

Harlan scowled at his youngest. "Win what?"

"We placed bets on how long it would take you to threaten to disown us. I figured less than ten minutes. Luke and Jordan thought you'd hold your temper longer."

"I was counting on Janet being here to keep him in line," Luke explained.

"Out of the will, every one of you," Harlan declared as he walked off and left them laughing.

Only after he was out of their eyesight did he allow himself to smile.

* * *

Harlan must have invited everyone within a hundred-mile radius, Janet decided as she stared at the throng of people filling their plates at the heavily laden buffet tables.

As if he sensed that she might be overwhelmed, he had stuck close to her side ever since her arrival, silencing gossip with a frown, introducing her to people who could bring her their legal business, shielding her from his sons' excessive teasing.

He'd left her just a moment before to greet the governor, promising to bring him back to meet her. The governor, for heaven's sake! At what Harlan referred to as a little backyard barbecue. Obviously he took such illustrious guests in stride.

To her, the sheer size of the event was daunting without even taking into account the importance of some of the guests. Her ex-husband would have had whiplash from looking this way and that to be sure he didn't miss anybody. The fancy New York parties they'd attended had been nothing compared to this assembly of Texas's rich and powerful.

"A little daunting, isn't it?" Jessie inquired, magically appearing by her side just when Janet was beginning to feel exactly that way.

"It's second nature to him, isn't it?" she replied, watching the ease with which Harlan escorted the governor from cluster to cluster. As many parties as she'd been to, she'd never been entirely comfortable with the small talk required.

"You wouldn't have thought that, if you'd seen him earlier," Jessie revealed. "He was like a kid throwing his first party and terrified nobody would come. Of course, in his case, I think you're the only guest he's been really worried about."

Janet couldn't get over the idea that Harlan might have suffered a bad case of stage fright. "He was nervous?" she asked incredulously.

Jessie nodded. "Because of you. He really wanted tonight to be special for you." She studied Janet intently. "Are you two involved? I mean, happily-ever-after involved."

Janet evaded a direct answer by asking a question of her own, "What does he say?"

"Not a darn thing, really. It's driving all of us crazy." She grinned. "I figure it serves Luke and his brothers right. On the other hand, I want to be in on the secret."

"There is no secret," Janet assured her.

Jessie's expression turned serious. "If he asks you to marry him, what will you say?"

Janet swallowed hard. It was clear that Jessie felt her question wasn't nearly as premature as Janet hoped it was. "I can't answer that," she said. To soften the response, she added, "And even if I could, you're not the one I'd be telling. Harlan would be the first to have an answer."

Jessie nodded approvingly. "Good. Now I know that all the bullying from these Adams men won't force you into a corner." She grinned. "It takes a strong woman to put up with them. I think you'll do just fine."

"Thanks for the vote of confidence," Janet said. "But sometimes trying to say no to Harlan is like swimming in quicksand."

"You ever need a lifeline, just let me know," Jessie offered. "The same with Kelly or Melissa. We've all been there." She glanced up and caught sight of Harlan approaching with the governor at the same time Janet did. "Whoops, I'm out of here. I voted for his opponent. I'd hate to have to admit that in front of Harlan."

Janet was still chuckling when Harlan reached her. She acknowledged the introduction to the governor and his wife with a smile and sufficient small talk to cover her nervousness. Fortunately, the band struck up a slower tune just then.

"That's my cue," the governor said, beaming at his wife. "Shall we?" As they headed for the dance floor, he said, "Call my office next week. I'd like to talk with you a bit about your interest in Native American affairs."

Janet stared after him openmouthed. "How did he know about that?"

Harlan shrugged. "I might have mentioned it. All that talk about Lone Wolf and his ancestors led me to think you might have a particular interest in the subject."

As if he thought he might have already said too much, he glanced toward the crowded dance floor that had been set up under the stars. "How about it? You willing to risk a turn around the floor with me?"

The request didn't give her time to wonder how a few comments about Lone Wolf had led Harlan to guess how deep her interest in Native Americans ran. Before she could even form a question, she was in his arms and they were swaying to the soft music.

The feel of his body pressed against hers made every inch of her flesh tingle. With her head tucked against his shoulder, she felt warm and secure and desired. His heat surrounded her, making her senses swim.

Suddenly she was no longer aware of anything but the provocative rhythm of the music and the feel of his muscles playing against her own. She could hear the steady sound of his heart pounding, feel the quickening of his pulse. A desperate hunger began to build deep inside her, a hunger that was clearly matched in the man who held her so tightly.

"You'll stay the night?" he asked out of the blue, his gaze searching hers.

"Jenny," she said, unable to manage another single word.

He nodded his understanding of her concern. "Not to worry. I'll speak to Cody. Melissa will think up an excuse to have her baby-sit. Will that do?"

"Yes," she whispered, sighing as she settled her head against his shoulder. She was grateful for his consideration, anxious to get this entire crowd on its way before she had time for second thoughts.

He leaned back and gazed down at her. "You want me to send everybody packing as badly as I want to do it?" he inquired, a teasing glint in his eyes.

"Yes," she admitted. "Isn't that terrible, especially when you've gone to all this trouble?"

"Wanting it isn't so bad," he claimed "We'll just have to think of it as a test of character that we don't act on it." He winked at her. "Besides, a little anticipation isn't all bad. It'll just make the rest of the night all the sweeter."

Janet regarded him skeptically. It seemed to her the next few hours were going to be the longest of her entire life. And if Harlan had a brain in his head, he wouldn't give her anywhere near that long to reconsider the decision she'd just reached in the provocative circle of his arms.

He leaned down then to whisper in her ear. "Don't look so impatient, darlin'. You'll be giving folks ideas about what's on your mind."

"No question about that," Luke said impudently as he

tapped his father on the shoulder. "I'm cutting in before you two make a spectacle of yourselves."

"Go away," Harlan said, refusing to release her.

Janet chuckled as the two of them stared each other down. "I think Luke has the right idea," she said, slipping out of Harlan's embrace. "Go dance with somebody else for a while."

Harlan frowned at his oldest son. "You'll pay for this," he muttered irritably, but he did start off. He hadn't gone more than half a dozen steps before he turned back to Janet. "You and I have a date, darlin'. Don't be forgetting it."

"Not a chance," she promised.

She looked up to find Luke chuckling. "What?" she demanded.

"Another five seconds I'd have had to hose the two of you down."

"I'm beginning to see why your father finds you so irritating," she muttered.

He laughed out loud at that. "Jessie was right."

"About?"

"You'll fit in just fine."

The approval behind the comment stayed with Janet for the rest of the seemingly endless evening. She was glad that Luke and Jessie thought she'd be right for Harlan. She couldn't help wondering, though, how they'd feel if they discovered what had originally brought her to Texas. Would they be as open and generous then? Or would they do everything in their power to see that she and Harlan never spent another single second alone together?

13

"We'll all meet here for a late breakfast," Harlan said to Jenny as she prepared to leave with Cody and Melissa and their kids after the party. He'd been trying to shoo people off for an hour now, to little avail. His sons particularly showed no inclination to go.

To Janet's surprise, though, Jenny didn't seemed particularly thrown by the change in plans. She was probably thrilled to be spending the night under Cody's roof. Fortunately her daughter had missed the earlier exchange of winks between Cody and his brothers when they'd learned that Harlan was sending Jenny home with Cody and his crew.

"You'll be back then, too, Mom?" Jenny asked sleepily as she climbed into Cody's car.

Janet nodded. "I'll be here," she promised.

Jenny yawned. "Okay. See you."

A moment later they were gone and Janet's heart climbed straight into her throat at the look of pure longing in Harlan's eyes. Despite the irreversible commitment she'd made to stay, despite her own yearning to make love to this incredibly gentle, thoughtful man, she was more nervous than an innocent bride on her wedding night.

She still had so many questions about why he seemed to have forgiven her for what must have seemed to him a hiding of the truth at least. That he still hadn't mentioned what Jenny had told him kept her from relaxing and falling entirely under his spell. She kept waiting for him to reel her in and then turn on her when she least expected it.

"What about the others?" she asked, delaying their return to the house.

His gaze never left her face. "What others?" he murmured distractedly, his attention clearly riveted on her.

"Jordan and Kelly, for instance," she said, though she was a bit distracted herself by the intensity of his gaze and the electricity arcing between them.

He stroked a finger along her cheek. "They've gone home. Slipped away a while ago, in fact."

Janet swallowed hard before managing to add, "And Luke and Jessie?"

"Upstairs in their suite." Her expression must have given away her trepidation, because he quickly added, "It's at the opposite end of this big old place from mine. Think of it as being like a fancy hotel. You wouldn't think twice about who was down the hall."

"But this room is occupied by your son and his family, not strangers."

He shrugged off her concern. "I promise you it's not a problem."

Janet disagreed. "How will they feel when they find out I've stayed the night?"

"For one thing, I don't think any of them had a doubt in the world that you would be here come morning.

Besides that, you seem to be forgetting whose house this is."

"Hardly."

"Okay, but whatever Luke's opinion might be, he'll keep it to himself."

Janet chuckled at the unlikelihood of that. "Are we talking about the same Luke?"

"Stop fussing," he soothed, cupping her face in his hands. "If you want to put this off, just say the word. You'll have your own room for the night. I can even fix you up on a different floor, if you'd prefer. Give you a key for the lock, too, if it'll make you feel better."

She wrestled with the offer. Eventually, longing and a deep sense of inevitability overcame doubt. With Jenny staying at Cody's overnight, there might never be another opportunity like this one.

She reached up and covered his hands with her own. Her gaze locked with his. "If I stay here tonight, it will be with you."

Rather than seeming relieved, he tensed as questions darkened his eyes. "If? You aren't seriously thinking of driving back into town, are you?"

She tilted her head. A smile tugged at her lips at the stark disappointment in his expression. She had another alternative in mind, one with which she was far more comfortable.

"I was thinking I'd have you take me," she said. She lowered her voice to a coaxing note. "My house might be a half hour from here, but it is totally deserted." Unspoken was the fact that there would be no ghosts in the bed or prying family members down the hall.

The tension in his shoulders eased the instant he

caught her meaning. "Well, why didn't you say so?" he said, grinning. "I'll get my car keys."

"Mine are in my purse," she said, already reaching for them and handing them over. "Besides, with only my car parked out front, no one will ever guess you're there. No gossip."

"Better yet."

They rounded the house, laughing like a couple of kids sneaking off to make out. Harlan gunned the engine in a way that would have had Mule sulking for a month about his disrespect for what the mechanic had declared to be an almost-classic car.

Then he shot down the lane and away from White Pines as if he'd been celibate for a decade and had finally discovered he was about to get lucky. Janet found his eagerness both touching and very arousing.

The drive into Los Piños seemed to take an eternity, especially after Harlan placed her hand on his rock-hard thigh and covered it with his own. So much heat, she thought as her senses spun wildly. So much strength. So much barely contained passion.

His blatant desire fueled hers, until by the time they reached her house, the last of her uncertainties had been stripped away. They rushed through her front door, barely taking the time for Harlan to kick it shut behind him before he dragged her into his arms. He kissed her with all of the pent-up hunger that had been held in check on the dance floor, on the long drive and for who knew how long before.

The kiss was commanding and all-consuming, wiping out every thought except for some primitive understanding of its wicked effect on her senses. Never in her life had she experienced such raw, untamed lust.

She was suddenly trembling from head to toe with anticipation.

She was fumbling with the buttons on Harlan's shirt just as urgently as he was stripping away the blouse they'd searched all over Dallas to find just yesterday. Then his mouth was covering first one breast, then the other, teasing, suckling in a way that sent shock waves ricocheting through her.

His skin was on fire beneath her touch, but her own was hotter. The caress of his tongue cooled, then inflamed, then cooled again in a devastating cycle. A moan of pure pleasure escaped, shattering their previously silent, passionate duet.

The sound brought his head up, leaving her feeling bereft. As if he had suddenly found his bearings, he tucked her tightly against his chest and sucked in a deep, calming breath.

"Whoa, darlin'," he murmured softly, as if gentling a skittish mare.

"No," she pleaded. "Don't stop."

He chuckled at the urgency in her tone. "I will not make love to you on the floor in the foyer," he said. "Not that I'm entirely sure I can get us both out of this tangle we've made of our clothes and into the bedroom."

If that was the only delay, Janet was more than willing to help. She shucked what was left of her clothing, kicked it aside and headed down the hallway stark naked. Only when she realized Harlan hadn't followed did she turn back. He was staring after her, looking stunned. The thoroughly masculine appreciation in his eyes made her knees go weak.

"You take my breath away," he said in a hoarse whisper.

"Ditto," she said in a voice only faintly louder. "If you get over here, though, I'll give you mouth-to-mouth resuscitation."

Amusement danced in his eyes at that. "You certified?"

"No," she admitted, then grinned. "I'll need lots and lots of practice."

Practically before the words were out of her mouth, he had joined her, scooping her up and carrying her into the bedroom with long, anxious strides.

"Then by all means, let's get to it," he said, lowering her to the bed, then settling down beside her atop the thick comforter.

The break had allowed just enough time for ardor to cool. To Janet's astonishment, it took little more than a sweeping caress of her bare hip with callused fingers to return it to a fever pitch.

But Harlan was clearly in no hurry now that they'd made it this far. He seemed intent on making each response linger, then build to a shattering crescendo before trying something new. In her head, Janet knew that this was the same body she'd lived with all her life, but under his gentle, tormenting ministrations it seemed entirely new and heart-stoppingly responsive.

She was filled with astonishment over each exquisite, devastating sensation. And when every nerve was vibrantly alive, when he finally, at long last, entered her with a slow, tantalizing thrust, she felt as if she'd finally discovered the true meaning of joy.

As their bodies played out this timeless ritual, over and over through the night, perfecting it, elaborating on it, exploring its every nuance, she wondered if she'd ever been alive before she met Harlan Adams or if she'd just been existing in some half-awake state, waiting for this moment.

Discovering such passion deep within herself should have been exhilarating, but in the silvery, moonlit darkness just before dawn broke she was overcome by an agony of indecision. She tried to compare these new, barely tested feelings for the man sprawled out half on top of her, his hand possessively circling her breast, with older loyalties to the grandfather she had adored.

If there hadn't been such a history in her family of mistakes, of choosing mates so unwisely, perhaps she could have reached a different decision. But neither her father nor her first husband had understood this gut-deep need she had to discover the Comanche side of her heritage. She doubted Harlan would be any different, especially when he realized that part of that discovery meant righting a century-old wrong if there was any legal means at all to do so.

Sighing, she resolved that this night would never be repeated. She knew with everything in her that it was a decision Harlan would never understand, one he would fight with all of his incomparable powers of persuasion. She also knew it was the only one she could make.

And knowing that broke her heart.

Harlan was the kind of man who usually snapped awake in an instant. He'd never had much interest in lingering in bed when there were chores to do and a ranch to run. Maybe the trait had been born of necessity decades ago, but it had become a habit he'd had no reason to break, not even when the whole day stretched out emptily ahead of him.

This morning, though, he seemed to be easing back

into consciousness, sensation by sensation. First it was the heat that tugged at his senses. Then it was the sweet, sweet smell of some light-as-air flowery scent, layered with an undertone of dark, musky sensuality. And then, dear heaven, it was the soft-as-satin brush of skin against skin, a teasing caress that had his blood pumping so hard and fast he thought his heart might flat-out explode in his chest.

That woke him, all right! His eyes snapped open to gaze straight into sleepy, dark eyes that struck him as far more troubled than they ought to be after such an incredible night.

"You're looking mighty serious," he said, brushing Janet's hair back over her shoulders so he could drink his fill of the sight of those rose-tipped breasts. The peaks pebbled at once, even under such an offhand caress. He might have lingered longer, intensified his touch, had Janet's gaze not seemed so fraught with worry.

"Regrets?" he asked.

"None," she swore.

Harlan wasn't convinced. "You sure?"

"I could never regret what happened between us last night," she said more firmly.

Though he was still doubtful, he decided he'd just have to take her at her word. "Then I think we ought to talk about making it permanent."

This time there was no mistaking the alarm that flared in her eyes.

"No," she whispered, touching a finger to his lips. "Please, don't say any more."

He couldn't take rejection so easily, not when he had his heart set on spending his future with this woman, not when he knew without a trace of doubt that deep inside that was what she wanted, too. He suspected he even knew what was preventing her from accepting his proposal.

"You don't even want me saying that I love you?" he said, keeping his tone light. "You don't want to hear that I won't settle for anything less than making you my wife, not after last night?"

A tear slid slowly down her cheek, even as she declined his proposal for a second time.

"I can't," she whispered.

"Of course you can," he insisted just as adamantly. "There's nothing to stop you, except some foolish willfulness on your part."

He knew as soon as the words were out of his mouth that they had been exactly the wrong thing to say. Whatever she was struggling with—and he was certain now that he knew what it was—he shouldn't have dismissed it as foolish or willful. A milewide stubborn streak would kick in over words like that. His own certainly would have.

"I'm sorry. I shouldn't have said that," he apologized at once.

"No," she said stiffly, retreating as far from him in the bed as she could and surrounding herself with layers of covers despite the room's more than comfortable temperature. "You shouldn't have."

Because he needed time to rein in his temper, Harlan stood and searched for his pants. When he'd yanked them on, he returned to sit opposite her on the edge of the bed.

"Can we discuss this?"

"I don't see why you'd want to," she said dully.

"Because this is too important for you to leap to a snap decision that could affect the rest of both of our lives, to say nothing of Jenny's," he explained, fighting to keep his tone even. "You know I care for her as if she were one of my own. You also know I've been a good influence on her."

She shot him a stubborn scowl. "I'm not going to get married again because Jenny needs a father."

"Then how about because you need a husband who loves you, almost as much as I need a wife who'll make me feel alive the way you did in this bed last night, the way you have every day since we met? Can you deny you felt the same way?"

"No, of course not. I would never lie to you about something that important," she told him. "But I came here to find myself. You're such a strong man. From all I've heard, your first wife doted on you. You were her first and only priority. I'm afraid I'd turn out to be just like her, that I'd lose myself in being Mrs. Harlan Adams, rather than Janet Runningbear, a Comanche lawyer in search of her roots."

"It's the last that's important, isn't it?" he said, experiencing the bitter taste of defeat in his mouth. "It's this thing you have about your great-grandfather."

Her gaze narrowed. "What if it is?"

"Why don't you tell me what really brought you to Texas?" he commanded.

Her gaze faltered. "I've told you a hundred different ways," she said. "You haven't been listening."

"You want to know what I hear? I hear you denying yourself a future you want because of some crazy notion that won't ever pan out the way you want it to."

She frowned at that. "Don't be so certain of that,

Harlan. There's very little I can't accomplish if I set my mind to it. I won't let you or my feelings for you stand in my way. I can't allow that to happen. I will never be like Mary, so you might as well accept that and move on."

It was quite likely the only argument she might have made that he didn't have a ready answer for. Words were too easy for a fear like that, especially when he couldn't deny that Mary had given up a part of herself the day she became his wife.

He resigned himself to taking a little time to show Janet that that had been Mary's choice, not his. He was ready and eager to have a strong and independent woman at his side. He was no young kid who'd mistake independence of spirit with a lack of love.

Patience, unfortunately, was not one of his virtues. More, he suspected that that would solve only part of the problem. Janet was still struggling with her conscience over her desire to get her hands on the land that she felt had belonged to her ancestors.

Until she could tell him about that herself, until they could work it through together, it would always stand between them and happiness. She'd almost said the words a moment ago, he was sure of it, but something had kept her silent. Whether it was fear of his reaction or a desire not to hurt him, he couldn't be sure.

"Okay," he said eventually. "I'll let it slide for now, if I must."

He walked around to the other side of the bed where she still sat huddled under the covers. He determinedly tucked a finger under her chin and tilted her face up until their eyes clashed.

"But I won't give up on us. I'll pester you until you see what I see, that we belong together."

A clearly reluctant smile tugged at the corners of her mouth. "That ought to scare the hell out of me," she said, then gave a little shrug of resignation. "But for some crazy reason, it doesn't."

"That's because you know I'm right," he said with satisfaction.

"I do not," she insisted.

"Argue all you want, but the end result will still be the same," he informed her. "Now get dressed so we can sneak back to White Pines before the whole gang figures out we're missing."

"It would serve you right," she muttered as she strolled off to the shower. "You're the one they'd taunt unmercifully. They're very polite to me."

"They won't be, once they know you're going to be family."

"I am not going to be…" she shouted, then sighed audibly. "Oh, never mind."

Harlan grinned as the bathroom door slammed behind her. Yes, indeed, no matter what she thought, no matter what kind of struggle she put up, it was only a matter of time.

Facing the entire Adams clan around the breakfast table—except for the youngest babies, who were being watched upstairs—was a heck of a lot more intimidating than their first meeting had been, Janet decided after several awkward minutes ticked by. Their fascinated gazes kept shifting from her to Harlan and back again. Only Jenny and the older grandchildren seemed oblivious to the undercurrents. Their unrestrained chatter was all that made the situation bearable.

The minute everyone had finished eating, Harlan

said, "I had Consuela's brother put up the wading pool out back. Jenny, why don't you take the little ones out to play in that and keep an eye on them?"

Jenny surveyed him speculatively. "My usual rates?"

"Yes, you little entrepreneur," he said with contradictory fondness. "I'll pay you your usual rates."

"Great! I'll be able to buy more CDs, if we ever get to a town with a decent music store," she said with a pointed look in Janet's direction.

"Maybe next weekend," Janet replied distractedly. She was too worried about the inquisitive expressions on Cody's, Jordan's and Luke's faces to pay much attention to Jenny's normal grumbling about the lack of shopping in Los Piños.

The reply seemed to satisfy her daughter, because she took off readily with the younger children.

"Well?" Luke said, his gaze fixed on his father.

Harlan tried to stare him down. "Well, what?"

"Isn't there something you two want to tell us?"

"No," Harlan and Janet replied in chorus.

Luke and Jessie exchanged a look filled with amusement that was promptly caught by the others.

"You know something, don't you?" Cody guessed. "Come on, big brother, share."

Harlan's gaze narrowed. "I don't know what you think you know, Lucas," he said, "but if you've got any decency in you, you'll keep it to yourself."

"He has a point," Jessie said, laughter dancing in her eyes. "I mean, we don't know for sure where they were going when they went sneaking off in the middle of the night."

Janet groaned and buried her face in her hands, sure that her complexion must be a fiery shade of red.

"That's it. I'm out of here," she declared, shoving her chair back and practically racing from the room.

"Now look what you've done," Harlan chided, sending his own chair scooting across the floor with a clatter. "When I get back, I want you out of here. Maybe the whole blasted lot of you ought to think about moving to Arizona or Montana, anywhere that's far away from here."

If she hadn't been so embarrassed, Janet might have chuckled at his blustery tone. As it was, she just wanted to disappear herself. She was already outside when he caught up with her.

"I'm sorry," he said. "You know what big mouths they have. I told you so myself before we came back here this morning."

"It's not that," she said miserably. "It's just so sweet the way they tease you. I know they wouldn't do that, if they didn't want something to happen between you and me. I feel as if I'm letting all of you down."

"Only for the moment," he reminded her with that trace of stubbornness that proved he still hadn't accepted that her no meant an emphatic *no*.

She lifted her chin and leveled a look straight into his eyes. "No, Harlan. Not just for the moment. I meant what I said back at my house. There is no future for us, not unless you mean it to be no more than friendship."

"I won't settle for that," he said with surprisingly little rancor. She knew why when he added, "And in time, neither will you."

14

Jenny's presence was the only thing that gave Harlan any peace of mind at all in the days after Janet had fled from White Pines. The fact that she continued to turn up every morning reassured him that there was hope. It enabled him to be patient.

Not that the teenager had suddenly turned into a saint or even a staunch advocate of his relationship with her mother, but she was showing signs of weakening. Her belligerence was sported more for effect than any real attitude on her part. He decided one afternoon to call her on it.

She'd thrown a fit not an hour before over some inconsequential task he'd asked her to do. She'd saddled Misty after that and taken off. He guessed he'd find her at the creek.

Sure enough, she was sitting on the grassy bank, her bare feet dangling in the cool water.

"If you wanted to come down here, all you had to do was ask," he said, dropping to the ground beside her.

She regarded him with disbelief. "You'd have let me come?"

"You know I would. You also know I would have come along. You just figured you ought to raise a ruckus so I wouldn't get too used to the more mellow Jenny, isn't that right?"

She slanted a look at him. "You think you're pretty smart, don't you?"

"I know I am. The question is, are you ready to admit it?"

She sighed heavily. "If you're so smart, how come Mom's dropping me off at the end of the lane again? It's her idea this time," she added, so there would be no mistake.

"Because she's sorting through some things."

"She's behaving like a ninny, you mean."

He grinned. "Is that what I mean?"

"Seems that way to me." She met his gaze evenly. "Are you in love with her?"

"Don't you think that's between her and me?"

"Not if I have to live with her while you two are figuring things out. I think I deserve to know what's going on." She shot him a sly look. "I could help you, you know. Mom listens to me."

Harlan hid a smile. "Is that so? What would your intercession on my behalf cost me?"

Jenny blinked. "Hey, wait a minute," she protested. "That's not the kind of thing I'd charge you for."

"Then that would be a first," he said dryly.

"Look, you don't want my help, it's no skin off my nose. You don't seem to be doing so great on your own, though."

"Trust me," he said. "I can handle this without any help from you." He studied her curiously. "But can I assume from what you're saying that you would approve of your mother and me getting married?"

She looked reluctant to make that big an admission, but finally she shrugged. "I suppose it would be okay."

He grinned. "Thanks for the endorsement."

"Would it mean I could stop doing chores and get an allowance?"

"I doubt it."

"Oh." She regarded him intently. "But you would want me around, right?"

"You bet," he said. "It's definitely a package deal. You comfortable with having me as a stepdaddy?"

To his astonishment, Jenny shifted and threw her arms around his neck. She didn't say a word, but the dampness of fresh tears on his neck told him all he needed to know. He had himself a daughter.

Janet was feeling besieged. Not by Harlan, bless his heart. To her surprise he was giving her all the space she'd claimed to crave. No, it was his family that wouldn't leave her in peace.

Every son, every daughter-in-law made some excuse or another to pay a call, to proclaim all of Harlan's virtues, to try to wheedle from her a reason for her reluctance to accept the proposal, which they had somehow discovered he'd made. She had the same answer for each of them: "Does your father know you're here?"

And when the reply was consistently no, she suggested that they talk with him if they had questions about the relationship. "He knows why I won't marry him," she repeated over and over.

Unfortunately, Jessie wasn't as easily dissuaded as the others. She popped in two weeks after that disgraceful scene Janet had caused by running out of the dining room at White Pines. The minute she'd walked through the door, she settled into a seat opposite Janet and showed no inclination at all to leave.

"I'm not going to talk about it," Janet declared for what must have been the hundredth time, hoping just this once to stop any questions before they started.

Jessie nodded. "That's understandable," she soothed.

It was, perhaps, the hundredth time Janet had heard that, too. Everyone who'd dropped by had said the same thing, then proceeded to butt in just the same.

"It's private," Jessie added, indicating a deeper understanding than most.

"Exactly."

"Harlan's probably done more than enough bullying himself without the rest of us getting in on the act."

"Precisely," Janet said.

To her relief, Jessie appeared willing to give up. She even stood, to indicate an imminent departure.

"Let's go to Dolan's and have a milk shake," she suggested.

Janet blinked. "What?"

"A thick, chocolate milk shake," Jessie added temptingly. "Come on. I never get anything like that at the ranch. Consuela's a great cook, but lately she's constantly worried about killing Luke with too much fat. There hasn't been so much as a pint of ice cream in the house in months. I have to sneak over here to Los Piños to get a milk shake, if I want one."

"And just this morning you decided you had a hankering for one and drove…what? Two hours? Three, just to get one?" Janet said skeptically, not believing for a minute that Jessie couldn't have whipped one up right in her own kitchen if she'd really wanted to.

"It's amazing the cravings that come on when a woman least expects them," Jessie said. "Chocolate milk shakes…" Her expression turned innocent. "A man, same difference. Once the idea's planted in your head, you might as well give in to it."

That sneaky little reference to men triggered all of Janet's alarm systems. "Are you suggesting that I should go ahead and marry Harlan, because he's like some sort of addiction I won't be able to break?"

Jessie regarded her with another innocent look. "I was talking about milk shakes. You're the one who brought up marriage." She tilted her head inquiringly. "Has it been on your mind a lot lately?"

"If I didn't like you so much, I'd tell you to go fly a kite," Janet muttered, but she stood. "As it is, though, now you've got me craving a milk shake, too. Let's go."

They walked down the block to Dolan's Drugstore and headed for the counter. Melissa popped out of the store room. She'd worked there before her marriage to Cody and still filled in several days a week to keep from going stir-crazy on the ranch.

"Hey, you two, what brings you in in the middle of the morning?" Melissa asked. "Jessie, I didn't know you were coming to Los Piños today."

Janet thought the greeting sounded suspiciously cheery, as if they'd plotted this little gathering. When Kelly strolled in not five minutes later, she knew it.

"Okay, what's going on?" she demanded.

"That's what we want to know," Kelly said, propping her elbows on the counter and leaning forward intently. "Harlan's been grumbling like an old bear for the last week. Jordan, Cody and Luke are practically busting with curiosity, but he refuses to say a single word to any of them. Cody told Jordan you've been dropping Jenny off at the end of the lane again."

"I had no idea everyone was so fascinated with my habits," Janet said irritably.

As if she sensed that Janet was about ready to bolt, Jessie laid a soothing hand on top of hers. "Look, we all like you and we love Harlan. You seem to make him happy. He's crazy about Jenny. I doubt the two of you would have gone sneaking off and tearing down that lane in the middle of the night, if you weren't more than fond of him. So, what's the deal?"

"It's complicated," Janet summarized.

"Nothing's too complicated it can't be worked out, if two people love each other," Melissa declared, distributing milk shakes without even being asked. "I can vouch for that."

"Me, too," Jessie said.

"And me," Kelly added. "We had three of the most reluctant bridegrooms in Texas and look at us now. We're all deliriously happy."

"Well, most of the time," Jessie amended. "After all, those Adams stubborn streaks didn't vanish overnight."

Two "Amens" greeted the comment.

"Anyway," Melissa said. "You clearly have Harlan in the palm of your hand, yet you're throwing away the chance to marry him. How come? Is Jessie wrong? Don't you care about him?"

"I love him," Janet forced herself to admit to these three women who were clearly so concerned with their father-in-law's future that they'd ganged up on her. "That's why I can't marry him."

"Huh?" Kelly said blankly. It was echoed by the others.

Janet pushed aside her practically untouched shake. "I can't explain. Not to you, anyway. I can't even make myself tell Harlan all of it."

"Are you still married or something?" Melissa asked, eyes wide.

Janet grinned. "No, it's nothing like that."

"Then you can work it out," Jessie said confidently. "Just tell him what's on your mind. Harlan loves to fix things up for the people he cares about."

Kelly nodded. "He doesn't lay on some heavy guilt trip like a lot of men would. He just takes care of things."

Janet wondered if she could bring herself to tell Harlan that she had wanted the very land he was living on. If she did, would he ever believe that she was marrying him for any reason except to get her hands on that land? It didn't seem likely.

"At least think about it," Jessie prodded. "You won't regret marrying Harlan."

That had never been her fear, Janet thought. She was far more concerned that Harlan would regret marrying her.

That night, now fully aware that her every move was being scrutinized by fascinated relations, she drove all the way up the lane at White Pines to the house to pick up Jenny. She had almost managed to convince herself to lay all of her cards on the table and tell Harlan everything. She would test Jessie and Kelly's theory that Harlan would somehow make everything right and forgive her.

When she arrived, he was nowhere in sight. Maritza answered the doorbell.

"You are here for Jenny, *sí?* She will be back soon, I think."

"Actually I'd like to speak with Mr. Adams if he's available," she said.

"He's in his office. Come, I will show you."

She led Janet down the hall and pointed to a heavily carved door. "In there. You would like me to tell him you are here?"

"No, I'll knock. Thanks, Maritza."

She stood outside the door for several minutes summoning up her courage before finally rapping softly. "Harlan?"

"Janet, is that you? Come on in," he called out so eagerly that she was immediately consumed by another bout of guilt.

He was on his feet and halfway across the room by the time she had the door open. His expression made her heart skitter wildly. There was so much hope there. So much love.

"I wasn't expecting to see you today. You've been making yourself scarce."

"I had some thinking to do." She looked into eyes so blue they reminded her of the summer sky. "Thank you for letting me do it in peace."

He looked as if he wanted to reach for her, but he shoved his hands into his pockets instead. "Reach any conclusions?"

"Just one, thanks to Jessie, Kelly and Melissa. I have to tell you the truth about something."

His eyebrows rose. "Sounds serious."

She nodded.

"Then come on over here and sit." He gestured to a big leather chair in front of the fireplace, then settled into the one beside it.

Janet liked the arrangement. She didn't have to look directly into his eyes while she talked. She began slowly, telling him about the summer she had spent with Lone Wolf. Then she repeated all of the stories he had told her about their ancestors being forced out of Texas.

"I resolved then that I wanted to make it right. I came here wanting to get that land back. If I could have found a legal way to do it—which I couldn't, by the way—I would have taken White Pines from you," she summarized.

There, it was all out in the open. She glanced over at him to gauge his reaction. To her astonishment, he smiled.

"I know," he admitted without batting an eye. "I've known for some time now."

"You've known," she repeated blankly, then wondered why she was so surprised. Of course he would have put all the pieces together. He hadn't become a successful rancher without knowing how to read people. What she couldn't seem to absorb was the fact that he had taken the discovery so well. Where was the ranting and raving she'd anticipated with such dread?

"And you still wanted to marry me?" she asked, bemused.

"How could I blame you for thinking of Lone Wolf and wanting to make amends for what happened to his father?"

"Why didn't you say anything?"

He shrugged. "Because you needed to figure out you could trust me enough to tell me the truth."

Tears stung her eyes. "Oh, Harlan."

"Hey," he protested, "don't start crying. I won't say I wasn't mad as a wet hen when I first figured out what was going on after Jenny spilled the beans about where Lone Wolf had once lived. Then I did a little research of my own. I discovered you had cause to come here and do what you were doing. I'm sorry you couldn't figure out a legal way to do it."

"But you see, then, why we can't get married," she said. "I just wanted you to know that it's not because I don't love you. It's because you'll never know for certain if it's you I want or White Pines."

"Darlin', my ego's in no danger of being deflated by uncertainty," he said, waving off that argument dismissively. "You'd never marry a man you didn't love. There's never been a doubt in my mind about that."

She refused to accept that. It was too easy. She deserved his hatred or, at the very least, his disdain. Yet he was still claiming he wanted to marry her.

"I have to go," she said, leaping to her feet and heading for the door.

He stepped in front of her. "Not without saying yes to my proposal. All our cards are on the table now. There's no reason to say no."

"I can't," she insisted, guilt and confusion tumbling through her. How could she say yes, when she didn't deserve the love of a man like Harlan?

"Mom!" Jenny wailed from the doorway.

Her gaze shot to her daughter. "How long have you been standing there?"

"Long enough to know you've flipped out completely. I can't believe you'd do something like this." With that she whirled and ran from the room.

Janet stared after her in shock, then turned back to Harlan. "I have to go after her."

He nodded. "Go. But this isn't over, Janet. Not by a long shot."

Jenny refused to say a single word during the entire drive home. She huddled against the passenger door and stared out the window, her expression sullen. Janet felt as if they were right back where they'd been when they'd first arrived in Texas. All of the progress she and Jenny had made over recent weeks had disappeared in an instant back in Harlan's study.

When they got home, Jenny headed straight for her room.

"Jennifer, get back here."

"I'm not in the mood to talk."

"Then you'll listen," she said. But once Jenny had reluctantly sprawled in a chair in the living room, she had no idea what to say. She wasn't even entirely sure why her daughter was so furious. She could hazard a guess, though.

"Look, I know you like to think of Mr. Adams as the enemy," she began. "But he's not. And there's no need for you to concern yourself that I'll marry him, anyway, because I turned him down."

Jenny shot her a look of disgust. "Jeez, Mom, don't you think I know that? I heard everything."

"Well, then, why are you acting as if I've gone over to the enemy?"

"You've got it all wrong. I think you're making the worst mistake of your life, if you don't marry him."

Janet's mouth dropped open. "What?"

"I know why you're turning him down, though. It's

not because of all that stuff about Lone Wolf and the land."

"Of course it is," Janet insisted.

"It is not. Not really. He told you that stuff didn't matter to him anyway. You're saying no because of your own stupid pride."

The accusation stung, not because it was unjustified, but because somewhere deep inside it rang all too true. "I don't have any idea what you're talking about," she said stiffly.

"Oh, puh-leeze!" Jenny retorted. "When you left Daddy, you swore you'd show him you could stand on your own two feet. You're afraid if he hears you're marrying some rich guy, he'll think you've sold out."

Before Janet could gather her wits to react to that, Jenny went on.

"Do you think it even matters to him what we're doing?" she said with adolescent bitterness. "He never calls. He never comes to see us. The only time you hear anything at all is when he sends a child support check. I think you'd tear that up, if you could."

It was true. Only the awareness that the money belonged to Jenny kept her from doing just that. Every cent was in an account in her daughter's name, meant for her college education.

"So what's your point?"

"Just that you're afraid if you marry anyone, much less a guy like Harlan Adams, Daddy will see it as an admission that you couldn't make it on your own. Like he really cares," she said with more of that angry sarcasm Janet had never heard before.

Feeling both bemused and under attack, she asked carefully, "Do you want me to marry Harlan?"

"I want you to be happy, Mom. It's all I ever wanted. And Harlan's a pretty cool guy. I knew that the minute he caught me after I stole his truck. He didn't freak out, like some guys would have. I've been pretty rotten sometimes since and he hasn't hated me for that, either."

She shrugged. "Maybe I was testing him, to see if he'd be like Daddy and abandon me just because I wasn't behaving suitably." The last was said in precisely her father's judgmental tone.

Janet sighed heavily. At last the reason behind Jenny's behavior for the past few months was coming clear. She'd lost her father, even when her behavior had been exemplary. She'd been testing, not just Harlan, but before that, Janet herself, to see if they would abandon her at the first sign of trouble. Now her gaze was fixed anxiously on Janet's face. "So, will you at least think about it?"

"I'll think about it," she promised.

She did little else for the next twenty-four hours. By morning, she thought she had figured out a way to prove to Harlan that it was him—and him alone—she loved.

15

When Harlan turned up to take Janet to lunch the next day, he sensed right away that something had changed. He couldn't tell exactly what it was, just a bit more color in her cheeks, maybe a glint of confidence in her eyes.

"I have some papers here for you to sign," she said when he walked through the door.

He frowned at her businesslike tone. Was she about to get into the land ownership issue, after all? Had she found some blasted loophole she hadn't admitted to the last time they'd talked?

"What sort of papers?" he asked suspiciously.

"It's a legal agreement."

His wariness doubled. "Who are you representing?"

"Myself."

His heart slammed against his ribs. So it was about the land.

"Suing me, are you?" he asked, keeping his voice light, when he wanted to lay into her at the top of his lungs for spoiling everything, for not trusting him to do what was right.

Her mouth curved into a sensuous smile that made

his heart go still. If that smile had anything to do with a land deal, he'd eat his hat. But what, then?

"You'd love that, wouldn't you?" she taunted. "You're never one to back down from a good fight."

"Gets the juices flowing, that's for sure." He reached for the papers and began to read. His eyes widened at the first line. "A prenuptial agreement? What the hell is this for?"

"It's an agreement between you and me, before marriage, guaranteeing that I won't take a dime of your money if the marriage ever breaks up."

"Like hell!" he exploded, too furious to even think about the fact that she was apparently agreeing to marry him. He didn't like the terms she had in mind. He didn't like 'em one damned bit! "I'm not going into a marriage thinking about how it's going to end. The day you and I get married it will be forever, Janet Runningbear, not one of those blasted things where one of us skedaddles at the first hint of trouble."

To his astonishment, she chuckled. "I had a feeling you were going to say something like that, so I made a few alterations from the traditional prenup agreement. Perhaps you should read the details."

He was about to rip it to shreds when a phrase caught his eye. Something about guaranteeing that White Pines would remain with his sons.

"What's this?" he asked.

"Just putting what's right in writing," she said. "I want to be sure there's never a doubt in your mind about why I'm marrying you. Read the rest. See how it suits you."

The next paragraph legalized his adoption of Jenny as his daughter. He couldn't have been more flabbergasted if they'd let him win at poker. He searched Janet's face for proof that this wasn't some sort of diabolical hoax.

"She's sure about this?" he asked, not able to control the hint of wonder in his voice.

"She and I talked it over this morning. It's what she wants. She wants to be your daughter." Her gaze caught his. "If you'll have her."

Tears stung his eyes. "It would make me proud to have her call me daddy. Your ex-husband, though, he won't mind?"

"He'll have to be consulted, of course, but I don't see why he would, especially if it would let him off the hook with the child support he sends so grudgingly."

He couldn't believe that everything was finally coming together just the way he'd imagined. He cupped Janet's face in his hands. "You're dead serious about this? You're not going to back out of this on me, are you?"

She shook her head. "Not a chance."

"You know we're going to be butting heads every now and then. That's just the way of marriage."

"So I've heard. Your daughters-in-law have informed me what it's like to be married to a stubborn Adams."

"Traitors," he muttered, but he was smiling. He knew he owed the three of them for making Janet take a second look at his proposal and forcing her to shed her conscience of that secret she'd been keeping. He had a feeling he might owe Jenny, too. She'd promised to intercede in his behalf and it looked as if she had.

He studied Janet intently, not quite able to believe that she was almost his. She was so beautiful she took his breath away. He'd be counting his blessings till the day he died.

"How soon?" he asked.

"How soon what?"

"When can we get married? You want a big to-do or can we sneak off and keep it from those brats of mine?"

"It doesn't have to be big, but I want those wonderful children and grandchildren of yours to be there. We're going to start this off as a family," she insisted. "No more secrets. Understood?"

"Don't look at me with those big brown eyes of yours," he accused. "I'm not the one who was hiding what I was up to. You knew from day one what I wanted from you."

She grinned and looped her arms around his neck. "And what was that?"

"This," he said, and settled his mouth over hers. He ran his tongue along the seam of her lips until they parted. The taste of her was sweet as peppermints and far, far more intoxicating.

"If you hadn't said yes soon," he declared when his breathing was finally even again, "I'd have had to kidnap you and haul you off to some justice of the peace."

"And what if I still hadn't been willing?"

"I'd have used all of my considerable influence to see that the ceremony came off anyway," he declared, liking the immediate flare of temper in her eyes.

"You can't expect to bully me into giving you your way, Harlan Adams."

"Who's talking about bullying?" he said, closing a hand gently over her breast and teasing the nipple until he could feel it harden even through the silk blouse and the lacy bra he knew was underneath. "There are other ways to tame a skittish filly."

His expression sobered then. "I love you, Janet Runningbear. I'll make you happy. For all my teasing and taunting, you can count on that as a solemn promise."

"I love you, too, Harlan." The smile she turned on him then was radiant. A bride's smile. "It ought to be downright fascinating, don't you think?"

"What?"

"Our marriage."

He grinned back at her. "I'm counting on it."

Janet stood at the back of the church barely a week later and fussed with her white antique lace dress. "Are you sure I look okay?" she asked Jenny for the thousandth time.

"You look beautiful, Mom. Every hair is in place," she added, anticipating Janet's next question. She twirled in her own dark rose dress. "How about me? Do I look grown-up?"

"Too grown-up," Janet declared, wondering where the time had flown.

It seemed only yesterday that her daughter had been small enough to rock to sleep in her arms. And yet she wouldn't go back for anything. Jenny was going to make her proud one day. She was bright, spirited and intrepid. With Harlan as a father, she could be anything she chose to be.

Lone Wolf would have been satisfied with how far his descendants had come and how far they would continue to go, she thought. Perhaps she had fulfilled her promise to him, after all.

"Isn't it time yet?" Jenny asked. "What's taking so long?"

"Blame me," Harlan said from the doorway to the church, taking them both by surprise.

"Harlan," Janet protested. "You shouldn't be back here. It's bad luck."

"You and I have one last detail to settle before you walk down the aisle," he said, pulling a thick packet of papers from his pocket and handing them to her.

Janet regarded him warily. "What's this?"

"It's one of those prenuptial things you seem to like so much. I ripped up yours," he said, handing her the shreds of paper as proof. "I set out a few terms of my own."

Janet allowed the remains of her prenuptial agreement to filter through her fingers, then took Harlan's papers with a hand that trembled. She wasn't sure what last-minute fears might have driven him to clarify the status of things between them in writing.

"Read it," Harlan insisted, putting an arm around Jenny's shoulders and giving her a squeeze as Janet began to scan the familiar legal language.

She'd read no more than a clause or two before her gaze shot up to meet his. "This isn't a prenuptial agreement at all. It's a will."

"I knew a fine lawyer like you would see that right off," he taunted.

"You're putting Jenny into your will as one of the heirs to White Pines?" she whispered, incredulous.

"She'll be my daughter," he said firmly. "She's entitled to her share, not just as my daughter, but as a descendant of Lone Wolf's."

Tears welled up in Janet's eyes. "The land should belong to your sons. They were raised on it."

"'Just putting what's right in writing'," he insisted, quoting her. "If things had gone differently a hundred years ago, maybe you'd have been raised on this land.

Maybe Jenny would have been born here. I just see that paper as bringing things full circle."

"She'll probably put a shopping mall on it," Janet threatened.

Harlan winced, but stood firm. "That'll be her choice," he said, gazing fondly at Jenny, who was staring at the two of them in stunned silence. "Thanks to you, she has a good head on her shoulders and good, decent values. She'll make us both proud."

Oblivious to wedding day conventions, which had already been shot to blazes anyway, Janet threw her arms around his neck and kissed him. "Oh, Harlan, I do love you."

He grinned. "It's a darn good thing, 'cause there's no way you'd get out of this church today without saying 'I do'. I can't wait to walk down that aisle in there, so the whole world will know how proud I am to be your husband."

"Even if I don't change my name from Runningbear to Adams?"

He winced. "Even then," he conceded. "You've worked hard to be who you are. I guess you've earned the right to call yourself whatever you want, as long as it's me you come home to at night."

"Count on it," she said softly, then took his hand. "Since we've already made a mishmash of tradition, how about walking down that aisle with me to stand before the preacher?"

"Mom!" Jenny protested with a wail. "What about me?"

Janet grinned. "You can still go first. You'll probably have to revive the organist. She won't know what's going on."

"That's exactly why I'm so anxious to get started on

this marriage," Harlan declared, winking at Jenny. "With your mom around, there's no telling what'll happen next. I expect there will be surprises in store for all of us."

The ceremony wasn't nearly as tospy-turvy as their arrival for it, Harlan reflected late that night while Janet was changing into some fancy negligee he was going to take pleasure in stripping right back off.

He let his mind wander over the days and weeks since she'd come into his life and counted each minute among his blessings. He was so engrossed in his memories, he never heard a thing as she apparently managed to sneak up behind him and circle her arms around him.

"I love you, Harlan Adams," she whispered.

At the sound of those sweet words, a tremendous sense of peace stole through him. They were going to be so damned good together. Family had always been the most important thing on earth to him. Now, after losing his beloved Mary and his son, Erik, both in terrible tragedies that had taken them too soon, his family circle was going to grow once more. His life was once again complete.

"I love you, Janet Runningbear. And I love the daughter you've brought into my life."

Her eyes lit with a teasing glint. "Who knows, Harlan? Maybe I'll give you another one before we're done."

It was a good thing she slid into his lap and kissed him then, because he was too darned flabbergasted to say a single word. A father again? What an astonishing, incredible idea! One thing for sure, any child they had together was bound to be a hellion.

He could hardly wait.

Epilogue

By golly, if Janet didn't go and make good on her promise. Barely nine months to the day after their honeymoon, Harlan found himself pacing the hallways at the hospital waiting for her to give birth. The whole danged family was there, fussing and carrying on, teasing him unmercifully about getting a second chance at parenthood.

"Maybe this time you'll get it right," Cody teased.

"There's not a thing about the way I did it the first time that I'd do over," he shot right back, then sighed heavily. "Except with Erik. I'd do that over if I could."

Luke put his arm around him. "Daddy, Erik made his own choices."

Jessie stood on tiptoe to kiss his cheek. "That's right. It's time to let it go. Besides, this should be a happy occasion. We should be concentrating on the new baby, not sad memories."

Jenny, who'd been standing impatiently in the corridor outside the delivery room for the past hour, came up in front of him and scowled. "I just don't get it. What's taking so long? And why aren't you in there with her?"

"Because he'd be telling the doctor what to do, that's

why," Cody chimed in. "The delivery room staff signed a petition to keep him out."

"But you took those classes with Mom and everything," Jenny protested. "Now she doesn't even have a coach in there with her. If I'd known you were going to chicken out, I'd have taken the classes."

Just then a nurse appeared in the doorway. She zeroed straight in on Harlan. "Mr. Adams, your wife is asking for you."

His breath caught in his throat. "The baby?"

"Should be here any minute now," the nurse said. "She says you'll probably only have to suffer through a contraction or two."

When his sons heard that, they hooted. "Now we know," Jordan taunted. "Janet was terrified you were going to faint in there, wasn't she?"

"We reached an agreement is all," Harlan said defensively.

The truth of it was, Janet had fought like a demon to keep him from seeing her in pain. He'd fought just as hard to be in that delivery room. He'd missed out on the birth of his sons, because that was the way of the world back then. He'd regretted it more than he could say. This time he wanted to be there for the miracle, just one of many to come into his life since the day he'd met Janet and Jenny.

As promised, he walked through the door of the delivery room just in the nick of time. Janet's face was bathed in sweat, but the smile she turned on him was enough to fill his heart to overflowing. He clasped her hand.

"I hear you're doing great," he said.

"So they tell me," she said, suddenly clenching his

hand in a grip so fierce he thought for sure the bones would break. "This is it."

"Sure is," the doctor agreed. "That's it, Janet. Come on. Just a little more."

Harlan's incredulous gaze was fixed on the doctor, watching his concentration, then the smile that slowly spread across his face just as he lifted their brand-new baby into the air.

"It's a girl," he announced. "A big one, too. Pretty as her mama."

If there'd been a chair close by, Harlan would have collapsed onto it. Tears welled up in his eyes as he turned a tremulous smile on Janet. "A girl," he repeated softly. "Another daughter."

"I promised, didn't I?" Janet whispered.

He leaned down and pressed a kiss filled with gratitude and love to her lips. "Thank you for my two girls," he murmured. "Most of all, thank you for loving me and making my life complete."

Just then a nurse approached carrying their daughter in a pretty pink blanket. "Here she is, Mr. Adams. Would you like to hold her?"

An awe unlike anything he'd ever before experienced spread through him as he took that precious bundle into his arms and gazed down into his daughter's tiny, scrunched-up face.

"She is so beautiful," he said, barely getting the words past the lump in his throat. "What are we going to name her? Have you decided?"

"I had a thought, but I wasn't sure how you'd feel about it," Janet said.

"What?"

"I was thinking of naming her Mary Elizabeth," she said, watching his face intently.

He was stunned by the generous, unselfish gesture. "Wouldn't you mind naming her for Mary?"

Eyes shining, she reached for his hand. "It's something I'd like very much to do for you and your sons. I was thinking we might call her Lizzy."

He gazed down at the child in his arms and grinned. "Lizzy, huh? What do you think?"

Mary Elizabeth Adams opened her tiny mouth and wailed. There was no telling if that was a sign of approval or dissent, but Harlan took it as a positive reaction. He smiled at Janet. "Lizzy, it is."

"So," she said, as they wheeled her and the baby to her room, "do you think there are any more surprises in store for us?"

"You bet," he promised. "They're around every corner."

* * * * *

Read on for a sneak peek of
The Littlest Angel,
The first book in the next
Adams Dynasty anthology titled
The Heart of Hill Country
from New York Times *bestselling author*
Sherryl Woods!

1

Angela hadn't wanted to come home like this, with her belly the size of two watermelons, and not one single proud accomplishment she could claim. She'd always meant her return to be triumphant, proof that she could succeed on her own without relying on the Adams name that meant so much in one little corner of West Texas. She'd envisioned a banner across the porch and a barbecue in her honor in the backyard and her name in lights, if Grandpa Harlan had his way.

Instead, it was the dead of night and no one even knew she was coming. Until she'd driven down the last stretch of deserted highway, anticipation mounting with every mile, she hadn't known for sure herself if she would have the courage to face her family. The car had settled that for her. It had conked out less than a mile from home. She sat in the rapidly chilling air and shivered, wondering if fate was on her side this time or just out to humiliate her further.

Home. The word had always conjured up a barrage of images for her, some good, some bad. Over the last six years the bad ones had faded until only the special memories remained. With her birthday tomorrow and Christmas just a few days away, it was no surprise that it was the holiday memories that came back to her now in a flood.

The celebrations always began early and lasted through New Year's, with everyone—aunts, uncles, cousins—traipsing from home to home for one party or another, but always, *always* ending up at White Pines. Grandpa Harlan insisted on it. He claimed he could spoil his grandkids rotten in his own home on Christmas Day if he chose to, while anywhere else he might have to show some restraint.

Rather than feeling deprived that her birthday was so close to Christmas, Angela had always felt as if all of the holiday trimmings made the day more special than it would have been at any other time of the year. Other kids got cakes and a single party. Angela's celebration included a huge tree, blinking colored lights, endless music and nonstop parties that went on for days.

She'd missed that while she was away, missed it when she'd noted the occasion all alone in a college rooming house already deserted by students who'd headed home for the holidays. Last year she'd almost forgotten it herself. She was too caught up in love, too excited about sharing her first Christmas with a man who really mattered to her.

Now, though, the memories were as vivid as if she'd never left. Even from her stalled car way out here on a lonely Texas highway she imagined she could see the lights twinkling on the ceiling-scraping Christmas tree, smell the aroma of Consuela's fresh-baked sugar cookies and bread mingling with the scent of fresh-cut pine. She could almost hear the sound of carols being played at full volume, while her dad chided her mom that she was going to deafen all of them.

She sighed as she remembered the angel of shimmering gold that was ceremoniously placed on top of the tree each and every year and the pride she'd felt when that duty had been given to her. At five she'd been too small to reach the top, so her father had hoisted her up on his broad shoulders so she could settle that frothy angel onto the tree's highest branch. Then and only then, in a room that had been darkened for the ceremony, did they switch on the lights, always too many of them, always so magical that she and her mom had gasped with delight, while her dad had grinned tolerantly. The same ceremony had been repeated at White Pines, where as the oldest grandchild she'd always been the one who'd put the angel on her grandfather's tree.

So many wonderful traditions, she thought now. How could she have run away from all the warmth and love in that house? she wondered in retrospect.

Rebellion, pure and simple. She had chafed at all the bright expectations and what she now suspected had been imagined pressures. Like all families, hers had only wanted what was best for her.

It was just that the Adams men, particularly Luke and her grandfather, had a tendency to think they were the only ones who knew what was best. No two men on earth could be more mule-headed once they'd charted a course of action, for themselves or someone they loved.

Ironically, they had rarely agreed on what that course should be. One plan would have been hard enough to fight, but two were impossible. Angela had wanted to decide her future for herself, and leaving—choosing a college far from Texas where the Adams influence didn't reach—had been the only way she'd seen to do it. She'd limited contact to occasional calls, an infrequent e-mail to her computer-literate father.

Now, with snow falling in fat, wet clumps and the roads turning into hazardous sheets of ice, she sat in her idled clunker of a car less than a mile from home and wondered if anything else could possibly go wrong. Even as the thought crossed her mind, she glanced quickly heavenward.

"Not that I'm tempting fate, You understand," she said wearily. "But even You have to admit my life basically sucks these days."

She was twenty-two, unmarried, unemployed and no more than a week or two from delivering a baby. She was virtually back on a doorstep she'd vowed she wouldn't cross again until she'd made something of herself and done it totally on her own without the Adams power and influence behind her. If she'd taken one thing away from Texas with her, it had been the fierce Adams pride, the determination to buck everyone and chart her own path.

She supposed, in a manner of speaking, that she had. She had made a royal mess of things. No other Adams that she knew of had gone so far astray. She'd skated through college with grades no higher than they had to be. She'd lied about who she was and run away more times and from more places than she could count. Rather than upholding the noble Adams tradition, she'd thumbed her nose at it. Oh, yes, she'd made something of herself, all right, but she wasn't especially proud of it, and this was hardly the triumphant homecoming she'd once envisioned.

The only thing she had going for her was the absolute

certainty that the two people inside would welcome her back with open arms and without making judgments. Luke and Jessie Adams accepted people for who they were, flaws included. That went double for their only child, the daughter they adored. They would be relieved that she'd finally realized that her heart and her identity were all wrapped up with the tight-knit family who'd been patiently waiting for her all this time.

As she huddled in the rapidly cooling car, she recalled the oft-told story of the joy with which she'd been welcomed into the world twenty-three years ago tomorrow. She had been born in the middle of a Texas blizzard with no one around to assist her mother except Luke Adams, her uncle at the time and the man who became her father. Luke had been blind drunk that night, but he'd sobered in a hurry when faced with the immediacy of those shattering labor pains. He had risen to the occasion like a true Adams hero.

From an early age Angela understood that they both considered her to be their Christmas blessing, a miracle on a cold and bitter night. With her natural father dead, her birth had brought Luke and Jessie together, helped them to overcome the anguish and guilt they'd felt at having fallen in love even before her father's fatal accident. Just as her name implied, she was their angel. Living up to such a lofty label had been daunting.

Admittedly, though, their expectations for her probably hadn't been half as exalted as she'd imagined them to be. She hadn't done a lot of listening before breaking the ties with home. At the first opportunity, she had fled Texas, first to attend college, then to roam the country in search of herself. It was time, she had thought, to do something totally outrageous, to discover what she was truly made of. Being angelic was a bore. She wanted to be wicked or, if not actually wicked, at least human.

Unfortunately, even after four years at Stanford and a year on her own the answers still eluded her. Over the past few months she'd had plenty of empty nights to examine her past. She was human, all right. The very human mistakes were mounting up.

She'd made the worst miscalculation of all in Montana with a rancher named Clint Brady, a low-down scoundrel if ever there was one, she thought bitterly. Her mound of a belly was testament to that. She wasn't looking forward to the hurt and worry that her parents would try their best to hide when they saw her and realized just how much trouble she'd managed to get herself into. She hated the thought of the heartbreak she would read in their eyes.

She was less worried about the reaction of her incredible grandfather, Harlan Adams. When it came to family, he was thoroughly predictable. He would probably set off fireworks to celebrate the birth of his first great-grandbaby. If he had questions about the baby's conception, he'd keep them to himself.

For the time being, anyway, she amended. As meddlesome as he was capable of being, he wouldn't be silent for long. By year's end he'd probably have a lynch mob searching for the baby's father, assuming he could get Angela to name him, which she had no intention of doing. Not even Clint Brady deserved to face the rancor of the Adams men, once they'd been riled up.

In addition to Luke and her grandfather, there were Cody and Jordan. They might be wildly different in some ways, but they all shared the Adams gene for pure cussedness and family loyalty. Clint wouldn't have a prayer against the four of them. He'd be hogtied and married to her before he could blink. She would have no more say in the matter than he did.

To her chagrin, just the thought of Clint and her wild and reckless behavior in Montana made her blood run hot. Until she'd met him, she'd had no idea that passion could be so overwhelming, so completely and irresistibly awe inspiring.

Nor had she known how quickly passion could turn to hatred and shame.

She was glad now that she'd lied to him, that she'd faked a whole identity so that she could pretend for just a little while that she wasn't Luke and Jessie Adams's little angel. It had been liberating to pretend to be Hattie Jones, a woman with no exalted family history to live up to, a woman who could be as outrageous as she liked without regrets.

The decision to lie had been impulsive, made in a darkened country-western bar where she'd stopped to ask about a waitressing job that had been posted in the window. Clint had had the kind of lazy smile and sexy eyes that made a shy, astonishingly innocent college graduate imagine that all sorts of forbidden dreams were hers for the taking.

The job had been forgotten as she'd succumbed to newly discovered sensuality she hadn't even been tempted to test with the boys she'd met at Stanford. By the end of the night they were lovers. By the end of the week, she had moved in with him. She supposed that there was yet more irony that after all her running, she'd wound up with a rancher, after all.

More than once in the blissful days that followed she had regretted the casual lie she'd told when they met. More than once she had vowed to tell him the truth about who she was and where she came from, but Clint had been the kind of man who lived in the here and now. He didn't talk about his own past. He never asked about hers.

As weeks turned into months, it seemed easier to live with the lie. She liked being devil-may-care Hattie Jones, who flirted outrageously and never gave a thought to tomorrow. She liked the way Clint murmured her name in the middle of the night, as if he'd never before heard a word so beautiful.

In Clint's arms she was ecstatically happy. His ranch was a fraction of the size of her father's or her grandfather's, the days were long and exhausting, but none of that mattered, not at night when they made magic together. She found peace on that tiny Montana spread and something she had thought was love.

Then she'd discovered she was pregnant, and all of the lies and secrets between them—most of them admittedly her doing—had threatened to come unraveled.

When Clint had reacted in stunned silence to the news they were expecting a baby, that famous Adams pride had kicked in with a vengeance. She'd shouted a lot of awful, ugly things and he'd responded in kind. Even now the memory of it made her shudder.

If he'd been that furious over the baby, she couldn't imagine what his rage would be like once he discovered that she'd lied to him from the start. In her entire life, no one had ever made her feel so low. Nor had she ever before wanted to hurt a person so deeply that he would never recover from it. Words were their weapons and they had used them well.

Angela hadn't waited for tempers to cool. She'd

loaded up her car and hit the road before dawn, determined to put Clint Brady and Montana far behind her.

That had been nearly seven months ago. She'd been in a lot of cities since. Few of them had even registered. She had no more than vague memories of cheap hotels and back-road diners.

She wasn't exactly sure when she'd realized that Clint was following her. It had been almost a sixth sense at first, a nervous knotting in the pit of her stomach, a prickly sensation scampering down her spine. She was too hurt, too sure that she'd been wrong to get involved with him, too ashamed of her age-old predicament to let him catch her. What was the point of one more argument, anyway? It was best to put him in the past, along with all the other mistakes she'd made. A fresh start beckoned from around every curve in the road.

To her surprise, Clint hadn't given up easily. He'd nearly caught up with her in Wyoming, cutting short the part-time waitressing job she'd taken to get gas money to move on. Warned about the man who'd been in earlier asking questions about her, she'd slipped out the diner's back door just as Clint came through the front.

The narrow escape had made her jittery for days. She hadn't felt secure until she'd managed to trade her beloved blue convertible in for cash and a sensible beige sedan so old she hadn't even been born the year it was made. No car that old should have been expected to survive the kind of journey she'd taken it on.

She had moved quickly on to Colorado, then doubled back north to Cheyenne, looped up to South Dakota, then headed west to Seattle, enchanted by the idea of living by the water.

In Seattle she'd found a one-room apartment in an area

called Pill Hill for all the hospitals clustered together. For the first time she had searched until she landed a halfway decent job as a receptionist. She'd found a kindly obstetrician to make sure she was doing all the right things for the baby she'd already learned to cherish. She'd vowed that the baby would never have to pay for the mistakes she'd made. Oddly enough, though being Angela Adams had daunted her, being a single mom did not.

In Seattle she'd even made a few friends, older, married women who invited her over often for home-cooked meals and the kind of nurturing concern she'd missed since leaving home. She took endless walks along Elliott Bay, bought fresh produce and fish at Pike's Place Market, sipped decaf cappuccino in every Starbucks she passed.

Clint seemed to have lost her trail or else he'd just given up and gone home, satisfied that he'd made a noble attempt to find her. No doubt that enabled him to sleep well enough. By then, he was probably sharing his bed with some other woman. At any rate, she'd felt it was safe to linger in Seattle. Contentment seemed almost within her grasp. She couldn't bring herself to admit that she was disappointed that he had given up.

Maybe, if it hadn't been for the Seattle weather, she could have made it work. But as summer gave way to fall and then to a premature winter, all that rain and gloom had finally gotten to her. She began to miss clear blue skies and the kind of heat that baked the earth.

When she packed up and moved on, she told herself her goal was merely sunshine. The undeniable truth was, she was heading straight for Texas, toward home.

For better or worse, was going back to become Angela Adams again. The spirited Hattie Jones had died in Montana. Like it or not, Angela Adams was a Texan through and through. Her baby would be, too. The heritage she had abandoned for herself, she had no right to dismiss for the baby. It should be up to her child to decide someday if being an Adams was too much of a burden.

Not that she ever sat down and listed all the pros and cons for going home. The choice was instinctive. She'd hardly even needed a map to guide her south along the Pacific Coast and then east. If she'd stopped to reason it out, she probably would have found a hundred excuses for staying as far away from Texas as she could.

She'd developed a bad case of jitters near the end and wound up in Dallas, bypassing the turn to the south that would have taken her home much sooner. For days she'd lingered, wandering around the stores that had been decorated for the holidays, pretending that maybe this would be the final destination. It was close enough to home for an occasional visit, but far enough away to maintain her independence.

This afternoon, though, she had gotten into her car and impulsively started driving, taking familiar turns onto back roads and straight highways that were unmistakably leading her back to Los Pinos. Her static-filled radio had crackled with constant threats of an impending blizzard, but she hadn't once been tempted to turn back or to stop. Not even the first flurries of snow or the blinding curtain of white that had followed daunted her. Home beckoned by then with an inevitability she couldn't resist.

It was ironic, of course, that it had been on a night very much like this that her mother had gone into labor practically on Luke Adams's doorstep, had delivered Angela in his bed, with his help.

That had worked out well enough, she reminded herself as she tried to work up the courage to leave the safety and comfort of the car for the bitter cold walk home. Their marriage was as solid and secure as a bank vault.

Maybe that was why Angela had run from Clint Brady, had kept on running even when she knew he was chasing after her, even when she realized that it was possible that he wanted her back. She had seen what it could be like for two people who were head over heels in love, who faced problems squarely and grew strong because of them. She wanted nothing less for her child. If she couldn't offer the baby that, then she could at least make sure there was a wide circle of family around to shower her son or daughter with love.

As if in agreement, her baby kicked ferociously. Boy or girl, she thought defiantly, the kid was definitely destined to be a place kicker in the NFL. She rubbed her stomach and murmured soothing words, then drew in a deep breath.

Exiting the car to face an icy blast of air, she shivered and drew her coat more snugly around her.

"Okay, little one," she whispered as excitement stirred deep inside her, overcoming dread or at least tempering it. "This is it. Let's go home."

The Littlest Angel
by New York Times *bestselling author*
Sherryl Woods, available now
wherever MIRA Books are sold!

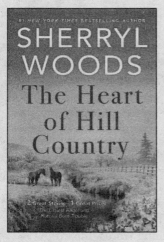